ALSO BY MARY HOWARD

*Discovering the Body*, a novel

# The Girl with Wings

**a novel**

**Mary Howard**

Culicidae Press

Culicidae Press, LLC
918 5th Street
Ames, IA 50010
USA
www.culicidaepress.com

editor@culicidaepress.com

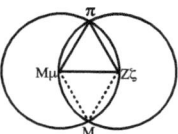

Culicidae
PRESS, LLC
culicidaepress.com

Ames | Gainesville | Lemgo | Rome

For more information, please visit www.culicidaepress.com

ISBN-13: 978-1-941892-23-7

ISBN-10: 1-941892-23-X

Front cover image: *Autumn Dress*, monotype, Chine-collé, etching by Marina Terauds, 2008. By kind Permission of the artist.

Cover design and interior layout © 2016 by polytekton.com

For Roger Mosher Brown
1947-2010

# Table of Contents

*If you would be a real seeker after truth, it is necessary that at least once in your life you doubt, as far as possible, all things.*

Rene Descartes


*And your doubt can become a good quality if you train it. It must become knowing, it must become criticism. Ask it, whenever it wants to spoil something for you, why something is ugly, demand proofs from it, test it, and you will find it perhaps bewildered and embarrassed, perhaps also protesting. But don't give in. Insist on arguments and act in this way, attentive and persistent, every single time, and the day will come when, instead of being a destroyer, doubt will become one of your best workers—perhaps the most intelligent of all the ones that are building your life.*

Rainer Maria Rilke
*Letters to a Young Poet*

# Chapter 1

Exactly thirteen days before Gracie Cantonwine was abducted, graphic artist Linda Garbo was in her studio. She was holding a rustic-red paper sample at arm's length, considering the way the slate-like surface took the light, when her phone rang. Distracted, she said, "Good morning. Garbo Designs."

The caller was Annie Cantonwine. She had a question.

"You want me to be Gracie's godmother?" Linda's laughter hissed across the telephone. Met with silence from the other end, she put the paper sample down. "Go on," she said gently. "I didn't mean to laugh. I was just making up my mind about a project here. I'm listening."

A fly buzzing the plate glass window of the studio barely registered.

"I'm serious," said Annie.

"I know you are. You caught me off-guard, making up my mind about a project. I told the client I'd get it done today." The fly dive-bombed mere inches from Linda's face, as if it had the wits to demand her attention, too. She shifted the phone to her left hand. "Let's start over," she said, closing her fist around a fly swatter's wire-loop handle. "I'm all yours."

Annie repeated what she'd said right after hello: "We're planning Gracie's baptism, and we want you and Will to be her godparents."

"Of course." Linda swung at the fly and missed. "I mean, of course I understand."

"It's important to me," said Annie. "You'll do it? You sound mad."

"Not at you," said Linda. "I'm just a little stressed, preoccupied. Sorry. We're talking about making a promise in church, to teach Gracie to believe certain things?"

Over the phone, Linda could hear the baby's cry in the background. Then the double-click of a door shut out the sound. "John said yes to the godfather part," said Annie.

"He did? Already? When?"

"Just now. Will talked to him. All you need to do is stand up with us when the baby's christened. My mom wants it to be right away, before something bad happens to Gracie. She keeps saying that, and it's getting to me. I know paranoia is part of her illness and I should keep in mind what she's like when she isn't so crazy, but she's upsetting Will, too. He's talking about banning her from our house. I never thought that would happen." Annie's voice dropped to an urgent hush. "She keeps saying Gracie's in danger until she's been blessed in church. I'm hoping the baptism will calm her down."

"Baptism will calm her," repeated Linda.

"I'm hoping so, yes," said Annie. "She calls Daddy at the bank all day long, and so now he's pushing me, too, to have the baby baptized as soon as we can. Mom thinks it's magical, a precaution of sorts, and we've been meaning to do it anyway. I put things off, I guess, especially when it has to do with her these days, the way she's been so—"

Linda waited for Annie to finish her sentence.

"So embarrassing," said Annie. "I need you there. My mom needs you there, though god knows if she'll realize it in the state she's in. You're not afraid of her like some people. You're normal-acting and relaxed with her these days when her other friends stay away. If she makes one of her scenes, you'll be there, and that would mean the world to me. You still haven't said yes. I was sure you'd say yes right off."

"This coming Sunday?" Linda asked.

"Right. Daddy's setting it up with the minister." Annie pled like a child: "It'll be the four of us, in front of everyone. You and John and me and Will. We're so lucky to have people like you as practically part of the family."

*A wish wrapped in flattery*, thought Linda. It wouldn't kill her to do this for Annie. Their husbands were best friends, and Linda had been meaning to make more time for the younger woman, to get to know her better, but she'd imagined a movie or a lunch downtown, not standing up in church together. She really wanted to find some common ground with Annie. Maybe this would be it.

Linda was sitting at the front desk in her graphic design studio, gazing at the sign in the plate-glass window—lime-green neon, LINDA GARBO DESIGNS, in an oval of pink and lavender. Beyond it on the parking stood another sign, this one lettered red: FOR SALE. "To be honest," she said, "I'm not godmother material right now, Annie, given that I've been questioning my beliefs."

"To me," said Annie, "it's just a matter of saying you'll be Gracie's friend, like an aunt or something, while she's growing up, someone she can count on. The main thing you have to believe is that we all love her more than anything."

"I do believe that, of course," said Linda. The fly was back, low over the drafting table. "Give me time to think about it."

"But not too long," said Annie, her voice an octave too high by then, needy and girlish. "It's in *four days*. I know it's short notice, but if I have to get someone else— I have my *heart* set on you, so, Linda, *please- please- please?*"

Linda glanced at the clock. She had so much work to do and needed to get on with it, so she raised her right hand and struck the fly one lightning-quick blow and watched it fall dead onto the dusty windowsill. "Okay," she said, "I'll lighten up. For you. For Gracie. Of course I will. Maybe it will calm me down, too. I'll do it. Yes."

On Sunday, September 8, 2002, the weather was hot and humid. A haze drowsed over the Linden Grove United Church of Christ. Linda tried to smooth the creases from the lap of her linen dress as she got out of her husband John's Toyota. She watched him pull his jacket out of the back seat and hang it by a thumb over his right shoulder. His long hair, still damp from the shower, was pulled back into a rubber band. At the temples he was gray. "Your tie," she said.

He hardly ever wore one. He wiggled the knot back and forth, observing her face as if it were a mirror. One nod from her and they headed up the steps of the redbrick building, hand-in-hand.

In the pastor's study, Will Cantonwine, a sturdy man with curly blond hair, held his infant daughter Grace. Beside him stood Annie, a pretty woman in her early twenties with long, dark hair and high color in her cheeks. A yellow sundress showed off the fragile folds of her collarbone. Seeing Linda, she hurried toward her. "I'm nervous," Annie whispered.

"Just breathe," said Linda, and Annie took a deep, deep breath, smiling with relief, then, as if it had helped.

The Reverend Gustavson was barrel-chested, tan, and sported a well-trimmed beard. He reviewed the meaning of the sacrament. While he spoke of water, "to wash away," Annie stroked the baby's cheek, and two-month-old Gracie opened her mouth toward the touch. She shook her topknot of wild, dark hair like a tiny exotic bird. "You respond, 'I will,'" said the minister. "Remember your cue: Will you endeavor—?"

"I will," said Will. "I will."

Annie groaned and rested her head against his sleeve. "Can't we just say yes? Or else I'll laugh."

"Works for me," said the minister, smiling. "Since the baby's quiet, you might as well go on in. Remember: listen for the word *endeavor*."

Linda's stomach lifted. Eating something usually helped the morning-sickness. She reached into her purse to finger a soda cracker as the two couples headed for the front pew.

"I'll be glad when this is over," Will said quietly to Annie, handing the baby off to her. Annie giggled. "I will, too."

*Annie's about to jump out of her skin,* Linda was thinking when Reverend Gustavson sailed through the side door, black robe billowing. He sank out of her line of vision, beyond the pulpit, as he sat, and she felt queasy.

She broke the corner off a cracker.

She savored the salt.

She looked around.

The sanctuary walls were blue; the pews were curved, the carpet worn. She took it in with a tourist's eyes and longed for something there to make her sure what to believe. The organ played a reedy tune with a baleful under-moan. Two oscillating fans sighed back and forth. Sulfur hanging in the air from just-lit candles on the altar made Linda want to stand and run from her uncertainty. Instead, she leaned forward slightly to look at Will, her husband's closest friend, who was confiding something to Annie that made her nod. He was smitten with his beautiful young wife. That was obvious.

The hard oak pew, too small for Linda, who was six-foot-two, pressed painfully into the soft part of her back, just below the shoulder blades, but at least her stomach had settled down. John's gaze met hers, and then moved beyond. "They're here," he whispered.

Annie's parents had arrived. Esther Hebring settled herself at the end of the pew, while Frank, a portly, balding man with patient eyes took Linda's hand in both of his to say, "Good morning."

Esther's lovely face was bloated, scrubbed, all the pinks and reds gone to her hands, to lacquered fingernails and ring — a ruby circled with diamonds, real, no doubt, but ostentatious, out of fashion, out of place. Her plum-colored suit looked beautifully made, but tight, too warm for the weather. Frank rested a protective arm along the pew behind her. When the minister raised a hand for silence and the organ came to a rest, everyone stood to pray with him.

All, that is, but Esther. "I told you this would happen, Frank." Her voice was an actressy, insistent whisper everyone in the place could hear. Annie stiffened, a sure sign of embarrassment, as her mother leaned forward and pointed a bright red fingernail at Linda, whose heart sank when Esther said, with more than a hint of venom, "What's that Garbo woman doing here?"

It was her illness talking, that intimation, delivered so dramatically, that Linda was not her friend. Linda didn't let it get to her. That would have been like abandoning Esther over an estrangement she couldn't help. Anyway, at the best of times, Esther was known for her theatricality. On her one-woman local radio show called *Willing Suspensions*, she read stories full of harried waitresses, gritty cowgirls, enthusiastic mayors, little children, thieves. She was amazingly good at dialects, from Mississippi drawls to the uninflected vowels of Minnesota, as well as many foreign accents. For her latest story, set on the western coast of Ireland, her west-country accent was so convincing—even when she ad-libbed digressions so seamless they seemed to be part of the story —none of her listeners would guess she was suffering a relapse of schizophrenia. Those who had seen Esther there in the front pew the last few Sundays had grown accustomed to her outbursts. Linda heard a ripple of sound from the worshipers behind her. *Unstable*, they might have been whispering to each other. *Poor Frank.*

Gracie shook her tiny fists and wailed along as the choir sang, *"Lead Me to the Water,"* processing up the center aisle. When the Reverend Gustavson led the Call to Worship, Linda was too out of practice to join in. She reached into her purse and broke the corner off another cracker. Will and Annie stood, and Linda took her place, with John, beside them as Grace's crying went up a notch or two.

"— baptizing them in the name of the Father, the Son —" The minister projected his voice above the baby's cries: "—and the Holy Spirit, with water, the sign of God's forgiveness."

Linda returned his gaze and longed for holiness. She wanted awe. She missed the grandfatherly God of her childhood, with his everlasting arms. Infant baptism was a lovely sacrament, she thought. *Maybe today will be a blessing for all of us, at the very least.* That's what she was thinking when the minister said, "Will you endeavor—?"

"I will," said Anne and Will and John.

Linda had missed the cue.

"I'll *try*," she said. The congregation was on its feet. They covered her mistake with the creak of floorboards, delivering their oath: "—and we promise our support."

By that point in the service, Grace's cry was loud and rhythmic. She arched her back as Annie passed her into the minister's arms where, like magic, she grew still. "What name shall be given to this child?" he asked. The answer: Gracie Ellen Cantonwine.

Then Reverend Gustavson carried the baby into the center aisle and raised her forward in both his hands. "This child is yours," he said to the congregation, "to nurture and protect, a reminder that we believe in a loving, caring God." He lowered the baby. He kissed her on the head.

And then he placed her in Linda's arms.

She wasn't expecting that. She hadn't held a baby for a long, long time. Gracie's weight in her arms, the Johnson & Johnson's scent of her hair, the formality of the four adults standing shoulder-to-shoulder facing a congregation of people who taught in the Linden Grove schools, sold groceries and hardware and used cars, plowed the fields along country roads, lightened her heart and, through her body, relaxed Gracie, too. The baby looked up at Linda without blinking for the longest time. Then she smiled.

The minister spoke enthusiastically. He asked them all to encourage her in the church until she reached the age of confirmation. Well, thought Linda, there were plenty of people in the room to share in that. If she could love Gracie — like an aunt, as Annie had proposed — she wouldn't be a hypocrite. Linda thought of the ham in the oven at home, the dinner she had prepared for the family — in part to keep in touch with Esther during the paranoid and angry summer days she'd had to be without her meds, a *washout period,* Esther had called it, to prepare for a change in medication. The sanctuary blurred with tears as the baby curled against Linda, and she felt maternal consolation right down to her toes.

But Esther broke the spell. Chin high and sighing over-dramatically, she stepped into the center aisle and hurried toward the minister, who had closed his eyes to pray in his commanding baritone. She paused, then walked around him toward the double doors. Halfway there, she stopped and raised her right arm to point toward the back. There stood two men in shirtsleeves — and a girl with long, fuzzy, wheat-blond curls and wearing black, perhaps a late arrival waiting to be seated.

The Reverend didn't miss a beat: "Loving this child will take us on a journey —" But when he paused for breath, Esther shouted, *"No you don't."* The eyes of worshipers flew open as she yelled toward the door, in an odd, atonal voice. *"Get out. I told you to stay away. Everyone here will watch out for her, in case the water's not enough."* At first Linda thought the angry words might be for her, but then Esther turned her face toward the congregation to her right and jabbed a red fingernail in that direction: *"The baby's cry made the devil run. Did you see that?"* She stage-whispered, *"The one with wings? I recognize her hair."*

A silence fell. Linda's heart was thumping. Someone coughed. The baby clung to her. The men at the back — one might have been an usher, printed programs clutched in a fist — moved aside, one to the left and one to the right. The girl with all the fuzzy curls rushed out between them, and the two men looked at their feet with embarrassment. *"Ah-men,"* Esther shouted in their direction, as if she'd won an argument.

She returned to her seat. She bowed her head.

Linda wished with all her heart she could help her friend. She'd never seen Esther so wild and outside of herself. Even here, among friends and neighbors, the world had gone dangerous in Esther's lovely, dark eyes.

When the congregation stood for the benediction, Esther Hebring took off in a hurry, down the center aisle. It wasn't her usual graceful walk, but the arm-pumping, belly-first march of an angry child. Frank followed her close behind. He inclined his head as if to hear her better, though she was still loud enough for Linda to recognize the same words she'd spoken before: *the one with wings.*

The organ filled the room with triumphant, brassy song. Someone slapped Will on the shoulder and got him to exchange his grim look for a grin. Friends shook hands over the backs of pews. Reluctantly, Linda gave Gracie up to Annie, hugging them both in the process, then stood motionless to gaze at the largest stained glass window, at the golds and greens of a dove descending, alighting on a leafy branch. What sort of creature, *the girl with wings,* had Esther seen in her psychotic state?

Outside the church, Esther pressed close to Linda on the wide front steps. "I've decided not to come to dinner, I guess you know." Her eyebrows were tweezed and darkened, pencil lines visible in the harsh sunlight. "I should be the one preparing it, not you."

"I hope you'll change your mind," said Linda gently. "We want you to see what we've done to the house since the last time you were there. The day wouldn't be complete without you and Frank. Annie helped me plan the menu. It'll be just the seven of us."

"Seven?"

"Including Grace."

"Of course," said Esther. "Including Grace. I'm afraid for her." Esther turned away to take Frank's hand and head for their car, parked right there at the curb. "I have my reasons," she said over her shoulder. "You'll find out."

"I wish you wouldn't talk like that," said Linda under her breath as she watched Annie carry Gracie down the sidewalk. There she placed the baby in the arms of Becka Gustavson, one of the minister's twin daughters, whose yellow shirt displayed a pointy design that looked like fire. Becka rocked the baby in her arms, showing Gracie off to her high school friends—under Annie's watchful eyes. Beside her, a girl in a black t-shirt took one of the baby's tiny feet into her hand. In bright sunlight, the girl's skin and hair were so pale as to seem almost translucent, dreamlike, barely real. Still, Linda probably wouldn't have noticed any of that at all, if not for what the girl was wearing.

Even at that distance — Grace was thirty feet away — Linda had eyes only for the baby's wide-open gaze, and that flag of unruly dark hair that made her look surprised. Holding Gracie's foot, the stranger turned and bowed her head to talk to her, and the silver design on her t-shirt flashed in the sun.

Linda looked around for John to ask him, "Who is that girl?" He never missed a Sunday service. He'd grown up in Linden Grove and was editor of *The Linden Times,* so he knew everyone in town, but when Linda turned to point her out, the girl was gone. She might have been one of Esther's apparitions, the way she vanished in a moment like that. Linda asked Annie—and Becka, too— but neither of them remembered seeing a girl in a black t-shirt embossed with a silvery horse in flight.

"It was Pegasus, the mythical horse." Linda tried to explain — just as Esther had, in her schizophrenic rage — "the one with wings."

Probably a coincidence.

*Mary Howard*

# Chapter 2

"**I** saw the girl with the winged horse on her shirt." Linda wiped sweat from her brow with a forearm. "I have a hunch she might have been the one who upset you. Am I right?"

Esther frowned. "I might have known she'd wear something like that to church," she said. Little more than an hour had passed since she had broken the spell of worship with her outburst. Now she stood in the doorway to Linda's kitchen and watched her lift a ten-pound ham from the oven.

"Was she the one you were shouting at?"

Esther walked around Linda and backed up against the counter so she could watch the door.

"Who was she, Esther?" Linda smiled.

Silence.

Linda tried again: "I thought maybe she was a high school friend of the Gustavson twins."

"Then you didn't get a good look at her face," said Esther.

"It wasn't her face that drew my attention." The flying horse on the girl's shirt had been one of those plastic, laminated designs, wings feathered with a glare of light.

"She's not as young as all that," said Esther softly. "She's a dozen years past high school, if she's a day."

"A woman, then. I saw her at a distance, after the service, outside."

Esther stopped blinking. "She was still there?"

"Yes, admiring Grace. All eyes were on the baby. John didn't remember seeing the woman. Neither did Annie, or Becka Gustavson, and they were standing right next to her. Who was she, Esther? I'm just curious."

Esther's expression gave nothing away. In recent weeks, she had suffered a cluster of brutally obvious symptoms of schizophrenia for the first time in years. Earlier in the summer she had managed to confide to Linda that she sometimes saw people at the periphery of things who probably weren't there, and that a rough, male voice commanded her at times to do things she didn't feel like doing. Esther drew the line at revealing what those things were, or if she obeyed the voice. "He scares the bejesus out of me," had been her last word on that.

Linda maneuvered the ham onto a blue and white platter. She had scored the fatty rind in a diamond pattern and then studded each diamond with a pineapple ring and a clove, just like the picture in *The Better Homes and Garden's Cookbook*. "If you shout about a thing with wings, in church—" said Linda. "Out loud when the minister's in the middle of a prayer. I admit I thought—"

"Of evil?" Esther asked. "Dark angels, or demons, is that it? Driving the devil out of church?"

"It crossed my mind."

Esther chuckled. "It crossed Frank's, too, and he knows I don't believe in devils."

"But you said something like, 'The baby's cry made the devil run.'"

"I don't know where that came from," said Esther. "I really don't."

"Who was she?" Linda asked again.

"It's the crack in her armor, so to speak. She never listens to reason." Esther's voice sped up with urgency. "I told Frank in the car that I won't be going to church anymore, now that she's figured out she can find me there. She ran from me fast enough, outside those double doors. Good thing. She was watching all of us make our promises, watching you as much as anyone. She dresses like a teenager. You're right about that. She hears me on the radio and thinks that gives her the right to call me day or night and hang around. I'm relieved you saw her, too."

"She calls you?"

"Yes. She hisses in my ear. Whispering can disguise a voice, but she doesn't fool me. I see her behind the house sometimes, back in the trees. She's stalking me. She wants the marrow from Annie's bones."

"That's horrible, Esther."

"You're telling me."

Shaken, Linda inhaled the salty fragrance of the ham. She wanted Esther to feel welcome — no stress, just an old-fashioned, country Sunday dinner. Linda's right hand gripped the handle of the carving knife. She sawed slowly, laying down the first slice, and then another, until half the rosy meat lay fanned out on the plate. After consulting Annie on the menu, she had prepared the ham, in its armor of fat, to honor Hebring family tradition. As she looked at Esther's hands, thinking to compliment her on her rings to change the subject, it occurred to Linda that if flattery is a cover for prying, it isn't sincere.

Esther looked depleted, standing there. "I stopped answering the phone," she said. "That's why she came after me in church. Someone must have told her it's practically the only place I go these days. I hope she doesn't turn up here." She gazed past Linda, toward the door. "Does everyone know now," she asked sadly, "that I'm crazy? Have I completely given myself away?"

"Your illness is nothing to be ashamed of," said Linda quietly. "In no time at all you'll be starting the new drug, and you'll be yourself again." Linda added one last pineapple ring, crusty from the pan, and handed the platter to Esther.

"It was good of you to go to all this trouble," Esther said with her normal flair, "all these circles and cloves, a real trip down memory lane." She lifted the plate chest-high and proudly carried it to the dining room as if it were a royal offering. Linda hurried to move a bowl of marshmallow-covered sweet potatoes to make room on the table. "Come sit," Esther said to Annie as she appeared from the hallway.

"I put the baby down for her nap," said Annie.

"Linda's made all your favorites, just like I used to do," said Esther to her daughter before she shouted: "Dinner's ready." She projected as if she were on a stage, and something shifted in her countenance. She actually smiled. The men below responded instantly, thundering up the wooden stairs from the basement toward the sound of her voice. "Annie, sit next to me," she commanded. "Just look at this feast. It's fabulous. Enough fat and sugar to carry us through till Tuesday. Will can sit on my other side. No telling where this meal might lead."

Annie looked startled. Then she seemed pleased.


After dinner was over, Esther and Linda sat side-by-side on the brown leather sofa in the living room while Annie checked on Gracie down the hall. The men were doing clean-up in the kitchen. "Annie has one of those," Linda said to Esther, who was studying a Fisher-Price Baby Monitor in her lap, in a rattle of tissue paper.

The sofa faced the fireplace, built of river-rock. On the mantle leaned one of John's college paintings — Kandinsky-like strokes of yellow, green and coral spun into motion by vibrating black lines. Shelves flanking the fireplace overflowed with John's books on residential architecture, American history and politics —along with Linda's mystery novels, books about art, and poetry. More stacks of volumes drifted along the walls and up against the side of a red leather chair. When the tissue paper went silent in Esther's lap, Linda turned to look at her.

Esther, eyes fixed on a point in midair, muttered something argumentative to herself. To Linda, talking to Esther when she went faraway was sort of like confiding in a photograph. Linda was never sure Esther registered a thing she said to her at times like that, but usually went on talking to her anyway. "My father had a brain injury from the Korean war," Linda said, her voice low as Esther went on talking to herself, a kind of weird duet.

Linda never talked about her father, but she'd been thinking about him all day.

"When he had trouble staying in the present moment," she said, "I was ashamed of him. He was the town character, making his rounds through the streets, slipping in and out of reality. He embarrassed me."

Esther fell silent.

"By the time I understood what he'd been dealing with," said Linda, "it was too late and he was gone. I felt guilty, and I longed to make it up to him, but of course I couldn't. Turns out, I learned a lot from him about compassion, at least I hope I did. You're still my smart, gifted, funny friend, no matter where you are right now. I know you haven't wanted to come over here to our house lately, the way you've been feeling, and that's okay. I'm glad you showed up today. I feel like we're family now."

Esther was still blank-eyed and oblivious — but a loud burst of laughter from the kitchen made her turn her head. Out of sight around the corner, in the kitchen, Will's voice rose and fell fervently, inaudible except for a word or two. And then John's deep voice took over. Only when water drummed loudly into the stainless steel sink, drowning the men's voices entirely, did Esther pull open the end-flap of the box in her lap and peer inside. The baby monitor was a gift Annie had brought for the baby Linda was expecting in the spring. The sound of rushing water ended with a shudder of old-house pipes, and John's voice came back as it had left, mid-sentence — just as Annie came into the living room.

She wanted to take a walk. Esther lifted both feet and pointed at her plum-colored, strappy pumps. She said something about the wrong kind of shoes for walking on uneven ground, the first words she'd spoken since dinner. "You two go on." She pulled a Styrofoam tray out of the box and slipped the receiver out of its plastic bag. It had a white antenna with a baby-blue tip. Esther gave her daughter an anguished look and spoke only to her: "They're laughing about me in the kitchen, those men. Your husband makes fun of me behind my back. I always knew it. Don't try and tell me otherwise."

In the kitchen, the men's voices fell silent.

"I believe you're mistaken," said Annie, continuing without out a pause to say," I have a baby monitor just like that. It's set up by Gracie's crib."

"Not that I'll ever see it for myself," said Esther loudly. "Your own mother, banished by that salesman." Esther stood, her face dark with anger. "It won't be enough, the water, to keep us safe. Not like he told me."

"Who—?" Annie gave Linda a defeated glance, then turned to her mother again and said, "The monitor is so Linda can hear her baby when she's working downstairs."

"Ah, yes," said Esther. She held the two parts of the monitor in her hands. "Downstairs," she said. And that's all she said. She'd gone away again.

Linda led Annie across the back deck and down the steps, toward the river, waving a hand in front of her face to shoo a swarm of midges hanging in the sultry air. "How long until she can get on her new medication?" Linda asked.

"Another couple weeks," said Annie. "Will hasn't banished her, you know, the way she said, at least not yet. She can come to the house and see the baby any time she wants, but she just doesn't. Daddy says she's afraid to leave the house. She was so awful, today in church. I just wanted to sink through the floor."

"But you didn't," said Linda. "We all stood up together, just like you wanted. All-in-all, I think it went rather well." She gave Annie a look, and they both burst out laughing.

Linda sat on the low wall beyond which the ground dropped off steeply to the river below. The stone was cool from being in the shade. She leaned back so she could peer down though the trees. Below the bluff, leaves drifted on a slow, brown current. "My God, it's hot. I don't know about taking a walk." She puffed out her cheeks, deflating them with a long sigh. "There's something you could do for me," she said. "Promise you won't take it the wrong way?"

"Not till I hear it," said Annie, sitting down beside Linda on the wall.

Linda reached out to tuck a strand of Annie's long hair behind her ear, so she could see Annie's face. "Well," Linda said. "I've taken on a lot of design work, and I'm not feeling that great, with the morning sickness and all."

"That will pass."

"Yeah, well, I hope so," said Linda. "Anyway, I have a lot of deadlines piling up."

"Will says you're driven."

"I don't know that I'd agree with that," said Linda. "I need to be protective of my work time, is what I'm trying to say. Once our baby comes and I move my business out here to the house, business hours will have to be off-limits for unexpected social calls here, too. When the time is right, I like it when you stop by the studio, but we might as well have an understanding. You could call first."

Annie leaned away from Linda and looked her straight in the face. "Your clients just drop in, don't they?"

"Yes, of course, Annie. But that's business. Maybe I'm not saying it well. You and I could get together in the evenings, or on a Saturday, just the two of us. We hardly ever do that. I know you like to be spontaneous and just show up, but it's been happening a lot."

Annie looked at her feet, silent for a full minute, maybe two. The cidery smell of fallen apples came from the orchard on the other side of the house. The river below made a whispering sound. Linda waited.

"Okay then, fine," said Annie. "I won't show up without calling first. It's fine. I get it. It's fine."

"Come on," said Linda. "Look at me." But Annie didn't. "I was afraid of this," Linda said, "that you'd take it personally. I maybe didn't pick the best time to bring it up. Just tell me you see this from my point-of-view." She hesitated. "No going back to the air conditioning until you do."

"Don't do that," said Annie.

"What—?"

"Patronize me."

"Sorry."

"You're not the only one who does it," Annie said. She took a breath and, angrily, she said, "Will thinks my body chemistry's run amuck and makes me lazy. And dissatisfied. Postpartum inertia. Something like that. I decided to prove him wrong a couple weeks ago and ended up proving something to myself instead. I'm about ready to show you the results." Annie stood. "That is," she said sarcastically, "if I can have your permission."

Annie walked away from Linda, along the path that led away from the house, apparently emboldened by the hiss she'd given to that word, *permission*. Linda followed her. "Will was on one of his sales trips," Annie said over her shoulder. "I ran straight to the basement when Gracie slept." She stopped and turned around so abruptly Linda almost bumped into her. "I was nervous because I'd been out of the darkroom for months. I didn't want to be around the chemicals because of the pregnancy. Now I'm getting ready to pass your test."

"What test?"

"Color from black-and-white? Turning straw into gold? Don't tell me you've forgotten."

"Oh," said Linda. "Straw into gold? Oh, yes." Months earlier she had asked Annie if she'd like to experiment with a way to process film in diluted developer — an overexposure technique called *lith* printing that could yield a print tinged with delicate color from a black and white negative. Linda had given her an instruction manual, some special tapestry-textured paper and a selenium toner, to shift the neutral grays toward blue or sepia. She had proposed to Annie that if she could produce some gallery-quality compositions of defining places and details around town, they might collaborate on a photo series — "Picturing Linden Grove: Old Town Develops New Life." It would be a project they could do together.

But nothing had come of it. "I let the grant deadline go by," said Linda. "There's no money for it."

"Daddy would fund it," Annie said. "I'm almost ready. It's a tricky process, but I'm getting close to some really good prints. I'd still rather try for the effect with Photoshop, though."

"Photoshop would miss the point of what I had in mind," said Linda, "and I know you love to work in the darkroom." They were standing out of the shade now, where it was really hot. "Lith printing takes lots of practice, Annie. I know. I tried it myself. I didn't have the time or patience to master it. It seemed like alchemy, getting subtle gradations of color out of black and white film. With your background in photography, I thought you'd be able to get some really beautiful prints. I'm not surprised if you're on the brink of that."

"Well, thanks," said Annie proudly. "I'd like to show you sometime soon." Will was on the deck, calling Annie's name. "But I'll call first," she said, head down, smiling up at Linda. "Sorry I got bent out of shape. I've been a bit on edge today." She glanced toward the house.

Will looked left, then right, and saw them. "The technique is to make the print look dreamy, like a watercolor," Annie was saying when Will shouted again. "Is Grace with you?"

It was Linda who answered him. "She's napping."

"Where?" shouted Will.

Annie reacted to the alarm in her husband's voice: "In the master bedroom. Why?"

"She's not there." Will leaned over the railing further, craning his neck "Is your mother with you?"

Annie ran toward the wooden steps, Linda right behind her. "Mom?" called Annie as she hurried across the living room into the back hall to see for herself. The baby wasn't in the crib by the big bed, where Annie had left her. Linda checked the spare bedroom, and she and Annie were back in the living room by the time Frank hoisted himself to his feet from the low sofa, calling out Esther's name. John put the TV on mute as Frank called her name again and then followed Linda toward the closed basement door. They all crowded onto the stairs.

"Christ, Esther," she heard Will say, from a few steps below. "Didn't you hear us calling you?"

Esther stood near the far corner of the room, her head and shoulders pressed against the wall, her chin tucked down. Gracie was cradled in her arms.

The entire back wall to her left was glass sliding doors. Beyond a concrete drive stood the low stone wall built of the same oval river stones as the house itself. "He tells me not to go out there until I'm ready," she whispered.

*Who?* thought Linda.

"Didn't you hear us calling?" Will said again. Annie and her father went back up the stairs.

Esther twisted her body to protect Gracie with a shoulder as Will approached. He kept his forearms straight and aimed at her, hands limp from the wrists as if poised to rush forward and catch his daughter in midair. "We need ground rules." His diction was excessively precise. "Look at me. Esther? Stop this, now. You don't just walk off with the baby without asking us."

At last Esther inhaled. When she spoke, she spoke to Linda: "We wanted to see what the big attraction was down here in this so-called basement. It's not at all dark like I thought it would be." Gracie gazed up at her grandmother, eyes wide in a liquid stare. "How can you think with all those lines?" Esther indicated the wall to her right with her eyes.

"Those are drywall seams," said Linda. "This will be my studio, as soon as I sell my building in town. It is a bit of a blank canvas at the moment."

"I don't get that," Esther said.

"John tore out a wall to make the space big enough. His workshop's at the other end. Will's been helping him. I've got it planned to the square inch where I'll put everything." Linda pointed out the taped outlines on the floor, showing where her lithography and etching presses, sink counter, and worktable would go. "I can have our baby with me while I work."

Esther adjusted Gracie in her arms.

Long seconds passed.

"Best to wait her out," Linda said to Will. "She just wants to hold her granddaughter. That's all this is about."

If Esther knew she was being talked about, she didn't let on. The room was bare except for a sofa the color of orange marmalade and stacks of cardboard cartons Linda and John had never unpacked in the eighteen months they had lived in the house. Heavy footfalls, probably Frank's, moved along the wooden floor of the hallway overhead. "Let's go upstairs," Linda said to Esther, gently. "You'd be more comfortable holding Gracie in a rocking chair. We have one in the back bedroom. I know you're not used to so much visiting."

Will backed up to sit on the arm of the sofa.

Gracie blinked sleepily in her grandmother's arms, her chubby legs dangling like a doll's. Even the baby's hair had gone limp, collapsed on her head like a tiny mop. Linda pointed out the new doors for the kitchen cupboards where they leaned against a distant wall, but Esther didn't look. It was then, not daring to pry the baby from Esther's arms by force, but restless to do *something* while they waited out the impasse, that Linda recalled Esther's *blank canvas* remark from a few minutes before. She walked to the workshop end of the room where she opened the flaps of a cardboard box and rummaged through a collection of drawing tools. She came up with a fistful of pencils, charcoal, and oil pastels.

With an old palette knife, she peeled the end off an oil stick and wiped it with a tissue from her pocket. The stick looked like a large Crayola, big around as her thumb. "A livestock marker, oil paint in a solid form," she explained to Esther, who still wouldn't look. "I haven't used this thing for years, but it makes its own skin, so it never dries out. I'm going to do a portrait of you holding Grace. The way the light falls on your face is perfect." She made a mark near Esther's head.

"You're going to draw on the wall?" Will was incredulous.

"Like a naughty child," said Linda, chuckling. "It's time for us to distract ourselves."

"No doubt," said Will.

The doggy musk of oil paint took Linda back to art school, where portraits had been her first love. She touched the marker to the wall again, making a thicker line this time, wrist held straight to draw with arm and shoulder. "Talk to the baby, Esther. Let's hear your voice."

"I don't want her holding Grace unless one of us is with her," said Will. "It has to be a *hard-fast* rule."

Linda had never seen his lips pulled so thin, his gaze so wide and worried. "Well, we're with Gracie now," she said quietly. "Everything's under control."

The planes of Esther's face were flat, emotionless — a portrait artist's nightmare, no show of healthy, quixotic spirit to try and capture. So Linda began by scribbling Esther's crown of tangled hair. The next line extended the curve of her right eyebrow to form the ridge of the nose. Esther murmured under her breath, then sang—something about *paddywack, give a dog a bone*. With the singing came a sudden flicker of uncertainty in her dark eyes, as if she had just stepped through a door into the present moment. Her whole face changed, as if something about the song had freed her from the frozen schizophrenic stare. She raised the baby's head closer to her own.

Linda caught Esther's smile in a quick, unfurling line.

After that, Linda's concentration blocked out everything but the movements of her hand. She was six inches taller than Esther, a difference that steepened the perspective and lengthened the shadows, which Linda rubbed in with her thumbs. Feature by feature, she stared at Esther. Such close scrutiny, uncivil under other circumstances, revealed something in Esther's physiognomy Linda had missed before, when gazing at her casually and half in fear: a tenderness, blunted, but palpable. It began to disappear.

Quickly, Linda sketched the curve of the baby's head and added Esther's hands, fingers spread to hold her. After refining a line or two with hatching marks of an oil pastel, Prussian blue — adding detail in small, quick strokes from her knuckles now — Linda noticed Esther stretching her neck to look at the baby monitor on the carpet near her feet, its red light on.

"I brought that thing down here for you," said Esther quietly. "You don't look pregnant."

"Well I am," said Linda happily.

"She'll be after the baby's, too," said Esther.

"The babies?"

"The marrow of her bones. A genetic thing. She's an impostor, the girl you saw outside the church. She's out to get me."

Will's sigh was contemptuous. "She's a *delusion*, Esther. You can't tell when you're seeing things."

"That girl's as real as you are," Esther snapped. "I don't see things that aren't there *all* the time. Linda saw her. She'll be back. And I do believe in devils. Some people are hiding withered-hearts under their handsome skins."

Esther lowered Gracie against her hip. Quick as a reflex, Linda lifted the infant into the shelter of her own arms, stepped backwards with relief, and hugged the child against her chest even tighter than she had in church. All the warm and damp and compliant weight of the baby went straight into her heart.

But Will was reaching for his daughter. "The woman should be locked up," he said, carrying Gracie up the stairs.

Esther looked enormously upset as she followed him with her eyes. She continued to stare at the top step even after he was gone. "Schizophrenia discredits me no matter what," she said to Linda at last, a flash of savvy in her quick glance. "It's my curse to tell the truth but never be believed." She ventured another glance at Linda, and held the gaze. She looked toward the top of the stairs again. "That baby's in danger," she said sadly, "but not from me. I should be on hand to help my daughter. She needs me now. But you can see how I've been demonized by the man she thinks she loves."

# Chapter 3

As Linda pulled into the parking lot behind her studio that Friday morning, she was startled to see the Girl With Wings by the back door of Blue Earth Archaeology, across the parking lot. There was something recognizable in her posture — feet set wide apart, a boyish stance. She unloaded a box that appeared to be heavy, judging by the way she bent her knees, out of the back of a pickup with a rusty dent along the side.

She cast a fleeting glance toward the sound of Linda's car door going shut, then proceeded to lift the tailgate of her truck and shove it home with a loud *ka-thunk*. Clearly, she was strong, despite her anorexic build. Sunday's froth of curly hair was held down by a green cap with a bill. The design on her black shirt wasn't a winged horse this time, but the orange and white Harley-Davidson eagle. Maybe the woman had a thing for wings.

Linda placed her left hand on the roof of her car. Morning sickness was ten times worse than ever before, and she felt a tiny, shooting pain. Straightening up, she managed a friendly wave.

This time the stranger's glance toward Linda stuck. She lifted the bill of her cap with a thumb — but not enough to remove the shadow from her face. Still, even at twenty paces Linda could see the lines around her throat. This woman was much older than Becka's friend from church.

"Hey," the woman shouted. "I remember you. You held the baby at the christening."

Linda nodded, swallowing.

"Tell me— I've wanted to find someone to ask. And here you are." The woman was approaching fast. "Esther Hebring must have some sort of mental problem, to go off like that." Up close by then, she cocked her head to study Linda's face. "Are you okay?"

Concentrating on the flying ear of corn embroidered on the woman's cap, Linda fought another wave of nausea, which made her blunt: "Esther told me you've been harassing her. Calling and showing up at her house. Making bizarre threats against her granddaughter. Esther is my friend. I feel protective. Who are you?"

"She said I threatened the baby?"

"Yes," said Linda. "She did."

"Then she *must* be crazy."

Linda steadied herself against the car.

"I mean that as a question."

"She suffers from schizophrenia," said Linda. "It's an illness, not a character flaw."

"Okay." The woman's green eyes widened and flashed with something that might have been fear, or treachery. "You actually believed her that I was a threat?"

"Enough to be curious about who you are."

"I'm hardly the devil, as you can see," the woman said, her features softening into a grin.

"Maybe in Esther's mind—"

"Apparently." The woman hesitated, and then she said, "I tried to talk to her once, a long time ago. I even went to her house a couple of times. I certainly meant no harm. I'm a big fan of hers. She refused to see me, but was never as rude as Sunday, if you could call that rudeness. It might have been her illness rejecting me, don't you think? And nothing personal?" She raised her eyebrows at Linda and waited a beat.

Linda was slow to react, but it didn't seem to matter. The woman had a lot more to say about Esther Hebring: "Some of the stories

I've heard her read on the radio have stayed with me for days," she said. "Her inflection is never sentimental, even if the story is, if you know what I mean. And those voices. Wow. She *becomes* her characters. She chooses stories that lead to the kind of revelation that could change a person, not preachy, but true to life. I'd really love to talk to her. I had no idea she was mentally ill. To tell the truth, with her talent I've always wondered why she didn't get beyond a little local radio station."

The woman didn't even stop to breathe: "I was gone from this part of the state for years, for school, but now that I'm back in range of the station, I'm a bigger fan than ever. I always try to take my break from work when her show is on. I never meant to set her off in church. I feel like I did."

A stalker, Esther had called her. Linda pursed her lips to ask, *Why are you so fixated on Esther? It can't just be the stories.* But she wasn't quick enough.

"I don't care if she has schizophrenia." Tears flooded the woman's light blue eyes. "I mean, I *care*. I'm genuinely sorry, but— She must really be paranoid if she thinks *I'm* a threat. Maybe you could tell her for me how much I admire her work."

The ground shifted as Linda held her throat to swallow. Dizzy, she soon found she had unlocked the door to her studio and was sitting in the straight-back, wooden chair that was just inside. For a few seconds her consciousness had blinked. Now the woman was kneeling in front of her, saying, "Can I get you something? A glass of water?"

"Morning sickness. It's really bad." Linda strove to get her bearings. A pain shot through her belly like a spark. "I've made a terrible mistake."

"You're sure there's nothing I can do? I could call someone."

"No, really," said Linda. "What you can do is leave Esther alone. She doesn't need a fan trying to talk to her. She'll misunderstand, and she has enough suffering — Maybe in a few months, when hopefully she'll be better. She's not this sick all the time."

"I'd never say a bad word against a baby," the woman said. "No one would."

"That's not the point," said Linda. "Esther had to go into the hospital Sunday night."

The woman stood, staring toward the bright expanse of the studio. The cords in her neck were long and precise, her elbows wrinkled, her arms sinewy, way too thin. Then she looked straight into Linda's eyes, a gaze of anxiety and yearning. It was like looking in a mirror. "I'll stay a minute till you're back on your feet. The color's coming back into your face."

"All right. Thanks." Linda extended her hand. "I'm Linda Garbo."

"Yes, I know who you are." The woman's handshake was weak, her fingers cold as ice, though the day was hot. "Your name's on the sign in the front window," she said with a weak grin.

Linda watched the woman hurry across the parking lot. She hoisted herself up behind the wheel of her pickup, slammed the truck door extra hard, gunned the engine, and drove away. Beyond the skid marks where she'd been parked, at the back door of Blue Earth Archaeology, were a long-handled shovel and a cardboard box.

As soon as Linda's stomach settled and the pain was gone, she walked to the front of her studio. She couldn't draw the stranger's face from memory, but she did a quick sketch of her wiry build, her green bill cap, and the faceless shadow under it.

Linda left a message on Austin Benn's machine: "A skinny, blond woman just left. She didn't give me her name, but she left a box by your back door. I'm guessing she's a client, or might work for you, but I haven't seen her around here before. I wonder what you can tell me about her. I'm curious. Give me a call."

By nine-fifteen Linda had eaten a couple of soda crackers at her front desk. Any shift to move the computer mouse gave her a faint, wobbly feeling, so she tried to keep the swivel chair from moving. Her work on Frank Hebring's ad for the local Farmers and Merchants State Bank, where he was president, wasn't going well. When the farm futures report came on the radio — *pork bellies up two-and-a-half from a year ago* — she turned it down, her mind already sore from probabilities, percentages of risk. By her due date she'd be forty, which put her estimated risk of having a Downs Syndrome baby at one out of seventy-eight. The day before, on Thursday, by having a procedure done for genetic counseling, she had increased the risk of miscarriage by one-percent. That last statistic, which had seemed so small, was haunting her.

A wiry pain shot low through her abdomen again, and she was heartbroken that she'd taken such a chance. In the hospital parking lot, John had tried to talk her out of the procedure. "Most Down's babies are born to women around my age, John," she had told him. "It's all I can think about. If something's wrong, I want to know ahead of time. So we can educate ourselves, and plan."

"And talk about abortion," he said. "You know how I feel about that. I believe in choice, but I've made mine."

"So have I," said Linda. "That's not why I want this done. I just need to know what the future holds. There are support groups these days, and educational aides. But the chances are, the news will be good. I need to know," she said again. "You know how I am."

"But if all we're after is peace of mind, how can we justify the risk?"

"It's small," insisted Linda.

"And unnecessary," said John. "That's my point. It's not too late to change your mind."

The technician who administered the ultrasound was named Mason, a man with dark-rimmed glasses and a mustache. He smeared Linda's stomach with a clear, warm gel and slid a wand around on her skin to make images swirl on a small, green screen. The probe felt frictionless and sensual. Like a penis.

"It's called a transducer," said John, as if he could read her mind.

"Well, it would be." She squeezed his hand. They'd both read the brochure, but it was John who could see a term once and remember it. *Chorionic villus sampling.* Her doctor's words from weeks earlier replayed in Linda's mind: "*We can do it as early as*

*Mary Howard*

*the tenth week and get results in seven days, much sooner than with amniocentesis. You'll be within the first trimester, so if you decide—*"

"Eyes on the screen," said Mason.

"*—if you decide to terminate.*" The tension in Linda's body tightened as a wedge-shaped blur fanned like a weather pattern, then settled down to show baby-embryo, tiny as a lima bean. At the shadowy sight of eyeholes and cranium, the discrete fingers and thumb of a friendly wave, Linda felt a *ping* of joy. She squeezed John's hand.

"Will you look at that," he said.

Tears of happiness stung her eyes.

Dr. Arul Mukerjea had come into the room with a kit for the procedure, her black hair bundled into a green, gauze cap. Her voice rose and fell with her Mumbai accent: "It's best if you don't watch my hands."

But Linda couldn't help it. She raised her head to see a shockingly long needle hover over her lower abdomen and come to rest. Deeply, slowly, she inhaled, tightening her grip on John's hand. "It won't be bad," he said as the needle went in.

The pain was terrible.

"Easy, now." The doctor announced each layer as the needle pushed toward the uterine wall and then through it, with a definite poke. She continued to explain: "This part of the placenta is furry with finger-like *villi*. They are fine as human hair and genetically identical to the fetus."

Linda forgot to breathe. The pain was bad. She was in the hands of strangers. Her panic rose. She whispered, "No," then took a shallow breath, impaled upon the straight, bright line of the needle in her mind. This was a mistake. Again she said, "No," but barely made a sound.

"Deep breath, now," the doctor said. "Are you with me?"

"*No,*" said Linda. "Take it out."

"You're doing fine. There's nothing to be gained by stopping." The doctor's voice was very calm. "I need to concentrate. Now talk to me. Please say, 'Okay.'"

Tears slid down Linda's temples as she said, "Okay."

The doctor continued her gentle coaching. "The syringe," she said, "is aspirating *villi* from the membrane outside the amniotic sac. These cells will tell us the genetic makeup of the fetus. There, now— Out we come."

Linda heard herself gasp. Tears ran into her ears, and John stroked the wetness into her hair. His face was close to hers. "I should have kept my mouth shut in the car," he said. "We did the right thing. It's okay."

The procedure had taken half an hour.

The cramps had started in the night.

Linda pushed her chair back on its castors. She rose to turn off her neon sign and close the blinds in the wide window over her desk — but forgot the OPEN sign, turned out and trembling on its string just inside the screen door. She needed to finish two projects today or she'd never catch up. She had to concentrate.

By eleven, she was tempted to give up and start over. The moment she deleted the word FORTUNE off the palm of the hand she'd drawn on the computer screen, the phone rang. She hoped it would be John, checking to see how she was after her breakfast of weak tea. She'd tell him about the Girl With Wings. Picturing his lively brown eyes that crinkled to half-shut when he smiled, she answered.

"Linda? Would that be you?" It was Esther Hebring.

"Of course. Hello. Where are you?"

"Frank brought me home last night from the loony bin. I had to have a bit of a visit to settle down. I want to see my girl." *Me girl* was how she said it, in Irish dialect. "She said she was busy this morning, meeting with you."

"You're looking for Annie?"

"Am I to think she's not there?"

"I'm here alone."

"She doesn't want her own dear mother to see the child. I guess we know whose refusal that might be. Might you be harboring her then, on account of Will?"

"Of course not. She's not here, honestly."

"I'm ready to go on the air," said Esther. "I'm wearing the hat and boots for it. You don't fool me, the way you lead my Annie on. You're going to be after dragging us into some kind of pain. I hear the ticking." Esther's words slowed to an awkward beat: "Her pho-ta-gra-fee is to art as what I do — is to ac-ting. It's way off Broad-way, let's just say. Go on with you, and hire the girl."

In that moment, Annie appeared beyond the screen door. "Esther," Linda said calmly into the phone, "Annie's never mentioned anything about a job. Photography can certainly be fine art, and what you do is acting of the highest form. I've been your fan since I heard you on my car radio, the first day I drove into town. Right now, my radio's on." She turned it up as Annie pushed noisily through the door.

An artist's portfolio case slid down the screen and Grace's car seat banged against the doorframe as Linda said, "Don't sell yourself short, or Annie, either," into the telephone. She stretched the phone cord full length to unhook the screen door.

Esther dropped the scornful tone, and the accent, too. "Don't help my girl avoid me. Please. I've got to go."

Esther's theme music began to play on the radio. Linda's heart went out to the woman. "Esther?" she said "Annie—" But the line was dead.

Annie was wearing one of Will's old sweatshirts, stretched at the wrists and down to her knees. She thrust Grace into Linda's arms.

"Your mother thinks we're conspiring—"

"Well, we're not, are we? Wait till you see what I brought."

"It was you she wanted," Linda said. "After her program's over, you might call her back. I have a lot of work on deadline. I told you that."

Annie opened her portfolio on the worktable. Gracie flinched with the zipper's rasp, and Linda hugged the baby tighter.

All energy, Annie ripped a black and white toy loose from its Velcro on the car seat and took the baby back from Linda. "The ones underneath are the trials, so you can see how touchy your method is." She pointed to a stack of photographic prints, then walked away.

"Okay, I'll give you a half-hour," Linda called out to Annie as she headed for the loft, "that's all. Thirty minutes, tops."

Annie's top print did show promise — an empty warehouse by the railroad tracks, ephemeral as a watercolor in a range of barely-pinks, near-blues and browns. A peeling sign — Millard's Hatchery — hung above a plate glass window, cracked and half-boarded up. On its sill sat three pots of bright pink geraniums. Linda looked up as Annie reached the top of the stairs.

Between the two women lay what had once been the heart of Linda's printmaking studio. A counter along the wall to the left held sink and acid baths, now dry. The long, glass-topped worktable reflected the skylight like water. Over the railing up above, where Annie stood, hung an antique quilt of blue and white. "How come you have a crib up here, if you're selling the place?" Annie called out. "Is it for Grace?" Hope was painfully obvious in her voice. "So I can work with you?"

"No, Annie, it's not. Originally I thought I could work with my baby here. We just haven't moved it yet, since I decided to sell the place." Linda checked the harshness in her voice.

Hearing Esther's voice, in story-telling mode, Linda looked at the radio. *"Ah, these needles of rain'll go to yer heart like shards of ice—"* Esther conjured the Irish shopkeeper with her voice: shoulders hunched into a shawl, hair flying all blowzy around coarse, ruddy features. She sounded nasal, too, for the character's head cold: *"You need to get back to thad cottage and build yourself a fire."*

Static sizzled, like sleet hitting glass. Linda shivered. On Monday, because Esther had been in the hospital, the station had started the story over, from the beginning. Now Esther was back to pick up the plot, live from her kitchen table. There was a gentler rhythm, now, beneath the roughness of the voice: *"Sure and it's not a chill you're used to, whad with the sea raging so. Best be going back where you come from, Linda me dear."*

Linda's heart sank. There was no Linda in the Irish story.

Annie came back downstairs empty-handed except for her baby monitor — an ivory-colored plastic unit the size of a phone, emitting Grace's soft murmur. Annie scratched at a milky stain on the shoulder of her yellow sweatshirt and said something about geraniums. Linda was busy trying yet another design idea on her computer screen. She hit delete and turned to Annie. "What?"

"The flowers set up a nice tension, being so out of place."

"Flowers?"

"On the window ledge." Annie pointed at a photograph.

Linda walked over to the glass-topped table and stared at the muted pink, blue and brown mid-tones of the print, and at the swooshes of color above the flowerpots. "You didn't hand-tint this, did you?"

"The colors are from the selenium toner and the special paper," said Annie. "Except for— I added a tint to the flowers," she said. "All the rest of the color came from the process, honestly. And the texture— Look at the whites and shadows on that weathered door."

Linda's computer went to asleep.

"I can't bear the thought of shooting senior pictures and weddings like I did last year at Danny's Fotos," said Annie, "but I want to work. I know I could help lighten your load, do all your photography. Part time's okay."

"You've never mentioned working for me," Linda said. "I didn't realize—"

"I'm terrible at this stay-at-home stuff," said Annie, interrupting. "The house is a mess." Her tempo slowed. "I'm having regrets." She pulled her bottom lip between her teeth again and lined up three warehouse prints, two of them too dark. "I love what this process is called, 'excitable overexposure,'" she said. "You mix the developer so weak it takes forever, but when the image finally shows up, the darker it gets, the faster it darkens — a race to the one, exact split-second it has to be stopped. Too soon and it's washed out; too late and the picture goes out like a light." Her eyes filled with tears. "Every failure's like a little death."

"Oh, Annie—" Linda touched her on the shoulder, near that sour-milk stain. "It takes time to learn a new technique, time and practice. Lots of practice."

"I *have* been practicing. That's what I'm *show*ing you."

"You need to stop it out sooner, that's all," said Linda. "These are too dark. I have a feeling there's something else you want to talk about besides wanting a job. What did you mean by regrets?"

Annie walked over to the radio, to her talented mother's voice, so convincingly Irish. "I have no regrets," said Annie quietly.

*"She folded a lump of cheese into a small brown sack,"* said the radio, *"the paper's mad crackle the only sign of her temper until—"*

Annie turned it off. "You wouldn't have to pay me very much."

"If I hired you, I would pay you fairly," said Linda firmly, "but I'm trying to cut back on overhead by moving my studio out to the house. You know that. That's why this building is for sale. I don't have a job to offer you, or anyone." Linda hunched her shoulders forward slightly. She didn't feel too well. "We'll have to finish this conversation another time, but I can tell you — these are not as good as you think they are." She swiped at the air, backhanded, over Annie photographs.

Annie, flinched, taking Linda's gesture like a blow.

"I thought we had an understanding," Linda said. "I don't have time for this. Right now I just want you out of my sight."

The juggler's arms, like propellers, flashed, sending a fountain of blades into the smoky stratosphere, then down in a crash. A body melted and ran red across the floor. Linda turned onto her side and moaned with misery. Far away, a phone was ringing. She surfaced from the dream and — reaching both arms into the cooler part of the sheets — remembered where she was. Alone, in her old bed, in the loft of the studio. Downstairs, someone was leaving a message on the answering machine, while in the parking lot a sound repeated like a tailgate shoved onto its latches. Her brain had ended the dream with everyday sounds outside her head.

Her heart pounded. She hadn't had a nightmare for years. What else was wrong?

There was something else.

She remembered feeling sick, the cramps. She remembered how cruel she'd been to Annie to get her out the door and felt ashamed.

By the way the light in the studio had changed, Linda knew she had slept for a long time. She sat on the toilet. She put her head down to look for blood in the water.

"Thank God," she whispered. Clumsy with relief, she forgot the worst part of the dream and staggered back to bed.

Around five, the looping wail of the volunteer fire department siren — mounted on City Hall three blocks away — sawed its way into Linda's consciousness. She got up to wash her face as the alarm wound down.

The voice on her machine was Austin Benn's. "*Yeah, that was Nina. She does work for me. Moving an archaeology lab is a bit like moving a desert in cardboard boxes. She must have left one of them by the back door. We've been hauling things in here from the old place bit by bit. I'm on the road right now. If you don't hear from me again soon, give me a call back, or stop over when you see my truck and we'll talk about your mystery woman. She's temperamental. If you think you offended her, join the club.*" The message ended with a dry sort of chuckle.

Linda called her doctor's service about the cramps. Then she headed for home, a route that took her right past the *Times*. John's car was still there, so she parked behind him, and locked her car. When she stepped into the newspaper office, John was standing in his cubicle, his back to the door. He was putting his right arm into the sleeve of his denim jacket. They were the same six-foot-two, but his shoulders were stooped. As he tugged his hair, held by a red rubber band at the nape of his neck, from under his jacket collar, it was that move, so familiar, that brought tears to her eyes.

He turned and saw her. "Hey," he said, but his smile didn't last. His expression went long with worry, deep lines from the sides of his nose past the corners of his mouth, as if he'd already heard enough bad news for one day. "There's a barn fire south of town," he said. "I'm headed there."

"I heard the siren. It woke me up."

"What's wrong? Are you sick?"

She moved into his embrace. "I haven't been sleeping well all week."

"You've been stirred up, I know, since Sunday." He loosened his hold enough to study her face. "Those pains. They're worse?"

She shook her head. "No, but this afternoon I got so scared I locked the doors and fell into one of those deep, deep sleeps—" She took a shaky breath. "—the kind it's hard to come back from. I woke up drenched. Like when a fever breaks."

"Scared of what?"

"I was scared I'd lose the baby because of the needle yesterday. I was so relieved when I woke up and there was no blood. I was mean to Annie to make her leave, when she needs understanding, especially now. She's depressed, so why did I treat her that way? I just lost it. I got no work done anyhow. I'm so far behind and worried about how that stupid genetic test with the needle might turn out to be the worst mistake I've ever made, and I was awful to her. Just horrible."

"I can't imagine that," said John. "I'm not sure I'm following all of this."

"It wasn't the siren that woke me up the first time. I felt like something was about to blow apart. It was the dream. You know how they are."

"Sometimes they tell the truth," he said. "Is that what you mean? We need to work on easing your anxiety. I've got to get going, but I'll cook tonight. Go home and put your feet up and listen to some music. You know that calms you down." He touched her forehead with his hand.

# Chapter 4

Annie fled in anger toward her shiny red Focus ZX 3, parked across the street from Linda's studio. Gracie's car seat pulled heavily on its handle in her left hand. Halfway there, the straps of Annie's purse and diaper bag slid off her right shoulder to her wrist, so she ended up dragging the portfolio. "I should just drop it," she muttered. "Let cars run over it." She was that upset about Linda's dismissal. It was shocking, really, that Linda could turn that nasty.

By that time Gracie was screaming. Otherwise the neighborhood was quiet. Unnerved, Annie tried to snap the safety seat onto its base in the back seat, but missed the mark again and again. By the time the mechanism clicked home, she was perspiring furiously, so she unzipped Will's sweatshirt, pulled it off, and tossed it onto the back floorboard. When she put the car in gear and took off fast, the baby fell silent. She didn't make another peep as Annie drove.

It was a few minutes after one when Annie parked in the five-minute zone in front of the post office. She got out of the car and bent down close to the hatchback-window, holding her hands to both sides of her face to block the glare on the glass. Gracie's lower lip quivered as she slept, like maybe she was dreaming. Annie didn't want to wake her and make her cry. It would only take a minute to run inside.

Annie's was the only car parked along the street. She rolled down the driver-side window for ventilation and then took another look at Gracie in her rear-facing seat.

Ten weeks earlier, a man Annie had known in Iowa City when she was a senior at the University of Iowa, an old boyfriend, had sent her a page from one of his business note pads printed *with J. Eliot Boisseau — Conservation of Books and Paper Documents.* He'd addressed the envelope "Anne Hebring Cantonwine." The local return address made her heart pound — 530th Street, north of Linden Grove, a road that had once been a Rural Route. He was that close.

The envelope was square, leading her to expect a greeting card instead of what she found: *Meet me? You say where and when. I've been spending weekends out here in rural Madison County. I'm thinking of moving my business to the area. I can't decide. You'd be doing me a big favor if you'd agree to see me so I can return the book you left behind. Do you remember it? I should have sent it to you long ago. I need to get it off my hands. I'm packing up to move.* He had signed it *JB*.

Not *Love, Jack.*

The same day Annie received that note from Jack, back in July, just a couple of weeks before Grace was born, she had composed an answer she thought made her sound sure of herself: *You obviously know I married Will, and where I live. Why not just pick up the phone and call? If he answers, don't say anything and he'll hang up. He'll think you're a telemarketer. We get those calls all the time. Anyway, he's out of town a lot. My friend Linda Garbo has a building for sale down town that would be perfect for your business. Call, and we'll figure out a meeting place.*

She had signed the note with the letter *A.* The stationery was cream-colored, classy, with a pebbled finish, something she'd received as a gift. She had zipped it into the inside compartment of her purse, lacking the nerve to send it, the way she'd made it sound like she wanted the meeting to be a secret from Will. Frequently, over the weeks to follow, she had felt a zip of excitement whenever she thought of the envelope hidden there, like a possibility.

Today, leaving Linda's studio, terribly hurt and royally pissed off for being shown the door, Linda having dismissed her photographs with an insulting, backhanded wave, Annie felt like mailing her letter to Jack. She'd come to the main post office in town because she needed to buy stamps, too.

Jack was vivid in her mind — his high forehead, blue whisker shadows across cheeks and chin, a cloud of inky-black hair — long-faced and exotic, not like the guys she'd known growing up in Linden Grove who'd been mostly blue- or green-eyed, sandy-haired, and pink around the ears — but he had turned her loose, too, in a cold sort of way, sending her straight into the path of Will Cantonwine.

Annie pulled the door to the post office open to consider the distance to the OUTGOING MAIL slot on the back wall, next to a bank of P.O. boxes. Stepping back, she held the door for a woman carrying a package up the steps. From where Annie stood, she could barely make out the white edge of the infant seat in the back of her car. *Jack*, she was thinking. She inhaled self-consciously, like the last deep breath before a dive. The air smelled like grape bubble gum.

Gracie would be fine. Buying stamps wouldn't take that long. The lady with the package was the only person ahead of Annie in line.

At two that afternoon, Annie stood in her dining room, in a patch of sun. Will was due back in three hours from an overnight trip to Omaha. She had put Gracie down for a nap in the nursery down the hall, her favorite stuffed toys, the black and white cow and a lamb named LuLu, nestled beside her head. The couch, just a few steps away, was occupied by two baskets heaped with laundry, as usual. Annie slid the screen door open and stepped onto the patio. A broom leaned against the siding, where she'd left it the day before.

The baby's sleepy cry idled over the monitor on the dining room table behind Annie, just inside the house. She poked the broom at a drift of yellow leaves, curled like tiny hands, along the foundation. Gracie's tinny murmurs died down, but then she hiccupped and cried louder than before.

As Annie stepped inside, the baby's cries grew louder. She had been fed, burped, changed, and cuddled. Annie didn't know what else to do. Panicked, she turned up the radio as her mother's theme music began to play. KSAI recorded Esther's program at ten and replayed it at two, Monday through Friday. Because she had been in the hospital that week, the station had covered for Esther yet again by backing up to the beginning of the story about an American woman waiting for her lover in Ireland and the old shopkeeper who was hostile to her. Annie knew the Irish lover would turn out to be a terrorist because she'd read the book.

After her rest in the hospital, Esther's voice was strong as ever. Annie could picture her mother sitting at the kitchen table, gesturing over her microphone, some scarf or hat or other on her head to help her stay in character: *"'Now aren't you just our darling child?' says I to her, herself so snug and warm-like in the corner of my arm."* Annie cranked the volume even more, cover for Grace's crying while she wore herself out. *"It's getting late,"* shouted the radio. *"I feel it coming on me like a chill. Ticking against the window. These icy rains'll be after piercing your heart like needles."*

The second character in the scene spoke up then, a twenty-something Midwestern American, modest and excessively polite. It was remarkable, her mother's talent for creating the illusion of two people in a conversation.

But not totally convincing at the moment. Annie heard a half-tone off in her mother's voice. *Willing Suspension* was supposed to mean going along with a fiction, forgetting a story hadn't really happened, believing a character was *real,* but Annie couldn't be taken in. She crouched to find her face reflected in the oven door before she sprayed it and scrubbed with quick, frenzied movements until it squeaked, while down the hall and through the monitor, the baby cried.

*"Give us a smile, if you hear me, now."*

Annie smiled into the black glass of the oven door.

*"By what right does she come for me?"* asked the radio. *"One of these days the world's going to close around us, Annie me girl? Are you listening?"*

Annie's heart pounded out the silence — a thousand-one, a thousand-two. *"Annie?"*

"For god sakes, Mother, stick to the story. It's not about *me*."

*"It's about your going places with your photography. You're not like me."*

"Mother—?"

*"One of these days, one way or the other—"*

The voice was out of tune, out of character and straying far from the plot. Annie stared at the numbers on the radio dial as Esther noodled around, back in dialect, riffing on *"one of these days, one of these days—"*

Annie faced the kitchen table littered with breakfast dishes — the stove top with its greasy, egg-crusted frying pan — the counter littered with smeared plates, a sprinkle of coffee grounds. Crumbs popped underfoot as she fled the kitchen. Esther had lost her way once or twice before — improvising on the air to drown out the voice in her head. That was Frank's theory, anyway. Annie stopped short at the patio door. "Daddy," she said, blaming him in exasperation. "You brought her home from the hospital too soon."

Out on the patio, the yellow leaves Annie had swept into a pile skated across the flagstones as the wind came up. The baby cried and cried, and Annie took ten more steps away from the house. She smelled the breeze, inhaling a hint of leathery, old-book mustiness from the dried-up garden, and a mannerism typical of Jack Boisseau — boyish, head bent forward to disguise his confidence — came back to her. Recalling him was an escape from all of this. She turned around to stare past that cluttered dining room table into the kitchen, at the scatter of coffee grounds and a few Rice Krispies from the box she had knocked over at two in the morning when she had stumbled upstairs from the darkroom into the light at last. *"Aye, it's a devilish thing. The Lord'll be after stopping me now, my Annie. Sure and it's a paradox."*

Annie had never heard her mother talk about devils until her rant in church on Sunday. Now here she was again, saying *devilish*, way off script. Listeners in south-central Iowa and part of Missouri could hear her talking crazy on the radio. Why hadn't anyone caught it at the station that morning when she'd done it live?

It was pathetic, really. Esther was going to have to be locked up again, and Gracie was screaming down the hall like a maniac.

When Annie turned her head she could see her purse, hanging by its strap on the back of one of the dining room chairs. The baby fell silent. Annie stared at her purse, just hanging there.

In no time, the letter to Jack — the one she had mailed at the post office ninety minutes earlier and then begged the clerk to return to her — "because mailing it would be the start of a mistake" — was in her hand. She put the cream-colored envelope in the mailbox outside the front door for the mail carrier to take. There. It was done. Grace began bawling again, as if — even over the rising volume of her grandmother's voice — *"hot as pokers to sear the heart"* — she had heard the front door open, then close.

The previous Friday, before Grace's christening, with Will due home from a four-day absence, Annie had stayed out of the basement darkroom. She had been excited about the baptism, when Linda and John would stand up with them. While Grace slept, Annie had straightened up the house and mopped the kitchen floor. Will walked in the door at four-thirty to find his home in order and his wife dozing on the sofa, a book turned over on her belly to save her place. When she opened her eyes, he said, "Don't rest a book like this on its bindings. You'll weaken the spine."

Frowning, he lifted the book from her body and closed it. He sat beside her, stroking a loose strand of hair back from her face. "You looked so contented, lying here. Bet I know why." He lifted the volume in his right hand. "You were remembering that day on the steps, when you were crying."

Will liked to tell the story, like it was foreplay. "I wasn't crying," Annie said.

"Amazing, isn't it, how a chance meeting like that changed our lives. Now we have each other. We have Grace. All because of your being there when I went to pick this up." When Will opened the book again, it fell open to the etching just inside the cover. The illustration showed a plant suspended mid-page, root-ball meticulously round and hairy. Stems waved like an underwater thing, bearing dark-veined leaves and three-petaled flowers. The blooms were a remarkable pink for the age of it: An illustration from Kreuterbuch by Dr. Gracenart Fuchs, 1543. "That why you took this off the shelf today?" Will asked. "To remember?"

What could she do, but smile? In truth, she liked the smell of it.

The volume was from Will's collection of rare books. She loved its complicated, woody reek and the warm scent of dust, like dry leaves. The old volume reminded her of Jack Boisseau's shop, up a narrow flight of stairs, and the work table where he had taken that book apart at the spine and scraped off the amber glue, made from the bones and hides of animals. He had worked on that very book, off and on, for the entire span of their affair, repairing torn pages, removing stains, re-sewing the leaves, bringing the leather case back to its former luster, explaining every step along the way. "If you take a book back to the way it used to be, slowly and patiently," Jack had said, that last time she had gone up there, "no one will know you touched it. No one will know you'd been there."

The book was ready for the customer. Jack was breaking up with her. "I've tried to explain to you it might end this way."

"I know," she whispered. "I suppose you couldn't get *her* out of your mind." His wife had cheated on him, and Annie had been there to cheer him up.

Jack was wrapping the book in brown paper so fast and noisily it made him seem angry. "We've made a mess of things."

"To *me* it's not a mess."

"I mean *she and I* have made a mess of things," he said. "I promised her I'd have this conversation with you. Today."

Annie stared at him in disbelief, tears standing in her eyes.

"You have your whole life," he said. "I'm too old for you."

"Not if you loved me," said Annie. "You said you did."

"All right—"

"You don't love me."

"No," said Jack. "Not the way you want me to."

"That's not very original."

"I'm a lot more ordinary than you think I am." A water-stained book about clocks lay on his table, waiting its turn to be stripped down to its antique glue and broken threads. He tensed his jaw, and rubbed his fingertips against his thumbs, like he was trying to rid himself of something sticky. He turned his face toward the sound of the door opening at the bottom of the stairs.

She wiped the corners of her eyes, not crying, really.

Someone was halfway up as she burst onto the landing at the top. Starting down the stairs, she could see she'd have to turn her body sideways to get past the man below her without slowing her headlong rush to reach the street. He was a tall, blond, featureless impediment. The way narrowed with every descending step; but as she reached the riser above him, he made an awestruck question of her name, "Anne Hebring?" She pushed his hand away as he announced his own name, "from church, back home."

After she reached the street, she pretended to study a dress in a store window, panting until her heart slowed and her mind returned to Jack, up there, endlessly restoring worn out books. She wanted him desperately, aroused by the thought of never touching him again. Tears spilled from her eyes. She hadn't recognized the man on the stairs, Will Cantonwine. He had wire glasses and meticulous hair. She figured maybe he was the father of one of her friends.

That night Will had called. "None of my business," he had said, "but I wondered if a good Italian meal would make you feel better."

It had. For their second date he had invited her home to Madison County to watch him be best man at John and Linda's wedding.


At suppertime, Will sat at the kitchen table holding Grace while Annie stir-fried chicken with strips of green pepper, carrots, onions. At the last minute she tossed in a handful of cashews. While they ate, the baby swayed transfixed in her bouncy swing. When the doorbell rang, Will rose to answer it.

Annie heard the front door open and then a man's voice. When the door closed a minute later, she swallowed. "Who was it?" she called out.

Will stepped into the doorway. "Ken Hansen, from the police department. He's asking for you."

She let her fork clatter against the plate and knew something had happened to her mother, something worse than talking crazy on the radio. Annie hadn't heard back from her dad all day, after she'd left a message for him at the bank. A stocky man stood by the front door. Behind her, Will was bringing the baby.

"There's no emergency," the man said to her, seeing her expression.

"Then what—?" asked Will.

"We got a couple of anonymous calls this afternoon."

"What kind of calls?" asked Annie.

"I'd like you to help me decide what to make of them. This visit isn't all that official. I'm not here to accuse you of anything." He kept his eyes on Annie's face as he went on: "I've known your dad for years, and I'm acquainted with Will, here, too. Let's just say I'm here out of personal concern, and to get your reaction, like I said. We get crank calls down at the station from time to time. This afternoon one of the clerks took two calls I'd put in that category, a few minutes apart." He paused to breathe, then let his shoulders drop. "The calls were almost identical, a woman's voice, a report you left your baby in the back seat of a red, '99 Ford Focus ZX3 with vanity plates, ANN CAN. I see it's in the driveway. The caller didn't identify herself, so we can't give this much credence." He raised both his hands as if to ward off what Annie might be thinking. "I feel protective," he said. "You understand."

"Not quite," said Will.

"Most nuisance-calls are tied up with some sort of immature joke. This one is more troubling. The clerk thought I should listen to the recordings."

Annie felt her lips part as Detective Hansen explained himself: *Child endangerment.* She took Grace from Will and rocked her from side to side.

The detective attempted a smile. "I do want to make sure you are aware of what the law says about leaving a child unattended in a car."

"We are aware of that," said Will. He removed both laundry baskets from the sofa, dropping them on the floor, then backed into his easy chair and sat on the edge of it, knees wide apart.

The detective stayed on his feet. So did Annie. She held Grace against her with both arms. "Who would say such a thing about me?" She knew the question contained her denial.

"Well, like I say," said Hansen, "we don't know. The caller gave your license plate and the location, in front of the post office. A precise time of day. Even the number of minutes the child was left alone, eleven." Annie felt her ribcage rise, thinking about the line to buy stamps, behind the woman with the package, who took forever. "Without the caller's name, of course," the officer said, "there's no cause for official action. At any rate, there's no harm done. The thing that gets me— The call could be taken as a threat."

Will rose to his feet. "What kind of threat?"

"It's in the attitude, the tone of voice, more than in the words themselves." The detective shifted his feet on the carpet. "Tell me this: was your car parked in front of the post office around one?"

"Yes," said Annie. "Grace was with me." Will was still frowning at the officer.

"If this were an credible report of child neglect," he said to her, "I would have the Department of Children and Family Services send someone around to investigate. As it is, please don't be unduly alarmed by my being here. Just be alert to anything unusual in terms of a stranger's attention to the child."

"Why? Exactly what did this person say?" asked Will. "It had better be convincing, for you to upset my wife like this."

"The most troubling part was—" He flipped a notebook open. "'Think what could happen to a baby left alone like that.' It's ambiguous. Could be a warning or a threat, if you see what I mean. So when in doubt— Well, here I am. There was a case in the northern part of the state, just two years back, you might recall, a baby taken from a car under just these sorts of circumstances. A car parked in front of a local business in the middle of the afternoon. The baby—" He licked his lower lip.

"I do remember," said Will. "That baby's body was found—"

"So I was nervous after I heard the recordings," said the detective, nodding.

Annie breathed carefully. She watched the officer observe the gentle way she held her daughter, right hand under her bottom for support, left hand stroking her silky hair.

"Just take the information for what it's worth." He started for the door. His last question seemed like an afterthought. Half-turned to face her, he looked Annie in the eye. "Did you leave the baby alone in your car this afternoon?"

"She's already answered that question," said Will.

Detective Hansen must know she had done no such thing. "I did go to the post office around one o'clock," she said evenly, "to mail a letter and to buy some stamps." Annie wasn't looking at anyone. "Gracie was sleeping in my arms."

# Chapter 5

A week later, on Friday morning, the twentieth of September, Annie answered the phone and Jack Boisseau said, "I got your note. When I can see you?"

Annie's heart lurched so hard it hurt.

"Don't hang up." Jack waited, but not long. "You still there?"

"Yes." She closed her eyes.

"Anne." His voice was deeper than she remembered. "Is this a bad time?"

"No. It's fine."

"I'm afraid I gave you the wrong impression when I wrote," he said. "I want to return your book to you, but not behind Will's back. *Jens Olsen's Clock,* remember? I never meant to keep it this long, but at first it seemed awkward, and then I just kept putting it off. Where can we meet? Your house? A restaurant? You name it. Annie?"

"I have a baby. She's two months old. Her name is Grace. I really can't talk to you now. I'm too embarrassed." Annie hung up the phone, then grabbed it back and listened to the dial-tone drone.

Before Annie left the house, she looked in on Will, who had been sick all night with fever and aches. He was asleep on his back, covers pulled down to mid-chest. His breathing clicked in his throat and his undershirt was damp. She touched his forehead, too, and his hands, where his skin was cool. He stirred, working his mouth like it was dry, but he didn't wake up. She refilled the water glass on the table next to the bed and whispered, "Gracie and I are going out."

He opened his eyes a little and managed a hoarse "Okay, Sweetie." She left him a note anyway, on the kitchen counter: Gone to take pictures.

When she returned, around ten-thirty, the bedroom door was still closed.

Around eleven, Annie sat cross-legged on her dining room floor, just inside the patio doors. Grace lay on a blanket next to her, a bubble of milk at the corner of her mouth. Will hadn't come out of the bedroom yet. The weekly *Linden Times* — already two days old — was spread out on the floor. The front-page headline was *Fewer deer would be just fine with rural Linden Grove man.* "David Sowers' truck sustained $5,600 damage when it struck a deer last Thursday night."

She skipped to a page-two article that told about how Linden Grove had paid a guy two thousand dollars to fog trees downtown with a mist that smelled like grape bubble gum. The spray was guaranteed to irritate crows' nostrils so they wouldn't roost in the business district and poop on the sidewalks. The *Times* had used the word 'excrete.' Annie remembered a sweetish, grape smell outside the post office on Friday the thirteenth, 2002 — a whole week ago, the day she had gotten away with leaving Gracie alone in the car. Feeling guilty, she scooted a few inches to the right so the length of the baby's body rested against her thigh. It was her job to fall in love with this baby, a job she wasn't good at.

Turning back to the front page, Annie began to read John Bender's article below the fold about the club drug Ecstasy: *X marks bad trip for local youth.* Bobby Milhous, a high school senior, had overdosed and undergone treatment at Iowa Lutheran Hospital in Des Moines. She knew Bobby, could see him in her mind, his pupils huge in her camera lens as she took his senior picture. Last spring, long before his overdose.

"Just X," he had told her as she raised her camera and told him what she saw. "No big deal."

She had moved him into the sun, so his big pupils wouldn't give him way. Bobby Milhous, stoned on god-knew-what. She might have killed him, keeping his secret. She saw that now. She'd been seeing a lot of things a bit clearer since Detective Hansen showed up at the door and spoke with the voice of the world about child endangerment.

Annie hunched over the newspaper. In John's story, Bobby rattled off all the illegal substances he'd gotten from older friends. She put her finger down to keep her place and remembered the time she took Ecstasy and danced in a sweaty crowd until she nearly died of thirst. "I hope Bobby Milhous," she whispered to Gracie, "is going to be okay." And then she added, "I love you, baby." She slipped a finger into her daughter's tiny fist and felt it tighten.

She read Bobby's drug-list in a musical, soft voice for Gracie, who seemed to like the gentle tone: "Marijuana, hashish, opium, meth, cocaine. Anything I can do without a needle." Those were Bobby's words: "I'm afraid of needles." He stole from his mom's purse if he ran out of money from working at the grain elevator. In the emergency room, he thought the doctors stole his thoughts by shining lights in his eyes.

The kitchen wall-phone rang. Annie jumped up to answer it, heart thumping.

It might be Jack again.

But it was Linda, sounding like she just won a prize: "Hey, Annie, it's such a gorgeous day. I've been thinking about you a lot. You caught me at a bad time last Friday. There's no excuse for my throwing you out like that. I was upset and took it out on you. I'm embarrassed."

"It's all right," said Annie.

"No," said Linda. "It isn't. Something just came over me, and it was a wakeup call that I need to get a grip." She waited. "Is this a bad time to talk?"

"No," said Annie. "I was just reading John's interview with the Milhous kid."

"The boy and his mom asked for that interview," Linda said. "It was supposed to be part of Bobby's rehab, tearing down the secrecy. That's what he told John."

"The way he told it in his article, Bobby made it pretty obvious he was mixing his drugs, but then John went on—" Annie thought better of finishing her thought out loud that John had blamed the love drug Ecstasy for Bobby's craziness, that he'd made the evidence fit his argument that X is totally dangerous by itself, that it gives you hallucinations. The worst it had done to her was give her a backache so bad she'd only tried it twice. Maybe three times. Once with Jack.

Now she wanted to please Linda, to overrule the bad impressions from all the times she had gone silent in the middle of a thought, out of nervousness. "The quotes are good," she said quickly, "like the U.S. attorney saying, 'It's a mistake to think drugs are an urban problem. Our cornfields don't protect us.'"

"You must have been pretty upset when you left here Friday."

"You hardly looked at my work," Annie said.

"That's what I'm trying to apologize for," said Linda. "You need to pull the prints sooner, but your efforts are very promising. I should have said so. I'd like to come over and take another look at that print, the best one, the shot of the warehouse."

"Now?"

"When it's convenient. I'd hate to see you give up on the brink of something spectacular."

Annie grinned and shrugged with pleasure. "I started experimenting with the other negative you gave me, the picture you used for the town logo, the linden tree?"

"How about tomorrow, then? Late afternoon?"

"Okay."

"I'm dying to see Grace, too," said Linda. "I'm wondering. Last Friday, after you left my place—" She paused.

*Linda knows about the visit from the cops*, Annie realized. "The amount of time I was in the post office," she said quickly, "that much of it was probably right, eleven minutes. A precise detail like that can make a lie ring true."

Linda didn't make so much as a breathing sound. Then she said, "I don't know what you mean."

Annie walked across the dining room to where she could see down the hall, to the closed bedroom door. Panic confused her so much that she blurted out the first thing that came to mind: "I mailed a letter, and then wished I hadn't."

Alarmed and confused, Annie remembered how the woman ahead of her at the P.O. window had taken forever choosing to send her package Priority Mail and then couldn't decide between Love stamps with hearts, or stamps with birds and flowers. Annie had shifted her weight back and forth, looking at her watch. When it was her turn at the window she had said, "I just dropped a letter through the slot over there, by mistake."

The uniformed man — his nametag said Dirk Askelsen — had smiled broadly. He had a wide forehead, dark-rimmed glasses.

She had turned her head to glance through the window that faced the street. She'd seen traffic moving and hoped to God Gracie wasn't awake and crying. "I'm in a hurry."

"Give me the name of the addressee," said Dirk Askelsen.

"Jack," she had said. "Boo-sew."

"You mailed a letter and wished you hadn't?" Linda's repeated over the phone, bringing Annie back to the present problem: how to keep Linda from asking about the detective's accusation.

"I hadn't seen this man for three years," said Annie quickly, "and he wrote to me out of the blue. He said he wanted to see me again. I knew right away I shouldn't have encouraged him by answering his note."

"Who—?"

"Turns out he lives just north of here now, at least part of the time. He has a business over a hundred miles away, so I don't know what he's up to, way over here. Last time I saw him, four of us — my friends Jack and Mitch, and this other woman and I — were in Jack's apartment when this thing happened that was the beginning of the end. I thought it *was* the end. I heard from him again. Like I said. In July."

"I see." Linda's tone implied she didn't see at all. "The end of what?"

"The four of us did things together."

"Okay." Linda sounded like she was giving in to something. "What kind of things?"

"Sometimes we made supper together, watched a movie, played music and talked. The place had a dining room with navy walls and a paper lantern floating over the table like a moon."

"Annie? What are you—?"

"That night," said Annie, raising her voice to override Linda's, "we were sitting around the table with some other people, playing Trivial Pursuit. I got the question 'What was the name of Khrushchev's wife?' I did this memory thing to remember it later — *Khrushchev,* like a sneeze. At the time, I thought maybe I'd come up with the answer if I thought hard enough. I'd done this report for History of Dance, about Russian ballet dancers who defected to the West. One of them had a baby with a movie star. I didn't think they got married, though, so technically she wasn't his wife. While I was jabbering away to show I knew some things, like I am now—" *Oh, dear god, please. What will Linda make of this?*

"It's okay, Annie." Linda sounded amused. "I can't name Khrushchev's wife either."

"You can't? Really?" Annie plunged ahead, still too panicked to stop now: "All three of them were older, so the game was stacked against me. I hated that. Jack used to tell me that was one of our problems. Too much age difference."

"Jack is the one who wants to see you again?"

Annie stared at the closed door to the master bedroom. "It's out of the question."

"Right," said Linda. "Okay, now see if I have this straight: You were playing a game of Trivial Pursuit with Jack." Linda paused. "And — what was the point again?"

Annie bit her lower lip, remembering how Mitch had looked right at her and said, "Are you so clueless you can't see who's running the show?"

"I was staring at Mitch," Annie said out loud to Linda. "I thought he was trying to help me with a clue. Then suddenly Jack stood up. He bumped the table doing it." Annie took a breath. "Next thing I knew, he was shouting at Mitch, 'Take her with you.' He pointed at the other girl." Annie bit her lip to keep from saying *Jack's wife*. "She was large and energetic."

"Large?"

*Oh, God,* thought Annie, picturing Linda's curvy six-foot-two. "I mean not *tall*, like you are," she said quickly, "but very plump. I never thought overweight women were supposed to be that attractive, but she was beautiful, really a star. Her hair was fine as corn silk — long, pinkish Botticelli curls. 'Take her,' Jack kept saying to Mitch. He was furious, telling Mitch to take her with him or leave her alone and never come back."

"Why did Jack—?"

"He was trying to bring something out into the open. Mitch had been sleeping with her for weeks. Right there in their apartment, while Jack was at work."

"So how many of you lived there?"

"I didn't live there. Mitch lived down the block from them. I lived in the Tri-Delt house. Jack was giving him an ultimatum, to take her away with him *right now*, or give her up on the spot."

"In the middle of a game of Trivial Pursuit?" Linda laughed, but uneasily.

"It wasn't the middle. It was pretty much the end. The game was over. Mitch didn't leave. He just pointed at me and said, 'What about *her?*' Jack didn't look at me or say a word to stop me. I was the one who had to go."

Linda was silent for a few seconds. "That's quite a story," she said finally. "You lost me back with the moon floating over the dining table. Jack was living with a woman, but she'd been sleeping with the other man, Mitch. So Jack tried to get her and Mitch to declare their intentions. Do I have that right?"

"I'd been seeing Jack in secret, to be sure we really loved each other." Annie's mouth was dry. She felt like crying. The only reason she had been in that room was so Jack could even the score. That's how it sounded. That's how it was. Loving her had been Jack's payback for his wife's infidelity. Retaliation. Annie straightened the phone where it had slipped too low against her jaw. "After I mailed my letter to him — last Friday, I mean — I realized I would be very wrong to encourage him in the slightest way. I mean, I *love* Will. He would never do me like that." Annie's heart was sinking. "I had to wait in line to get the letter back."

"On Friday. After you left my place," said Linda. "A week ago."

"Yes. That's why I was in the post office so long. You can ask the guy in the post office, Dirk Askelsen. He'll remember giving the letter back. Gracie was sleeping in my arms." There it was, the lie she had thought she'd never have to tell again. Annie closed her eyes and said, "Ask Dirk, if you don't believe me."

"Why wouldn't I believe you?"

Annie hadn't heard the bedroom door open. Will was in the hallway, still in the v-neck undershirt and briefs he'd slept in, his left cheek creased from the bed. "Tomorrow afternoon, will be fine, Linda," she said into the phone, "for you to come over."

"Why wouldn't I believe you?" asked Linda again.

Annie watched Will's tender expression as he hunkered down next to Grace and said, "How's my girl?" Gracie's arms flew out to the sides. She drew up her knees and kicked, with a happy, crowing sound. Will gave his glasses a quick push against the bridge of his nose and studied Annie's face while she invited Linda to come by and take a look at the print again. Down the hall, Will's business phone rang.

He looked in that direction, still crouched down. In Annie's ear, Linda said, "I can make it by three-thirty or so. We can talk some more about this if you need to, if that Jack person is still on your mind."

"Well, he won't be."

"I won't be what?" Will's voice was brittle, congested.

"Will might have to stay in the bedroom while you're here." Annie smiled at him. "He looks contagious."

"On second thought," said Linda, "tomorrow isn't good. It'll have to be today. I have some onsite work to do for a client at two-thirty. How about four, maybe a little after? Will that work? I've got a busy week."

"Okay, and— I took Grace out this morning," Annie said, "with my camera. There's an old, deserted bank between the grain elevators and the tracks, across from that empty warehouse I took that picture of. It's unlocked, and I went inside. I think I dropped a stuffed animal in there, on the way up the stairs. I remember hearing that ripping sound when the Velcro let loose, but it didn't register till I got home. I got spooked by the place and just took off. That black and white cow is her favorite toy. She sleeps with it. Could you do me a favor and look for it on your way over here?"

After Annie hung up the phone, Will kissed her on the top of the head. "What did I tell you?" he said. "She wasn't really mad at you the other day. Linda doesn't hate you. She was just preoccupied."


"Who was Khrushchev's wife?"

Will looked up from his computer and grinned. "Nikita Khrushchev?"

Annie nodded. She stood in the doorway to his office, Grace in her arms. "You sure you're feeling well enough to go?"

He had rescheduled the afternoon's appointment in St. Paul, Minnesota, five-hours north, for the next morning, and was about to leave. "I'll get something from room-service tonight and turn in early," he said. "Come sit a minute." He rolled his desk chair closer as she opened her shirt and Grace began to nurse. She felt a pinch and tingle in her breast as the milk came down. "Nikita Khrushchev was Premier of the Soviet Union, in the sixties and seventies," he said. "How did this come up?"

"I've heard of him, Nikita Khrushchev, I suppose."

"He visited Iowa, believe it or not," said Will. "Rode in a motorcade through campus up at Iowa State and visited a farm near Coon Rapids. Along with six hundred members of the international press. It was a big story, a head of state visiting an Iowa farm in the middle of the Cold War."

"Why did he do it?" Annie asked. "Come here, I mean."

"It had to do with farm trade, corn and wheat."

"What about his wife?"

Will grinned. "Khrushchev brought her along." He bucked his head back abruptly, and raised a Kleenex to his face. "Nina," he said. He sneezed.

"You're not better. You shouldn't go."

"I'm just lucky the guy I'm going to see works on Saturday. I'll be fine. The fever's down."

"Nina Khrushchev," she said, trying to fit the name into a puzzle. She looked at her husband. His eyelids were puffy, and the tip of his nose was pink. She teased him: "I suppose you were there."

Will sneezed again. He made a honking sound when he blew his nose. "Not quite," he said. "My folks saved the Des Moines paper the day I was born, September 23, 1959. I still have it somewhere, a front page picture of Khrushchev riding in an open car, waving at the crowd." Will crossed the room to a file cabinet and in less than a minute he had the paper in his hand. A leafy smell drifted from the old newsprint as it broke along a fold line. He opened it flat so she could see the entire page of gauzy photographs. "Look at this. People hanging out of windows, like he was a pop star." Will frowned at the portly, waving man. "A controversial moment. A tyrant-celebrity."

"I thought he was a dancer," she said quietly.

In a few days, Will would be forty-three, and she was twenty-two. She studied the fine lines around his eyes, and a name popped into her consciousness: "Baryshnikov," she said. "He's the one who had a baby with a movie star."

"Yeah, Jessica Lange," said Will, relaxing backward in his swivel chair. "I saw her in *King Kong* when I was seventeen and fell in love. She was something, camping it up, wrapping Kong around her little finger with those sweet, sweet eyes. 'Hey, big boy,' she'd say. I hear they're remaking that movie again, real camp. I'll make sure we see it. They revive it every generation or so. I guess it'll be your first time."

*Jessica Lange,* Annie was thinking. *Of course. But who's King Kong?*

After lunch, Will packed his favorite picture of Grace on top of a change of clothes in his overnight case. Because of his cold, he pointed to his cheek. Annie kissed him there, which left a rubbery taste of after-shave on her lips. "Did you tell John about that policeman coming here?" she asked him.

"No, I haven't seen John for a few days." Will closed his case, and zipped it. "Why?"

"Something Linda said on the phone just now made me think she knew what that anonymous caller said I did."

"She couldn't know, Annie. I haven't mentioned it to anyone. I don't plan to."

"I hate it when you leave." She raised her eyes to his. "I'm afraid to be alone."

"You've never said that before, Sweetheart." He waited. "What brought this on?"

"When Gracie cries," Annie said, "I don't know what to do."

"That's not true. I've seen you change her, feed her, rock her to sleep."

"She cries anyway, for hours sometimes, when you're not here. It's like I haven't won her over. I might have lost my chance because we didn't bond the first time I held her. It was so awkward. I never even babysat or anything, and I've read that babies have different cries for what they need, when they're tired, or hungry, or need to be changed. All her cries sound alike to me."

"You're doing fine with Gracie," said Will, in a gentle voice. Your mom should have been able to help you with your doubts. I'm sorry, Babe, that she can't do that."

*Mary Howard*

"Besides," said Annie, "even when Gracie's fast asleep, I never get anything done. I'll try to work in the darkroom some while you're gone, instead of napping when she naps. Maybe that will help."

"You're not afraid to be alone down there, are you?" he asked.

"Not really."

"Sounds like you need friends right now," he said, "not a hobby that shuts you off by yourself. If you don't want to be alone, call your friend Tiffani while I'm gone."

"It's not a hobby," said Annie. "It's more than that. It's really what I want to do someday."

"Maybe you and Gracie can get together with Tiffani and—what's her baby's name?"

"Luther."

"Promise you'll call her?"

"Sometimes it seems like I'm paralyzed," said Annie.

"You're not paralyzed," Will said. "You're fine. When I get back tomorrow night I'll expect to hear you've made plans to get together with your friend. And why don't you call Ruthie Gustavson, see if she can baby-sit next weekend so we can go out, okay?"

He didn't turn his head to see her nod. "Will you do these things for me?" he asked again.

"Okay."

When he headed for the car, she stood on the threshold to watch him go. The neighborhood was quiet. Birds must have been singing, but she didn't hear them. On the island in the middle of Isabella Circle, planted with pampas grass and a ring of flowers, Margo, the old woman from next door, watched her dog nose around in the marigolds. He raised his head, but didn't bark, when Will started his car. Gracie cried like her heart was broken. Annie wiggled the baby's little hand, and Will waved back.

After putting Gracie down for her afternoon nap, Annie hurried down to the basement, a warren of cement-gray rooms with cracked floors and hanging light bulbs. The air smelled of chlorine and laundry detergent. She stood outside the darkroom for a few long seconds before she stepped inside and closed the door. The Fischer-Price monitor in her hand filled the small room with Gracie's screaming, drowning out the distant echo from up above. She had never napped without her black and white cow before.

Annie switched off the incandescent bulb, breathing deeply to fight the fear of enclosure in such a tiny room. Grace's cries grew slower, softer. In the ruby glow of the safe light, Annie got right to work. She placed the negative of the linden tree in the enlarger and worked fast, dodging and burning to brighten the sky and darken the corners of the foreground. She repeated the actions for a second print. Bending forward over the sink, she felt the cold liquid on her fingertips. She set the timer for twenty-three minutes, and slipped the papers in.

Waiting for a mirage-like image to rise under the surface of the liquid in the tray, Annie relaxed until she felt herself yield backwards onto the world's ugliest, oldest sofa, moth gray, shaggy with snags. In memory her head came gently to rest on a pile of newspapers that shifted under her weight. Jack had kissed her, and she had kissed him back. The avalanche of papers that slid her over the edge had made them laugh as they sank together onto the floor. Now, in the darkroom, remembrance of his mouth on hers was so palpable she longed to abandon herself to him, if she ever had another chance, no matter what it cost, but then she caught herself on a recent fact: On the phone he had protested he hadn't meant to go behind Will's back to see her again. Nothing can cool desire like ambivalence.

Quickly, she wiggled the prints with her fingers until Jack Boisseau's face came clear again, to her mind's eye. "You can come back tonight," he says, and she *is* back, in the rapture of a small, white pill. She had swallowed it for nerve, for the rush of bright red feelings from knees to mouth when they kiss. "Ah, that's more like it," he says. "You're trembling. Such a lovely girl." His sentences are short, as if he's talking to a child. He thinks he knows everything about her. She doesn't mind.

Now faintly, through the monitor, the doorbell rang.

Her hands dropped to her sides.

*Mary Howard*

It rang a second time. The number on the timer was down to twelve. The darkroom smelled vaguely of vinegar.

Her arms and fingers glowed in the rosy safe-light as she snapped open the can of Diet Coke she'd brought into the dark with her and counted another doorbell ring, and then another. Altogether, there were five. Grace made a sound through the monitor.

Annie took a long drink, letting bubbles spark on her tongue.

That obscure, high-energy *lith* process Linda had dared her to learn took a longer time than most. The dots on the timer pulsed: ten minutes to go. By now, Grace was fussing rhythmically. "Get those darks darker," Annie whispered, and tried again to conjure up Jack Boisseau. "Some anonymous woman called the cops," she imagines telling him, "and tried to make me look like a bad mother. I can't stop thinking that something about that phone call doesn't add up."

"Yes, it does," he might say. "It adds up to your word against hers. Look who they believed. Don't you feel how safe you are here?"

Smiling, alone, her memory of Jack's arms around her made her swell with pleasure again, but she kept one eye on the timer. Five minutes passed as Annie struggled to concentrate on what was happening in the development pan while Gracie cried. The night before, while Will had rested — sick in bed, watching a football game — Annie had completed three trial prints of the linden tree. With a little cooperation from Grace, she'd get the result she wanted before Linda showed up at four. Her breathing quickened as she watched the emergence of blacks around the tree trunk, roots, and the bottoms of the branches. Soon the texture of the earth would turn grainy, the clouds would bubble around the tree's crown. Grace's complaints slowed, then revved again, more shrill.

"Come on, baby, said Annie to the monitor. "Shhh. Give it up." The timer had five minutes to go. Then she could stop the first print, then the second, and open the door.

Gracie's cry grew weak. She was wearing down.

With less than a minute to go, Annie watched the seconds tick, tick, watched the shadowy parts of the picture sprout dots that grew and grew. They'd merge to solid black unless she pulled the print in time, to stop it out. The emulsion grains developed faster as they got bigger, a combination of size and speed that would lead to a sudden rush. Annie was ready for it, staring at the image of a linden tree that floated under her hands. The precise moment it matched the tree in her mind, she'd immerse it in the stop bath. Now she was sure of herself, counting, counting.

At last, Grace was quiet. In the dim light, Annie's fingers found the wheel on the side of the monitor, turning down the white noise coming out of it, like the whisper of breath in a seashell. Slowly she filled her lungs and exhaled. This was her place, this small room, a haven, safe. Two o'clock in the afternoon. She'd get it right this time. Her fingers touched the rim of the sink. Sometimes the snatch-point will pass you by.

# Chapter 6

Linda was buoyant, full of light. She had sobbed with relief when the letter had arrived at her office after lunch with the results of the *villus* procedure. The tears had washed something out of her, some sort of dread. She hadn't had a pain for a week, and the morning sickness was easing, too. Now, beaming with happiness, she powered all the car windows down and signaled left to head for Market Street. When a breeze lifted her hair, she raised her chin and closed her eyes for a split-second, savoring the caress on the back of her neck. Passing the post office, she felt the car slow down. Someone in a white pickup behind her honked, the driver's face obscured by a glare of sunlight. *The Girl With Wings?* she wondered.

Linda grinned into the rearview mirror, waved as if to say, "Sorry I'm so slow," and pressed the accelerator down. Behind her, the truck turned right. Over her shoulder Linda could see a company logo on the side and the beefy, denim-clad arm of the man at the wheel.

Earlier that September, Linda's pitch to the vice president of Holliwell Sign Company east of town, out by I-35, had secured a lucrative job designing their annual report to stockholders. For the past hour she'd been shooting photographs in their main workroom with her digital camera. Now, for the first time in days, she felt optimistic and confident. She didn't mind that Annie's errand would take her to the south edge of town, way out of her way.

The sky was especially blue, the air a crystalline lens that sharpened all the greens and golds of trees along Railroad Street. She turned onto Market, which runs parallel to the railroad tracks, and parked within sight of the place Annie had described: a small brick building dwarfed on three sides by grain elevators — The Heart of Iowa Co-op. On the huge sign facing the tracks, the O in Iowa was shaped like a heart.

Linda tilted her head back to locate the tops of the towering structures armored with corrugated metal. Networks of ladders, conveyers, and chutes made triangles against a sky too bright to stare at.

She watched her feet for balance as she crossed the shiny tracks, inhaling the piney, creosote stink of railroad ties. The building ahead was only about thirty feet wide, with not so much as a blade of grass around the foundation. Like the railroad bed, that ground must have been treated with some powerful herbicide, like Roundup, maybe.

Around front, high on the facade, the word BANK was worked in darker brick above a wooden door. Combed rough by years of weather, it stood ajar. It scraped against the floor as she pushed it open. She stepped onto a black and white checkerboard floor, marked in lines of sepia stains — where file cabinets used to be, perhaps. Odors of mice and mildew, of something left in the refrigerator too long, made her swallow hard. She hurried toward a door at the back and squinted up the unilluminated stairs. Halfway up lay Grace's black and white cow.

She brushed it off and shook it free of whatever disgusting bits of who-knew-what it had been lying in, which made it moo. What was up with Annie, bringing Gracie to this awful place? It made no sense. The light wasn't right for camera work. The sidewall windows were boarded up, and the pale sunlight falling through windows to the front was grainy with air-born dust. Something skittered overhead. Linda couldn't wait to get back outside.

Yet she stood there, remembering the way Annie's story on the phone had veered off according to some unspoken logic — or none at all. An incoherent story that had seemed at first to be a confidence she was desperate to share, until it got obscured by extraneous facts— such as a paper lantern hanging like a moon over a dining table, the sort of dead-giveaway detail a person might feel compelled to dwell on if she were backing off some point she'd started out to make. An out-of-the-blue story that had started with the post office and ended with an old boyfriend named Jack.

Outside in the fresh air, Linda slid her left hand into the pocket of her skirt, touching the letter from the clinic: *no anomaly*.

Grace's cow mooed again as Linda tossed it onto the passenger seat of her car and started the engine. When she turned onto Isabella Circle a few minutes later, she saw two police cars and an orange pickup marked Linden Grove Power and Light.

Her body went cold with thoughts of catastrophe. *Gas leak? Danger of fire?* A black-haired man leaning against the passenger door of the orange truck straightened up as she put her car in park. The front door of the house stood open. The guy gestured that direction with a fistful of yellow flags on wire stems. "She say her baby vanish right under her nose."

Linda slammed the car door hard.

"I went around back to start working, and the lady was there, by the patio. She looked very scared, and she keep saying, 'Oh, God, oh, God,' and her arms were bleeding. He lifted his shoulders. "Somebody took her out of her own bed."

"What do you mean?"

"Somebody stole the baby girl. They think I might have seen something, but I never did." The golden-brown irises of his eyes were full-round with shock and concern. His mustache was waxed to lift at the ends. "I know one of them, Ivan," he said. "He told me not to leave. I bet they forgot I'm here." Linda was aware of a slow arc of color as the man lifted his bundle of yellow flags and placed it on the hood of the truck. "I have two kids," he said. His eyes were full of tears.

# Chapter 7

All Linda heard was a rushing sound. Her hands were freezing and her heartbeat was ponderous in her chest. A white movement drew her attention from John's face to the street, where a police car was backing up to block access to the drive.

"Did you hear what I said?" John asked her. "Look at me."

"I heard you," she said to him. "You said Will left around noon."

"He headed up I-35 for an appointment in St. Paul."

"I thought he was sick."

"He should be there by now," John said. "He doesn't answer his phone."

"You think he could have Gracie with him?" Seeing the anguish in the way John shook his head, Linda turned her face away from him. She didn't want to cry in front of a skinny cop named Ivan Bold, standing not ten feet to her left, on the patio. He had raised the flat of a hand to signal *no further* a minute earlier, when John had appeared.

Now Ivan was busy with a roll of yellow barricade tape. By the back corner of the garage, a young man with a pinched-together mouth probed a pile of dirt. With each gentle lift of the garden spade, the rushing sound blew louder in Linda's ears. Her body felt too light. Her head filled with heat, and then the moment passed. *Oh, my God, Gracie, where are you?* She looked around.

*Mary Howard*

Beyond Will's shade garden, the neighbor's lawn to the north was a flat expanse of green interrupted only by a clothesline. Sheets and towels hung flat. "Must be old people live there, to still use a clothesline," Linda muttered, as if it might matter. John opened his cell phone again, and pressed it to his ear. "What if Will forgot something?" she asked. "What if he came home and kept calling out to Annie and got no answer, so he took the baby with him?"

"No," said John. "He would have known Annie was in the darkroom, and she'd have heard him on the monitor." John's hand went up as he said, "Call me. It's urgent." into the phone, his voice pitched a half-note higher than usual. He flipped his phone shut, a flicker of anger in his eyes. "I don't know why I can't get a hold of him."

"The word is, no one's home on Isabella Circle," said Linda. "Detective Hansen had his people checking around the neighborhood. Annie was sitting on the sofa with a basket of laundry when I arrived." Linda looked at her watch. "Twenty minutes ago." It was almost four-thirty. She inhaled with a jerk, remembering how small Annie had looked, how her shoulders had bowed forward. "'Find her,' she kept saying to me, 'Find her. Hurry,' over and over. And, 'I want Will.' I kept nodding like an idiot. I didn't know how to help."

"Did she say anything else?" John asked.

Linda took a deep breath. "Before Hansen asked me to wait outside, Annie managed to tell me that when she came upstairs from the darkroom she thought Grace was asleep, so it might have been as long as a half- hour before she checked on her and found the crib empty. Gracie could be a hundred miles away by now. Ivan here—" Linda nodded in his direction. "He says they'd searched the house twice before I arrived. It seems to her that nothing else is being done. It seems like that to me, too, John. The baby's second-favorite stuffed animal is missing from the crib, she told me, and a stack of diapers off the changing table."

"They have bulletins out," said John. "There's a TV satellite unit on its way."

"LuLu the lamb," said Linda.

"What?"

"The stuffed animal that was taken from the crib with Gracie. Why wouldn't Hansen let me stay with her, at least until her dad gets here?"

"Frank and Esther were right behind me. They're probably with her now."

"Hansen thinks they're going to find the baby by talking to Annie. While we just *stand*—"

In that moment someone behind the garage shouted, "It smells like beer back here." The incongruity of the words aroused Linda's attention so that other sounds broke through at last — the choppy talk of a police radio out front, a burst of happy music, a Doctor Pepper commercial, from next door. "Ivan says there's no one home." She pointed toward the muffled sound from the neighbor's open window: *Wouldn't you like to be a Pepper, too?* "If no one's there, then why is the TV on?"

John wasn't listening. "The beer's for his slug traps," he was explaining to Ivan the cop, on the patio. "He keeps a quart stashed back there. In summer they come out at night to eat his hosta lilies. Beer attracts them, and they drown in it. *It's not a God-damn clue.*" Ivan reared his head back from John's outburst with a look of abject puzzlement on his narrow face. "You're right," John said to Linda. "We can't just stand around. Maybe Will does know something that would tell us where to start." John turned to Ivan and said, "The guy doesn't even drink." John flipped open his phone again.

Linda could guess what he was thinking: There had to be an explanation that, in a word, would end the nightmare. From around the corner of the house came a familiar voice: "Let's see my girl."

At the mouth of the driveway stood Esther Hebring, wearing a white t-shirt, yellowed at the armpits, and gray sweatpants. Her nose and cheeks were florid, shiny. "It's designed to be difficult," she said to no one in particular. Linda walked forward into the sunny heat beyond the house's shadow. Esther lifted her chin defensively as Linda approached. "Greatness falls on those who rise to the occasion," Esther said to her. "No, that's not it. When the occasion presents itself," she said. "The stage is set." She turned toward the TV van. "If I'm not allowed to talk to Anne, I'm certainly not talking to *them*."

"We have to trust the officers," said Linda even as a seed of doubt began growing in her mind: *What has Annie been telling Hansen to keep him with her so long?* "You'll be able to see her pretty soon," Linda said to Esther.

If Linda's tone was patronizing, it didn't seem to register with Esther, who placed two fingers over her mouth. Her nails were ovals, lacquered red. A ring with a square-cut, emerald-green stone glittered on that right hand. Linda followed the woman's gaze to the roofline of the house. Esther nodded her head three times. She smiled an inward smile. Maybe she saw a message from God up there. Maybe she knew where Gracie was.

In a rush, Linda remembered holding the baby's weight in the crook of an arm, the comic innocence of her plume of hair, and the way she rocked her hungry mouth against whoever happened to be holding her. Tears sprung to Linda's eyes. "Esther?" she said. "Where should we look for Grace?"

Esther's lips parted, but that was all. No more shakes of the head. No signs of fear in her body language.

Linda's skin went cold. She lengthened her gaze to watch people from Des Moines Channel 8 set up their equipment at the intersection of Cantonwine's front sidewalk and the street. The blue and white van — with the landmark CHANNEL 8 water tower airbrushed on the side — ran its satellite dish up a thirty-foot pole. Linda recognized reporter June Sanderson, dressed for the camera in threadbare jeans, a cranberry-colored blazer, and a tailored shirt. Frank Hebring stood with John in the middle of the street, talking with Reverend Gustavson. Other people had arrived. No one Linda knew.

When she caught Frank's eye, he broke away from his conversation and hurried up to her, close enough to confide. He was sweating. "Esther needs a bathroom."

"Have the police questioned her? She could have taken Grace, like she did at our house the Sunday she was bap—"

"—No, she couldn't have," he said. Muscles tensed inside his loose-skinned jaw. "They've already grilled both of us. They searched our house, from top to bottom, apparently their first priority. I told them Esther never leaves our house without me these days. You know that. Anyway, right now she needs a bathroom. If you could help her find one it would free me up. I need straight answers about why my daughter's out of our reach in there like a prisoner." His eyes were wide.

"My car is blocked, or I'd take Esther to my studio for the bathroom. It's just six blocks away."

"Take my car."

Linda ignored the keys Frank offered. She turned to Esther. "Do you know the people next door?"

"She does," said Frank. "The woman is kind enough to bring Esther books from the library. What's her name, Esther?"

Esther wasn't talking.

"The police haven't been able to get a rise out of anyone in there," Linda said to her, "but their TV's on. Let's try. We'll use their bathroom. Come."

Esther obeyed, clasping her hands, twisting her flashy emerald ring, smiling that inward smile again.

Linda rapped on the front door of the brick bungalow with her knuckles. She poked at the doorbell six or eight times. She pounded the wood with both fists. At her elbow, Esther was breathing tightly. From inside, TV voices argued.

Next the lock clicked and a chubby boy with round cheeks and swollen eyelids opened the door. He squinted and blinked as if he'd been asleep. His skin was dark, blue-black in the lines under his eyes. His hair was matted to one side. His focus shifted beyond them, to the activity on the street. The news about Gracie made him loosen his grip on the sheet around his shoulders, revealing the red and yellow Superman shield on a blue t-shirt. "This is Mrs.

Hebring, Gracie's grandmother," Linda explained. "Do you know each other?" The boy raked his lower lip with his front teeth and shook his head. He appeared to be about thirteen. "Did you see anyone, anyone at all, next door this afternoon?" Linda asked him. "Between two and three?"

His *no* scraped out so hoarse and deep she didn't have to wonder why he had slept the afternoon away. She asked if Mrs. Hebring could use the bathroom, and he shook his head *no*. "My mom's not here."

"These aren't ordinary circumstances," said Linda gently. "If you have a guest-bath on the first floor, she can just use that. I'm a close friend of the Cantonwines. I'm sure your mom wouldn't mind."

This time he nodded instead of trying to talk, swallowing with such a bob of his head she knew his throat must be very sore. His nose was darker around the nostrils, and his upper lip was shiny. The house smelled of cold remedies: camphor, turpentine. He pointed the way to the half-bath in the front hallway. Esther's large ring knocked against the frame as she pulled the door shut behind her. She locked it with a double click.

*She's mentally ill,* Linda wanted to say to him, but the poor boy looked confused enough as it was. Linda followed him to the sun porch, where the loud TV featured an argument between two overwrought women with perfect hair and vivid makeup. When Linda turned it off with the remote control, the boy frowned, the corners of his mouth turned down as if to say, *Why did you do that?* His name was Burton Mack. He sat on the sofa in a tangle of sheets and bed pillows while she explained what was going on in the neighborhood outside. He glanced at the windows and looked bewildered.

"Do you think we could call your mom? Is she at work?"

"At the library."

"Yes. What's her name?"

"Cleo. Cleo Mack."

"And your dad?"

"He's a service mechanic at the airport. He also flies crop-dusting planes." The boy nearly smiled. "Sometimes he takes me up with him, on Saturdays." The smile failed, and he swallowed hard. "The dusting season is almost over. He's going to teach me how to fly."

"You don't have to talk, if your throat hurts."

"Someone took Gracie?" the boy whispered. He coughed six times.

"See that man?" Linda pointed at Ivan Bold, outside the double windows of the TV room. They watched him walk past Annie's car, around the back corner of her house, and onto the patio. "Try and remember," Linda said to Burton. "Did you see anybody go around to the back of their house like that this afternoon, or did you hear a car in the driveway?"

"Only Annie." He seemed to catch himself. "Mrs. Cantonwine."

"What time was that?"

"I don't know. I think maybe— Two o'clock? After my mom left. She came home to fix me some soup."

"You saw Mrs. Cantonwine walking, or driving?"

"Getting in the car," he said.

"What were you doing, when you saw her?"

"Watching TV."

"Lying there like that?"

He nodded.

Linda lowered herself to sit on the floor beside the sofa. Eyes level with his furrowed forehead, she could see only the roof of Annie's red car and the top inch or two of the driver-side window. "How did you know it was Annie?"

"Mr. Cantonwine never drives her car."

"He left on a business trip around noon," said Linda. "Did you hear him leave?"

The boy shook his head *no,* then raised his eyebrows, as if remembering. "She was wearing that yellow sweatshirt with the hood."

"Mrs. Cantonwine, you mean."

He nodded.

*Mary Howard*

"But it was really warm this afternoon."

He shrugged.

"Did she have the baby with her?"

He nodded again.

Linda pointed toward the window. "And then you saw the roof of her car back up past here?"

"I think so."

"And you heard it back onto the street and drive away?"

"Yeah, I guess."

Linda was vaguely aware that she was leading him and that she should be getting a cop to do the questioning. "How long was the car gone?" she asked.

"I might have been asleep when she came back."

"You're sleepy now."

"I took some of that." He pointed to the Nyquil bottle. It's supposed be for night, but my mom gave me some and then I took some more."

"After lunch?"

"Yeah."

Linda told him to rest and she would call the Linden Grove Public Library. The voice that answered said that Cleo had heard the news and was already on her way home. Then Linda helped him remake the sickbed on the sofa, smoothing the bottom sheet and building an incline of pillows so he could lie with his head and chest elevated. He was shivering, his breathing labored. She pulled a blanket up to his chin.

"Well," she told him, "you just take it easy. I'll get you some fresh water."

Linda picked up an empty glass from the table at the end of the sofa, where the triangular bottle of green Nyquil squatted between a box of tissues and a blue jar of pungent Vicks VapoRub without a lid. She headed for the kitchen at the back of the house, visible from the entry hall, but paused by the bathroom door when she heard Esther pant, then wail softly, as though her heart were breaking. As Linda touched the doorframe lightly with her hand, Esther fell silent, then uttered a descending moan. Linda tried to think of reassuring words, but all she could manage to say was, "Everything all right in there?"

Esther didn't answer. She didn't make a sound.

Linda filled the glass at the kitchen sink and went back to Burton, who clutched at his blanket and sat up enough to take a drink. He looked miserable.

Linda fought to keep her face composed. "The police will find the baby. They'll come and talk to you soon as your mom gets here. I'll stay with you till then." Another wave of terror hit, but she took a deep breath and asked another question: "People call you Burt?"

"Sometimes," he whispered. "Mostly they call me Big Mack."

"You don't mind?"

"I do a little." A pudgy hand clutched his throat as he swallowed again.

Linda sat in a chair and waited for Esther to come out of the bathroom, for Cleo Mack to get home from the library, only a few minutes away. The boy's breathing slowed, and then he jerked, opened his eyes. "What was that?"

"Nothing," she said. "Someone talking outside."

He closed his eyes again when she put her hand on his hot forehead, and said, "She'll be here soon. She probably had to park a block away or so. There's a traffic jam out there."

When Linda heard the bathroom door open, she went to meet Esther in the hall. Her hair was wet at the temples and her face was blotchy, but the set of her shoulders and the lift of her chin showed she felt better. She even looked Linda in the eye. Moving close to her, Linda said, "I'm sure we'll find Grace very soon, and you can hold her in your arms again. We have to figure out some way to help."

Slowly, Esther shook her head. Linda watched as Esther's right hand rose to press against her mouth.

*We need to find Gracie right away, or it will be too late,* was what Linda meant to say as Cleo Mack rushed through the door, clearly startled to find Esther and Linda there. She was as tall as Linda —

over six feet. Elegant dark features. Extremely slender. Prominent eyes like her son's. When Esther extended her right hand for Cleo to shake, it struck Linda that Esther's fingers were bare. After Burt called out in a broken voice from the other room, and Cleo went to him, Linda said, "Esther?" If only she could get her to talk. "Your ring, Esther, the green one. You were wearing it when you came in here. Where is it now?"

Esther lifted her chin another quarter inch.

"Okay, then," said Linda. "I'll find it."

The bathroom smelled of lavender. Linda tugged on the mirror's gilt frame, but there was no medicine cabinet behind it to search, which made tears spill from her eyes at last. Sobbing, she crouched down to inspect the floor behind the toilet, even lifted the heavy lid of the tank to look inside. Desperation rose to her throat and she let out a shuddering hiccup. *What the hell am I doing?*

"Esther?" she demanded, as she stepped back into the hall. "It doesn't matter, about the ring. You have to talk to me."

Esther threw her shoulders back and swept out the front door, down the steps, and straight into the eye-line of the lead reporter from Channel 8, who tilted a microphone toward Esther's mouth. She turned her face away, lips locked between her teeth. She held the pose, like a child rejecting a spoon at feeding time.

Startled, probably by the sound of the mailbox lid going shut outside, Annie looked up from the socks she was matching on her thigh as Linda came through the door with a bunch of catalogs and envelopes in her hands. Detective Hansen said something like "get her away from here soon as we can" into a walkie-talkie as big as a shoe. He motioned Linda in.

She put the mail on the end table. Then she crouched to be at eye-level with Annie and asked, "How are you holding up?"

"Not too well." Annie lowered her gaze to the laundry basket heaped with whites at her feet. Tear-tracks puckered on her cheeks, dry and tight.

"What happened to your arms?"

From wrists to elbows, Annie's skin was latticed with fine, red marks, like an addict's. "I pushed through that tall privet hedge at the back," she said, "into the neighbor's yard. I was not thinking too well, I guess. I didn't even realize I was hurting myself." She matched the socks on her thigh, then rolled them into a small bundle with difficulty. Her hands were shaking and so was her voice as she explained how she had run around the neighborhood, looking for someone, anyone, who might have seen something, but there was no one in sight, no one home. "I ran until I could barely breathe."

"I just walked by your car," said Linda gently, "and noticed the safety seat is missing from the back. Had you noticed that?"

Annie shook her head no, her face crumpling into a terrible, silent cry, holding her breath until she gasped. Linda put her arms around Annie's shoulder.

Linda's eye contact with Detective Hansen made sure he was listening to what she said to Annie next. "The Mack boy next door told me he saw you leave in your car this afternoon, with the baby."

"Hold on," Hansen said, into the walkie-talkie. "Say that again, Linda."

"The Mack boy next door," said Linda, "saw Annie back out of the drive this afternoon around two or so."

Annie stopped bothering with the socks, but her hands still shook with fright—which made Linda want to hug her close, comfort and disarm her so she'd say the thing that would get them all moving.

Annie pulled away. The air of the room was heavy with mistrust. "What the boy remembered for sure," said Linda, "was that he saw Annie go out to the car with the baby this afternoon."

Annie's hands tightened into fists and stopped their shaking.

"Around two or so," repeated the detective.

"Around then, yes," said Linda. "That's what he said. He's sick with a cold. He's been lying on the couch all day in front of the TV."

"He's wrong," Annie said emphatically. "He's mistaken. He's a good kid, but it was this morning I went out, not this afternoon. I was gone for an hour or so. I told you that, remember? Down by the tracks to take pictures? And anyway, I was down in the dark-room till after two. While I was down there someone came into the house. Burt is confused about the time. Let me go talk to him."

The detective shoved the walkie-talkie into a holster on his belt and gave Annie a look that made her sit down again. Linda walked around the laundry basket and sat beside Annie so she could take hold of her hands and still them in her own. They could hear voices outside, a police radio. "She's hungry, and she needs me," Annie said to Linda, sobbing. "We can't let this be happening."

A few minutes later, Detective Hansen went next door to question Burton Mack and another officer walked Annie toward a police car, pausing part way there to address a microphone: "We do not want questions at this time. Detective Ivan Bold is the information officer at this stage of the case. He will give you a statement after we've left."

The TV crew continued interviewing people in the crowd. Linda stood in the street and listened as KCCI reporter June Sanderson faced the camera for a live spot on the six o'clock news. She introduced a woman with shiny glasses, Margaret Oliver, who lived across the circle. "We moved here because we wanted the small-town atmosphere. We don't even lock our doors when we go out during the day. When I heard about the baby, I came right home from work. I just got here. I'm scared to death. Annie and Will are lovely people."

The reporter turned to the camera: "Isabella Circle is a cul de sac with only five houses, where typically most of the residents are at work or school on a Friday afternoon. We noticed an officer going into the house next door to the Cantonwine's a few minutes ago. We'll keep you posted on any developments. Police are asking citizens with any information to call the number on the screen."

Linda looked around for John and saw him back by the garage. She wanted to tell him she'd follow Annie downtown and stay by her side. She needed the comfort of family, but Frank and Esther were nowhere in sight.

John was explaining something to Elsa Silk, the pretty, blonde forty-something owner of the local jewelry store, and Reverend Gustavson. Linda watched John poke his cell phone and hold it to his ear and knew that he had hit redial one more time, trying to reach Will. They had known each other since they were five, and were like brothers. Linda stared at him until he gave up, folded his phone and put it in his pocket, still talking to Elsa Silk and the minister.

Turning around, Linda saw that the guy from the city had moved his orange truck to the far side of Isabella Circle. The yellow flags still lay on the hood. He reached to turn his radio off when Linda approached. She picked up a flag and unfurled the rectangle of thin plastic to read the words printed in black: UNDER-GROUND GAS.

He stuck his hand out through the open window of his truck so she could shake hands with him. "Tom Alvarez." No smile. "Guess I forgot my manners before."

"Linda Garbo. Is there some problem with the gas?"

"No, just a routine job to mark utilities so they can have a fence put up."

After Linda had crossed the street, she realized she still had the yellow flag in her hand. She meant to return it to Tom Alvarez, but then she saw Gracie's stuffed cow on the front seat of her car where she had left it earlier. She started her engine, then saw that a Madison County Sheriff's car was blocking the entrance to Isabella Circle.

She stood in the street and raised her voice, Gracie's cow mooing in her fist. "Can you get someone to move that car? I need to get out of here."

# Chapter 8

Heading across town, Linda sat rigid, fists gripping the steering wheel. Her throat was dry. At the first stop sign, she clicked on the radio: *"bulletins out across Iowa and adjoining states. At this early stage, police are going in a broad general direction, interviewing neighbors, searching every yard and alley in town, and out into the country. Teams of volunteers are being organized."*

Linda drove to the Heart of Iowa elevators and parked at the back of their gravel parking lot, not ten feet from the door to the abandoned bank. The light was starting to fail, especially inside the building, with most of its windows boarded up. The flashlight from her car was barely adequate. She stood in the middle of the black-and-white tiled floor and wished she hadn't come alone. *Don't touch anything.*

She was thinking *evidence.* She was hearing mice, or birds, skitter across the floorboards overhead. She strained to hear a human sound. A weak line of light from her small flashlight swept across the ceiling and found the door to the narrow stairs. Steep wooden steps rose to the left, to a closed door. Halfway up, at the point where she had found Gracie's cow earlier in the afternoon, she stopped. Shaken by an adrenaline chill, she wondered again what had possessed Annie to bring her baby to such a place. 'To take pictures,' she had said, but of *what?*

Linda yelled, "Hey, anybody here?" She climbed the rest of the stairs. She rapped sharply on the door at the top, which was ajar, then pushed it open. The place smelled of something chemical, like fingernail polish remover, and she knew what that meant. John had written at least a dozen stories on the dangers of methamphetamine in rural Iowa, but a meth lab right in town?

It certainly looked like one. Casting loops of light around the shadowy room led her to a battered transistor radio on the floor next to a green camp stove, a mattress with an ugly shadow down the center, and a kitchen sink stained brown around the drain. Someone had been cooking meth all right: two rusty cans of Draino and one of Gas-line de-icer sat on a shelf. On the drain board lay a couple of coffee filters, stained the same bright red as the plastic flowers on the windowsill.

Dreading what she might find in the next flick of the flashlight's beam, Linda felt the muscles in her throat go rigid. Her skin felt cold. Annie had said, *"Find her. Hurry."* The beam of light jerked in Linda's hand toward the three-note warble of a siren, across town and diminishing. The window glass reflected her looming shape back to her until she jerked the filament of light toward the second room, this one darker than the first. She gave a window shade a jerk and sent it rolling up with a terrible snap. Behind it, black plastic covered the window entirely, duck-taped to the frame. The still-dark room was empty except for a cardboard box from Mona's Pizza and a dozen beer cans, stomped flat. Waves of roaches fled the flashlight beam.

The bathroom reeked of mold and urine. When she twisted a faucet on the sink, what came out was a stream of something silvery with a million legs.

At the bottom of the stairs, Linda took stock of her pounding heart, her cottony mouth, her confusion, her relief. Annie's incoherent story on the phone that afternoon came back to her: An old boyfriend, a game of *Trivial Pursuit,* something about standing in line at the post office to get a letter back, a story that had ended before it made a point because Will had come into the room.

Back outside, she tilted her head back to look at the sky — a cold opalescence above the roof of the towering grain elevator. The wind had risen, pushed by the predicted cold front, and it smelled like rain. It was starting to get dark, and at that moment lights went on to illuminate the corrugated walls. A backlit sign leaned in a window: OFFICE. And an angry man was hurrying her way. Shouting something.

"You want to tell me what you were doing in there? It's private property." Before she could answer, he'd rushed past her and jerked hard on the door, forcing it tight into its frame. He batted the broken, metal hoop and then crouched down to retrieve a padlock from the gravel. "Smashed to hell," he said, turning to glare at her as if she were responsible. He raised the lock in a beefy fist. "I saw you flashing a light around in there. Explain yourself."

"A baby's been kidnapped, the other side of town. I was looking for her."

"Here?" The man's jaw drooped, his expression blank. "Why in the hell—?"

"Her mother brought her here earlier in the day."

That confounded him to silence for a count of three. Then he said, "Ned Milhous," and stuck out his hand.

"Linda Garbo. I take it this building's yours."

"You got that right. First time I've caught anyone back here, and you don't look the type. I heard about the kidnapping. A baby missing from her own bed, in broad daylight. It was my first thought, too, that the mother done it."

"I didn't say that."

"Seems you did," he said.

# Chapter 9

At Wendy's drive-up window, Linda reached for a paper sack. The smell of French fries filled her car. "Where are you?" she said into her phone.

"On I-35 north," said John, "going around Des Moines. I was ready to hit redial for the hundredth time when my phone rang and it was Will. He's sick as a dog in a motel up by Story City."

"Talk louder," Linda said.

John raised his voice over the highway moan, but still sounded husky, like a man under great duress. "I should get to Will in less than an hour."

Linda pulled her car forward, her phone pressed desperately tight to her ear.

"Poor guy'd already heard it on the six o'clock news," said John. "He had his head over the toilet when he heard his baby's missing. He got to the TV screen, and there was Annie being escorted into a police car, his house fenced off with crime-scene tape. He thought she was under arrest, until I told him otherwise. I made him promise to stay where he was and let me come get him. He didn't argue, so he must be really sick."

"So no one could reach him by phone because—?"

"He'd left it in his car, until he finally woke up and thought he'd better get a hold of the client he'd been set to see tomorrow. He's got some kind of stomach flu. He mentioned he was burning up."

Linda switched her headlights on. "I'm in my car, too, heading home," she said. "My body's telling me—"

John interrupted again, and they spoke at the same time. She said, "I need to eat," just as he said, "Why don't you—?"

She licked the salt of a French fry from her lower lip. "Why don't I what?"

"Go over to the county hospital. In the middle of all the commotion on Isabella Circle, Frank called an ambulance for Esther."

"Really? When was that?"

"Must have been right after you left. She's hurting, but that's not all. He told me she'd given the cops consent to search their house when they showed up at their place with the news about the kidnapping." John was using his confident reporter's voice now, a blow-by-blow account, his diction clipped, all business, emotions under control. "By the time Frank arrived to take her to Annie's," he said, "one man was in the basement, another was searching the attic, and Esther had locked herself in the bathroom. Frank's got a lot to deal with. If you could stop by and talk to him, it might help you both."

"Can you tell if they've ruled Esther out?"

"Frank says no, but I'm not sure he really knows. Who can think straight with all that's happening?" The emotional strain returned to John's voice: "He helped them search the house for Gracie. It must have broken his heart to have to do such a thing."

Linda took a deep breath. "What does he think? Does he think she might have taken the baby?"

"He's avoiding such a thought by virtue of knowing his wife so well, is how he put it to me," John said.

"That sounds like him. Why does he need to stay with her in the hospital? She's there for her own protection, right?"

"I wouldn't say that, no," said John. "She was in agony. I saw you drive away and wondered where you were going."

"What kind of agony?"

"Physical," he said. "She bent double and groaned so loud everybody turned to look. I admit I didn't credit what was happening to her right away. You know how theatrical she can be, but Frank knew the difference between one kind of pain and another. She seems to have lost the power of speech."

The light turned green, and Linda turned left to head for Winterset, the county seat, twenty miles away. One of the trees along that part of Maple Street had a pink ribbon tied around it already, and the sight of it jacked Linda's terror up a notch. Fear pressed close, almost a hum, a vibration that made it hard to breathe. By her watch it was seven-o-five. Gracie had already been missing at least four hours. "She could be two hundred miles away by now," said Linda into the phone, tightening her left-hand grip on the steering wheel. "I'll go to the hospital and tell Frank that you'll be bringing Will back very soon. I can do that at least. I don't know what else I can say to him. Frank's so self-contained. He's not at all reticent in business dealings I've had with him, but personally he can be unapproachable."

"He likes you, though," said John. "You made quite a hit with him when they were out at the house after the baptism. You'll find a way to help him open up about her illness. See how much he knows about her delusions. You never know how that might help solve this horrible—" He left the sentence unfinished. "It obviously wasn't a stranger who did this. Esther was alone this afternoon. Their housekeeper Jessica Mann usually arrives at one, but she wasn't there today. Some sort of out- of -town accident with her car."

"What do you know about her, this Jessica person?" Linda asked. "She's never been there when I've gone to have coffee with Esther, always in the morning."

"I think she works for them in the afternoon until after dinner, something like that. She's the organist at the church, so you must have seen her at the baptism. She has a music degree from Oberlin College in Ohio, I believe. She's a widow. She's worked part-time for Frank and Esther for years, a combination cook, maid, and companion for Esther. Her husband was an air-traffic controller at the Des Moines Airport."

"She was hurt? In this accident?"

"Couldn't have been too bad," he said. "She was there in the crowd on Isabella Circle. She wears her hair in long braids, like an Indian."

"I don't remember seeing anyone like that."

"Might have been when you were inside the house next door," said John. "I saw her talking to Ivan Bold. Her car was towed to a shop in Des Moines, an easy thing to check. I'm sure the cops are on it. But, back to Will. I wasn't the first person he called when he saw the story on TV. He got a hold of one of the detectives and told him about Esther taking Gracie out of her crib at our house. He's blaming Esther one-hundred-percent and wanted me to tell you that."

For long seconds neither of them spoke. A mile west of town by then, Linda switched her headlights to low beam as she came up behind a combine going ten miles an hour, taillights flashing through halos of dust. The dense cloud in its wake turned her windshield the color of smoke, gray-white, from the crushed limestone on the road. In the low light, with her vision obscured, it was impossible to pass. Barely moving, the car crept along. "Maybe you'd better go home after all, and forget the hospital," John said finally. "Eat something. I forget you don't have your usual stamina."

She braked almost to a stop. "I stopped at Wendy's. I've got food, which I can barely look at. I'm feeling guilty I didn't wait until the cops were done with Annie so I'd be there for her. She's probably still alone with that detective, and I'm stuck here behind a slow combine while Gracie is—" She inhaled a sob.

"We're in shock," he said.

"I know, but I mean—"

"I'm trying to help, Linda, by giving you an idea of what you can do. Most of—"

Static rained noisily over the phone. "—situation," he said, his voice fading out, then in again: "—prefer to be there in the thick of things. Frank's called me twice since I hit the road to fetch Will. He was telling me about how good you were with Esther at our house the Sunday of the christening. He noticed you didn't argue with her in her crazy state, a mistake he's made at some time or other, I take it. She'd be more likely to talk to you than to a police officer. You usually jump at a challenge like this. Where did you go in such a hurry, by the way, when you left Isabella Circle?"

Linda took her foot off the brake and let the car inch forward. Dust crawled up the windshield. "Hold on a sec." She put her elbow against the steering wheel to free a hand. She pulled a cheeseburger from the Wendy's bag. "I was finding—" She swallowed, though she hadn't managed a bite. "—finding out that I can't trust myself to think clearly right now."

She told John about her first visit to the boarded-up building by the railroad tracks, to retrieve Grace's toy cow and take it to Annie. "When you saw me drive away from Isabella Circle, I was headed back to Market Street for a second look. I was convinced I was about to find a body." John didn't make a sound. She took a breath. "Are you still there?"

"Yes."

"If I'd been thinking straight this afternoon," she said, "I'd have remembered I heard Will talking to the baby when I called Annie this morning. That was *after* she'd gone to that empty building and lost Grace's favorite toy. She asked me to retrieve it because it helps the baby sleep. She wasn't sending me off to find her body. Esther's not the only one who's paranoid. I'm a little unhinged by the shock. Now I'm stuck here."

"Linda, listen—"

"You know how you read about people shaking their babies," she said in a rush, "or slamming them— horrible, chilling things like that — and then they make up stories to blame the baby's injuries on someone else."

"I don't believe Annie would do such a thing."

"What about the man digging in Will's compost heap in their back yard? What do you suppose *he* was thinking she might do?"

*Mary Howard*

"They saw loose dirt with a spade stuck in it and suspected the worst. That's their job."

"That's my *point*, John." Linda steered the car to the middle of the road and leaned her head to the left. Inching along behind the combine was making her feel more and more helpless. Traffic noises at John's end escalated in her ear, the sound of semis running through their gears. Her right foot pressed down hard.

She steered farther to the left, then forward, blind, her heartbeat in her mouth. Just when her headlights broke through the wall of dust, a pair of lights veered out of nowhere. The oncoming driver hit his horn, and she accelerated hard to pull ahead into her own lane as the road curved to the north.

"What's happening?"

"A slow combine."

"A *what?*"

Linda felt a surge of energy. "When I stopped by the police station earlier," she said breathlessly, "the clerk at the front desk said one of the cops had been listening to some recordings from their phone system, so maybe they have a lead. A girlfriend of Annie's by name of Tiffani was waiting in the hall, to stand by Annie when Hansen lets her go, so I didn't feel I had to stay. Anyway, I couldn't sit still. I had promised Annie back at the house that I'd keep her company so she wouldn't feel so alone, and then I ran off to that empty building without so much as a good-bye. I had no hesitation in suspecting the very worst of her. Now I don't know what to think."

Linda's tires went quiet as the gravel road gave way to blacktop. "Of course I'll talk to Frank," she said. "I'm feeling more clear-headed now." The adrenalin rush of nearly hitting a car head-on had that effect.

She looked for the hospital up ahead, the tallest building around. "Maybe we'll hear from the kidnapper," John was saying in her ear, "some sort of demand."

"Like for a ransom, you mean?"

"No. Not really." The melancholy of his voice was barely familiar over the hiss and whine of eighteen-wheelers braking and revving up again. A truck horn blared, a tuba sound. "I've had the same thoughts about Annie you have, Linda," he shouted over the highway noise. "We'll have to find—" There was static. "—what attraction that old building — for her."

"You're breaking up again," said Linda. "I'm turning into the hospital parking lot, anyway. There's a Linden Grove police car here."

Six columns, caged in scaffolding, supported an unfinished bridge canopy over the main entrance to the Madison County Hospital. Linda tossed the cold cheeseburger into a construction dumpster and followed a chain-link fence to a side door. Inside, a narrow, plywood-lined hallway took her through the building's unfinished wing to an atrium waiting room. Frank's brother Leonard and his wife Helen were sitting in a group with three men in suits and a couple of other women. One of them was Elsa Silk, a client of Linda's. Elsa was owner of Starlight Jewelry: *Gems for every occasion of your life.*

Len Hebring was a leaner version of Frank, with the sunburned, big-knuckled hands of a farmer. Linda had seen him at city council meetings, where he'd argued against the color and signage guidelines she'd proposed for Old Town storefront restoration. He'd called her guidelines the first step on a "slippery slope" and accused her of "too much goddamn artsy-fartsy messing around with the rights of property owners." Now he rose eagerly from his chair to shake her hand. His grip was powerful. "You have news?" he asked.

"No." She shook her head.

"Here comes Frank now," he said, looking past her. "He's been in the cafeteria talking with a cop. No one's told us a thing so far."

Linda turned to see Frank approaching down a wide hall. "Let me talk to him a minute privately," she said to Len. She hurried toward Frank's wide-open arms.

He tucked a manila envelope under his arm so he could grasp her hands in both of his. "I'm so sorry," she said.

"Will had me paged here a few minutes ago," said Frank. "I hoped to God he'd have some kind of explanation for us, but he's set on blaming Esther. I'm afraid he's got company, but pointing at her is a waste of time we can't afford to lose. Can you make any sense of what's happening?"

"Not yet, but we will," said Linda. "Tell me about Esther. Why is she here? Will told me she's in pain."

"The doctor's ruled out appendicitis," said Frank. "She kept holding her fists against her midsection. When she's in and out of a psychotic state as she has been these last few weeks, she tends not to register pain in a normal way, so I didn't know what to make of it. She hasn't said a word since we arrived at Anne's this afternoon."

"I know," said Linda.

"At first I thought she'd had a stroke," he said, "but the doctor pinched her to make her say *don't.* Now she won't even nod her head for *yes,* or shake her head for *no.* It makes her look bad, refusing to answer their questions. Mentally ill people aren't always believed, anyway. It's one of the things she hates most."

"I'd like to see her."

Frank frowned, shaking his head. "You'll have to wait. Like I say, she's literally not talking, to anyone. I've been through a lot of things with her, but never silence." His attempt at a smile gave way to a grimace. "Will is right about one thing. I shouldn't have checked her out of the hospital last week." He looked into Linda's eyes. "Who'd have believed she'd ever in her life need an alibi."

Linda averted her eyes.

"I want you to understand," he said, his urgency bringing her gaze back to his. "At the start of the summer, we took her off a medication that wasn't agreeing with her. She'd been accepted into a clinical trial for an atypical antipsychotic drug, so since then she's been through what they call a titration period in order to not pollute the new drug with carryover from the old. Now I wish we hadn't decided to put her through all that. I've demanded that her doctor get her meds sorted out as soon as she's out of the woods with this stomach pain." Frank took a sudden, nervous intake of breath. "I thought she could focus on her radio show if I brought her home, and that would be the best thing for her. Work is her lifeline."

*Lifeline,* thought Linda. The word rang a bell. She didn't know why.

"Putting on a hat," he went on, "taking on the voice of someone else, entertaining the folks out there on the radio. People write to the station, praising her." He pulled a white handkerchief from a pocket.

"Esther has ferocious concentration when she's performing her stories," he said. "Her doctors theorize her acting uses a different part of her brain." Frank looked down at the envelope in his hands. "That business about going to the bathroom a lot — I should have taken it seriously. It looks like we've missed a physical illness, not that mental illness isn't physical. It's a brain disease. There's nothing psychological about it, the way people tend to think. The fact she isn't talking doesn't mean she has anything to hide, no matter how it looks. It's a coincidence this terrible thing should happen just at a time she's so symptomatic after years of being on an even keel. She did not do this thing."

Linda had never heard him speak at length about anything besides land development, or the bank's marketing campaign, always with such confidence. Now he seemed so fatherly, so powerless, and so utterly bereft, she was moved to put her arms around him. He hugged her back, tightly, and for long seconds didn't let go.

"What's in the envelope?" she asked.

"Personal effects," he said. "Her wedding ring, her diamond, and her watch. That sort of thing." He took a single step toward the waiting room, then stopped, turned back to Linda. "I've set up a twenty thousand dollar reward, but that's too damn little for me to do. I have to stay here until they figure out what's wrong with Esther's stomach, but I need to see my daughter. This is tearing me in two."

When they reached the waiting area, Frank's friends widened the circle so someone could pull up one more upholstered chair, for Linda. Frank introduced her to the men in suits and to Elsa Silk as an old friend of his and Esther's. "She has the jewelry store downtown."

"We know each other," Elsa said to Frank. "Linda and John bought their wedding bands from me. You were with that policeman a long time."

"He wanted to know if Esther neglected Annie when she was a child. Of course I told him no. He wanted to talk about the time I took Esther to the station, back in May." Elsa nodded as if she knew just what he meant.

Frank turned to Linda, to explain how Esther had complained she kept seeing a woman behind the house, staring at her through the kitchen window. Esther kept her microphone on the table there, for broadcasts. She practiced dialects with her tape recorder, even in the middle of the night when she couldn't sleep. I hated to bother the police with her complaints, but she made the initial call to them herself. She can be mighty convincing. Neither I nor Jessica, our housekeeper, ever saw anyone out there. Esther claimed the woman was stalking her, that she had talked her way into the house a few times, insisting she was a fan of the radio show and wanting to watch Esther do one of the programs, but Jessica knew it never happened. She's always there when Esther is on the air." He straightened his posture. "Detective Hansen was very understanding that day we went to see him. The officer I've been talking to just now is another man, by name of Bold."

"I met him at Annie's house this afternoon," said Linda.

"He's wondering if the person harassing Esther last spring might be someone who wishes the family harm. Detective Bold, trying to use a sick woman's delusions as evidence, does not impress me. My poor wife's hallucinations are muddying the waters."

Linda reached out to touch Frank's broad shoulder so he'd turn and look at her. "I don't think the stalker is a delusion, Frank. I've talked to her. She works in the neighborhood of my studio. Seeing her is what set Esther off at Gracie's christening."

"Oh, I know," said Frank. "Esther told me that, too, that you saw the person who was stalking her." Frank paused to swallow. "She can transfer her delusions to real people and see them as threats, Linda, so let's be careful. For a while Esther was convinced that *you* were plotting to do her harm."

Frank bowed his head and pressed his broad fist to his mouth. His forehead crumpled. In a moment he recovered himself enough to say, "Esther's been afraid to leave the house without me for months. She doesn't recognize faces very well, so she avoids seeing people all she can. She sure as hell didn't go out today." He was on his feet. "She loves that child."

Linda frowned at Frank's brother Len, who was grumbling about Esther's craziness. Then Linda turned to see Elsa touch Frank's arm and gesture toward a doctor in green scrubs entering the lobby. Frank hurried to that end of the room, where the doctor held a large blue X-ray film to the light. As the doctor turned to go, Frank made a circle, with thumb and finger, which Linda took to mean, *OK*. Walking up to Elsa, he explained: "She swallowed one of her rings. One of the biggest ones. That's what's been causing her abdominal pain."

Voices murmured: "She did what?" "Good God."

"Her emerald," said Linda.

Frank turned to his brother as Len said, "Why do such a crazy thing?"

Frank said, "We won't know that—"

"Because she's mad as a hatter, of course," said Len. "I had to ask. Sorry, but I don't know how you put up with it. Maybe this had to happen, Frank, for you to *see*. She needs to be put away."

Frank ignored his brother's anger. "They're treating her with mineral oil." The group emitted a collective sigh, the start of a laugh that they all stifled, checking each other's faces, then staring at their hands. "I'll arrange for private staff so she can stay here tonight," Frank went on, to no one in particular. "They have no psych ward, but I won't move her till this ring crisis—until it's passed." His dawning look was part grimace part grin, a vain hope that something, anything, might be the slightest bit funny at such a time. Someone's chuckle turned into a cough. Frank's face loosened and sagged terribly as he raised his handkerchief to his face.

*Mary Howard*

Len muttered an apology for his "mad-hatter outburst at a time when everything's come down on you." Elsa rose from her chair. "I'll wait for you in the car," she said to Frank. She walked toward the plywood hallway, the windowless way out, without a word. She slowed down to let Linda catch up with her. "What makes you think it was the emerald?" Elsa asked.

"She was wearing it earlier today."

"He bought that ring at my shop," said Elsa sadly, "years ago. We used to be best friends, Esther and I. Did you know that?"

Linda shook her head. They continued walking, slowly.

"We started the community theater together. Our girls played at each other's houses. My husband was a close friend of Frank's. Being discreet doesn't matter now, until we find that baby, so I'm going to say this: It's not true that Esther never did Annie any harm. I suspect Annie's still struggling with certain things her mother has done." She paused, as if waiting to be asked.

"What kind of things?"

"She locked Annie in an outbuilding behind their house one summer afternoon," said Elsa, "when the poor child was not yet five. Must have been, oh, twenty years ago. Frank came home and found the child half naked, decked out like a little tart in a skimpy outfit, her face and body all painted up in gaudy colors— exhausted and dry as a bone from crying. She'd fallen and cut her chin, so there was blood on her clothes. She still has a scar from it. Esther was in the kitchen, arguing into the microphone, convinced the radio had stolen her thoughts.

"She had to go away for weeks that time, to Clarinda," Elsa went on. "That's the closest lock-down psych facility, a couple hours from here. Turned out she'd stopped taking her pills because she hated not feeling her emotions the way she used to. Having her mother gone was terrible for Annie. I stepped in to help. She stayed with us. She was just starting school that August, two years younger than my daughter. Hayley's in law school now, at Northwestern." Elsa smiled, then looked sad again. "Annie would wake up crying in the night. I'd sit with her and try to reassure her. For a long time she was afraid to be alone.

"Annie stayed with me again a few years later," Elsa went on, "when Esther hit a bad patch again, not long after Duane, my husband, died. Esther hasn't spoken to me since, not even in church. The past few months, she's been wearing those rings night and day — the entire collection at once, sometimes. And now she *swallows—?*" Elsa's voice caught. "I'm sorry. Frank will say it's nothing to do with me. Esther's crazy like a fox sometimes."

"Crazy like a fox? You don't mean she *fakes* her illness?"

"No, of course not. No," said Elsa. "But at her best she's colorful, all that histrionic charm. I swear she parodies herself sometimes as a way of saving face. Nothing embarrasses her anymore. If she has a fatal flaw, it's jealousy."

"Esther and I became friends the moment we met," said Linda. "Until the problems with her medications this summer, I would not have guessed she had schizophrenia if she hadn't told me. I have found her colorful, dramatic, eccentric and delightfully outspoken. I admire her."

"Still," said Elsa, "when she's off her head, she can turn mean and blame others for all kinds of things."

"Paranoia's part of the illness, Elsa."

"Maybe not entirely. Frank says it is, but I can't help taking it personally. She's obviously very sick right now, but even when she's doing fine, she accuses me of turning her daughter against her. Annie doesn't dare be friendly with me, for fear of distressing her mother." Elsa turned her face toward the exit, thirty feet away down the narrow hall. "Maybe the doctors can straighten Esther out and get her to talk. Her reality isn't the same as ours right now, according to Frank. Neither is Annie's, if you ask me."

"What do you mean?"

"I know he used to be afraid she'd inherit her mother's illness. She might be hiding certain symptoms from us. Voices, that sort of thing."

"Frank said that?"

"Not in so many words. He's talked to Will about getting some counseling for her, but I don't know if anything's come of it. Frank thinks she's been withdrawn since Grace was born."

"That's a far cry from being psychotic," Linda said.

"Yes, well, we don't know what being psychotic is like, do we? He's been worried about Annie spending afternoons in the darkroom while the baby sleeps instead of getting some rest herself. The baby still wakes up in the night, he tells me, and Annie's exhausted."

Both women turned their heads toward the sound of a doctor being paged. Frank was coming up behind them with his brother and sister-in-law. "I want to run by home for a minute," Linda said to Frank. "Then I'll meet up with Annie and stay with her."

"Of course." He watched Len and his wife until they disappeared through the door to the parking lot. He put his hand on Elsa's back. "I'll be out as soon as I'm sure Esther's in good hands," he said to her. "Or—" He turned to Linda. "I wonder if you'd give Elsa a ride back to town. She drove my car over so I could ride in the ambulance. I may be here a long while."

Linda nodded. "Yes, of course."

"I'll see you later, then," Elsa said to Frank. They gazed at each other steadily. "We need to keep our faith strong," she said to him, her tone so hushed and fervent that Linda felt embarrassed. His face moved toward Elsa's until he seemed to catch himself. "I know we'll find Grace very soon," she said to him gently. "The police are doing everything they know how to do. The rest of us are praying."

Her words didn't seem to comfort him. His walk was slow-footed and pigeon-toed as he made his way back across the waiting area, which was empty now. He was wearing a gray cardigan, and the slope of his shoulders and the dip of the sweater's hem across the back made him look older than his fifty-some years. He slapped the envelope full of his wife's personal effects against his left thigh with every step he took.

# Chapter 10

"We'll head straight for town, and I'll drop you off at your car," Linda said to Elsa as they pulled out of the hospital parking lot. The dash clock read 8:48 p.m.

But Elsa said, "You know, it just occurred to me. Your home is the only place Esther has ventured out to lately, except for church."

Linda let up on the accelerator. The two women exchanged a glance. "I heard the minister say earlier that the church was being checked," said Elsa. "Has anyone thought of searching your place?"

"No," said Linda, a little too emphatically. "Not that I know of." At the intersection with the next county road, she took a left.

"Why are we going this way?"

"We'll head up along the river," Linda said to Elsa. "It's shorter than going by the airport."

For the next mile of dark countryside, yet another rising tide of panic for Gracie flooded Linda's consciousness over and over. Elsa fell silent, too. Linda tried to keep her speed slow enough for the winding, loose-gravel road, but her right foot kept pressing down.

Elsa's face was turned away, toward a rough field of corn stubble off to the right. "I wish Frank were with us," she said softly.

"Yeah, so do I." Linda turned the heater on, and the radio, and drove faster. It was a moonless night — frost predicted, according to the radio. She turned it off. Her house would be warm, a haven for Gracie, safe, if she was there — but it was locked up tight.

Linda gave Elsa a sidelong glance and, to distract herself, turned her mind to images of Frank. As an artist, Linda had learned to pay attention to every lack of symmetry in a person's face — the quirky emotional muscles, the temperament in the fix of the chin. Now, a half-mile from home, she concentrated on a line-portrait of Frank in her imagination, planar forms softened by folds of flesh between the eyebrows, under the eyes, at the edges of nostrils and mouth.

He looked like what he was, an old-fashioned banker. Usually commanding and self-satisfied, he had allowed Linda to see another side of him back in the hospital, with Elsa. He might not appreciate a likeness of himself that showed such vulnerability behind the eyes, a hint of internal isolation. He was usually so stoic. Gracie's abduction had blown his cover: his face had revealed his suffering — and his deep affection for Elsa.

The minute Linda turned into the long drive that led to her front door, she was shocked to see that half the lights inside the house were on. They hadn't been on when she'd left that morning, ten minutes behind John. Now the night breeze whipped her clothes as she and Elsa raced up the steps onto the wide front porch.

Linda's heart beat even harder when she discovered the door was unlocked. The fear as she entered the house was the worst of all. Her every muscle tensed, the body's way to brace itself for being startled. "Someone's been here," she whispered. She saw her own living room as if for the first time, searching for something out of place. A lamp at the near end of the sofa was on. So was the light in the hall that ran off to the left, to the bedrooms. Linda walked slowly, touching a wall with her fingertips. *Please*, she thought again, as she reached the bedroom doorway, *let Gracie be here, sleeping, warm and safe.*

Disappointment is one of the most painful emotions, right after despair and grief. Linda felt all three, standing beside the empty crib in the master bedroom. She caressed her belly with her right hand. "John can't wait to be a father," she said dully, as if she had to explain the crib.

"I didn't realize you were expecting." Elsa was breathing so hard she had to sit on the edge of the king-sized bed.

Linda headed for the basement as she pointed Elsa toward the other bedroom.

With every quick creak of a cellar step, with every basement light switch she clicked on, with every out-of-the-way shadow she peered into, Linda's skin prickled with another chill of apprehension. Under the watchful eyes of the portrait of Esther she'd drawn on the wall thirteen days earlier, she checked to be sure the sliding doors were locked. They were.

"Anything?" she called out to Elsa when she reached the top of the stairs again.

"She's not here." Elsa had tears on her pretty face.

"Someone has been." Linda entered John's number on the phone.

He answered on the first ring, a couple miles north of Des Moines, more than halfway home. Yes, he told her, he had made a fast stop by the house before getting on the interstate and driving north. "For cold remedies and aspirin and Gatorade," he said, over the highway noise. "I cleared out the medicine cabinet. I thought it might help get Will back on his feet by the time I get him home." Linda could hear Will coughing in the background.

"You left the house wide open and all lit up," Linda told him, desperation in her voice. "I couldn't talk to Esther. She's not speaking to anyone. I'm going back to town."

With a flashlight, Linda searched the old machine shed they used as a garage. Together she and Elsa poked into every shadow around the house.

"Now I understand that old cliché," Linda remarked to Elsa as she started the car. "The one that goes, 'Their hearts were in their mouths.'"

Halfway to town, Linda slowed for a left-hand curve that followed the river bend, spooked by sudden movement off to the right where the roadbed gave way to a wide ditch. It was only tall grasses blown sideways by a gust of wind. "On the way to the hospital," she said, "I passed a combine on a curve like this and nearly hit someone head-on."

She glanced at Elsa.

Elsa's eyes were closed. "Sorry," she said, "I wasn't listening. When I don't know what else to do, I say a prayer. I'd rather not talk just now."

So in the silence that followed, Linda went back to her earlier reverie about Frank, about how Esther wasn't able to give him much in the way of companionship these days, and Elsa had been a widow for more than ten years. Linda glanced at Elsa's profile, at the ghostly, dash-light-shimmer around her short, blond hair. Now *there* was a face with contradictions: an easy smile, an habitual head-tilt to the left, and then the chill of those gold-green eyes. She was slender, Frank's physical opposite. *Lovers?* Linda was wondering when Elsa said, "Slow down. Watch out." She pointed as the headlights picked up two disks of light, and then two more. The tires spit gravel as Linda braked hard, the rear wheels sliding to the left as they came to a stop. Four deer bounded over the road no more than five feet in front of the car.

Linda gripped the steering wheel, her heart practically turning over in her chest. She slammed the car into park. Panting, she managed to say, "I need to sit here a minute and calm down. This is unbearable. I won't be any help to anyone if I fall apart."

They sat in silence, Linda with her eyes closed and her attention on the furious thub-thud, thub-thud of her heart. After taking a few long, deep breaths, she reached for the ignition key to restart the car, but then changed her mind. "Better not rush it," she said under her breath.

She turned and stared at Elsa, and Elsa stared back at her as a new sound from outside the car began to register. When Elsa opened the door on her side, the feeble cry grew louder.

In an instant, Linda was out of the car and running. A yellow bundle stood out in the headlight's beams as if it were phosphorescent; such was Linda's shock. In one long move, she slid downgrade and knelt to fumble with straps in the darkness of her own shadow. When she slipped her hands underneath the baby, the child whimpered. "Thank God," said Elsa as Linda turned around to face the light, cradling the baby in both arms. Elsa helped Linda up the sloping side of the ditch to the roadbed.

"Oh God," Linda murmured, echoing Elsa's words: "Oh *god, who would do this? What kind of person?*" Tears streaming, Linda pushed the seat of her car all the way back so she'd have more room between herself and the steering wheel. Gracie's face and hands were cold. She didn't cry. Linda unwrapped her and, before she realized what she was doing, removed the baby's clothes to be sure she was unharmed. Her diaper had soaked up all her wetness into a chilly ball, so Linda pulled that off, too, and warmed the pears of Gracie's bottom in the palms of her hands. Both women rubbed the baby's limbs, to warm them as the heater blew full-blast in the already warm car.

Somehow Linda managed to unbutton her blouse and draw the cold little body against her skin, arranging the blankets the baby had been bundled in and closing her own shirt over it all — staking her protective claim to this child who had been exposed to such unspeakable danger. *Godchild,* Linda thought. She stroked the baby's back and rump, rocking her side-to-side instinctively. She talked to her: "Gracie, Gracie, you're all right now. You're safe." Her fingers pushed the cold teeth of a zipper away from Gracie's soft cheek. The garment smelled of dust.

"It's a miracle those deer made you stop the car right here," said Elsa. "She seems all right, do you think?"

Linda nodded. "Yes." There was nothing more to say. She savored the feel of the baby's soft head against her collarbone and tried not to think about raw weather and wild animals. Elsa's head was close to Linda's shoulder and the three of them were breathing like one person. When Linda turned the dome light on to examine the baby more closely, Grace made a sound. Her face was pink, her fingers no longer cold; but the look she gave Linda was pitiful and she was rooting desperately for milk. Linda managed to get her cell phone out of her pocket. A message on the screen that said 'One missed call' barely registered.

Pressing nine-one-one with her right-hand thumb, Linda was ready to say: "If we hadn't come along and seen those deer—" But when the dispatcher picked up, Linda kept it simple. "We found the baby. She seems unharmed. It's unbelievable."

# Chapter 11

Holding onto Gracie in the warm, dome-lit car on that dark road, Linda breathed from the stomach so the rising and falling would calm them both. Then she noticed something. Out at the end of the headlights' beam, where the ditch-weeds were trampled, lay something she had missed before. She pointed it out to Elsa Silk, who got out of the car to investigate.

Linda watched Elsa bend from the waist to pick up the thing, lying next to the baby's safety seat. She brought it back to the car: a magazine, *Traditional Home.* A perfectly appointed living room, all taupe and gold, filled the cover behind the words "Decorate like a DESIGNER." Elsa touched the image of a lacquered table with a finger, dragging a clean mark along the edge of it. "We shouldn't be handling it," said Linda.

"Fingerprints. I should have thought of that." Elsa was out of the car in an instant, balancing the magazine on the palm of her left hand. She placed it on the hood of the car and came back in where it was warm. "Oh, God," she said, "I'm still in shock. It's a powerful feeling, isn't it, finding Grace — and the *way* we found her?"

Linda didn't feel powerful. She felt horrified. Grateful. And relieved. When she reached to turn the emergency blinkers on, the baby began to cry, but quieted right down — exhausted, probably — and relaxed against Linda's chest again. Before long, way back in the rearview mirror, Linda thought she saw three lights hovering high above the surface of the road. She stared at the floating lights as three men on horseback materialized behind her car, phantoms in a haze of dust. Searchlights bobbed with the horses' gaits.

It was like a dream, the men coming alongside and dismounting. A walkie-talkie cackled on the first man's belt. He had white hair and a close-cropped beard. Said his name was Terrence Bird. He and his buddies were Madison County Sheriff's deputies, an off-road search party called out because of the predicted cold front. They had been looking for the missing baby along North Onion Creek when Linda's call for help was relayed to them. "Let's see the child," he said to her. She powered the window all the way down. He looked ready to bite someone in half.

His face changed when Linda uncovered the top of Gracie's head. Linda introduced herself, and Elsa. "I've got the baby against my bare skin to warm her up." Linda tried to smile, but the man's expression stopped her. Her own face might look like that: relieved, but wary, haunted by what they still didn't know.

"We've been looking for a body," he said, clearly moved.

All three men crowded closer to see Gracie for themselves.

"She seems fine," said Linda. "We've looked her over pretty well. We're friends of the family. Did they tell you that?"

"That didn't come up," said Terrence Bird. "I take it you were searching for her along here. You one of the volunteers?"

"Not exactly, no," said Linda. The baby drew up her knees.

"Then I guess I don't understand," said Bird, his drawl extra-slow with skepticism.

Linda turned her emergency flashers off to stop the ticking, and the baby relaxed. "I had to apply my brakes suddenly, and the car swerved on the gravel. I was probably driving too fast."

"There were four deer, officer," Elsa volunteered. She leaned close to Linda so she could peer up at Bird through the driver-side window. "I had my eyes closed, praying for a miracle, so I didn't see them on the road until Linda hit the brakes after the curve back there and slid in the gravel, like she said. The headlights shone right on the baby then. That's how it happened, a miracle, those deer. An absolute miracle."

"Mmmm," said Terrence Bird. He kept his eyes on Linda as he leaned sideways to listen to something one of the other men was saying. Gracie pedaled her feet against the waistband of Linda's jeans and lifted herself in such a way that the men could see her entire face as they bent down close again. The horses stood motionless off to the side while Elsa explained where she'd found the magazine, now lying on the hood, that it might be important.

Just then a car flooded the scene with its headlights and parked at an angle, blocking the road, an official shield on its side. Linda was glad to see the driver was Ivan Bold, the detective she'd seen at Annie's house that afternoon. In a moment he opened the passenger-side door and asked Elsa if she'd mind moving to the back seat so he could see the baby better. He slid in beside Linda and placed a broad hand on Gracie's head. "She was on the shoulder of the road?"

"No, in the ditch. In her car seat." Linda pointed. "It's still there. She was wrapped up pretty well. She's hungry, but we couldn't find any marks on her." Gracie began to cry in earnest, rocking her open mouth against Linda's shoulder hungrily.

"We'll get her to a doctor."

"First she needs her mother," Linda said. "She needs to be fed. And tell that guy Bird I'm not a suspect. The best thing in the world has happened, and he hasn't even smiled. Why can't we head straight to town?"

"Soon," said Bold, ignoring the impatience in her tone. "We need to check out a couple things before we move your car. Is there someone who can verify where you were this afternoon, from two to three-thirty?"

"Yes, a client. Holliwell Sign, out by I-35. You can check."

"And you?" He was asking Elsa.

"Me? I closed my store as soon as I heard the news from one of my customers." Up until that time, she explained to Bold, she'd been open for business since nine o'clock. "I was praying hard for Gracie at the very moment we found her. Did they tell you about the deer?"

"Yes, ma'am," said Ivan Bold.

"When you saw me at the Cantonwine's this afternoon," Linda asked him, "why didn't you ask for an alibi then?"

"You were a bystander," he said, looking down at a small notebook in his hand. "Now you're involved. Five minutes, tops, we'll be on our way, and get this baby to her mother."

At that point, Terrence Bird opened the door and asked Linda to stick out her left foot. "We have a clear print in the dust. If it belongs to one of you two ladies, we can rule it out," he explained, pulling off her shoe. Then he walked around the car and opened the back door for one of Elsa's. "Left foot," he said.

Through the windshield, Linda watched the other two deputies examine the magazine on the hood of her car. They seemed far away, in another universe. Underlit by their flashlights, their features were ghoulish. One man fanned pages with his thumb and opened them flat.

Linda moved her face forward, wishing she could see that page up close for herself, the one the man lifted as he cocked his head; but with Ivan still there beside her, reaching to cup his hand over Gracie's head again, she was aware of her nakedness under the baby and her blanket. "Look how they're handling that magazine," said Elsa.

Linda fingered a buttonhole of her blouse and watched Officer Bold get out of the car and disappear into the dark. As light fell through the open page of the magazine there on the hood, she stretched her neck again to see: a neat square, at least a third of the page at the bottom corner, had been torn away. She watched Officer Bold place the magazine, holding it by the edges, into an evidence bag.

*Surely five minutes have passed by now*, thought Linda, *and we can go.* Someone was shining a bright light on the ground. Someone else had a camera. Linda's shoe came back with the news that the print was not hers. "Smaller, I bet," she guessed.

"By quite a bit."

"I wear a twelve," she said. "Why are we just sitting here?"

No one answered her. One minute Gracie was sucking her fist with pathetic urgency, the next she was fussing in frustration. More long minutes passed before Ivan made a winding motion in the air for Elsa to roll her window down. "That footprint turned out to be yours," he told her. He returned her shoe through the window. I'll drive you two back to town while the others look for additional evidence. You want to scoot over, Linda?"

"Evidence like what?" asked Linda as Bold got in behind the wheel.

"People dump trash in these rural ditches all the time," he said. "It's quite a problem. This magazine's a help, though. We need to sort through whatever else we find within fifty feet of here that might connect this crime to one particular individual."

"We're to head for Hebrings," said Ivan Bold as he drove Linda's car forward at last, with a crunch of gravel. He turned the windshield wipers on, which horrified Linda all over again with thoughts of what might have befallen Gracie, exposed to such weather. Linda looked off to the right, into a darkening indigo sky over a coppery soybean field. Linda entered John's number on her cell. "The temperature's really dropped," said Ivan. "We may not have an Indian Summer after all."

John answered his phone, and Linda's throat closed with emotion. "Gracie's in my arms," she managed to say.

"Will got a call from downtown that it was you who found her. I've been waiting to hear from you."

"I've been in a horrified state of relief," Linda said. "Where are you now?"

"In Will's driveway. We got back just a few minutes ago. He's sitting here beside me."

Next she heard Will's broken voice, hoarse with fervor and congestion: "Gracie really is okay?"

"She really is." Linda's voice was brisk but quiet, nearly a whisper: "She snuggled right up for warmth and her eyes were big and round with curiosity when the deputies came along. Hungry as she is, she hasn't even cried that much since we got her into the warm car."

Then John's voice was back. "You're holding her?"

"She's spread out on my chest like she's part of me. She seems perfectly fine. She's very hungry."

"Fine, but very hungry," John repeated — for Will's sake, she realized. She took a big breath and held it. "How did you happen to look for her there?" John asked.

"We didn't. I was just driving from our place back to town." In memory, the four deer performed their graceful leap over the road again. Gracie's soft head bobbed against her throat. Linda's voice began to break. "It's just so wonderful that she's all right."

"Save the rest of the story for when you talk to the police, John said quietly. 'I'll hear it then."

"No, wait—"

"I'm listening," he said.

"Out here in the dark," she said, "with all the dust and lights and horses, it still seems unreal. The suspicious way some of these guys have been looking at me keeps me grounded, though. We're headed for Frank's house. I take it Annie's there."

"They're headed for Frank's," John repeated off to the side, to Will. "Linda's asking about Annie."

Will got back on the phone. "We'll be right ahead of you. Right now she's inside our house gathering up diapers and things for Grace. That Detective Hansen is with her. They've impounded her car and they're designating our house a crime scene. She gave consent for it to be searched again, but Gracie's safe. That's all that matters."

It was John who said good-bye. "See you soon," Linda said to him, her voice an intimate whisper.

Ivan drove all the way to the outskirts of Linden Grove before anyone spoke. It was Linda who broke the silence. "You said that magazine would be a help. Is that because part of a page is missing?"

"No, it's the subscription label," he said. "It's addressed to Mrs. Esther Hebring."

# Chapter 12

The Hebrings lived in the oldest part of town. The brick pavement glittered with damp before the headlights as Ivan parked Linda's car at the curb. A fine mist fell. Car door open, she tasted the iron bite of rain and smelled the char of wood smoke in the air. The house loomed huge, Victorian, and brightly lit, all roof angles and gingerbread. At a glance, every detail registered: a wraparound front porch, transformed at the corner into a round, gazebo-like space with a conical roof; a fan-shaped opening between the windows on the second floor; three dormers on the third. Before Linda reached the steps, Annie and Will burst through the doublewide front door. They threw their arms around Linda and the child. She twisted sideways so they could see Gracie squint and turn her face from the sudden light.

They drifted into the warm house in a three-way embrace. Annie scooped Gracie from her wraps and carried her off to the right, pink and naked, crying, into the living room. To the left, a phone trilled, then stopped mid-ring. Linda held her unbuttoned blouse together with both fists and watched Annie settle on a sofa with her baby, watched Will pull an afghan from the back of the sofa and cover the three of them. The worst part of something unspeakably horrible was over.

*Mary Howard*

"I can't stop shaking," Linda confided to John. He was right there, his eyes bright with tears. She felt lost without Gracie's heat against her chest, until he embraced her.

From the library to her left she could hear Frank's voice on the telephone. In the long living room to her right, a half-dozen lamps cast light onto polished tables crowded with objects made of shiny metal, tortoiseshell, and glass. Picture lights illuminated paintings on every wall. On the hearth a fire burned low. In front of the fireplace, two sofas faced each other, an oversized square coffee table in between. The room was quiet except for the out-of-sync ticking of three clocks on the mantel and Gracie's murmurs while she nursed. Linda crossed her arms over her chest and led John toward a shadowy part of the room, back in the corner. There was a grand piano there. A feathery plant in a large red pot.

Linda's trembling fingers fumbled for a buttonhole. "Here," John said, helping her. He sighed with concentration, his breath familiar on her cheek. He cupped her shoulders in his hands and waited for her to tell him what it had been like on that dark road. It wasn't like him not to ask.

"It was instinct, I guess, to warm her up as fast as I could, skin-to-skin," she said. "It's all a blur. I didn't think. I just undid myself and wrapped her in. It made one of the deputies nervous, I think, the thought that I was naked under the baby." Linda was afraid she might laugh hysterically, but the moment passed. "What if we hadn't found her before it started to rain?"

"Well, you did. She's safe. The cops seem to be working double-time to figure out all the rest." A door closed somewhere in the house. John stroked her back.

"Where's Elsa?" she asked him. "I thought she was right behind me."

"She was. She's here somewhere."

"It was blind luck," Linda told him, "our coming around that curve at just the right time. I had to slam on the brakes. The ditch is wide and deep along there." In Linda's mind she saw the deer, their silver eyes in the headlights' beam. She had so much to tell.

But Frank was calling to John from the entry hall. He stepped into the room to make eye contact and say John's name again, and Linda's, urging them toward the back of the house. "Let's give them some time alone with her," Frank said. "We've got some coffee on."

But then the doorbell rang.

"Doc Gilder's here." Frank opened the front door to admit the doctor, and then stepped into the library to answer the phone again.

Detective Hansen arrived, too, letting in another burst of cold, damp air. Elsa slipped out before the door could close.

Doctor Ralph Gilder, a slight, freckled man with reddish hair, was asking Linda how Gracie seemed to her. He had to ask a second time. "Unusually quiet at first," she told him, "but not too subdued to fuss when she got warm. Whatever she's been through, it wore her out. She'd worked her outside blanket loose. She was bundled up for wintery weather, in two or three blankets and something with a cold zipper. I'll say that." Linda pointed at a heap, on a chair in the entryway.

Detective Hansen held up a yellow sweatshirt by the shoulders. A hood, a zipper up the front, an ivory-colored stain on a shoulder. He looked at Linda over the tops of his glasses. "This, you mean?"

Every face turned to Linda's. "Yes," she said, her heart quickening. "Gracie was wrapped in that." She recognized it now.

"It's mine." Will stood in the archway from the living room.

"Annie wore it a lot when she was pregnant," Linda explained to the detective. "She still wears it sometimes." *And the boy, Burton Mack, saw her wearing it this afternoon,* was what she was thinking.

Judging by the knowing look the detective gave her, he was thinking the same thing. He folded the sweatshirt into a plastic bag. "So it came from your house," he said to Will.

"Yes." He turned to go back into the living room.

"You're shaking," Frank said to Linda. He took her hands in both of his, which were enveloping and warm. "Let's get you something hot to drink. Here." He handed a slip of paper to the detective. "I said you'd return this call as soon as you arrived. Use the phone in the library. Then I need to have a word with you."

*Mary Howard*

Linda, Frank and John sat at the kitchen table, waiting for the doorbell to ring again. John adjusted the root of his ponytail at the back of his neck, where a red rubber band held his hair in place. Down the hall in the living room, the doctor was examining Gracie. The baby let out a single cry, then a series of weak, complaining sounds. Frank left the kitchen long enough for Linda to ask John, "What's going on?"

John was whispering, "The baby monitor was in Annie's darkroom, like she said, but it was turned off," as Frank came back into the room.

Frank drank a glass of water at the kitchen sink. "That detective's on the phone again. He asked for privacy to make the call. He's closed the door to the library." Frank opened the refrigerator, then let it go shut with a rubbery slap. His lips were pulled between his teeth.

"Do you know why they searched Annie's house again tonight?" Linda asked Frank.

"They took some of her shoes, some other things that didn't make sense to her. More coffee?" John shook his head. Frank had sandwiches to offer, too, each one cut into a triangle, brown bread and white, arranged like flower petals on a big, blue plate. Linda wondered out loud who had made them.

"Jessie," said Frank, "our housekeeper. She's gone upstairs to gather some of Esther's things so I can take them to the hospital in the morning. More tea?"

"No thanks," said Linda. "I've never met Jessie. Seems odd that I haven't, as many hours as I've spent with Esther here in this room, but it was usually on Saturday mornings."

"Jessie is rarely here on Saturdays," said Frank. "She comes and goes, when Esther needs her. She does all the cleaning and grocery shopping and makes our evening meal."

"She was in an accident this afternoon?"

"Yes, and she got stranded a couple hours from home. She was pretty put-out about it, but otherwise she's fine." He lifted the plate of sandwiches toward Linda.

"I'm not hungry," she said. "Tell me about this again." She pointed off to her right as he sat down. He lowered the plate to the tabletop. He looked where she was looking.

The wide window over the kitchen table was covered with old *Linden Times* dated the previous April. Esther had taped them there, Frank explained, so no one could see her from outside.

Linda felt for pockets in the baggy sweater she was wearing. Frank had pulled the garment from a peg on the wall behind her while waiting for the tea water to boil, determined to stop her shivering. Now she turned in her chair to view the wall of costumes. Lined up neatly were two shelves of shoes: flopped-over, red-tooled cowboy boots; stiletto heels with pointy toes; scruffy work shoes stuffed with thick, gray socks; white, laced oxfords like a nurse might wear.

Hanging on hooks above the shoes were lots of sweaters, jackets, scarves, and hats. Linda fingered a lacy cloche, pulled out of shape by a fist-sized rose. These were the shoes and hats and bits of clothing that helped Esther get into character. "She always sits there," Frank said, pointing at an empty chair, "so she can watch the doors. She doesn't like surprises."

Abruptly, he stood. He walked to the center of the room. "What's taking the doctor so long, if the baby really is all right? Maybe I should go in and check."

"Let's just hold tight." John glanced across the room toward a loud-ticking Regulator clock with a pendulum. It was eleven-thirty. "Could be he's examining Will, too. He's got quite a rattle in that cough of his. And Annie's still in shock. Ralph has a good idea what they've been through. The guy's two-thirds psychologist."

Frank had paused at the wall phone by the sink. Now he returned to the table and pulled the phone book out from under a pile of books by the microphone. He ran his finger down a page and then ripped it from the book with an angry jerk. Back at the phone he listened for the dial tone, punched in numbers, raised his chin and said, "Gus, it's Frank. Sorry if I woke you. I guess you've heard—"

He was talking to Jon Gustavson, the minister. Frank looked up at the clock, then down at his watch. "Oh, good. I appreciate that. — Yes, thanks. Anne's here at my place, and Grace seems fine, but we can't entirely lower our guard, if you see what I mean." He nodded. "Right. He still is, pretty sick. John Bender brought him back. John and Linda are keeping me company." Frank turned and looked at them, balling the phone book page in his fist. "Now the problem is, the detective in charge of the case— Yes, that's right. He's still here. I have an idea he doesn't plan to leave any time soon. He intends to talk to my daughter and Will as soon as Gilder's through with his examination. Hansen's locked the kids out of their house. He's been talking to a social worker, and he's asked me if he can use the library to consult with her when she arrives. He intends to take Gracie into protective custody."

Linda felt her eyelids open wide as Frank went on: "He hasn't talked to Anne and Will about it yet. We're all waiting for something to happen here, and it's damned unbearable. We should be celebrating that the child is back. — I know, yes, I agree. I want you over here in case we need a character reference or two to satisfy the woman from Human Services. Maybe we can change their minds. — Well, I'm not sure of anything, but the situation's stacking up to be as baffling as it is offensive. There can *be* no motive for exposing an infant like that to the elements. — Pure moral corruption. What sort of person would do a thing like that? Not my daughter. Not my wife. We're missing something."

Frank turned and met Linda's gaze, holding it while he said, "We're missing an essential piece to the puzzle, that's all I can say. One of the men who questioned me implied Esther is responsible, but she doesn't drive anymore, and Grace was found way up north of the airport." He narrowed his eyes at Linda, then shifted his gaze to the wall of hats and boots behind her. "Frankly, if I were Ken Hansen I'd want to protect that baby above all else. That part I understand. He's doing his best, but I intend to stand up to him. I'd like you here."

He paused to listen. "Sure, I wager there's a *lot* he's not saying at this point, but listen to this: I asked him if he's prepared to accuse my daughter of having some part in this awful business, and he told me no, but he can't rule that out. To my ears, that's a yes. Anne is sitting in the living room oblivious to what's about to happen to her. He wants her evaluated by a psychiatrist." Frank listened to the minister for a few long seconds, and then he said, "My thoughts exactly. Yes. Just come on in the front. The house is full of people. — Thanks. I know you do."

Frank looked from Linda to John as he replaced the phone on the switch hook. "A good way of bringing you up to date, having you hear all that. Hell of a thing." He turned away again. His shoulders were in more of a slope than usual.

John walked over to put a hand on Frank's back and said, "The three of them could stay with us. We're set up for a baby, you know, a bed and so forth." He looked at Linda.

"Yes, of course," she said, "if it comes to that. We'll do anything we can to help."

"Just for the weekend, I gather." For a moment, Frank sounded like Esther at her most cynical: "Our detective needs to put Gracie somewhere while he follows up on five pairs of shoes from Annie's closet and some magazines."

Again the doorbell rang. Frank rushed from the kitchen to answer it. John seemed like he might follow, but then he stopped. From where he stood, in the doorway to the dining room, he could see into the foyer. "This has to be the social worker," he said to Linda. "Ralph should be about done examining the baby. I'll go talk to him."

Linda rose to her feet, touching her fingertips to the table to steady herself. She'd gone to bed early every night for weeks, sleepy from her pregnancy. Now she was really tired. She opened her eyes to a newspaper headline, at eye level: *City and countryside collide: Houses replace cattle as Madison County grows.*

Two-handed — right, then left — Linda ripped the paper off the window, laying bare the window glass, black with darkness outside the house. Poor Esther, so sure there was someone out there, stalking her.

All Linda could see was a ghostly reflection of herself, crushing newsprint in her fists. She dropped the balled-up paper to the tabletop. She crossed her arms over her chest. In memory she could feel Gracie, spread out in five directions against bare skin. Linda stared at her hands, gray from the newsprint and still shaky.

The door to the library was closed. Inside were Detective Hansen, Reverend Gustavson, and a social worker.

Three adults sat quietly in the living room, as if they'd been told to wait. Ralph Gilder's medical bag sat on the ebony coffee table, an oversized platform that squatted on cabriole legs so exaggerated they had knees. He sat on a straight-back chair, talking to John, who was on the sofa opposite Annie. Grace, her topknot of hair in a finger-curl, slept in her mother's arms. A woman Linda guessed to be Jessica Mann — she had a white bandage on her forehead — put more wood on the fire, then walked back toward the grand piano. She wore her dark hair in two long braids. The three clocks on the mantle made a syncopated rhythm like the *pock* of popping corn. All three had the exact, same time: twelve minutes past midnight.

Linda's attention drifted to the large painting above the fireplace — a woman gazing into a fishbowl. Even from across the room, the water in the bowl flickered with light and golden fish. The exotic pattern in the painting's background glowed with blues-on-blue. *Matisse,* thought Linda. She observed all this from the doorway, her cell phone forgotten in her hand.

Then, remembering, she looked down at the screen, which displayed MISSED CALL, an unfamiliar number from outside her area code. To her left, Will came down the stairs and walked over to rejoin Annie on the sofa. Annie whispered something to him, and he said, "Not now." He slouched to settle his head on her shoulder. He coughed and closed his eyes.

Annie's neck pinkened, a stain that rose to her cheeks as she stared at the surface of the coffee table. *What did Annie just say to him?* Linda wondered.

"Did you take a look at Will?" John asked the doctor.

"He's got the flu that's going around," Doc Gilder said. "I've given him a prescription for something to knock the cough and help him sleep. His being overtired and stressed to the max isn't helping him. The rest of you want to drink lots of orange juice and wash your hands a lot. The strain you've all been under will make you susceptible to whatever he's got. But then you know all that." The doctor leaned back in his chair. He didn't seem to notice Linda standing in the wide doorway. "Wonder what's taking so long." The doctor pulled his lips between his teeth the way Frank had earlier.

Jessica Mann was playing a slow, soothing piece on the piano, something vaguely familiar. Behind Linda, the French doors to the library opened. "John," said the detective, signaling to him. "Linda? I'd like the two of you to come on in here." He put a hand on Linda's arm as she came near. "I got a hold of Holliwell," he said quietly, "who owns that sign company out by the interstate. He verified you were out there this afternoon, when Grace Cantonwine went missing."

Linda looked the detective in the eye. Neither of them blinked.


The library smelled of stale cigarette smoke. The room was richly appointed: dark wood, three walls of books, four maroon-leather chairs around a low table heaped with magazines. Overseeing it all was the head of a six-point buck, mounted high on the wall. On a roll-top desk a gilt clock kept perfect time under a glass dome. The painting above it caught Linda's eye. *Mysterious Water.*

She had written a college paper on Paul Gauguin's obsession with that image. A graceful, androgynous person leaned forward to drink from a thin trickle of white that fell straight down into the blue pool at the bottom of the picture. Gauguin's waterfall. She moved closer, looking for the weave of the paper, but it was a poor reproduction.

"Linda," said Detective Hansen. She turned around. "Candice Torrey, here, is with Child Protection Services." A woman in a red sweater and faded jeans extended her hand to Linda first, then John.

Reverend Gustavson rose to his feet to offer Linda his chair. I've done my part in here," he said. "I haven't said hello to Will and Annie yet. I'm eager to hold that baby in my arms again. We can't let go of our joy to have her back." He shook hands with the social worker.

She had long brown hair and small wire glasses. "I'll go break the news to the parents," the detective said to her. The minister went out with him, letting in the sound of the piano, and closed the door.

"We've been talking about you, the Reverend and I," Candice said, looking up at John. "Please, sit down." John sat. "He thinks a lot of the two of you," she said to Linda.

"We're all good people, everyone in the house," said John. "It's the situation that's bad. What's this about?"

Candice Torrey leaned forward, elbows on the arms of her chair. "I need to go over a few things with you," she said steadily. "According to Iowa law, a peace officer can take a child into protective custody without the parents' consent. That's what's about to happen here." She raised a hand in John's direction as he shifted in his seat. "Forgive me if I tell you some things you already know, but I need to cover this as clearly as I can. Officer Hansen called my supervisor earlier tonight and made his case for placing Grace Cantonwine in protection while he follows up on certain details of the abduction case." She raised two hands this time, one palm toward John and one toward Linda. "I don't know what those details are. You'll need to save those questions for him, I'm afraid."

John leaned forward, mirroring the woman's posture.

She leaned back. Chair-leather squeaked. "Right now, in the other room, he's basically going over with the parents what I'm about to tell you. Then I'll visit with them for a few minutes. You can ask him then, any questions you may have." She worried the brass nails on the arms of the chair — fast, tiny circles with her thumbs.

"Anne Cantonwine is not a person who would leave her daughter by a country road like an unwanted pet," said John. "It's a cruel suspicion, unless there's some pretty damning evidence."

The social worker's hands grew still. "My role is not to pass judgment, but to place Gracie in a safe home. Please let's just focus on that. In the morning Officer Hansen will file a written statement with juvenile court which outlines his reasons for taking this protective action." She looked at the clock in the corner. They all did.

It was after midnight, twelve-thirty-three.

"Because it's Saturday," said Candace Torrey, "chances are there won't be a court hearing on the custody matter until Monday. A judge will decide then whether to return baby Grace to her parents or continue the protective order. He'll base his decision on input from the police, since this is a criminal investigation. Normally when I get a call like this, there is clear evidence of neglect or abuse. In this case, the only thing I'm sure of is that Gracie is the nine-week-old infant of a nursing mother. It's important that we not disrupt that bond. That's where you come in."

"They can stay with us," said Linda.

"Mr. Hebring told us you had agreed to that. That's wonderful."

"I hear the police have put Annie and Will's house off-bounds. They must have found something incriminating there."

"I really can't say, Linda," said Candice Torrey. "I mean, I truly don't know." She paused. "At any rate, the grandfather has a sick wife to get situated in some long-term care. He's extremely upset by this custody decision. The calmer we can be, the better for him, for the whole family."

"Where is Frank?" asked Linda.

"I think he went upstairs. Having you in the picture is a great help to him. Reverend Gustavson tells me I have nothing to worry about if Gracie and her parents stay with you. Detective Hansen and I are comfortable with the arrangement, but there are a couple of things I need to ask. "

"We have a crib," said Linda. "We have a spare room and a rocking chair. Do we need to get a safety seat for one of our cars? Gracie's, as I suppose you know, is evidence."

"I didn't realize that, but yes. These are the sorts of things we need to talk about. You'll be representing the state of Iowa in protecting this child. One of you must be with her every minute, even when the mother is nursing, no exceptions. Even if, based on your friendship with the parents, you think this protection order is unnecessary. Even if you trust the mother completely. She's the one the detective is concerned about. I do know that. This is going to feel very unnatural to you, the twenty-four-hour-a-day proximity. The vigilance. The appearance of mistrust, regardless of your personal relationship." She leaned forward again. "Now let me ask you this." She looked at John and Linda, each of them in turn. "Let's say one or both of the parents takes off with the baby while you're in the bathroom, or asleep? Let's say they leave a note, 'gone to the grocery store.' Something like that. What do you do?"

"Go after them," said John.

"Or what if one of them simply declares an *intention* to take the baby for a ride, insisting you're not to go along?"

"We talk them out of it," said Linda.

"But failing that—"

"We wouldn't fail," said John. "Will is my oldest, closest friend."

"'Call the police,' is the right answer here, to both my scenarios. You don't hesitate. You don't even *think* of going after them. You don't argue with them if they test you. If their feelings are hurt by the situation, you just have to remember that it's your job to keep the child in your presence, *period*. When she's nursing Grace, one of you stays in the room. The baby will sleep in your bedroom, and you're right, the child-safety seat will be in your car, not in theirs. I have one with me. I'll see it's properly installed before I leave."

"This all seems unnecessarily rigid," said John. He turned his head as Frank's voice grew loud in the living room, unintelligible, but clearly angry. The housekeeper stopped playing the piano, and Gracie began to cry.

"She won't leave our sight," said Linda.

"Right," said John. He was on his feet, checking out the expression on Linda's face. "Whatever it takes, we'll do it. Fine. Yes, I agree."

It was Annie who introduced Linda to Jessica Mann as they were about to leave. The woman was about Linda's age, friendly and efficient in jeans and a man's oversized white shirt. "Jessie's been looking after us since I was ten," said Annie, "on top of another part-time job, plus playing organ for the church. She cooks the most wonderful meals and keeps the house looking like a stage."

"I've been wanting to meet you," Jessica said to Linda, shaking her hand. "Esther talks about you all the time."

Linda shifted her gaze to the woman's forehead. There was a blue bruise below the six-inch white bandage. "Frank told me about your accident. You feeling okay?"

"Five stitches," said Jessica, "but my car will be out of commission for a few days. I got rear-ended in a slowdown for construction around noon. They patched me up at Iowa Methodist in Des Moines. I was headed for the Graziano Brothers. Have you ever been there?"

Linda shook her head.

"It's an old-time Italian grocery store on the south side," said Jessica. "There's nothing like it anywhere around. If you're wanting to make a killer Italian meal, it's a great one-stop shop. I was after a bag of their frozen homemade meatballs and some bread and olives, plus some of their special sausage and cheeses." She turned to Annie. "You're dad's been asking for his favorite Italian dinner, complete with a big old jug of their table wine. I never made it that far, needless to say. I imagine no one here even ate dinner tonight. I feel terrible I wasn't with your mom this afternoon."

"So do I," said Annie. "Thank God you're okay."

"And thank God our little Gracie is safe. We should be focusing only on that." Jessie embraced Annie and smoothed her hair as if Annie were a little girl. "Really, baby, the rest of this mess will work itself out."

Annie pressed her face into Jessica's shoulder for another hug.

"What was the music you were playing?" Linda asked.

Jessica brightened, despite the tears in her eyes. "It's called *Butterfly in Reverse*. 'Everything that hurts you is locked up inside you.' Those are some of the words."

"Really. I've never heard of it. For some reason it seemed familiar."

"Probably because it's on the radio a lot," said Jessica. "I sometimes listen to top-forty when I'm driving. It's by a group called Counting Crows."

"I would have guessed it was something classical," Linda said. "It's in waltz time, right?"

"Yes, it is," said Jessica. "It's become one of Esther's favorites. She asks me to play sometimes, to calm her."

"Jessie can play by ear," Annie said to Linda proudly. "She's a mimic like my mom, but with songs instead of dialects. Hear a song once, and she can play it."

"I played by ear when I was a girl," said Jessica, "before I ever took a lesson. I may start with tonal memory, mimicry, like Annie says, but then I work with the chord progressions and phrasing to develop a distinctive style."

"Well, you certainly have done that," said Linda. "Your playing tonight was just right, unobtrusive and yet remarkable, really — consoling, under the circumstances."

Jessica chuckled. "The lyrics are a love song to a girl named Maryann — 'Maryann, you're better than the world.' I guess I turned it into something else, losing the words and making the music my own. It's not plagiarizing, you know, if I do it only for my own pleasure. I'm glad if it seemed just right for tonight. A song for Gracie. We can call it that. A song for Gracie," she said again.

Jessica pointed to a small suitcase on a chair nearby. "I'll leave this here by the door for your dad," she said to Annie. "Just lotions and makeup and your mom's nightgown and such. He can take them to her in the morning." She gave Annie another hug. "Try not to worry, Sweetheart. We all know you. We know your heart, and how you love that baby. It's a nightmare, that's all. The police have to be afraid of what they don't know, so they're trying to blame you, but it won't hold water. We all know that." She turned to Linda. "Lovely to meet you. I'd like to get better acquainted, Esther loves you so." She turned her head to look into the living room. "I'd better go. Doctor Gilder's offered to give me a lift home, and I see he's putting on his coat. I don't live that far, but I do have a bit of a headache, and I think it's misting out there."

Once Jessica was out the door, Annie looked lost and scared. She pointed at Linda's chest and, in a wavering voice, she said, "That's one of the sweaters from Mom's costume wall in the kitchen. It's one she uses to get into character for the radio. I don't want you to wear it home."

Linda looked down at herself, at the shapeless, loose-knit sweater with its tangle-edged hole in the sleeve.

"Take it off," said Annie.

Linda crossed her arms and gripped the bottom hem. "Your dad brought it to me when I first got here," she said. "He could see how cold I was from all the emotional distress. I forgot I had it on." She pulled the sweater over her head. "I'll put it back."

"No, I'll do it," said Annie wearily. "It has to be in a certain, exact place when she gets home. Order is one of the things she needs."

Linda read the sweater's label: *McDevit, Cork, Ireland. Size: XL.*

"I know just where it goes," said Annie. "Don't tell me you forgot you had it on." There was a hint of resentment in Annie's tone, and then she broke down. She lifted her mother's sweater and buried her face in it.

# Chapter 13

Instead of hanging Esther's sweater back on its peg in the kitchen, Annie pulled it on over her own head. The familiar scent of cigarette smoke and spicy perfume brought with it a curious recollection of her mother wearing a lacy hat with a fat, pink rose and speaking with a French accent — a memory of another mad period Esther had suffered, years before, when she'd refused to take her pills. Annie rubbed her nostrils free of an itch and hurried out to where Will slouched in the passenger seat of his silver-gray Lexus. The hood was spattered with beads of rain. He had the heater on full-blast. His eyes were closed.

"John's gone to look for an all-night pharmacy to get a prescription filled," he said as she slid behind the wheel. His voice broke like a teenage boy's. "Terpin Hydrate with Codeine." He covered a cough with both his hands.

As soon as Linda pulled away from the curb, Annie backed out of the driveway and followed. Passing under the streetlight at the corner, she said, "Everyone in town will know Gracie can't be left alone with me. I can just imagine what Linda thinks."

"She's happy she can help us hold together."

"Don't try and talk."

"I have to talk," said Will. "This is the first we've been alone since I got back. John and Linda are our friends. We have to stay strong together, Annie."

"I'm being blamed."

"Maybe not. Only for the moment."

"I have no way to defend myself."

"I talked myself blue," he said, "trying to change Hansen's mind, but Gracie was in your care when she was—"

"You don't have to remind me of that."

Will shifted his body, as if all his muscles hurt. "He's doing what he thinks he has to do. What matters is, our baby is back. We're together."

"How can he get away with this protective custody thing," she said, "without making some kind of announcement about who his suspects are? He *has* no evidence. He's bluffing. He doesn't trust me because of that night he came to the door and practically accused me of neglecting Gracie. He obviously thinks—" Annie paused for a sudden, jagged breath. "What if he never figures this thing out? We'll be scared every minute from now on, for months — for *years* — wondering if, or when, whoever did this will try and take Gracie again. Everyone in town will always wonder if it was me. Hansen's made it so I have to feel ashamed, even though I've done nothing wrong. Why are you defending him? Do you think he's right to protect Grace from me?"

"I think anyone who doubts you will be put straight in no time at all."

"Does that include you?"

"Don't do this," he said. The base-note of his voice was flat and guttural, and he coughed before he could go on. "I've never doubted you. You and I need to stay as close as we can to each other right now. It'll be a comfort to be with Linda and John for the weekend. By the time John writes up the story for next Wednesday's *Times*, everyone will see this custody issue for what it is, a terrible irony. By then we'll have all the answers, some of which should be obvious to the cops right now."

"Like what?"

Will stared toward the taillights up ahead, where Gracie was secured in Linda's back seat. It took him three tries to clear his throat. "I just want to get there and go to sleep."

"In a strange bed."

"It will feel pretty good."

"It's so unfair."

"Tomorrow I'll be worth more to you," he said. "The worst of this ordeal is over. Just think of that."

They'd reached the town limits. Annie eased up on the accelerator and steeled herself for what she had to say. "When Detective Hansen held up your old yellow sweatshirt tonight, my heart nearly stopped." She glanced at her husband. His face was turned away from her.

"Your mother is very ill," he said.

"Will, you're not listening."

"Just let me say this," he said.

Annie let the car slow even more.

"The mentally ill," he said, "can't be trusted to tell the difference between their delusions and the reality the rest of us live in."

"That's way too general. You *know* that, Will. I love my mom."

"But you know her illness takes her away from her true character."

"I don't know any such thing," Annie said. "It's how she reacts to situations that changes. She wouldn't do something against her beliefs. She never has."

"Okay, we won't debate that right now, but 'a danger to themselves or others' — isn't that the rule for putting delusional people away?" He bent forward to better see Annie's face. She took her eyes off Linda's shrinking taillights. "Wasn't I patient with her," he said, his voice a congested growl, "until Gracie came along?"

"Not always."

"Okay—"

"I know she's hard to be around sometimes, Will. That's hardly the point you're trying to make now."

"Hansen needs evidence. We need an eyewitness, or Esther's own admission."

"No."

"Until we have that," Will said firmly, "Hansen wants the community to be assured he's doing all he can to protect our baby. Someone will come forward who saw her driving your car, just wait and see."

"That's ridiculous."

"I don't think it is. I'm sure that's how it happened. Someone *must* have seen her. Let Hansen have his couple of days, and it'll be over. It's understandable you're having trouble letting go, after being terrified for hours. I wish I could help you more than I can."

Annie couldn't look at her husband. She gazed off to the left, to where a mature cornfield was ready for harvest, whispering like a river current. "Even if my mother got up the nerve to leave the house on her own again, let alone drive," said Annie softly, "she wouldn't leave Gracie in a *ditch*."

"What's the alternative?" said Will. "That some sociopath lay in wait for an opportunity to terrorize us, for no reason? I don't think so."

"I do." Annie let the car slow even more. "In fact, I'm sure of it."

Will coughed once, and then couldn't stop. She pulled onto the shoulder of the road, unscrewed the top off a bottle of water from the cup holder between them, and held it out to him. She waited until he could talk again.

"You have to wonder—" His voice was barely above a whisper. "—why she had to be hauled off to the closest hospital the minute Gracie was missing. And why does she refuse to speak? If she had been on a locked ward yesterday, this never would have happened."

"Hansen's not protecting Gracie from *her*, Will. Look at me. Your old, yellow sweatshirt. It *means* something that Gracie came home wrapped in it."

In the light from the dash, Will's face was greenish-pale.

"This is the thing. Back on that Friday, a week ago— The thirteenth?"

"Yeah?"

"I went to see Linda that morning," said Annie quietly. "It was chilly when I left the house, so I had that sweatshirt on over my

*Mary Howard*

t-shirt. By the time I left her studio later, it was hot in the car. I pulled the sweatshirt off and tossed it into the back. Then I drove downtown to the main post office." She turned her head to face the steering wheel.

He waited.

Annie explained how she had stood in line at the window while some woman was choosing stamps. "It seemed like forever. The anonymous caller was probably right about that. Hansen had me listen to the tapes down at the station this afternoon. A woman, a wimpy voice, turning me in for child endangerment."

"What do you mean, she was probably right?"

"About the length of time I was inside, eleven minutes. Which sort of proves she was really there and didn't make that part up. The thing is, Will— What I'm trying to tell you— The woman who made that call took the sweatshirt out of my car. I *know* she did. She must have. It's the last time I saw it until tonight. We've had so many warm days since then, I didn't miss it. I told Hansen that, but he didn't write it down or anything. That woman who called is the one he should be looking for."

Will drank from the water bottle, slowly. He swallowed with a lift of his chin, like his throat was killing him. "Why would anyone steal such a thing?"

"I don't *know* why."

"No one would, Annie," he said gently. "Steal a worn out sweatshirt? On a warm day?" He paused. "Sweetheart—? If you didn't miss it, it was probably on the floor of your car, or lying around the house. I seem to remember seeing it on the back of the chair in our room."

"When I was pregnant, yes. I wore it as a bathrobe sometimes. I wore it a lot when I was huge. But not recently."

"Okay. But it doesn't really make sense, does it? That someone took a rag of a shirt that should have been burned months ago and then stole our daughter and wrapped her in it? It doesn't matter if the shirt was in the car, or in the house. Your mother could have picked it up either place. I understand why you'd be desperate for someone else to blame, but only a crazy person could have committed a crime so depraved. You need to let yourself consider that."

"My mother didn't do it." Annie lifted her foot off the brake and sped into the twin tire-paths worn smooth in the gravel road. "As long as you think that, Will, our baby won't be safe."

Hours later, slow-flipping numbers on a digital clock gave Linda and John's second bedroom a greenish glow, 1:31 a.m. Will lay on his back. Every so often he twitched and sighed, as if something hurt him in his sleep.

Unable to lie still, Annie thought of taking some of Doc Gilder's medicine to help her sleep, too, but she knew Gracie would wake up hungry any minute. Annie lay on her side in the queen-sized bed, her back to her husband. As she listened to the scratches and moans of an unfamiliar house on a windy night, she closed her eyes and sent a prayer-like message to her mother. *Okay, let Will be right, if that's what it takes for us to know for sure what happened. Tell on yourself. Tell us why — whatever crazy story you believed would end well with Gracie in a ditch. Whatever voice made you think you had to do it.*

Then Annie took it back — that wish that would lock her mother out of sight for a long, long time.

On a nearby rocking chair lay Esther's sweater. Annie pulled it into the bed with her. The scent of it triggered a vivid, well-worn memory of the first time Esther had gone away. The rejection was awful. Annie began reliving it:

*"It smells—"*

*Hayley is a blond-headed girl of seven.*

*"—like cigarettes," she says, swinging a crocheted hat between finger and thumb. "You wear it." She's a couple of years older than Annie. "She'll get lung cancer and die. My mom says so."*

*"She won't," says Annie.*

*"You'll learn all about cancer when you're in second. I'm never going to smoke, are you?"*

*Mary Howard*

"No." Annie lies. She has already imagined the taste of it, leaning her head back, blowing air through her pinched-together lips the way her mother does. Now she flops the hat, limp as a net, onto her head and pulls it down, gripping its single flower in her right-hand fist. The cap smells glamorous. It's so big on Annie it covers her eyes and nose and fills her with a familiar scent of flowers and smoke. Through the crocheted holes, she spies the lemon-green of her own back yard. "We have to finish our rocks today. I hope you didn't forget the paint."

"First we have to practice your song."

"You did forget," said Annie.

"No, I didn't." Hayley pats the pockets of her bright red shorts. She wears a band of blue and white fabric around her head. She's been wearing it every day since her mom took the two girls to see Karate Kid. "I hope you have a costume figured out. If we're going to sell tickets to our show, we have to be good."

Annie drags open the door to the screen house at the edge of the trees, a charming gazebo with cupola and dome. It's almost too shadowy inside to paint, but at least it's cool on this sweaty day in August of 1984. The radio is set on KIOA, a Des Moines Top Forty station. "Girls Just Want to Have Fun" is number eight. She goes into her act as it starts to play. She lifts one knee, and then the other, moving her shoulders to the beat. "You're the only one—"

The screen house is their clubhouse, and they always have to start the afternoon with an art project. It was Hayley who made that rule. "Get down to business," she says. She is Annie's best friend and president of their Summer Vacation Craft and Drama Club. Annie's mother named it that.

"—to shine in the sun," sings Annie. Her right knee burns under its band-aid as she scrambles onto a wooden bench. "Fuh-hun." She fingers the rocks and pebbles on the tabletop. They have magical shapes.

Hayley tugs tiny jars of paint from her pockets. "This is the best. It has stuff floating in it that makes it look like real gold. I'm painting both of mine with this. Smell it, though."

"Don't."

"Isn't it gross?" Hayley pushes it under Annie's nose.

"There's only one brush."

"I brought Q-tips for you. — No, Annie, you have to shake it up first, like this. It stays all watery on top if you don't." Hayley makes a fancy arc in the air, raising her wrist to show off her new gold watch with a leather strap, from her mother's store. "I'm getting my hair cut at three, so I have to keep track of the time. Here comes your mom."

Annie snatches the hat off her head and sits on it.

"I saw that, Sweetie. You can't have that one. C'est Francais. Anyway, it makes you look like a lamp." Esther smiles with her teeth clenched, like she's about to start laughing out loud — and then she does, a musical trill that makes the two little girls join in — even though Annie doesn't get what she meant about a lamp.

Esther is thirty-five years old, but looks younger in a white bathing suit. Her skin is tan and shiny. Her belly button is halfway shut. "Come here, into the suh-hun." She laughs again as she drops a cardboard box onto the ground. "You can do your secret rock and roll stuff later, until You-Know-Who shows up."

The three of them have a conspiracy against Hayley's mom, who doesn't allow MTV. Annie watches it every day at four in the library at the front of the house. Hayley, too, if her mom lets her stay long enough.

Esther lifts her hands straight up from the box and tosses some flimsy fabric that floats from her hands and settles slowly on the grass. "I used to wear this, look. Here are the shoes. I have something for you, Hayley, too. Come here," she says to Annie again. Esther smells of coconut, like the beach. She has a lipstick in her hand and she rubs a slippery circle on Annie's mouth. "I always loved to play dress-up when I was a little girl. Do this." She slides her lips together.

Annie does as she is told. "But I need red hair."

Esther laughs her throaty laugh again, rubbing Annie's cheeks with both her thumbs. "Wait until your dad sees this," she says. The clothes piled on the grass are dreamy, with huge red flowers, or shapes of blue and yellow, or long, black stripes. "Hey, turn that up," Esther *shouts in her rich contralto. Head tilted back, she squints up her eyes and sings in a girlish voice, a perfect imitation of Cyndi Lauper.*

*Annie's neck is getting hot. She looks back at the screen house where it's cool.*

*Hayley claps her hands. "Annie needs dangly earrings and lots of beads around her neck," she says to Esther. "She knows how to fling her arms like Cyndi Lauper. Show her, Annie."*

*Esther doesn't seem to hear. She is twisting an orange scarf in both her hands. "We can fringe this up with scissors. I'll go get them. And I've made you some lemonade. If only you had Hayley's coloring, Annie-girl. You're brown as an Indian." She beckons with her hands, then twists her daughter's hair to one side and ties it with the orange scarf, ties it and ties it again, and fluffs it. "That will have to do, I'm afraid. Take off your top and turn around." She rips a strip of fabric and ties it tight around Annie's skinny chest. She sings a line that ends with run. "Now, turn that off," she says, meaning the radio. "Let me look at you, Hayley."*

*Annie runs to the screen house to switch off the radio while behind her back Esther says, "Oh, you'll look so cute in that. And look at that tummy. Why don't you give up the Karate Kid and be Madonna?"*

*"Material gull," sings Hayley. Even the accent is right.*

*"You were born to be a rock star, Hayley," says Esther. "You remind me of myself before I gave it up for all of zees." The sweep of her arm is probably French. Every th has turned to zee.*

*Annie knows what that means.*

*Esther turns her beautiful face away and strides toward the patio. From inside the screen house, Annie watches her mother settle herself at the picnic table, watches her pull that lacy hat with it's fist-sized rose onto her head. Now Esther is not Annie's mother, but someone else, talking into thin air, for the radio.*

*"She forgot the lemonade again," says Hayley Silk.*

*Annie paints her rock green. She turns the bumps on the top into yellow eyes. She adds a hint of tongue to the frog's wavy smile. When*

Hayley's mom calls from the street, Hayley looks at her fancy watch. "I'm really going to get it now."

Mrs. Silk is striding up the path through the trees, saying, "Get a move on. Don't dawdle." She jerks open the screen house door. "What did I tell you would happen? We're going to be late, and whose fault is that?" She casts an impatient look toward the house where Esther — in her bathing suit and her French hat — is talking to a girl in a dress. Annie has never seen the girl before. "Hayley, now. Scoot," says Mrs. Silk. "Straight to the car." She gives Hayley a swat on the seat of her bright red shorts.

Hayley doesn't even tell Annie good-bye, running away, running through the trees. Annie wonders why Mrs. Silk is still standing there, her hand on the door latch to the screen house. She says to Annie, "Your father would die if he saw you like that."

Like what? Annie has no idea what Mrs. Silk means. As soon as she's gone, Annie puts her Q-tip down and picks up Hayley's brush. She jerks her shoulders to the song that keeps running through her head: she-bop, she-bop. The rock-frog looks excellent with a flash of gold in its greeny eyes.

*Your father would die if he saw you like that.*

*Esther points with the hand that holds her cigarette. She strides toward the screen house. The girl she has in tow is plump. She hardly ever blinks her eyes.*

They stop in the middle of the grass and talk some more, and then Esther moves into the shade and says, "Annie, show us what you can do. You don't need the radio. Stand up on the table. Sing by yourself, like you did before." Esther claps her hands in a regular beat. She sings the first three, descending notes. She's looking so proud that Annie feels herself flood with some kind of light. She pouts her slippery mouth into the rectangular shape of Cyndi Lauper's. She scrunches her eyes and sings with a hiccup sound. She flings her arms. She bends her knees. She gets it right.

The girl walks up close, peering through the screen. "Who is she supposed to be?"

*Mary Howard*

"Guess," says Esther. Annie cocks her head to the right and squints her eyes. She sings every one of the rhyming lines. Moving her shoulders like Cyndi, she stutters the words: Gotta have fu-un.

"Stop." Esther rattles the frame of the springhouse door with the flat of her hand to make sure Annie does it: "Stop."

Esther is angry. "I told you who she is," she says to the teenager, who follows Esther past the heap of dresses on the grass, toward the picnic table. Annie hears the girl say, excitedly, "I love your show on the radio, something, something— autograph." Then the girl runs away, around the corner of the house. She actually runs.

"Annie, my beautiful daughter," Esther shouts after the girl. "That's who she is."

The door to the screen house locks from the outside. Annie screams for her mother: "Let me out." She cries to herself and then bangs on the table with both frog rocks, one in each fist, and gets green paint all over her hands. She calls to her mother some more. She can see her at the kitchen table, still in her white bathing suit and the hat with the rose, smoking cigarettes.

After a while the kitchen light goes on and Annie can see Esther even better, sitting behind her microphone. When she moves her hands and lifts her chin, the gestures are someone else's. Every time she stands up and vanishes from the window, Annie yells, "Come back, come back," till she reappears. Esther moves in and out of the window frame until shadows slide across the lawn and Annie can no longer see her own hands in the failing light. She holds the green rock-frog she painted for her dad in her right fist and rubs it against the screen for the rasping noise it makes, till her knuckles bleed. Cars on the street have their headlights on. "Help me," she yells for the hundredth time. In the dark it's hard to hold herself steady. Still, she stands on the table to sing, loud as she can, and falls horribly forward, hitting her chin on the way down. She curls on her side, her chin all sticky, but the floor is cold and spidery, and still no one hears. She stands up again and silently watches the window.

After hours and hours, her father appears there in the kitchen window, dark hair shiny. He's slim in his business suit. She screams, "Daddy, out here." Lights go on all over the second floor, then all the way to the attic. After a while, the back door opens and the yard light goes on. He runs toward the sound of her voice. His necktie divides. It flies off to both sides.

He holds her and tells her, "It's all right, baby. How did this happen? Sweetie? What happened to your hands?" He pulls a high-up chain that lights a single bulb. He moves her out of his shadow. "Your chin?"

"I'm thirsty," she manages to say.

"How long have you been out here?"

"Since three. Hayley was late to get her hair cut then"

"It's after eight," he says. "You must be hungry, too. I'm sorry." He pushes Annie away just far enough to study her face, and raises his eyebrows to say, "What's this?" He touches her cheek. He shows her his fingers, which have come off red. He pulls the orange scarf off of her head.

"Cyndi Lauper is the best girl singer on MTV." She sobs. "I'm terrible at her."

"I know something you're good at, though."

"What?" asked Annie.

"Grilled cheese. Your mother forgot to make your supper, didn't she?"

"She locked me up. She's mad at me."

"Oh, I don't think so, Anne. She's not feeling well. Let's go wash your face, get that green stuff off your hands. We'll put a Band-Aid on your chin. I'll open a can of soup and you can help with the sandwiches. After supper we'll see if your mother wouldn't like to take a ride. She needs our help. She's confused about the radio."

They walk across the grass, past the pile of dress-up clothes. "You had a meeting tonight?" she asks her father in a grown-up voice.

"County Board of Supervisors."

Annie has no idea what that means, so she just says, "Oh."

"Tell me about Cyndi. Who is she again?"

"You know. My favorite singer. You should hear Mom do her. I'll never be good as that."

*They've reached the warm light of the kitchen. "Look at me," he says, down on one knee so his face is level with hers. He is looking her right in the eye. "It's nothing you did, Annie. Always remember that. Your mother loves you. She'll be herself again soon. It's not your fault."*

Will, curled on his side, no longer snored; but he moaned loud enough to pull Annie out of her reverie. He made a dry, sibilant sound that was almost a word — *dresses*, it could have been. Or *confesses*. Alert to what might come next, Annie snuggled up to his feverish back. He bent his knees and settled his rump, which was cooler than the rest of him, against her belly, and her anger changed to loneliness. She'd never told him what it had been like, having a mother who was not herself sometimes.

"It will never be over," she whispered.

Even though he was asleep, and not accountable, she almost felt forgiven by the willingness of his body to seek hers for the first time in more than three weeks. She *needed* to be forgiven — for her sexy-cheating daydreams about Jack Boisseau, for wishing she'd never married Will in such a hurry, for being afraid of Gracie when she cried and cried and wouldn't stop. There were other failures, too, that could never destroy his love for her as long as they went unspoken. "I won't ever let you down again," she whispered.

She reached around him and took hold. She felt him swell. His shoulder pressed against her as he turned onto his back, his slurred voice a tease: "What'reyoudoing?"

"I thought you were asleep," she whispered.

"I was."

She rose up to see his goofy smile in the shadowy room. She kissed him on the cheek and in the hollow under his ear where he used to like it, going slow, hoping he wouldn't pull away, as he often had since Gracie was born.

"You've never," he said, turning his cheek to her for a kiss.

"Never what?"

"Let me down," he murmured.

She kissed him on the mouth, just lightly, tasting the bitterness of Terpin Hydrate with Codeine. He whispered, "Now you'll get what I have for sure."

"Promise?" She raised her right leg over and settled him in. "Just lie there and — yes, like that — let me try."

It took a while. She made a sound that might have been heard down the hall. He groaned happily.

"Shhh." She laughed with a soft *huh-huh* that turned to weeping, but sounded the same.

He held her. "I think I might be cured," he whispered when their hearts slowed down, and she said, "Me, too." Within a minute his breathing was methodic, in a feverish sleep. She gave him room to cool down.

*Was that Gracie stirring?* she wondered, listening. No, the house was completely still. For weeks she'd been wanting Will back the way he'd been before, first married, when they'd drowsed and then reawakened to after-sex talk, whispering, face-to-face. Everything had changed with Grace. Their whole life had changed. Maybe when he got well, got over this flu, things would be better.

She could smell his forgiveness on herself. Her nightgown was wet in the back. Her shoulders itched with wakefulness and she remembered the Irish wool. So she put both feet on the floor to pull on her mother's sweater, and just like that — one arm in a sleeve and one arm out — her mind caught a glimpse of herself as a child, there in the screen house, a girl of many colors.

Mrs. Silk had rattled the door latch to the screen house, saying, "Your father would die to see you like that. Your father would die—"

He would die to see me with red mouth and cheeks, thought Annie now. With bright orange hair, and green fingers. *That's* what she had meant.

That's *all* she had meant.

That didn't explain why her mother had locked her up for hours, then gone away the next morning, for weeks and weeks, without saying good-bye.

So much for the secrets hidden in memories.

Now Annie was wide-awake, restless with thought, even after making love with her husband. She wasn't dumb. She *knew* sex was a fleshly comfort, not a conversation. She wouldn't be forgiven until she *told* him how afraid she was of Gracie when she cried, how sad she was that marriage was lonely — but maybe then he'd turn away, and everything would fall apart. "Use your words," her mother used to tell her, but it had never been that easy for Annie.

Her weight made the floorboards creak all the way to the door of Linda and John's bedroom. "Ummm, what? Gracie awake?" asked Linda, a rising shape in a mound of covers. She must have pushed the crib against the side of the bed like that so she could slip her hand through the slats and touch the baby, like she was doing now. Like Gracie was hers. *Linda knows how to take care of her,* Annie thought. *She's naturally maternal. Not like me.*

"I just wanted to look at her," said Annie, head bowed to gaze at Gracie. *My beautiful daughter.* "She's never slept through the night before."

# Chapter 14

Linda's basement was so dark Annie had to pause to take her bearings from the glass doors off to her right. Beyond the planes of silvery light, rows of great, black trees, backlit by an eyelash moon, stood stark and colorless as a photographic negative. She found a floor lamp and turned it on so she could search the walls.

So this was the drawing Will had raved about.

No wonder. Annie walked up close to it. Linda must have caught something fleeting in Esther's gaze, a kind of tenderness Annie hadn't seen for weeks, the way a camera can preserve a split-second, guard-down moment purely by accident. Surely there was love in that shoulder as Esther held the baby and looked down at her.

A sudden wind swooshed around the house and changed direction, rattling the trees. It might as well have been the *hiss* and *Ah* of schizophrenia for the dread it inspired in Annie. She shivered from the cold. She shoved the couch around so it faced the back corner by the wall of glass, so she'd be able to see her mother's portrait when the sun came up. Then she tucked a blanket around her feet, hoping she might be able to fall asleep. The sketch on the wall was barely visible in the shadowy room. *Please start talking, Mother,* she prayed again: *If you took Gracie, tell us. Use your words.*

Annie closed her eyes. In a few moments — more like a dream this time, an insomniac memory — she was sitting on one of Hayley's twin beds.

*Hayley sits on the other. Annie feels her tongue curl against the roof of her mouth. "Schith—" The syllable makes her lisp. "I can't say it."*

*"Schiz-o-phren-i-a," says Hayley. "She went crazy on the radio. My mom heard her."*

*"She's not crazy. She's eccentric. She's an actress."*

*"That's a stereotype." Hayley's voice is full of scorn. "What will happen to her if she loses her show?"*

*Annie feels her shoulders lift. "She has her ups and downs, like everyone, but she always gets better." It's what her father always said.*

*"Your dad gives the station a ton of money," said Haley. "He buys that show for her."*

*"So? What's wrong with that?"*

*"I bet she sees things," said Hayley. "I've heard she does. That must be scary. Don't you wonder what it's like?"*

*"No," says Annie. "She just needs a different medicine. You can't believe everything you hear."*

*"It's like a non-secret no one's supposed to act like they know, but everyone does," says Haley.*

*Hayley is almost sixteen. Annie is thirteen. They haven't been best friends for a while, not like when they were five and eight. Annie has been praying to God to bring her mom back like she used to be. "You can stay with us as long as you like," says Hayley.*

*"My dad wants me home."*

*"I mean after school, or nights like this when he has a meeting. My mom is nicer to me when you're here. She sucks at being a widow." Hayley's dad died at Christmastime. "She just wants to blame someone," says Hayley, "and that someone is me. I don't see why." Hayley looks around her room. She might be seeing her makeup mirror ringed with light bulbs; or the movie poster for* Ghost, *with Patrick Swayze kissing Demi Moore on the throat; or the ballet shoes hanging on pegs. Hayley looks dazed, as if her own things are unfamiliar. She*

*has tears in her eyes again, but she's trying not to let it show. "You know that time you got locked in the gazebo?" she says.*

*Annie nods.*

*"I never dreamed your mom wouldn't let you out."*

*"Neither did I," says Annie. "Neither did anyone."*

*"I didn't know she was so sick she'd leave you there. I'm sorry, if you know what I mean."*

What year was it, when Hayley said that? Annie wondered, sitting there in Linda's basement, missing her mother, eyes scratchy and mind a blur, memories making sleep impossible. She shivered.

The trees outside the glass doors creaked again. A single star of farmyard light marked the darkness beyond the river. John had reported in the *Times* that he'd seen a bobcat come up the ravine from the river one night, seen the paw-prints, big as his hands, the next morning outside the door. Shuddering, Anne pulled the blanket up to her chin. Many minutes passed until her eyelids drooped and it came to her: the year Bill Clinton first ran for president. What year was that?

Her eyes opened extra-wide. Nineteen ninety-two. So it would have been the Christmas of ninety-*one* when Esther left the table in the middle of Christmas dinner to watch a political video called *A Place Called Hope.* Hayley and her parents, Elsa and Duane Silk, were there. So were Reverend Gustavson and his wife — and the twins, of course. This is another memory Annie has played over and over, letting it grow and elaborate in clarity and color:

*The minister's five-year-old daughters Rebecca and Ruth have left the table and are thundering up the stairs to the attic room where Annie's old toys are kept. The house smells of turkey, cinnamon, and sage. Hayley takes a fastidious bite of her Christmas pudding, making it last. She hasn't said a word during the entire meal. She refuses to look at anyone. "May I be excused?" asks Annie. Her father nods.*

*Annie heads for the stairs to check on the girls, who are probably pulling the heads off dolls. She glances through the doors into the living room where blue lights sparkle in the branches of the*

Christmas tree. "She hasn't been going out much," she hears her father say. He's talking about me, Annie realizes. She feels her face heat up. "She's happier at home," he says. He's talking about her in front of Hayley, as if Hayley were grown up. "She's lost friends," he says, "one by one."

Annie stands on the carpeted bottom step and leans over the banister, glaring into the dining room. Then he says, "When I do get her to go somewhere, she tells me strangers look familiar to her, but she can't place who they are." And Annie realizes he's been talking about Esther all along. "She hasn't meant to close you out, Elsa," he says to Mrs. Silk. "You mustn't think that. It's her illness returning, and nothing you did. We've adjusted her meds, but it hasn't helped." Annie wants to scream: Don't say meds, like it's a normal thing. Through the glass doors to the library, Annie sees her mother bend forward toward the television screen. The long ash of her cigarette falls to the floor.

"Maybe today wasn't a good idea. Too much for her." Elsa Silk's voice is so soft it's hard to hear from the stairs, but Anne concentrates.

"It's as if she goes away," her father says, "even though she's still in the house with us. She has come back from these episodes before, and when she does, she gets that wonderful radiance back." Silverware clinks on their plates. "Thanks for your contributions to the meal."

"We had no idea — at least I didn't." That is Mr. Silk's deep voice. "I admit I'm never sure what to say to her these days." He's a handsome, dark-haired man, president of Des Moines Area Community College. "As much as I've shied away from her, Frank, I've ignored your dilemma by doing that. You've got a lot to contend with. I feel ashamed for the way we've backed away little by little, of late. You deserve the same sort of loyalty you give your wife."

"We won't abandon you," says Mrs. Silk.

"Think of it like this," says Frank. "She has relapses just as people with Parkinson's do, or multiple sclerosis, or many other physical diseases." Annie has forgotten about going upstairs. "It's her brain," he is saying, "not her mind, and not anything any of us did." Why does he keep saying that, as if he doesn't quite believe it? "It's a brain disease," he says. "She's had a long stretch of good health, but as you can see, *this is a serious setback. We'd hoped that as she got older, the illness would subside, but she's not one of the lucky ones. At least not yet."*

*In the library, Esther has been talking along with the videotape. She knows it by heart: "Hope is more than a town in Arkansas." Now she calls out in a louder voice, "You see? Look at that." She is pointing. "He knows."*

*"Knows what?" asks Annie, as she enters the library.*

*"Now I know what he wants of me."*

*"Mother—?" Annie clicks the door shut behind her. "You're getting kind of loud."*

*"William Jefferson Clinton," Esther recites along with the tape. She puts it on pause.*

*"It doesn't mean he knows you, Mother. Every person on the street got one of those tapes. He just wants you to vote for him."*

*Esther opens the French doors so hard they hit the walls. She holds the videotape behind her back. "Walk ahead of me," she says to Annie, "We're going back in there."*

*No one speaks, in the dining room.*

"I didn't hear you," said Annie, startled by a light going on. "Is Gracie—?"

"Asleep. Still asleep." Linda stood at the bottom of the stairs. "I touched her little back a couple of times, and she was just fine. Just worn out, I guess. It's a quarter to five." Linda's long hair was tangled at the crown of her head. "What are you doing down here in the dark?"

"Thinking. Sorry I woke you up before."

"You didn't." Linda's voice was husky with sleep, and way too kind. "I was still awake when you came in our room to check on her. John finally went to sleep, and Will is snoring. It's cold down here. So you've been thinking."

"You drew my mom the way she used to be."

"I drew what I saw," said Linda.

"I wouldn't have had the presence of mind to think of drawing her to keep her calm. Will was impressed."

"He was frantic about your mom bringing Gracie down here that day," said Linda gently, "but we couldn't very well pry the baby loose by force. Portraiture is one of the few excuses in life for staring at a person's face up close without being rude. While I scrutinized her from an arm's length away, I could watch over Grace."

"I was also thinking," said Annie, "about the Christmas my friend Hayley's dad died."

"Hayley?"

"Hayley Silk. The Silks and the Gustavson's were at our house for this potluck dinner we used to do for holidays. I guess a lot of things started to change that night. It was one of the few times I remember my mom being sick. When it did happen, I got terrified."

"The Silks were close friends?"

"Um-hmm. And the Gustavsons, with Ruthie and Becka Sue. The girls were holy terrors then, especially Ruthie. She used to be the rowdy one."

"Ruthie's the blonde," said Linda.

"Right. Becka's the one with dreads."

"Different as they are, I get them mixed up," said Linda.

"Ruthie, the blonde, baby-sits with Gracie sometimes. Anyway, I have this memory of all of them milling around in the entrance hall, putting on their coats and saying good-bye. *Silver Bells* or something was on the stereo. The twins didn't want to go home, and Ruthie was pitching a fit. I was in the library with my mom. She'd gone in there again to smoke and play this tape from the Clinton campaign."

"I thought your folks were Republicans."

"My dad is," said Annie. "My mom is pretty independent."

"She still smokes, doesn't she?"

"She self-medicates with nicotine. It calms her down. Anyway, they're glass, you know, those doors. I could see out into the front hall. She refused to go out and say good-bye. 'That man is dying,' she whispered, pointing at Mr. Silk. He clapped my dad on the shoulder, and they shook hands and said 'Merry Christmas.' Mom put her finger against the glass and said it again, 'That man is dying. His ears are blue.' That was the last time we saw him."

"If he hadn't died, you wouldn't remember her saying that," said Linda gently. "Your mother was very ill, and you were very young."

"I know." Annie nodded. "I used to think she was one of those oracles, like in Greek plays. They could reveal mysteries and see into the future. I wanted her to be magical, not crazy. I tried to believe it for the longest time." Annie exhaled with a sigh, remembering how Hayley and her mom had stayed to help her clean up the kitchen that Christmas night. When they went home they had found Mr. Silk. A heart attack. "I never hear from Hayley," said Annie. "She graduated from high school early. She's in law school now, in Chicago. I don't even think she comes home for Christmas. My folks never have company anymore."

"She was how old then?"

"Hayley? About fifteen. Sixteen, maybe. My mother was gone for weeks that time. I stayed at Hayley's house, like I had another time Mom was sick. I was thirteen then. I had my first period while I was there, and her mom—"

"Elsa."

"Yes, she talked to me about how women have cycles like the moon. I thought it was funny, but it's true, isn't it? Those twenty-eight days. We're like clocks."

"More like the tide. We're not machines."

"What was Mrs. Silk doing with you," asked Annie, "when you found Gracie?"

"I was giving her a ride."

"From where?"

"The hospital," said Linda. "Some of us gathered to give your dad emotional support."

"Oh."

"Actually, Elsa and I had stopped by my house on the way. That's why we were on the river road. I have to ask you about Gracie's cow," said Linda.

"But how did Mrs. Silk *get* to the hospital?"

"She drove your dad's car over so he could ride in the ambulance."

"Ummm." Annie frowned. "What about Gracie's cow?"

"What I'm really curious about is the place you sent me to find it, that old boarded-up building by the railroad tracks. I didn't make it to the second floor the first time because the cow was on the stairs. I went back there a second time, after I knew Gracie was missing."

"Why?"

"Someone has cooked methamphetamine in an apartment on the second floor," said Linda. "Recently, I'd say."

Annie stopped blinking. "How do you know?"

"Not all of the smell is gone, Annie. I recognized other signs: cans of Drano, coffee filters with red chemical stains, windows covered over with garbage bags so no one could see in. Ned Milhous, Bobby's father, owns the building. He came out to see what I was up to — enraged, I'd say, that I'd been inside. It's occurred to me he might be protecting Bobby from charges of making the stuff. Otherwise the building would be posted as unsafe, or cleaned up, by now. I went straight to the police station after that to find out where you were, to keep you company."

"Was I still with Detective Hansen?"

"Yes. I completely forgot about reporting the meth lab then. I was in a state of shock, I guess, terrified for Gracie. I still am, to tell you the truth. Reporting what I saw in that awful place is on my list of things to do today. What shall I tell the cops about why you took Gracie to such a place."

Annie sat up straight, threw back the quilt. "Why did you go back a second time, after Gracie was missing? What did you think I had done to her? Did you think you'd find Gracie there? — Well, did you?"

"That building is contaminated," said Linda. "No one should be breathing the air in there." She glanced upward. "Especially a small child."

Annie rose to her feet. A phone was ringing upstairs, and Gracie was crying. "Thanks for showing your true colors," she said to Linda with all the sarcasm she could muster.

Annie fled up the stairs, and Linda followed. They met Will in the hall, puffy-eyed and confused with sleep. Frank had finished leaving his message by the time they crowded into the master bedroom. Linda hit the play button as Annie lifted Gracie from the crib and Will began to cough so hard he had to sit on the edge of the bed. Down the hall, a toilet flushed. John stepped into the doorway, wearing nothing but his briefs.

After a *beep*, and FIVE-SIXTEEN A.M., Frank's message began to play: "This is for Anne. After everyone left the house, I was missing your mother. I couldn't sleep all night. I happened to remember the envelope they gave me at the hospital, with her personal effects — her wedding ring, her diamond, her watch, that sort of thing. In the mix I found your car key. I'm sure it's yours. Just one key, on one of those clips that can be undone from a larger set of keys. I take this to mean she might have driven your car, with little Gracie in the back. That's one of that detective's theories. I called him just now. As soon as he verifies the key fits your car, I'm sure they'll call off the protective custody. Like I say, I haven't slept all night. I need to hear your voice. Give me a call."

*Mary Howard*

# Chapter 15

That Monday Linda and John accompanied Annie and Will to Juvenile Court. Social worker Candice Torrey was there, wearing the same red sweater she'd worn Friday night. At the hearing, Judge James Chapman, acting on information from the Linden Grove Police Department, ended the protective custody order. Will raised his chin and thanked the judge, his voice rough from the flu that still had him by the throat. It was his forty-first birthday. Grace looked especially tiny in Annie's arms. The baby's unruly hair escaped its pink ribbon and sprang straight up.

The Cantonwines headed home to Isabella Circle, John took off for the newspaper office, and by eleven-thirty that morning Linda was at her studio for the first time since Friday noon. One of the messages on her machine was from her realtor, left on Saturday: "Hi doll. It's Ruby. I know this is a difficult time for you, so I'm not calling you at home. I need you to give me a ring soon as you can. I've got an offer on your place. I think we need to pounce."

Linda called her back and, after a brief conversation, rejected the bid, too far below her asking price. She refused to let Ruby argue with her decision, ending the conversation more abruptly than she meant to. Linda was eager to turn her full attention to the annual report for the Holliwell Sign Company. All the photos she had taken at the company's facility on Friday afternoon, at the very hour Gracie was abducted, were of designers working at drafting tables or computer desks. Taken from the top of a stepladder, looking down, or from a crouched position, looking up, the images gave Linda a series of foreshortened, geometric angles to work with.

By the end of the workday on Monday, using Photoshop and Quark XPress, she had rendered some of the photos as shadowy, posterized images and run a band of them across a two-page spread. The client had limited her to the black and red of their corporate identity. They wanted this report to stockholders to be classy, but they also wanted a lot of pages for their money. To create excitement with such a limited palette, Linda knew she would have to be clever. She had promised a presentation on October first, only a week away.

That night she dreamed in black and red.

On Tuesday, she finished a mockup of two sample inside spreads, with dummy text. Turning to the cover design, she soon felt elated about the way the barn-red uncoated stock she had chosen would enhance the grainy look of the photographic imagery. One minute she was smiling about the way a *sans serif* called Neutraface, screen-printed in white ink, would compliment the ghostly photo-image on the red-ochre paper. The next minute she found herself staring at a sketch of Gracie pinned on the wall, admiring the button of flesh that graced the arch of the baby's M-shaped upper lip. Gracie's wide-open gaze showed all irises and very little white, like all babies' eyes, the very portrait of innocence.

She's safe now, Linda told herself for the hundredth time. She shivered.

The next day, Wednesday, September 25, 2002, John Bender published, on the editorial page of *The Linden Times,* a full-page report of Grace's abduction and Esther Hebring's recent struggles with mental illness. The account was impassioned and personal, the prerogative of a small-town journalist, and ended with this:

Will and I have been through a lot of tough stuff together since we were kids, including the deaths of his parents in a car wreck when we were in college, a divorce apiece, and the loss of my dad to cancer five years ago. Nothing has come close to being as heart-wrenching as this ordeal.

Even after Grace was back safe and sound last Friday night, we struggled to imagine a motive for her abduction. Thank God Annie's car key was found. She has long had the habit of leaving it under the floor mat of her car. The key was in Esther Hebring's pocket when Frank checked her into the hospital late Friday afternoon. Also, the police found her fingerprints on the driver's-side door of Annie's red Ford Focus ZX3. Sunday afternoon, under questioning, Esther admitted to the police that she had taken Gracie from her crib. Officials theorize that she must have driven the baby out into the country, returned the car to her daughter's driveway, then walked the five blocks back to her own home. Esther hadn't driven a car for years, so why now?

Well, her motive, which we may never know, may be beside the point. The words and actions of mentally ill individuals often arise from a delusional reality that conceals meaning and motivation. Repulsed, we're quick to brand such behavior 'crazy,' and damn the person along with the disease. The label is often contemptuous, or a way to tease someone whose antics are confusing, offensive, or off-the-wall. I for one won't be able to use the word lightly for a long, long time. 'Crazy,' in my lexicon, has become a terrible brain disease, from which Esther Hebring and her family have suffered deeply, particularly in recent weeks as she's been undergoing a change in her drug therapy.

It will take a better understanding of schizophrenia than most of us possess to make sense of Grace's abduction and brutal abandonment by a grandmother who loves her. Voluntary mental health treatment is a reasonable alternative to the use of criminal sanctions in the case of this disturbing crime. The family has asked me to express their gratitude for all the prayers and support from so many in the community. The pink ribbons can come off the trees now. Gracie is safe, and her grandmother is getting the best of care.

Linda practically knew the piece by heart: *motive, delusional, disturbing*. John had not mentioned that his own wife, along with

Elsa Silk, had found Gracie — an odd omission from such a personal account — but that wasn't what troubled Linda about the editorial.

It was the word *safe*. She didn't trust it.

As a break from the annual report, Linda turned to another task she'd been putting off, a complete reworking of Frank's ad for the Farmers & Merchants Bank. She had settled on a curvy silhouette of nineteenth-century storefronts from downtown Linden Grove, backed by a grain elevator-skyline. She couldn't get it right and couldn't keep her mind on it. Even as she studied the photographs she was using as drawing guides, she recalled Esther outside Annie's house, staring skyward, sliding her gaze from left to right along the roofline as if reading a message there.

The ringing phone brought Linda back from her reverie. She rested her fingers on the handset for a moment before picking up.

"I think you'll like this," said Ruby Best.

She paused just long enough for Linda to utter a distracted "Oh?"

"The buyer's come right back with a counter offer of one-sixty-five, and I think you should take it. Just listen, now. If you want to set up shop in the country, kiddo, you are on your way. He's an ideal buyer — no credit problem, raves about all your improvements to the place. Let's make him happy. What do you say? He's done his homework. I mean, he knows you've lowered your price twice since you listed it. He's been biding his time, I would guess, but now he's ripe to make a move. He really wants the place. He's from Johnson County, but he's been driving over here on weekends for a while to test the idea of relocating here. If you turn him down, you'll lose him. I'm showing him another property, too, but yours he wouldn't have to renovate. I've got him pegged as the impatient type. What do you say?"

Linda cast her glance all the way back to the railing of the loft, to the blue and white quilt hanging there. She was remembering Esther in Annie's driveway, wearing tight sweatpants, lost in an absentminded stare. "That's nice," said Linda.

"Nice?" Ruby gave the word a slide of irony. "This is the answer to your dreams, a guy who'll appreciate the place. He kept commenting on all that natural light. He wants to come by later to take some measurements before he leaves. He's due back in downtown Iowa City by suppertime. That's where he'll be moving his business from." Ruby's excitement brightened the inflections of her naturally quick voice. "All I need from you is a firm okay, and we can polish this deal off. I hardly opened my mouth, if you can believe that, once he got started ticking off the wonders of the place. He was looking at the drawings you have pinned up along the wall. All those faces. He thinks you're very talented. I didn't realize you'd done one of me. With my mouth open, wouldn't you know?" She chuckled. "I like it, though. It was like looking in a mirror."

"I didn't know selling the place was going to be so hard on me."

"You should be tickled."

"I am, Ruby. The news is great, but still—"

Ruby sighed with exasperation; but when she spoke, her voice was gentle. "Think of this: we've seen three established businesses move into town the past couple years, a great boost for our local economy — plus that new sewing shop down the street from you. This guy buys and sells old books, mostly over the Internet. I'm looking at his business card. He restores books, too. Takes them apart and puts them back together, just like new. He talks about it like he's writing symphonies. You'll like his attitude. Okay if we come by between two and three so he can do his measuring?"

"Sure, but I'll have to be here. I'm playing catch-up on a project I've had on hold. At any rate, you can tell him we have a deal." Linda tried to smile at her name in the window, LINDA GARBO DESIGNS. She could rig up the lavender and lime green neon sign at the end of the lane to her home-studio and print a map of how to get there on the back of her business cards. She exhaled fast, a kind of laugh. She had moved to Linden Grove from Minneapolis seven years earlier because she had thought a small town would give her a calmer, slower-paced life and help her get over a broken heart. "What are his reasons, do you think, for his wanting to relocate here?"

"All I know is, he's bought a bindery," said Ruby, "so he needs a ground-floor shop big enough for some new equipment. He wants that long table, if you'll leave it for him."

"I had it custom made for my height, so I could stand up and work at it. So no, tell him the table's not negotiable. I've got a place reserved for it at home." Linda pictured the rectangle of duct tape on the basement floor. "Will he live in the building, too?"

"I dunno. He checked out the loft pretty carefully. Even turned the shower on. What made you say this is hard for you?"

"I've had a lot on my mind." Linda swiveled her desk chair around.

That time of day, the entire workspace — from the iron stairs leading up the left wall to the loft, to the front desk where she sat — was illuminated by the long skylight. Those details barely registered before Esther came to mind again, her lacquered fingernails, the obsessive fussing with her rings. Linda turned to face the loop of neon at the front again. She must have made a sound.

"You okay?" asked Ruby.

"Yeah."

"I know you've been through a lot with the Cantonwine baby," Ruby said. "People are locking their doors more, I can tell you that. Before we knew who did it, my daughter was set to take a week's vacation and stay home with her two-year-old, thinking some kidnapper was at large. But little Gracie is back where she belongs, and her grandmother's locked up where she can't hurt anyone. The whole thing's a terrible shame. You having trouble letting go of all that worry?"

"No, I'm fine."

"I shouldn't wonder if you were still a little shaken, but just think. Selling your building will make life easier. You'll have the money to fix up your place in the country before your own baby's born. You can run your business without all that overhead. You can draw your pictures, make those linographs you talk about."

"Lithographs," said Linda, lisping the word softly on her tongue.

"*Lith*-o, yes, okay. You can ease up on your business until your baby's older. It's what you told me you wanted, right?"

"Yes. It's what I want."

"There you are. You see?" Ruby paused. "For a possession date—"

"It'll take a few weeks to get the studio at home ready. Let's say December first."

"He'd like it sooner."

"I'm swamped with deadlines piling up, things I've let go the past few weeks." Linda thought of poor Esther again, her uncombed hair, the t-shirt she wore, too tight to her body. The sweatpants. No pockets.

An electronic signal trilled at Ruby's end. "Bye. See you at two," she said.

As soon as Linda pressed the switch hook down, she pushed the numbers for John's cell phone. When he didn't answer, she flipped the OPEN sign in the front door to CLOSED. She turned off the neon in the window. As she shut the back door behind her, she looked at her watch.

It was after one. She hurried across the half-empty parking lot, down the short alley between the Grubstake Cafe and Ace Hardware. Down Main Street to her left, beyond the cafe, a man on a ladder was applying colonial blue paint over the red storefront of the former Little Read Book Store. The new sign, Blue Earth Archaeology, leaned against a parking meter. Linda took off in the opposite direction, walking past Montross Pharmacy, Ben Franklin, and Quilting from the Heart — the new sewing business Ruby had just mentioned. At the corner of Main and Third, Linda crossed against the light. The police station was two blocks away.

*In her pocket,* she kept thinking. John had that wrong.

From behind the shiny lenses of his glasses, Detective Hansen gave Linda a *you-can't-be-serious* look. "Hebring found the car key among the personal effects the hospital gave him."

"I realize that," said Linda, "but there were no pockets in what she was wearing Friday afternoon. She wasn't carrying a purse, and she didn't have the key in her hand. Whoever put it in that envelope didn't get it from Esther."

"You're sure about that," said Hansen. It wasn't a question.

"I'm positive. Esther talks with her hands. She has a sort of fetish about her rings and her bright red fingernails. To me, she was noticeably empty-handed."

"A fetish."

"I'd say so, yes. Part of her illness, maybe."

"I never noticed," he said. "You're suggesting someone planted Anne Cantonwine's key among her mother's personal effects?"

"I don't know what else to think," said Linda.

"Who? One of the nurses? Or Frank?"

"Elsa Silk was with him in the waiting room Friday night. Also, Frank's brother, his brother's wife, some other people I didn't know. There is a kind of rivalry between Elsa and Esther. All I'm sure of is that Esther didn't have any key with her when she was put into the ambulance."

The detective sat down and gestured toward the oak chair across the desk from him. Linda stayed on her feet. He shook his head. "Maybe she tucked the key in her waistband, or in a sock. Maybe she hid it in her underwear. She's nuts, you know."

"I'm serious."

"Sorry. I know she's ill, but considering what she did with that ring, who knows where that key might have been." Perhaps it was Linda's frown that brought the detective up short. "Sometimes I get a little flip when I'm—"

"Unsure of yourself?"

"Tired. When I'm tired." He pulled off his glasses held them up to the light. Once he'd adjusted them back on his nose, he again invited Linda to sit. She stared down at his scalp through his thick, brown hair, cut military-short. "Let's think this through," he said.

"Maybe the nurse who put the items in that envelope will remember if the key was there."

"We could look into that." He wiped all expression from his face with a muscular hand. "Look, Linda, I know Mrs. Hebring's illness is a terrible thing. In this business we deal with disturbed

*Mary Howard*

people more often than you might think. Mrs. Hebring is a lot more protected, more refined, than most I've run up against. I appreciate John's call for compassion. I agree with him. Remember, I interviewed her at the county hospital, so I've witnessed the state she's in." A deep V formed between the detective's eyebrows. "Don't lose sight of the nature of the crime. You seem to be suggesting someone risked the life of an innocent baby in order to have Esther Hebring put away. That someone planted that key to implicate her, to set her up to be another victim of this crime."

"What about that magazine in the ditch, which seems to point to Esther? Isn't that way too convenient to be reliable evidence? It seems obvious it was a plant. I'm simply not convinced Esther took that baby."

"She told me she did." Hansen's glasses came off again. This time he folded them. Without lenses, his green eyes appeared small. He held her gaze. "Go on."

Linda lowered herself into the varnished oak armchair facing the detective's desk. "Esther Hebring couldn't have hidden anything in her socks because she wasn't wearing any. She wore barefoot sandals that day. Sweat pants, a t-shirt, clothes that were way too tight. Her hands were flawlessly manicured, but the rest of her was really let go. The point is, someone—" Linda felt a catch of panic as her logic began to come undone. *When in doubt, ask a question,* she remembered. "You questioned Esther at the County Hospital on Sunday?"

"In Frank's presence, yes. We asked her about the ring that showed up on her x-ray. She said she had to perform a series of tasks, to prove she was worthy of being First Lady of the United States. Swallowing that ring was one of them."

The detective twisted his torso in his chair as if he couldn't get comfortable. "She wasn't able to make much sense of what she was doing before three o'clock last Friday afternoon. She did remember the Channel Eight television crew at her daughter's house, and she did admit taking Grace out of her bed. She felt no remorse or fear, as far as I could see, no emotion of any kind." Hansen jutted his jaw forward slightly. "She said Grace was 'quiet as a lamb, so no one

heard us.' That was about it. The rest of what she had to say was un-
related. That's the kindest way to put it. When I talk with her again,
I'll ask her how she managed—" He was writing something down.
"Key. Without. Pockets."

"Why do you have to talk with her again?"

"Because of her general state."

"Which you have to consider unreliable, right?"

"She shut down when I showed her that magazine, the one
found at the scene, with the piece torn out of it. It appears to have
been a recipe. Anyway, the interview was over, just like that. We
found other back issues of that same magazine in her daughter's
car, by the way," he said. "Unfortunately the one you found got handled a lot before we could dust for prints." He cleared his throat.
"We think the sweatshirt the baby was wrapped in may have come
from Anne Cantonwine's car, too, rather than from the house. That
strengthens the theory her own car was used in the crime. I asked
Mrs. Hebring about that, and she said something about how being
wrapped in a parent's garment keeps a baby safe, some sort of su-
perstition I've never heard of. Next week I'll set up a run to Clarinda. She's been moved to the mental health hospital there."

"Yes, I know."

"It takes days, sometimes weeks, I'm told, for a medication to kick
in and calm down the psychotic voices and the such, if it works at all.
It's a two-hour drive to the hospital. That means an entire afternoon to
go down and back and have time to talk with her. We're shorthanded,
so I can't spare the time for any aborted attempts before she's up to
it. Point is, I don't think there's any rush at this point, Linda. Frank's
convinced his wife will tell us the whole story when she's functioning
better, if she can. Her memory of that particular day may always be
scrambled, though. She's still in and out of some sort of delusional,
parallel world. I'm not sure how all that works. Frank's pretty much
resigned to what happened. Still, you should know we haven't closed
the book on this." He paused to clear his throat. "On another note, Ned
Milhous has agreed to hire a hazardous material contractor to clean up
that vacant building of his. Thanks for the tip on that."

"You're welcome. Why haven't you closed the book on the abduction case?"

The detective put his glasses back on. They exchanged a long and steady look.

"You have doubts too, don't you?" she asked.

"Loose ends," he said, "not doubts. Mrs. Hebring had that key tucked in her waistband, would be my guess."

"I suppose it's possible."

The detective simply nodded.

Linda inhaled deeply. "Annie told me about the crank call you got here at the station," she said, "accusing her of leaving Grace in her car. Do you think the caller could have been right?"

"No, I looked into it. It was a mean-spirited prank."

"Whoever made the call might have been trying to cast doubts on Annie's character, so you'd mistrust her later on when Grace was missing."

"There were two calls. My guess is the caller was a high school girl up to a grim sort of mischief. The voice sounds young. The afternoon Gracie went missing, I had Anne Cantonwine listen to the tapes of the phone calls, thinking she might recognize the voice. She didn't. At that point, I was afraid she might have made the whole abduction thing up to cover the fact she'd harmed her child. When the baby came back healthy a few hours later, that theory went out the window. It left a residue of suspicion, I have to admit. That might be what you're experiencing."

"Gracie didn't come back on her own. We found her, Elsa and I." Linda placed both hands on the edge of the desk between them.

"I could make a guess about Anne Cantonwine's timing, in telling you about those calls," the detective said. "I'm betting she told you *after* you had brought the child home wrapped in that sweatshirt. Am I right?"

"Yes. She told me Saturday afternoon, while she was nursing Gracie. She was still having trouble believing her mother did this thing. Annie's fixated on that caller."

"And so are you."

"Yes. So am I."

"Annie can't even pronounce the word schizophrenia," the detective said. "I dare say it's harder for her to deal with her mother's actions than for anyone else. I expect we'll have enough to charge Mrs. Hebring with abduction, pending the outcome of my interviews — when she's feeling better, of course. Since the baby was not injured, the charge would be an aggravated misdemeanor. I doubt she'll ever be arraigned. Assuming that she will be willing to comply with a condition of long-term treatment — we can't coerce her — I'm sure we can keep her out of prison. There's a judge up in Sioux City who holds a Mental Health Court. My guess is she'll be in institutional care for a long, long time. Hebring will no doubt find a private hospital. He has the money." Hansen gave Linda a hard look. "I hear that place is pretty bleak."

"Clarinda, you mean?"

He nodded. "This is a sad business, all the way around."

"I may go see it for myself." Linda stood. "Visit Esther."

The detective moved his face forward slightly, his upward gaze at Linda suddenly more intense. "I can't stop you from visiting her, but I'd hate to see her made defensive before I've had another chance to question her. I've still got a man assigned part-time working on this case. He's looking for someone who might have seen the car that afternoon, that sort of thing. Don't go off like a loose cannon."

"Just back off?"

"Remember," he said, "this is the kidnapping of a two-month-old baby we're dealing with — an insider crime, and one that makes no sense. Think motive. *Motive.*" He said it gently. "I caught the implication you were making about Elsa Silk. She's a longtime friend of the Hebrings. She closed her shop the minute she heard about the kidnapping and rushed to see what she could do to help. She has customers to verify that. To think she'd plot against Esther Hebring is absurd. Bottom line? Only an insane person, disconnected from the dire consequences of her actions, would leave a baby exposed to the elements like that. I still lose sleep over it myself."

The detective broke eye contact and studied his thumbs.

"I've managed to befriend Esther," said Linda, "despite her condition."

"That would be pretty hard."

"Not really. Not for me. She's a fascinating woman, great company when she's in her right mind. My father had mental difficulties, too. I suppose that makes a difference to my attitude." Linda felt herself color slightly. Her family took a lot of explaining, so usually she didn't even try. "My dad would have these spells," she said. "Every once in a while he'd stop what he was doing and get an empty look in his eyes. 'I relive scenes with you when you were little, singing a Christmas song,' he'd say to me. I wouldn't stick around to hear him try, yet again, to recreate how cute I'd been, getting it wrong: 'I'm dreaming of all-right Christmas.' I'd hurry off to be with my friends, escaping the father everyone knew came back crazy from the Korean War."

"I'm sorry—"

"John calls it a 'mondegreen.'"

"A what?"

"A mondegreen. A misheard lyric. Cute, when a child does it, as in, 'I'm dreaming of all-right Christmas. All-right instead of a white—"

"Yeah, I got that. Okay."

"I guess that's the sort of thing my dad told the VA doctors, that he was haunted by me as a little girl in a red dress, singing a song wrong, over and over. His problem seemed psychological. The diagnosis was Post Traumatic Stress Disorder. For a while he was hospitalized for some kind of talk therapy. The correct diagnosis wasn't made until the autopsy. They found something in his brain."

The detective waited.

"All along he had been having seizures," said Linda, "triggered by a metal fragment in the frontal portion of his brain, a wound from combat in Korea. It's the part of the brain that stores complex scenes from memory — scenes complete with music, smells, texture, color. He could have been helped with anti-epilepsy drugs, if only they'd known what was wrong. I had been ashamed of my father out of ignorance." Linda paced three steps, then stopped. "I was never able to tell him I was sorry, but at least I can have compassion for another brain that doesn't work so well because of injury, or illness, in Esther's case. I'm not about to abandon her now."

When she turned to face the detective, he was looking at his thumbs again.

"He died when I was seventeen."

"That must have been very hard." Detective Hansen stood. His gaze was tentative. He looked embarrassed. "You want to see that magazine?"

She nodded.

He left the room.

When he returned with the *Traditional Home* magazine found in the ditch near Gracie, she sat in the chair across the desk from him and reached for it, then hesitated.

"One of the sheriff's deputies handled it at the scene, I'm afraid," he said. "Most of the prints we lifted were pretty muddled. We have only one thumbprint that's unaccounted for."

"Elsa handled it, too. She's the one who fetched it from the ditch."

The detective didn't react to that. Linda turned all her attention to the page with the piece torn out. A cooking article started one page back, promising recipes for 'Diva-liscious Hummus, Pesto Tenderloin Crostini, and Baked Brie with Brandied Cranberries.' "Not very helpful, is it?" she said to the detective.

"I wouldn't say that. We found a stack of these same magazines in Anne Cantonwine's car, and a few more in Anne's dining room, all with her mother's name on the address labels."

"With recipes cut from all of them?"

"A few."

"Hand-me-downs," said Linda.

The detective raised his eyebrows. "Come again?"

"A mother trying to inspire domestic skills in her daughter, don't you think? Not too subtle. Sounds like Esther gave Annie all her back issues. The Hebrings house is a showplace." Linda closed the magazine. "Their living room could be on this cover. Annie's place still looks like a dorm room, and she barely cooks. Maybe her mom tries to change her."

The detective shrugged. He slipped the magazine back into its evidence bag. The conversation seemed to be over except for some kind of closure.

So Linda leaned forward and said, "Listen. When I found Grace—" The memory was quick, as four deer stood motionless again at the edge of the headlights' glow, then leapt. Detective Hansen ventured a wary look, over his glasses. "It was just the most wonderful luck," she said, leaning back again. "Gracie is a part of me now. I'm going to keep bugging you until I'm satisfied we have the truth and that she's really out of danger."

She stood up and tried to make her tone dismissive. "I can't wait around for Esther to get better and fill in all the details. What if she never does? We have to find other ways to know for sure. 'The crazy woman did it' is just too easy. Magazines don't just fall out of cars and land in ditches."

"But a mentally ill person might have a delusional reason to put it there," said detective Hansen.

"Let me listen to those crank-call tapes before I go," said Linda. "See if I recognize the voice."

"Think what could happen to a baby left alone like that." The voice on the tape was a whispery, country drawl, vaguely familiar. A second call was nearly identical, but added new details: "It was eleven minutes before she came out of the post office again. Think what could happen to a baby left alone in an unlocked car."

Unlocked? Had the caller tried the doors? Linda played the recording over and over. She memorized the voice until she began to believe every word.

Finally, angry, she took her finger off the rewind switch. She didn't want to hear it again. The earnest hiss of the girlish whisper had lost its familiarity. If it was *not* a prank, and the danger was real, why call the cops and not leave your name? Why not just take Grace into the post office and say to Annie, "Here. Don't ever leave your baby alone again"?

Why not just take Grace?

Linda walked so fast she got a stitch in her side. When she reached the alley leading to the parking lot behind her studio, she saw Ruby Best's car by the back door, about eighty feet away. Beside it was a shiny black vehicle with the word JEEP on its spare tire cover. Ruby was unlocking the door. The man standing behind her looked up at the second story, shielding his eyes with his right hand. When he turned around so that Linda could see his face — a blur of high forehead, wiry dark hair, an angular jaw — she backed-up and walked past the Grubstake to the door to Blue Earth Archaeology. The sign had been mounted. The painter was gone. The facade was completely blue, no traces of red from The Little Read Bookstore that used to be.

She was going to miss her own building something terrible. *Might as well get a look at the guy,* she thought.

In the alley, out of the sun, the air was cooler. A red cola can rattled along the stone foundation of Ace Hardware to her left. Though the buyer had gone inside the studio with Ruby Best, Linda could envision him, just as plain. He wasn't much taller than Ruby, who was five-six or five-seven. A small man who loved books for their pages and spines. She imagined him in there right now, measuring her worktable, realizing it was much too high for him.

# Chapter 16

The moment Linda stepped from the alley into the parking lot, a thunder-like sound snapped her attention to the right. Austin Benn was dragging something across the bed of his pickup. It looked like a posthole digger. With the long handle in his fist, he let the heavy bucket-end drop to the asphalt by his back door. Benn was a bearish man with a muscular upper body. He didn't see her until she called out, "Hello."

"Hey, Linda." He leaned the tool against the tailgate and hung his bill cap on the end of it as she approached.

"Your sign looks great out front."

"It's up? I haven't seen it."

"Just this afternoon," she said. "The painter's done. The colors are just right. I like the burgundy and ochre trim with the blue."

"Ochre, is it?"

"Okay. Tan."

He grinned back at her. "We'll have curb appeal, anyway. We're getting there. It's a nightmare moving a business like this. Boxes of rocks and bones and broken dishes, tons of reports." The red of the bandana around his forehead made his eyes look greener than usual.

"I haven't seen your truck here all week," she said. "I've been watching for it."

"Oh?" He took a swig from a bottle of water. "We've been pushing to finish up that survey along the Des Moines River for the Corps of Engineers."

"And did you succeed?"

"After a few interruptions with other work we have going, yes. We got her done this afternoon."

Linda glanced through the propped-open door into the interior of Benn's archaeology lab, piled waist-high with boxes. His partner Tom Alex was in there, talking on the phone. He waved.

"Hi, Tom," she shouted in to him and turned back to Benn. "Remind me which project this one is."

"It's a site on a Skunk river bank that was partly washed away in the '93 flood. The Corps plans to increase water flow from the Cedar dam during wet periods, starting next year."

"For flood prevention."

"Yeah. We've got a beautifully preserved Oneota village in jeopardy. Dates from the 1300s." While Benn went on talking about *village boundaries* and *mapping the site,* Linda's attention shifted to the black Jeep nosed up to the back wall of her studio. "We're hoping to shore up the bank with truckloads of rock," he said, following her gaze. "Someone looking at your place? I noticed Ruby over there. I see the guy has Johnson County plates."

"I think I've finally got the building sold." Even at that distance, she could see someone moving around inside the back window over there. "Sorry." She looked at Benn again. "I really am listening."

He chuckled. "You say hello and I give you a full-length report. Thing is, I've been out every day the past two weeks. We're a little shorthanded, so I had to help Tom finish up this job myself. Even camped at the site a couple nights." He hefted another bucket auger out of the truck and swung it ahead of him through the door of his lab, where he leaned it against the side wall, out of sight. "That's it." He returned to the tailgate of his truck and sat again. "I'm waiting for him." He tilted his water bottle toward the sound of his partner's voice. "To go check another job."

"I called you the other day," she reminded him. "I noticed a woman parked right here by your door. You said her name was Nina, when we played answering-machine tag. I recognized her from church, but at first I wasn't sure." Linda smiled, setting him up: "I found I had paid more attention to the wings than to her face."

"Oh yeah?" Benn laughed, a teasing chuckle.

"On her shirt," she explained. "The only reason I happened to notice her at all, first time I saw her—"

"In church, you said."

"Right. Was the way she was dressed. A t-shirt with a shiny design of Pegasus on the front. The mythical horse with—"

"Wings," he said.

"Right."

He tucked his chin and raised his eyebrows

"Clothes can tell you a lot about a person," she said.

"If you say so."

"The woman I saw with the shovel over here," said Linda, "had on a Harley-Davidson t-shirt, the kind with the eagle. She drove a white pickup with a rusty dent. That sound like Nina?"

"Yep." He stopped smiling. White lines fanned into the sunburned skin at the outside corners of his eyes. "When was this again?"

"Two weeks ago. Friday morning — about eight, I think. She left a shovel here by your door, and a cardboard box that was heavy, judging by the way she handled it."

"Yeah, that was Nina Sorba, I'm afraid."

*Afraid?* thought Linda. "I take it she works for you."

"She did."

"Oh."

"I can't see her going to church," he said.

"Well, she was there a couple weeks ago," said Linda, "the Sunday of Grace's baptism. The baby who was kidnapped? It's because of the kidnapping that I'm so curious."

"Yes, I've been following it, like everyone else. I saw John's article last night. An awful thing, mental illness. Horrible, what that lady did."

"We're the baby's godparents." Linda paused. "About this Nina — I'd never seen her around here before, and I haven't seen her since."

"She met us on the job sites. At this point, all our jobs are a ways from here."

"When I called you," said Linda, "I was wondering about a connection between her and the baby's grandmother." *Like playing a part in Esther's delusions,* was something she stopped herself from saying. "I'd like to talk to her again."

"So would I," said Austin Benn. "She left me in a bind. She was a hard worker, very professional, fascinating to talk to, if a bit cynical. Then all of a sudden—boom—she's gone. I've been worried something has happened to her. I can't get her to return my calls."

"She just walked off?"

"Must have been the day before you saw her. I found her tools here outside the door when I came by that Saturday — a shovel, a soil prob*e, this.*" He slid a white pole partway out of the truck. It had black numbers painted along its eight- or nine-foot length.

"Did you say something to set her off?" Linda asked him. "I ask because that's what happened to me. I apparently said something to upset her, and she was out the door without a good-bye."

"Yeah, I'd never realized she'd be that easy to offend." Benn turned around, propped a foot up on the tailgate, and retied the laces of his boot. "She liked to talk about her research trips to South America. She's a talker, like me."

"I know what you mean," said Linda. "I found her really outspoken when I spoke with her that one time. If I could have an address for her, or her phone number—" He nodded. "And then I should get going," she said.

Austin Benn glanced at Linda and seemed to reconsider something. "Come on inside. I'll look for her number."

"I'd rather stay out here where I can keep an eye on my back door. I'm curious to get a look at the buyer."

Benn glanced across the parking lot, then back at Linda. "Be right back," he said.

He was inside for three minutes, maybe four. She heard him talking with Tom, deep inside the shop. Finally, he returned with a sheet of paper in his hand. "Her resume," he said. "You got a pen?" He patted his shirt pocket.

"No."

"Just take the whole thing, then. That's her local address I wrote there on the top." It was scrawled across the paper in a bold hand, 11623 530th Street. "The cell number is the only one she gave me."

"Thanks. I'll bring it back."

But Benn was not ready to let her go. "You're right about her taking offense to something I said. She broke out in a sweat and went pale around the eyes. It worries me, the more I think about it."

"When she left, you mean."

"Yeah." Benn's green eyes opened wider. "It was almost time to quit anyway, because the light was fading. Tom was there, too, and another guy who works for us part-time. I was just making conversation the way we always did. It was a way to pass the time before we packed up at the end of a long day, a pleasant way to decompress from fieldwork. Kind of like I'm doing now. It's a pretty place, with a bike trail along the river, all the grasses and trees. Lots of birds. The mosquitoes were gone because we'd had that early frost before it got warm again."

Linda shifted her weight from one leg to the other. Benn was a talker all right.

"Her research area is pre-Incan burial practices in Chile," he said. "You can see that on her resume."

Linda glanced at the vita in her hand and saw that Nina had earned a Ph.D. the previous May from the University of Iowa.

"I told her I would like to read one of her articles," Benn was saying, "and did she have an off-print I could see? That's when it happened. Her mouth got small, if you know what I mean."

"Small?"

"A hurt sort of look. Then she demanded to know what I was really asking. I was floored. The other guys just looked away. She hadn't used that angry tone of voice with us before. She's a cultural anthropologist by training, something of an expert, I take it, on the effects of certain interviewing techniques. She accused me of trying to get her to reveal something I already knew was true. I guess my questions struck some kind of nerve that was painful enough to drive her away. I certainly didn't mean to."

"What was it you asked her? Can you remember?"

He paused to take another swig of water. "First you have to know that her doctoral research has to do with tiny, statue-like mummies from a pre-Incan tribe."

Linda made a face.

"I know, but it's interesting stuff. She's used to scholarly research, a far cry from the sort of short-term contract work I hired her to do for us. I only took her on part-time until the end of this season, when the ground freezes. This year that might mean after Christmas, if this warm weather keeps coming back. I had hopes she'd be available after the spring thaw. I was thinking that maybe then we could hire her full-time, with benefits — though I assumed she probably wanted to get closer to her specialty. That's what got me in trouble.

"I asked her if she was hoping her new degree would lead to museum work, or a professorship. You'd have thought I'd insulted her. I tried to compliment her to bring her back around, but that just made it worse. I asked, 'Isn't it a great feeling to have such a long personal bibliography?' She's got articles up the wazoo."

Behind her, Linda heard two car doors slam, an engine start, and then another. She didn't turn around. Benn was staring over her shoulder, his mind on what he was thinking. "She threw some tools into her truck," he said, "and drove away without a word. We haven't been able to reach her since."

"Do you think she could have been ill?" asked Linda.

"Interesting you should ask. My assistant Tom thinks she was strung out on something, but it didn't look like that to me. I liked her, see? My theory is that she was too proud to say working on her hands and knees in the dirt was just too much for her. Not what she was used to at all."

*Mary Howard*

"Do you think you'd recognize her voice if you heard it on a recording?" she asked him.

"Sure. She talks with a certain attitude. Sort of whispery."

The conversation with Austin Benn had lasted sixteen minutes. It ended with her talking him into going down to the police station to listen to the crank call tapes that were part of the Cantonwine baby case. Linda had let Ruby Best drive away, the guy from Johnson County right behind her. When Linda unlocked her back door and stepped into her sun-drenched studio, she saw it as an outsider might — a bright, cavernous space waiting to be filled with books and glues and whatever equipment goes with book conservation and a bindery. The long, glass-topped table down the center was immaculate — sterile, to her own mind's eye — no charcoal dust, no scraps of paper, no piles of pencils or pots of ink. It didn't look like an artist's studio. Not even a visible fingerprint. The untidy part of her that daydreamed portraits and drew faces on walls had moved out already. None of her client's projects seemed important now. She wanted to go home.

But it was only three o'clock. From the clutter of drawings pinned to the wall up front, Linda pulled down the portrait of the Girl With Wings she'd drawn the day the woman had parked her pickup by Benn's back door. Under the bill of her cap lay an oval of shadow. Linda erased it.

Beginning with strokes of rubbed graphite, she sketched a narrow facial structure, defining areas like nose and chin with the pencil's tip. Darker, thicker lines tightened the lips, jacked up the cheekbones, and sharpened the crevices of a small, coiled ear. She added splinters of mirrored light to the deep-browed eyes she imagined would be a malevolent amber, like a cat's, though she couldn't remember their actual color.

Linda tried Annie's phone number, but got no answer. So she sat at her drafting table up front, determined to finish the bank ad by hand. It helped that the Farmers and Merchants Bank was a local landmark, a corner building with a turreted tower. She practice-sketched it from memory, with a brush and India ink. Then she drew the entire skyline of Linden Grove's restored storefronts downtown with a single gesture, sweeping it off to the right with a flourish, like a signature. For typography she chose a bold Stone font. When she finished assembling the ad, she was surprised to see it was after five. She picked up the phone and pressed the tune for Nina's cell phone number and let it ring until she got an answering service. She left her name and number.

Ruby Best 's business card lay by the phone with another one, from John Eliot Boisseau: Rare Books Bought and Sold. Linda put it in her wallet. She read Nina Sorba's resume and saw that Austin was right. The woman was impressive. She'd published nineteen articles. Then Linda stared at the phone number scrawled across the top of the page in Austin Benn's bold hand. She searched on her phone for "Missed calls" and found the identical number. And Linda remembered: that call had come into her cell phone during the hours Gracie was missing.

The address crossed out on Nina's resume was in Iowa City, where in June she'd received her Doctor of Letters in Cultural Anthropology. The address written in above it was in rural Madison County.

John answered his phone on the second ring. "Isn't 340th Street out our way?" she asked him.

"It follows the river, across from us," he said, "then crosses over and turns south."

"The road where I found Grace."

"Yeah. Why do you ask?"

On her way home, Linda turned north onto 340th. It crossed a bridge, then curved east. She drove slowly, reading numbers on mailboxes. When she came to the address in the top margin of Nina Sorba's resume, she pulled onto the shoulder and put the car in park. The house was back too far in the trees to be seen, except for a steeply slanted roof she recognized. A FOR RENT sign had been tacked on a nearby tree.

The drive was narrow and rutted, the remnants of a crushed rock bed worn so thin that her car rocked back and forth as she drove toward the house — an A-frame cottage with a wraparound deck.

She cupped her hands against the window glass. An ancient chrome and plastic kitchen chair faced her from the middle of the room. A push-broom leaned against the back of it. She followed the deck around to the river side of the house.

From there she could see the stream at the bottom of the ravine, leaves drifting on a slow current. Mud and sand bars. Lifting her gaze, she caught a glimpse of a stone wall on the other side. Beyond it, in the fading light, gleamed the glass wall of her own basement studio.

Back in the car, she flipped open her cell phone and called the number on the FOR RENT sign. Nina Sorba, the disgruntled male voice on the other end told her, had left a message a couple of weeks earlier to say she was moving out. "Not much of an advance notice, so I'm keeping her deposit. If you're a friend of hers, you can tell her that for me."

Heading for home, Linda dialed her phone again. On the third ring, Annie answered.

"I've been wracking my brain," said Linda, "trying to come up with a plausible explanation for why anyone would steal a sweatshirt out of your car on a warm day." Linda's car moved very slowly down the gravel road. "I've come up with one. Want to hear it?"

"Of course."

"That anonymous person was threatening you. 'This time your sweatshirt, next time your baby.'"

There was silence on the other end.

"Of course, that only makes sense," said Linda, "if Gracie was alone in the car."

"I can't talk right now."

"Annie?"

"My friend Tiffani is cutting my hair," Annie said. "Our babies are on a blanket in the sun. You should see how cute they are together."

"If she could take the shirt, it would have been *that easy* for her to take Grace, left alone in an unlocked car. That warning, that threat, was the message. That was her point. The caller is the kidnapper."

"Detective Hansen doesn't think so," said Annie.

"But it makes sense to you, knowing what you do, doesn't it?"

"No. I don't know. Part of what you said—" Annie fell silent.

"Your mother is taking the blame for this. Help me here. Tell me you lied when you denied leaving Gracie alone. My theory only makes sense if you did. Tell me yes, or no."

"Yes."

"Okay, then, someone was watching you days before the kidnapping, Annie, waiting for you to give her an opportunity to take Gracie. She warned you ahead of time. What does that mean, that she warned you? Or threatened you? Think, Annie. Who would do that?"

Silence.

"Don't let the baby out of your sight."

There was a rustling of discomposure at Annie's end, then a door-closing kind of sound. When she spoke again, her voice was hushed, but forcefully distinct: "That detective was talking to Daddy again this afternoon. They think Mom had that car key in her mouth and that's why she wouldn't talk. She was into swallowing things, so who knows? It's a nightmare, but it's over. Just let it be. I have to go." She hung up the phone.

# Chapter 17

That Friday afternoon, the twenty-seventh of September, Linda drove south on I-35. She exited west on Highway Two. Frowning into the afternoon sun, she pulled her sun visor down and drove ten miles over the speed limit. As she passed a highway sign that said CLARINDA — 2 MILES, she bumped the brake to release the cruise control. Maybe she should turn around and go back home.

Maybe she was wrong to doubt Esther's culpability. Everyone else seemed satisfied.

Still, Austin Benn had listened to the tapes that morning and called to say, "There's something about the way the caller talks that reminds me of Nina Sorba, a regional kind of nasal sound. But I really can't say it's her."

Linda tightened her grip on the steering wheel and sped up again.

Frank had told her to take Business Route Two past the Page County Courthouse on the Clarinda town square and then turn north. After three or four tree-lined, residential blocks, the road meandered by a cemetery on the left, a horse pasture on the right. Beyond golf courses on either side, there it was, in the wide valley up ahead: a sprawling complex of institutional-looking structures and concrete parking lots. Linda spotted a clock tower at the center of a long, brick building.

Box hedges lined both sides of the walk leading to the main entrance of the Mental Health Hospital. The date carved in stone above the double doors was 1895. To both right and left of the landmark tower, the wings of the building spread for two hundred feet, a stately facade broken by recessed window bays. Inside the aristocratic front entrance, walls were paneled to the ceiling with golden-brown oak. Ornately carved doors rose ten feet tall. The mosaic tile floor lay patterned like a Persian carpet, tiny hexagons of terra cotta, crimson, green, and gold.

But twenty feet ahead there was a line to cross, beyond which dun-colored linoleum gleamed unadorned and the walls were white. Handrails ran along both sides of the corridor. The place smelled of talcum powder and incontinence. VISITORS CHECK IN AT THE NURSES' STATION demanded the sign.

She did and was told to wait.

In five minutes, a nurse wearing pale blue slacks and a white blouse came into sight, shoes squeaking on the shiny floor. "I'm sorry. She isn't up to having a visitor."

"But I called ahead," said Linda.

"I'm Nadine Hale, the one you talked to." She reached to shake Linda's hand. "We did talk about how questionable a visit might be for her just now."

"I know we did, but it's a long drive."

"It upset her, hearing your name just now," said Nurse Hale.

"Why? What did she say?"

"She's very tired. She's been agitated today, pacing. She wears herself out when she gets going."

"We're friends," said Linda. "She'll warm to me if I can just see her. It's happened before."

"Let's give her a few minutes. Try not to get your hopes up. I'll get you a magazine."

Linda took the September *National Geographic* to the front of the building, to a parlor with floor-to-ceiling windows, an ornate stone mantle, and heavy Victorian furniture. There was a picture of a Meer cat on the yellow-framed magazine cover. Reading was out of the question.

She couldn't concentrate. The oak rocker she sat in was big enough to fit her long legs and the curve of her back. *She'll see me,* she hoped. *I'll test her confession of taking Grace. I'll ask her about Nina Sorba, somehow. But no leading questions,* Linda reminded herself. *No leading questions.*

Before leaving that morning, Linda had sent an e-mail to a Professor Leticia Munizaga, Department of Anthropology, University of Iowa:

```
I noticed on Nina Sorba's vita that you co-au-
thored some of her early papers. I found your
address on the U of I web site. Could you call
me, please, at the number below? I've left
messages on her cell phone, but she hasn't
returned my calls. Her employer here in Lin-
den Grove has had the same experience. He's
worried she might be ill. She moved out of
the rented house she's been living in north
of Linden Grove two weeks ago. I'm hoping you
might know how I could get in touch with her.
It's terribly important that I find out what
she knows about last Friday's kidnapping of
a baby in our town. My number is—
```

Rocking absentmindedly in the once grand front-parlor-to-a-madhouse, Linda's mind returned for the dozenth time that afternoon to a detail in John's article from Wednesday's *Times*: "Under questioning, Esther admitted to the police that she had taken Gracie from her crib."

*Admitted,* Linda repeated to herself. *Under questioning.* She wondered what sort of question had finally loosened Esther's tongue. *Do you recall taking your granddaughter from her crib?*

Linda imagined a silent nod of the head.

"Okay." The nurse was back. "I reminded her of what you said, that you are a good friend. She's even combing her hair."

Nadine Hale led Linda up a flight of narrow stairs. A tall window brightened the landing. "Wait," said Linda, staring at the heavy, locked door. "I'm not sure I should have pushed for this."

The nurse paused, keys in her hand.

"Does she understand why she's here?" Linda asked her.

"Esther was admitted voluntarily," said the nurse. "She's been here on that basis before. She has an unusual amount of insight into her illness. Degree of insight is a quality that varies widely with schizophrenia. We've been instructed we can ask her about her voices — if they're louder, if they're bothering her, that sort of thing. She hasn't been willing to tell us much. We're not seeing the full effects of her new drug just yet."

"Has she mentioned the baby? Grace?"

"The granddaughter, no. Perhaps to her doctor. She's not much more connected to her surroundings than when she arrived. We can tell that from her eyes, that schizophrenic stare. Getting the dosage on the new meds may take some time. If she does actually talk to you, don't let it throw you if she starts a thought in the middle, or ends it before it's clear. You might say her brain has its own narrative that overrides what's going on in the room. How long has it been since you've spoken with her?"

"Six days."

"Then you know what I mean."

"I got cold feet there for a moment," Linda said.

"It happens." The nurse unlocked the heavy door.

It was warmer inside. "There's lots of light," said Linda, hopefully.

"We're always thankful for sunny days."

They were in an extra-wide hall that intersected with a common area — a huge, rectangular space with a television and a lot of chairs to the right, a table and the nurses' station to the left. "I don't know if you noticed the architecture of the building when you drove up, the way the facade steps in and out. The 19th-century architect planned for every unit to have windows facing in all directions, to catch the greatest amount of sunlight possible. Of course, back then they didn't have the drugs we have today. Sometimes I think sunlight is still the best mood-lifting remedy of all."

The nurse was walking slowly, talking low. She stood still to explain that a hundred years earlier the building had housed over two thousand mentally ill patients. Now they were down to three units of twenty beds each. The other two units were geriatric, people who would finish out their lives there. "Most of the folks on this ward, though, are transient," she said, "with us until they're stabilized. Now-a-days most people who once would have been institutionalized are drug-managed well enough to live useful lives, or they're in group homes, or on the streets of cities."

"Or in prison."

"Sadly, yes. Now much of the building is leased to a private academy, a high school for adjudicated teens."

A man with a burgundy shirt stretched tight over his stomach spoke as they approached. Linda returned his, "Hello," but her greeting didn't register on his face. In the TV area patients slouched in oversized, oak rocking chairs like the one she had sat in downstairs. Her eyes passed over every face in the group — quickly, as though they might catch her looking. Nadine led her past a bed where a man lay with his face to the wall — so staff could keep him in sight, the nurse explained, her voice a careful murmur. Now they were in the hallway beyond the day area.

Nadine raised her voice to a normal volume again: "And then of course we've got the prison on the grounds," she said, "to share our kitchen and maintenance staff." They arrived at a door with a foot-square window. "This is one of our visiting rooms. You can wait in here. I'll get her for you."

The room was small. Linda couldn't hear the TV from in there, but she could still smell the feeble, sweetish odor of the place. An ancient, boxy, black and chrome pay phone hung on the wall. Scrub marks lay in chalky arcs on the white surface of a table surrounded by four black plastic chairs, the molded kind that could be stacked. A sash window — three feet across, and almost to the ceiling — filled the room with light. Linda rested her fingers on the windowsill and waited, eyes fixed on the prison buildings in the distance — until the door opened, and Esther was standing there. "I'm glad you're willing to see me," Linda said to her.

The pink smock Esther wore over gray slacks had a zipper up the front. She pulled out a chair that faced the door and sat. She adjusted the fabric of her loose slacks around her knees. The green walls cast a pallor onto her clean-scrubbed face. "Annie would never visit me in a room this little," she said. "I'm surprised you came."

"Annie's doing fine," said Linda, "now that Gracie is back."

Esther didn't react to her words, so Linda made herself keep talking: "One of Annie's girlfriends cut her hair. Will's pretty much over his flu, but he still has a cough. He's taken the rest of the week off. John and I are meeting at their house for supper tonight. Annie wants to start entertaining more. That's a good sign, don't you think? I baked a couple of pies to take, with apples from our orchard. I talked to Frank this morning and he wanted me to tell you he'll be here tomorrow afternoon. He has a question."

Esther's lips parted as though she might be about to speak, but she didn't.

"He'll bring the book you asked for," said Linda quietly, "but he needs to be reminded which one that was."

"I'll tell you a story from that book," said Esther. Her gaze settled on Linda's face and lengthened, as if she could see right through her. "Ishmael—" she began. "No, that's not right," she muttered under her breath, "Ishmael was the archer. Mic-*hael*-ovich," she said, "was the insomniac."

Baffled, Linda let long seconds pass, waiting for Esther to speak again. *Don't ask direct questions,* she reminded herself. *Just make simple statements. Get her back on track.* "A policeman came to see you here in the county hospital on Sunday," she said finally.

Esther bent forward in her chair, reaching to press her right hand palm-down on the tabletop. She stared at the back of that hand as if it meant something, then released her posture quickly, like a spring. "Wrapping a baby in her mother's garment protects her from harm. I told him that."

*Mary Howard*

Linda's heart quickened. "Detective Hansen might have told you what the baby was wrapped in when we found her."

Esther lifted the splayed-out fingers of both hands this time and pressed her palms to the tabletop. "They took my rings. I'm not allowed clothes with buttons." She turned her hands over. Her fingers curled up. Her voice was flat: "Misha Michaelovich was the insomniac. That's my story. It's in the book I want. I need to practice it for the radio."

With a softening of her features, Esther began speaking from the chest, with a heavy Slavic accent. "Misha Michaelovich paced up and down the streets all night. The wind was harsh as blades. It lashed out with the kind of arctic cold that makes it hard to breathe. Misha pulled his collar over his chin. He knew that well before dawn he would smell the baker's loaves. Sun would begin to warm the cobblestones. The barber's window would put out a golden light."

Esther turned to face Linda again. "That growl in the back of my throat for Misha's voice sets my teeth on edge," she said. "This is a story about ways of being cold. 'I've lost my boy in the war,' says he. He can't shed his tears, can't stop grieving: 'my boy, my boy.' At last a lamp flares in a window. The barber opens his door to give his striped, wooden pole a spin. It's warm inside, warm as the nave of an Eastern church. Ishmael sits in the barber chair."

"Misha, you mean," said Linda softly.

"Misha, yes. Michaelovich." Esther placed her hands on her forehead. "I can't remember how it ends. It's the ending that matters. It's an old, old story. If I knew the end of the story, I could feel my grief, like Ophelia."

No feeling registered on Esther's untroubled features now, but Linda was moved to touch the woman's hand, and Esther allowed it. "Yes," she said. "Tell Frank it's on the kitchen table, under the microphone. He'll bring it. Tell him it's green, a green book. Green." She grasped Linda's hand. "He always talks about Grace. I knew you wouldn't abandon me."

"I never will," said Linda. "Gracie's been found, Esther. I found her. Elsa and I. She's safe at home."

"Oh, no," said Esther loudly.

Shocked by the long silence that followed that *no,* Linda waited. Finally, she rose from her chair and looked out the window at the penitentiary in the distance. She watched the second hand on her watch for one full minute, two, three, until she couldn't stand the quiet any more. "It's your illness the police are blaming for Gracie's abduction, Esther," she said, "not your true character. I'm on your side, believe me, but I need to ask. I need to know if you're the one who left Grace out by a country road like that. Try to remember last Friday afternoon, the day you went to the hospital with a stomach pain. Esther?"

"I'm not going to eat buttons, for God's sake. I may be mental, but I'm not an idiot. That emerald nearly killed me. He won't persuade me to do that again." Esther looked down at her hands, inhaling audibly. "I do remember a black boy."

"Burt Mack, yes."

"He smelled like Vicks."

"You used their bathroom," said Linda.

"There were television people in the street."

"That's right," said Linda. "Channel 8 was there to cover Grace's abduction. When Detective Hansen came to see you Sunday, he asked you if you remembered taking Grace from her crib, and you said yes."

Esther placed her fingers over her mouth. Her fingernail polish was worn off in red, striated lines. "Will wasn't fair."

"He wasn't there."

Esther covered her ears. "He came downstairs. He's had his way. He wanted me locked up, and now you see? I am."

"That was at my house, when Will came down."

"Yes," said Esther.

"But I'm talking about another day," said Linda. "Last Friday."

"We have to consume the things that consume us," said Esther. "He was very upset it was taking so long. He's still upset. He followed me here, and he talks all night. He says someone will steal my rings if I don't wear them. Someone is stealing me blind."

Linda had lost track of whom Esther was talking about, but didn't ask. A voice, she supposed. One of Esther's voices. "You told

Detective Hansen about swallowing the ring. And you told him about the baby monitor. You told him you took Grace out of her bed. You told him she didn't make a sound."

"The one that Annie gave you," Esther said. "Little blue antenna and a tiny red light."

Linda could *see* it, in her mind's eye, on her basement floor. "You took the receiver downstairs and plugged it in for me."

"You drew me on your wall."

"That was three weeks ago. Do you realize that?" Linda took a breath and held it for a count of two before she tried again: "*One week ago someone stole Grace from her own crib, in her own house, drove her into the country five miles from town, and left her there. When Frank took you to the county hospital, when you had that stomach pain, you weren't wearing anything with pockets. So I wonder how you could have had Annie's car key with you. I would have seen it if you'd had it in your hand."*

Esther turned her hands over on the table, palms up. "Ishmael was the one who became an archer."

"Archer? As in bows and arrows, you mean?"

"This was in ancient times," Esther said. "Abraham banished Hagar and Ishmael to the desert. She hid the boy under a shady bush and walked away so she wouldn't have to see him die of thirst. She lifted up her voice and wept. 'Let me not see the death of my child.'" Esther had gotten very loud. "An angel told her the way to a spring of water," she cried, "and so Ishmael was saved. He dwelt his whole life in the wilderness."

*Dwelt?* thought Linda. *An angel told her?*

"He grew up to be an archer. He founded a nation."

Nurse Nadine Hale's face appeared in the window in the door.

"Everyone knows that story," said Esther, in a quiet voice.

"It's new to me," said Linda.

"I'm not surprised."

Nurse Nadine rapped on the door three times and opened it. "It's time for you to see the doctor, Esther. A couple more minutes," she said to Linda.

"Look at me," Linda whispered a little desperately, but Esther refused. "We're almost out of time. The police believe you drove Annie's car. That you drove Grace into the country. That you brought the car back to Annie's driveway and then walked three blocks home. They think you hid the car key in your mouth and kept it there all the way to the county hospital. I'm wondering if all that can be true."

Esther pulled at the finger where her wedding ring used to be.

"Okay." Linda inhaled deeply. "Tell me if this name means anything to you: Nina Sorba."

Throwing up her hands, Esther reared her head back and then stood up, fists at the ready. "She's a goddamn spy," she roared. "She's a so-called fan of my show." Esther strode to the window and looked out, scanning the landscape, left to right. "She snoops around my house," said Esther, still loud, turning back to Linda. "One good thing about the radio is — I can't see the audience. They can't see me. I like it that way. They're up for a good story, and that's enough. The paintings in the living room have been growing bigger. The colors change, the reds and greens. They shrink inside their frames. That's how I know she's been inside the house again, robbing me blind. The new medicine, olanzapine will change all that. Just give it time. That's their lie. He's still here, my gravely god. He sounds like Henry Kissinger, and he's back in charge. Doctor says to ignore him if I can. Don't listen to him, doctor says. Listen to someone else. What do you say? Should I listen to you?"

"I don't believe you would leave Gracie in a ditch."

"Of course I wouldn't," Esther said quietly. "I didn't have any car key in my mouth. I'm not that crazy, but I do miss the happiness I used to feel. I used to be full of every emotion there is." Esther checked the pay phone for forgotten change and left the room.

*Mary Howard*

# Chapter 18

Linda didn't get home from Clarinda until six forty-five. Running late, she hurried to put the two pies she'd baked the night before into a long basket on the dining table. She greeted John in the bedroom with an abbreviated kiss. He was sitting on the edge of the bed in his boxer shorts, pulling on his socks. His long, damp hair was loose from its ponytail. Entering the bathroom, she raised her voice. "I was right," she said over her shoulder. "If Detective Hansen had been with me today, he'd be convinced Esther hasn't confessed to any crime. He didn't have all the background facts when he questioned her. When she told him she took Gracie out of the crib, she meant at *our* house, not at Annie's. She conflated the two events."

John's silence probably meant he was realizing how such a misunderstanding could happen. The bathroom, humid from his shower, smelled sexy from his after-shave. "She skips around from thought to thought," said Linda, "and her memory is out of whack." Linda leaned so she could see John. He was tying a shoe. "You listening?"

"I get it. She's out of whack." He pointed to the watch on his left wrist. They were late for supper at the Cantonwines'.

"I know. I'll hurry." Linda ran a comb through her long hair. Making her voice loud enough for John to hear in the next room, she said, "Esther thinks Nina Sorba is stalking her. The moment I spoke Nina's name, Esther got loud and agitated, like she did in church."

"You can tell me all about it in the car."

When she and John faced each other at last — Linda in the bathroom doorway, still elated from her day, their eye contact didn't last. He was still sitting on the edge of the unmade bed. She saw at once that his mind was not on what she had just told him. She watched him put his head back and shake it side-to-side to make his long hair fall behind his shoulders, where he gathered it in his long-fingered hands — a series of smooth, almost womanly gestures that never failed to move her. For a manly guy, he had a certain gentleness. He pulled his wet hair extra-tight to his head, which gave him a stern look around the eyes. "The pies are on the table, ready to go," she said to his back as he left the room, still securing his ponytail with a rubber band. "The cupboards, by the way," she shouted after him, "look great." He didn't respond.

He must have come home from his office early to install the kitchen cabinet doors. Now she could hear him slamming the deck door shut in the living room, locking up the house a little too enthusiastically. "You mad at me?" she shouted.

"We should have been at Anne and Will's a half-hour ago," he yelled at her from the front room. He *was* angry. He definitely was.

She followed him out to the old machine shed they used for a garage. As soon as he started to back the car into the gravel drive, she told him she had forgotten to check her e-mail. "It could be important."

"Go on, then. I'm sure it can't wait."

"I won't be a minute," said Linda, ignoring his sarcasm.

While John pulled out his cell phone to let Will know they were getting close to being on their way, Linda ran for the house. And, sure enough— Two clicks of the mouse, and there it was. The answer from Professor Leticia Munizaga was *yes*.

```
You are correct. I was Nina's major professor
for her doctorate. I will be in my office in
306 MacBride Hall on Tuesday afternoon from
two to four. It would be best if we could meet
```

*Mary Howard*

```
here face-to-face. Perhaps I can help you get
in touch with her. But I must tell you I have
not had any better luck reaching her than you
have in the past couple of weeks. I'm most
worried, too, by the way she's chosen to make
herself out of touch, but she's not capable
of kidnapping an infant. Surely you don't
mean to suggest that, but that's how you make
it sound. I read all about the abduction in
the Des Moines Sunday Register. That case is
settled, isn't it?
```

Linda typed a quick reply:

```
I'll be there Tuesday at three. I'm two and
a half hours away, in Linden Grove. If I run
late, I'll call you.
```

*Face-to-face. That's what I want too,* thought Linda, running back to the car. *So I can see the woman's expression at all times, in case she lies to protect her protégé.*

Linda told John about the message from Professor Muniza-ga while he drove the quarter mile from their house to Limestone Lane. Turning left toward town, he cleared his throat. "Sorry I was late getting home," she said. "Is that what you're bent out of shape about?"

"I'm not bent out of shape."

"I've never known you to hold back when you're upset," she said to him. "What's different this time?"

"Frank called this afternoon," he said. "We talked things over."

"And?"

"Do something for me?"

"That depends," she said, smiling. He didn't smile back. He kept his eyes to himself. "*What,* John?"

He drove another mile in silence before he said, "This morning Will heard back from Barb and Jon Gustavson that they can join us for supper. They'll bring the twins. And Annie invited Elsa Silk. Annie's terribly grateful to you and Elsa for being in the right place at the right time to find Grace."

"Annie knows I suspected *her*, at first. I doubt she's forgotten it."

"I think she's gotten past that," he said. "I think tonight might be a good opportunity for you to get some feedback about this woman you're hoping to find in Iowa City. Everyone who'll be there was at the christening. Ask them what they remember about the woman with Pegasus on her t-shirt. See if any of them has seen her since. I think you should do that before you run off to Iowa City to question the professor."

"Sounds like a plan," said Linda. "Sounds like a set-up."

"When you get an idea in your mind," he said, "you bear down on it and won't let go. I admire you for it sometimes, Linda, but right now I worry you're putting everything else aside but this obsession. You need to take a breath and think it through before—"

His sentences unwound — *"a habit of suspicion..... blind intuition.... talent for denial..."* Angry, Linda had stopped listening. Instead, she pictured faces as she went around Annie's dining table, starting with Elsa Silk's ivory complexion and golden hair, ending with the minister's golf tan and close-trimmed beard. "I had no idea there would be ten of us," said Linda. "It's lucky I decided to bake a second pie."

They didn't speak again until John parked the car on Isabella Circle and said, "Smells like the steaks are already on the grill."

It was time for them to regain their cheerfulness, or fake it. "Okay," said Linda flatly. "Let's celebrate."

There was a lot of laughter coming from the patio behind the house. Will was turning meat with a long-handled fork. He wore a red apron that said KISS THE COOK, a late-birthday gag-gift, he told Linda, from the Gustavson girls. Ruthie, the pretty twin with the soft blond curls, was tying it behind his back while Becka, the one with the dust-colored dreads, clipped a yellow ribbon to Gracie's crest of hair. Will added two more steaks to the grill and then beckoned to Linda with a forefinger. "I'm well enough," he said, "for you to obey my apron without fear of contamination."

Linda kissed him lightly on the mouth. He reared his head back in mock-ecstasy, and she laughed with the rest of them. Gracie looked around wide-eyed, as if the big folks were amazing for making such raucous sounds. Then she chortled, which made everybody laugh again. It was Linda's turn to hold her.

In Linda's arms, Gracie hunched her little body into a ball before she stretched and settled, eased her knees, and nestled. The steaks sizzled and the party stayed loud. Linda carried the baby into the living room.

There, where it was quiet, the baby breathed a slower, perfect rhythm. Soon she drowsed, her eyelids a pearly-pale, veined peachy-blue. Linda smelled her hair and stroked her cheek. She wished she could forget that someone had stolen this precious child and left her out in the open where it would take something like a miracle to save her life. Just remembering brought tears to Linda's eyes. Obsession or not, she was going to do all she could to find out who that person really was, knowing it might be Esther after all.

The patio door slid open and everyone filed in — Reverend Gustavson; his red-haired, freckled wife Barbara and their daughter Becka; Frank and Annie and John and Elsa Silk. Will, still in his red apron, brought the platter of steaks. They all took their places at the dining room table. By their easy banter, it seemed to Linda they had entirely dismissed the possibility that the person who had come so close to taking Gracie away from them forever might be free to attempt it again. "Where's Ruthie?" Linda asked, missing the twin with blue eyes and curls.

"She had to leave," her sister answered rolling her eyes. "She had a date with Mr. Not-So-Wonderful."

Linda decided not to ask.

Not until it was time to serve dessert, when there was a lull in the conversation, did Linda remember to share the good news about selling her building. She told the happy group what Ruby Best had said about the buyer, that he made the act of restoring worn-out books sound like writing symphonies.

Will's eyebrows rose above his rimless glasses.

Linda placed a piece of apple pie onto a plate. "I understand he sells rare books over the Internet." She licked some sticky sweetness from her thumb and went to get the business card out of her purse. "He's from over in Johnson County," she said, returning. "I'm not sure how to pronounce his name."

"Let me see." Will took the card Linda handed across the dining table. While Reverend Gustavson's quiet wife Barbara cleared the plates away, her husband was visiting with Frank. John handed desert to each of them.

Will tilted the card toward Annie, sitting next to him. "It's pronounced Boo-so," he said.

Annie lifted Grace higher in the crook of her left arm and took the business card from her husband. With her new short haircut, Annie looked even younger than usual, despite the vee of worry lines that creased her forehead. Gus and Barb Gustavson and Frank Hebring and Elsa Silk all spoke at once, congratulating Linda for selling her building. Becka Gustavson called out to John, a few steps away in the kitchen, "No pie for me."

"The fruit's from our own trees," John said, returning to his place at the table. "There's a piece with your name on it, Beck, if you change your mind. Linda makes the best apple pie in the world."

His compliment echoed around the table as forks lowered to plates. Becka was shaking her head. "No, really. I'm on a diet." She looked like she weighed maybe ninety pounds. She pushed back her chair and asked Annie if she could be excused.

"I know this guy Boisseau," Will was saying to Linda. "He keeps an eye out for botany editions for me — eighteenth, nineteenth century. I've collected rare books since I was in college. I used to stop in to see him whenever I got to Iowa City, but it's been a while."

Annie put the business card by Linda's plate. "He sent me a book the other day," she said. "He'd repaired some water damage and some ripped pages. He kept it so long, I figured I'd never see it again. In fact, I'd forgotten all about it."

"What book is that?" asked Will.

"A present for Dad," Annie whispered to her husband.

"Umm?" Frank glanced her way. Annie said, "Nothing," and he went back to arguing with Elsa and the minister about improving the tax base vs. preserving the rural character of the county.

"Jack Boisseau is a perfectionist," Will said, "slow at finishing a project, like Annie said. I think he gets a lot of restoration work from libraries to keep him going. He's forever getting distracted by one of his inventions. Last year it was a polyester welder, for sealing documents between two sheets of Mylar." Will lifted his fork, contemplating apple flecked with cinnamon. "Could be Jack made some money with that one. Enough to get out of that rat hole he's been working in. He'll think he's in heaven in your building." Will turned to hear something Barb Gustavson was saying.

Annie got busy with her dessert.

As Becka lifted Gracie from Annie's arms, the baby seized a handful of wooly dreads, which made Becka laugh as she headed for the living room. "Jack's in cramped quarters," Will said to Linda. "Plus, he was living back in a corner, to all appearances, last time I was in his shop, way last winter. I'm headed that way sometime next week."

"If you go on Tuesday, maybe Linda could ride along with you," John said. "She has an appointment."

"That would work for me," said Will. "What have you got going on in Iowa City?" he asked Linda.

John moved his empty plate away from him with both thumbs. "Linda's convinced herself the cops took the easy way out and settled on Esther by mistake. The cops don't agree with her, of course." John's glance moved around the table. "So she's headed to Iowa City on Tuesday to look for a woman she suspects of taking Gracie, the only evidence being the design on a shirt she wore the day of the christening."

All eyes were on Linda.

It was Frank who asked, "What woman is that?"

Becka had just come back into the room, rocking the fussy baby in her arms. "Yeah, what woman?"

Linda let her gaze escape beyond the faces across from her, through the patio doors. A new fence of brazen-new copper-colored wood enclosed the back garden. Linda focused on Frank. "We all assumed," she said to him, "that when Esther made that scene in church, the person 'with wings' she shouted at was part of her psychosis. But the object of all Esther's anger that day is a real person. She had a Pegasus design on her shirt that day. You know—the winged horse?"

Linda explained that the woman Esther drove out of church had turned out to be a former employee of Austin Benn, that she had walked off the job and moved out of her rented house north of town right before Gracie's abduction. "Her name is Nina. When I asked Esther about her this afternoon, she panicked." Frank tried to interrupt, but Linda wouldn't let him. "She graduated from the University of Iowa last May. I've tracked down her major professor, and she's agreed to see me Tuesday afternoon. Nina's the woman Esther complains has been stalking her."

Did anyone else here see a woman run out of the church when Esther had her shouting fit?" asked John. "I didn't."

All heads moved side-to-side.

Linda looked at Reverend Gustavson, across the table from her, at his broad forehead and steel-gray beard. "You were praying in the aisle," she said to him, "facing the front, when Esther made that scene. Your eyes were probably closed. That's why you didn't see the woman leave. You had your back to most of the congregation."

"*I* didn't," said Becka. She lowered Gracie into Annie's arms, and watched Annie carry the baby out of the room. "Mom and I were on the platform with the choir, facing the back."

"So was I," said Elsa softly.

"All I remember," Becka said, "is Mrs. Hebring sweeping into the aisle like it was a stage. I couldn't take my eyes off her. If it hadn't been so scary, it would have been kind of magnificent. She was so, like, I don't know, in *charge*. Like she was protecting Gracie against all the bad stuff in the world. In a weird sort of way it was totally part of the baptism. 'In case the water's not enough,' is one thing she said. I don't remember anything about wings." Frank leaned forward in his chair. "I didn't see anyone leave," Becka said to him.

"Neither did I," said Elsa.

"No one did." Frank's eyes flashed with indignation as he turned to Linda. "'A baby's cries drive out the devil.' I remember that rubbish well enough. Esther's paranoia is a symptom of all that's wrong, not some sort of *clue*. When Esther was cursing the devil out of thin air and driving him into the street, there was clearly no devil there. If Esther said the devil had wings, and the girl you noticed had a winged horse on her shirt, that was a coincidence."

Linda took a deep breath. "I hope you're right," she said.

"You're welcome to ride with me on Tuesday," said Will. "Maybe the trip over there will settle the matter for you."

After dinner, Linda looked for Annie and found her in a room across from the nursery. She had settled into a rocking chair to nurse Grace. Annie pointed to a corner of the room. "Come look at some of my pictures. On the top is the one I got out to show you."

The room had a twin-sized bed piled with books and papers. A drafting table in the corner had its lamp turned on. A clutter of unframed, black and white photographs was tacked on the wall. "The one on the table," said Annie.

Linda looked down at a face, or part of one.

"It's Bobby Milhous," said Annie, "the boy John wrote that drug article about. Doesn't it look like a lithograph? I had it out to show Ruthie, too, before she left. He's her boyfriend."

"I didn't know that."

"I thought you did," said Annie.

"So he's the reason she left early tonight?"

"Right."

In the twelve by fourteen photograph, the boy looked upward and slightly to the side, his features foreshortened by the camera angle. A sky streaked with clouds covered the top two-thirds of the composition. He had his hands up level with his ears, as if under arrest. "I like the way you cropped this at the bottom, Annie." She had cut the picture off at the middle of the boy's chin and captured a look of surprise and apprehension in his half-open mouth. Perhaps Bobby had just looked away from the camera lens to escape into all that sky. The palm of his right hand bore the tiny word MILIEU, as if he'd just scratched it there with the ballpoint pen in his other hand.

"Ruthie loves it," said Annie. I took some regular senior pictures to make his parents happy. Then some spur-of-the-moment shots, like this. It's my favorite."

Linda took a long look at it. "This really is brilliant," she said finally, "the way you framed this, shooting up at the face, getting mostly sky. It shows the displacement this boy seems to feel. That's how I see it, anyway. Wonder, or loss, or maybe both. You've stumbled on the fact that it sometimes works to catch subjects in odd situations. Brings out the personality. The optical realism of the face played against unexpected details sets up a narrative, excites the viewer's curiosity. The writing on the hand is a nice touch."

"That was just luck," said Annie. "He'd had a vocabulary test that day. We were down by the railroad tracks, out in the open where the light was good, behind the building where you found Grace's cow. Bobby works for his dad after school, so we walked out back to take a few shots looking down the rails. I happened to look up at the second story window of that old bank. All but one was curtained, black. 'Hands up,' I said. 'Look up there.' He did, and got that mysterious look on his face."

"I've met his dad," said Linda. "He manages the grain co-op."

"That's right."

"When did you take this?"

"Late last spring," Annie said.

Linda stared at Bobby's upward glance, at his hand that spelled MILIEU. She noticed his eyes, more black than white, pupils crowding out the irises.

"I framed the shot that way," said Annie, "to cut his face off in the middle of the chin. I cropped the left-hand margin so the vertical mid-line of the composition would go through his left eye. The 'center line principle.'"

Linda smiled at Annie. "I'm impressed."

"Thanks. It gives the portrait a hidden symmetry." Annie colored slightly. "About the reason I went back to that location with Gracie the other day, you know? You asked me that. I was hoping to shoot from the second story of that abandoned bank. I'd noticed that the lock was busted and I could actually go inside. I was looking for a high angle camera shot to feature in our photo show *Old Town Develops New Life*. But when I started to go up the stairs, I got freaked by the gross smell and panicked. I couldn't wait to get Gracie out of there. That's when I dropped her cow. You want to put her in her bed?"

Linda lifted the baby into her arms — her supple warmth, her caramel smell — and carried her across the hall. When she laid Gracie on her back, her eyelids trembled. Her little temples showed her heartbeat. Linda arranged Gracie's black and white stuffed cow beside her and made sure the monitor was on. Turning to the door, she said, "Annie, why are you looking at me like that?"

"I just want to say," said Annie, "that if you try to make sense of all the things my mom does, you'll lose your emotional boundaries. You'll be taken in by her disease. I know how that can be. I think it's happening to you."

Linda took a couple steps down the hall toward the sound of laughter in the living room and the clatter of cleanup in the kitchen. An old, familiar outsider-feeling stopped her from going further. She allowed the sight of Annie's photograph of Bobby Milhous to draw her back into the small workroom for another look. After staring at Bobby's face for a full minute, a padded envelope lying next to it on the drafting table caught her eye because of the return address: J. Eliot Boisseau, Conservation of Rare Books and Paper Documents. It was addressed to Anne Hebring Cantonwine. There were no stamps on the envelope. There was no postmark.

The envelope had been torn open hastily, judging by its condition. Inside was a fifty-page, eight-by-ten, hardbound volume, *Jens Olsen's Clock.* The copyright was 1923, but it didn't smell old.

Linda had seen that envelope before. It had been on top of the other mail on Friday, a stack of letters and catalogs Linda had brought into the living room from the mailbox beside the front door. She saw in her mind's eye the way Annie had folded socks while Detective Hansen ran his department's investigation through a walkie-talkie. "Annie?" she called out now, stepping into the hallway.

Annie appeared instantly, fingers crossing her mouth with a, *"Shhh. You'll wake the baby."*

"This was with your mail on Friday afternoon," Linda whispered, "in your mailbox. But it didn't come through the mail. There are no stamps. Look."

Annie stared at the envelope.

"I brought it into the house for you, remember?" Linda asked. "It was on *top* of the delivered mail. The mailman usually comes — about what time?"

"On top?"

"What time, Annie?"

"Between two and three."

"Somebody brought this after that because the other mail was underneath it. It must have been your friend Jack."

Annie nodded. "Surely you don't think he abducted Gracie."

"No, but he might have seen whoever did."

# Chapter 19

Tuesday morning, on the way to Iowa City, Will made a phone call from his car. He wore headphones so he could keep both hands on the wheel. Linda figured he was calling his client until he said, "Hey, Jack, it's Will. Will Cantonwine," in a tone of voice more buddy than business. "No kidding," he said. "Yeah, I'll look at it sometime, but to tell the truth I've been concentrating on other things besides old books. I get your on-line newsletter. Sometimes I even read it."

He listened. He laughed. "Okay," he said. "I hear you're moving to Linden Grove. — Yeah, it is. Great little town." His tone evened out, all business now. "We're close enough to I-35 that people can commute to Des Moines, so our population is growing. The mall out on the interstate hurt us for a while, but now our business sector is humming again. The town attracts people like you and me, whose customers aren't local. I'll be glad to fill you in about the community if you like. I'm a little hurt you haven't asked. — Sure, I know the building. In fact, the woman you're buying it from is sitting right here in the car with me. — Garbo, right. — She's a good friend of Anne's and mine, and—"

He glanced at Linda. "—she's married to my buddy Bender. You've heard me talk about him — editor of *The Linden Times?* —

Oh, well, that was a good idea. — Yeah, it was Annie's mother. The baby's fine. — Thanks. This is my first day out on the road since it happened, and I miss my little girl. Anyway, we're about an hour from Iowa City, so I thought I'd give you a call. — No, I'm meeting a client at the med labs at twelve-fifteen, and I'll need the whole afternoon. I was wondering if you could join us at the Linn Street Diner at six-thirty. Give you a chance to meet—" Will broke the sentence off with the inflection high, as if the voice on the other end had interrupted him.

He adjusted his hands on the steering wheel. "Annie got the book you left," he said. She actually didn't see it for a few days, given that it landed in our mailbox the very afternoon all hell broke loose and it got buried. It appears to us you dropped it by in person instead of trusting US Mail. — Yeah, it was for her dad. He's the clock collector. Did you ring the doorbell when you brought it by? — Sure, okay, but I wish you had come forward, anyway. — Well—" Will was silent for long seconds before he said, "I didn't realize that. The cops don't tell us everything."

The line of Will's mouth grew thinner against his teeth as he checked the mirrors to change lanes. "All right," he said. The next pause to listen was even longer than the last. "Well, see if it works out. We'll be there anyway. If you find you can join us after all, dinner's on me."

He pulled the headphones over the back of his head so they hung around his collar.

"So," said Linda.

Will looked to the left at a passing car. When Linda could see his profile again, he was smiling to himself.

"What did Jack have to say about leaving *Jens Olsen's Clock?*"

She was about to repeat her question when Will said, "I ran into Annie on Jack's steps." Here it came, the how-we-met story she'd heard before. "She was wearing—"

"—one of those little tank tops—" said Linda.

"—that shows the belly button, right," said Will. "I was a goner."

"You asked him if he rang the doorbell when he delivered—" Linda began, to change the subject.

"The great way she smelled, slipping past me, in a hurry to get away, her eyes shiny with tears."

"She was crying? Why?"

"That was my first question when I got upstairs. The guy knew nothing about any tears. None of my business, apparently. And yes, he rang the bell."

"I didn't realize you were going to invite him to have supper with us."

"I thought you'd like to meet Jack."

"When did I say that?" asked Linda. "I just want to know if he left that book at your house in person. Apparently he did. And rang the doorbell."

"Yeah. That's right."

"I have no burning desire to share a meal with him, Will. A real estate deal doesn't require us to be friends. What else did he say? He rang the doorbell and—? What happened?"

"No one answered, of course," said Will. "He saw the mailman on Isabella Circle, but no one else. He followed the TV coverage. Also, he subscribed to *The Linden Times* a few months ago to familiarize himself with the town while he considered moving there, so he read John's story about how the kidnapping got resolved."

Will pulled the earphones off his neck and placed them onto the console with the same care and precision he used turning steaks over on a grill, or lifting Grace onto his shoulder. "As for your reluctance to meet Boisseau, I do get that." He gave Linda a sympathetic glance. "You fixed up that old building to suit yourself and made a damn good job of it. But someone else can make better use of it now. You don't need a place to go back to."

"No, I don't. You're right. I'm home for good." She paused to swallow hard. She and John had argued again at breakfast and left the house in angry silence, no good-byes. "John's feelings are pretty transparent," she said quietly. "Lately he stops talking when he can't change my mind. I'm not sure what's up with him." Will glanced her way, his eyebrows up. "Did you ever think both you and John would be starting families at forty?" she asked.

"No, said Will. "We always were competitive, though. Once he married you, I did feel like the odd man out. I didn't see him nearly as often after you and he hooked up."

"So you set out to find a wife of your own."

"Not exactly. Although, with hindsight I admit I envied the goofy way he acted around you, the way settling in with you filled him with energy. That gave me ideas, I suppose. I still think marrying Annie will turn out to be the best thing I ever did. Gustavson has referred us to someone over in Winterset, for counseling. We start tomorrow night. I didn't realize until recently how hard it's been for her to tolerate my absences without feeling abandoned. It hasn't helped that we both held back on affection, after the baby came. I was walking on eggs in that area. I see that now."

"Sex, you mean?"

"Yep, I mean sex." He grinned over at her. "I thought she was avoiding me, because of some sort of hormone thing. Turns out she thought I'd lost interest because she'd gained some weight. Actually, I like a little more padding on her bones. You know how something happens to love after a year of marriage, a sort of natural letdown? A time of normalizing, I suppose. I don't think she was prepared for that. It doesn't have to mean the dance is over. She lives a lot more inside herself than I do, I've discovered."

Linda chuckled. "Sometimes her stories don't make sense because of what she leaves out. Sometimes I have to say, 'Back up, Annie. You've lost me again.'"

"I know. That's why she can't tell jokes. She skips over half the plot to rush to the punch line."

They exited I-80 in silence. As they approached downtown Iowa City, where he was going to drop her off at the edge of campus, Linda tried to remember the turning point of the story Annie had told her about Jack Boisseau. Something about *Trivial Pursuit*. "Annie asked me a question recently—"

"Linda?" Will interrupted her: "I have to say something before I drop you off."

"Okay."

"I know you were upset Friday night. It was never my intention to try and talk you out of your suspicions. I know you better than that. So does John, but he has reason to feel extra-protective. He's worried you aren't eating or sleeping as much as you should." He pulled over to the curb in front of the College of Business building. "Whatever you find out today, you'll want to talk about it all the way home. Am I right? You'll be glad for my company, I hope."

"I haven't thought that far ahead." An impatient driver behind them honked his horn. Linda's hand was on the door handle.

Will was looking at the rear view mirror. "Annie asked you a question?"

"A question? Oh, yes. I keep forgetting to look it up. Who was Khrushchev's wife?'"

He laughed. "She asked me, too."

"And the answer is—?"

"Mrs. Khrushchev."

"*Will!*" The driver behind them honked again. "Come on, I've got to go."

"Nina," he said. "Her name was Nina. I'm not making this up. The same name as the woman you're so convinced is the enemy." His eyes were still on the rearview mirror. "Linn Street Diner. Six-thirty. I'll see you there."

"I'm not the one who turned her into the—" Linda slammed the car door on her last word, "enemy."


At a quarter to one, the sidewalk in front of the University of Iowa College of Business was crowded with students wearing baggy shorts, backpacks, flip-flops. Fallen leaves rattled in their wake. A sky blue city bus parked beyond a black pipe fence.

Across the street was the Pentacrest, four classical buildings at the corners of a square dominated by a fifth, the Old Capitol. This nineteenth century structure, the original seat of government for the state of Iowa, was undergoing renovations. Workers in hard hats were busy erecting scaffolding around the limestone facade. Inside its cage, the gilded dome was streaked but still glorious in the sunlight, impressive against an azure sky shot through with threads of pure white vapor.

Linda made straight for the Registrar's Office, in the basement of Pearson Hall. There, she spelled the name, Sorba, "S-as-in-Sam," for the pretty, gray-haired woman behind the counter. "First name Nina."

The woman's fingers clicked the computer keys. "Oh, yes." She lifted her chin to read: "Ph. D. in Cultural Anthropology. 5-4-2002."

"Can you give me a current address?"

"I can give you the address as of her last semester of enroll-ment. If she's moved since May, you'd have to go to the Alumni Of-fice for that. But there's more here on her degree." The woman kept her eyes on the screen, "Ph. D. rescinded 8-12-2002."

"Rescinded?"

"Did you know that already?" the woman asked.

"No. The University granted her a doctorate, then took it back?"

"Caused quite a stir."

"Can I see the transcript?"

"Not the entire thing, no. Not without her written release."

"She received a doctorate last May," said Linda, "and it was taken back in August?"

"That much is public record." The clerk swiveled the computer screen so Linda could read it. Above the words *Degree confirmed... Degree rescinded,* Nina Sorba's last semester appeared: six credits of ANTHRO 699, RESEARCH, and three credits of PORTUGUESE 690, INDEPENDENT STUDY. "Is she trying to get a job with you?"

"No, she's a friend of a friend," said Linda. "His employee, ac-tually. He's concerned about her. You promised me her last known address. That's public information, too. Is that right?"

"Yes, it is." The woman typed again, tilting her head back to read the screen through her bifocals. "Dodge Street, 317 1/2."

Linda wrote it down.

Linda left the Registrar's office for the short walk to Phillips Hall, east of the Iowa River on Clinton Street. With luck she'd find the professor who had taught Nina Sorba Portuguese last spring. Then she'd go find some lunch before her appointment with Dr. Munizaga at three.

As she walked along, she reviewed what little she knew for certain about Nina Sorba. *Fact one:* She walked off her job with Austin Benn on September twelfth, a week and a day before Grace was abducted. *Fact two:* She moved out of her rental house north of Linden Grove at about the same time, without giving the landlord notice. *Fact three:* She did something to cause her Ph.D. to be withdrawn in August. *Fact four—?*

There was no fact four, nothing to connect Nina with a terrible crime. There was only Esther Hebring shouting superstitious nonsense about someone with wings, giving the appearance of driving Nina from the church — though no one else around the dinner table the other night saw it that way. There was nothing surprising in that. All their eyes were on Esther's wild histrionics.

In front of Phillips Hall, black wire-cage benches encircled a huge tree that hadn't yet dropped its chartreuse, pointed leaves. Mounting the steps to the front entrance, she thought of Grace lying on her back, plump cheeks flushed with sleep, so easily lifted from her bed and carried away. Linda could almost feel the baby's lively weight against her arm and chest — and she entertained again, for the thousandth time, her darkest fear that the kidnapper had meant to kill or injure the baby, but had second thoughts, or lost her nerve. If that was right, the person was sadistic, of two minds and, even worse, someone who had committed an unfinished crime.

There was no evidence of any of that. Linda felt a wave of self-doubt, even as she opened the door to the main office for the Department of Spanish and Portuguese. The department secretary told her that the instructor of record for all graduate level students in the Portuguese language for the previous Spring Semester had been Victor Sanchez. He was currently on faculty leave to study in northern Chile. The secretary did not hesitate to give Linda his e-mail address. "I know he checks his messages frequently," she said. "I hear from him all the time."

"What is he working on down there?"

"Entomology of words, evolution of vocabulary." A sign at the front edge of the desk read SUSAN SHIELDS. Her phone rang, and Linda waited while she took the call. When Susan hung up, she smiled up at Linda. "Perhaps you'd like to talk with one of his grad students."

"What about Nina Sorba? Is she around?"

"I haven't seen her for a while. This isn't her major department."

"It's very important that I talk to her as soon as possible." When Susan was slow to react, Linda said, "I know about the problem with her degree."

"Yes, well, I'm not the person to ask about that," said Susan quickly. "Maybe you should talk to her major professor."

"Munizaga."

"Yes. I don't think it's right to steal people's ideas. I'm not defending that, but I can't believe Nina would do such a thing. She's absolutely brilliant. I smell a rat." Susan stopped herself and glanced around the office, empty but for the two of them.

"Her trouble with the Ph. D. isn't what I need to discuss with Nina, anyway," said Linda. "A baby was kidnapped south of Des Moines, in Linden Grove."

"Oh, my god." The muscles of Susan Shields face relaxed with surprise. "Yes," she said. "Yes. I saw it on the news. Kidnapped by the grandmother. Left out in the country. That's horrible."

"The grandmother's name is Esther Hebring," Linda said. "I'm hoping Nina can help shed light on why Esther would do such a thing, something she's too ill to do. She and Nina know each other."

"So you're a detective, huh?" asked Susan. "And Nina's a material witness?"

"Something like that."

"Wow."

"So, are you friends with Nina?" Linda asked.

"In a way," said Susan. "She and her boyfriend used to live upstairs from us."

"On Dodge Street?"

"Yeah, they were quite the pair. She was gorgeous, in that earthy way of hers. They had some really rockin' fights after their parties broke up. I can tell you that. He was one of those guys who graduates from university and keeps hanging around, without much ambition. She married him, though, and set him up in a printing business. She has money, that girl, some sort of inheritance. Jed and me hung out with them way back when. Now we have a kid. If I didn't work here I wouldn't have kept up with Nina at all."

Susan's smile softened. "Nina helped me get this job. Why she wanted a Ph.D. anyway is beyond me. She never was made for scratching around in the dirt. She likes the mystery of deciphering the past, but she likes her gratification *fast,* and you have to have tons of patience in anthropology. Rumor has it she's left Jack, no surprise, and moved back home for the summer. The place with the covered bridges?"

"Madison County," said Linda.

"That's it," said Susan. "She got some kind of part-time job."

"When did you see her last?"

Susan flipped pages on her desk calendar. "Middle of August. Here it is. The fourteenth. She's determined to get her good name back. She was trying to get the graduate college to let her resubmit her dissertation. She had a meeting with the dean and stopped in here first to say hello."

"Did she look okay?"

"She was really hot to go to bat for herself, and she looked wonderful. She had on a skinny dress with a matching jacket. I don't think I'd ever seen her legs before. She's always worn baggy pants. She's lost a ton of weight, and she was dressed to impress. That's the last time we saw her around here."

"I'm assuming Jack knows where she is." Linda opened her wallet and held Jack Boisseau's business card out to Susan Shields.

Susan turned the card around in her hand and studied it. "Book restoration," she read from the card. "Well, good for him."

Linda began to say her good-byes, but then she had a last-minute thought. "Back when you and your husband were partying with Nina and Jack, did you know a girl named Annie Hebring, from Linden Grove? Long dark hair. A dancer's body."

Susan's brain had to compute a moment behind her eyes before she said, "No, I don't remember anyone like that."

*Facts four, five, six--* Linda began ticking off her thoughts once she reached the street again. *Nina is married to Jack Boisseau, a business acquaintance of Will's and a college boyfriend of Annie's. Recently, Jack has been spending weekends in Linden Grove. He subscribed to* The Linden Times *to learn more about the town, and now he wants to buy my building. He was at Annie's front door right about the time Gracie was abducted.*

"Who *are* these people?" Linda said, right out aloud. A bearded man carrying a briefcase turned his head to stare at her as she passed him on the sidewalk.

*Nina,* she thought, picturing Grace, asleep in her bed. Linda imagined Nina as she had drawn her: that thin, bracketed mouth. Those deep-set, watchful eyes. *Where are you now?*

# Chapter 20

In office number three fourteen, on the third floor of MacBride Hall, a woman sat at her desk, her back to the door, gazing out the window. Linda cleared her throat. "Dr. Munizaga?" There was no response.

Linda stared at the back of the woman's gray head, then took in details of the book-lined room. The professor's desk was angled to face a corner where two windows met. Orange drapes breathed forward and back in a breeze through those open windows. Down to the right, an electric kettle sat on the floor. It was plugged into a power strip that was tethered to a computer table by a tangle of electrical cords. Linda spoke louder this time. "Professor Munizaga?"

At least a dozen framed photographs leaned in a row along the back edge of that well-worn desk. Perhaps the anthropologist was gazing at one of those, not out the window at all. A low whistle — breathy at first, then shrill — sounded in the room.

The electric kettle on the floor gave up a puff of steam.

The woman swiveled the desk chair to look down at the kettle. Seeing Linda standing there, she shot to her feet with a startled, "Oh good. You're here." The professor was sinewy-thin, her shoulders bowed. She hunkered down to unplug the kettle, then rose to extend a hand to Linda, all in one smooth move. "You look like you've been standing there a while."

They introduced themselves. Linda sat in the wooden chair that Leticia Munizaga dragged into the center of the room. The air smelled pleasantly of steam.

"I wasn't expecting such a beautiful smile." The professor pronounced it be-*yoo*-ti-ful, with a south-of-the-border accent Linda couldn't place. "Would you like some tea?"

Linda shook her head. "But you go ahead."

"I only put the kettle on to pass the time while I waited, in case you decided to come anyway. I should apologize if you didn't get my message and made this trip for nothing."

"I got the one e-mail from you. Was there another?"

"Yes, this morning." The woman nodded. "I thought you might have heard from Nina, too."

Linda shook her head.

"She's gone back to Linden Grove, and now you're here, two ships passing. I should have had my secretary call you. I'm too deaf for telephones." She made an upturned gesture with her hands. "I've been sitting here stewing about Nina. She hadn't responded to my messages for weeks, but this morning she did. All it took was the mention of your name, and your insinuation she has something to do with a crime against a baby. If you put that in to get my attention, it certainly did, so I used it on her, too. She thinks you suspect her of being a kidnapper."

"I didn't say that."

"You came close," the professor said. "I let her think you did. You'll hear from her as a result. I thought that's what you wanted."

"She'll avoid me for sure now."

"Oh, quite the opposite," the professor said. "If I know one thing about Nina, it's that being put on the defensive really sets her off. She said she learned something shocking about her own life from the kidnapping."

"What did she mean?"

"I don't know. She likes to bait me. It's part of her personality to draw people in that way, a passive-aggressive quality, I would say."

The professor paused to lick her lips, which were thin and dry. "You did that, too, in your message: '—the disappearance of Nina Sorba.' That bit amused her, apparently. She's been withdrawn, avoiding those of us who care for her, but missing? She just doesn't want us to know where she is."

"Why not?'"

"It must be what she needs right now." The professor's blue eyes were clear and bright, set into a maze of wrinkles. Her skin was brown as a nut, as if she spent a lot of time in the sun, her hair white and unruly as dandelion fuzz. "Your reason for being here isn't a police matter, I take it."

"That's right. Just my own curiosity."

The professor looked skeptical. "In the email you said her employer has been looking for Nina, too. Do I have that right?"

"That's true. He's an acquaintance of mine. Austin Benn. You know him?"

"No."

"I thought you might. He's a contract archaeologist back home." Linda raised a hand to her mouth and cleared her throat. "He thinks she may have walked off the job because of something he said to her."

"Because of what?"

"Something he said." Linda raised her voice. "He realized the job wasn't a good match for Nina. He asked about her research articles and her plans for a career in a museum or university. She took offense. I went to the Registrar's Office just now, hoping to find a current address. To my surprise, I discovered her degree has been rescinded, which would probably rule out the sort of career Benn was asking her about. Could that have been the nerve he struck? Could that be why she's hiding out? Because she feels ashamed?"

The change in the muscles around Professor Munizaga's eyes was subtle, but made her look sad. "After years of work," she said, "Nina has ruined her career. I don't understand what made her do such a thing, but it's quite a jump from academic dishonesty to stealing a baby. I really can't take that seriously, it's so far-fetched, from what I understand about the case. Does this Austin fellow harbor such suspicions, too?"

"No. He thought she might have overdone it, working the ground during an Indian Summer heat wave. He's afraid she might be ill. He hadn't provided her with benefits and wonders if she needs a doctor."

"Sounds like she showed good sense to leave that job behind. She doesn't need the money. Her folks left her well off. You work for a living, Linda?"

"I'm a graphic designer."

"So you took a whole day off work to come all the way over here?"

"Yes, I did," said Linda. "It's that important. I would have come to see you," she added, "even if I'd seen your second e-mail about Nina being back in Linden Grove."

"I doubt it. You'll probably find a message from her when you get home. She's in a panic to defend herself. When are you going back?"

"Tonight. After supper."

"She's a compulsive person. I have to warn you. When she wants something done, she wants it *now*. For a time she would turn up at my door in the middle of the night. No matter the lateness of the hour, even if my lights were all off, she'd pound on the door and shine a light in my bedroom window until my dog would wake me up. My hearing was fading even then. I'd put a pot of coffee on and listen to her enthusiasms. It seemed to calm her down. A mark of narcissism, that disregard for others. I didn't see where it would take her at the time. She's brilliant, or I wouldn't have put up with her."

Linda kept nodding. What luck that a litany of Nina's faults was spilling out without the need of a single prompt. Or was it something else, the professor's eagerness, this seeming lack of loyalty to her own student? "She was like a daughter to me in those days," the professor said. "I should have kept a professional distance. I see that now, in hindsight."

"You didn't have to let her in."

The professor cupped her right ear with crooked fingers. "What's that?"

"When she showed up in the middle of the night. You didn't have to let her in."

The professor seemed to realize something and looked abashed. "This employer, this Austin fellow, he has some grievance against her, too, besides his concern for her health?"

"No, nothing like that. He probably owes her some back pay. I'm here of my own accord. My husband says I'm afflicted with a 'cynical curiosity.'"

"You're a lot like Nina then," said the professor. "She'd push a hunch way over the line of reason."

"Could be the mark of a creative mind," said Linda softly.

The professor leaned forward in her swivel chair, which made a creaking sound. "Where Nina had trouble," she said, "was in finding concrete evidence to support her arguments. I wouldn't mind talking to her myself — not e-mail, mind you, but sitting face-to-face, like this. She owes me that. Last week she filed a grievance with my department, claiming the bad example of my own professional standards. She was my star student at one time. I was probably a little bit in love with her. Not that way—" The professor glanced at Linda sharply, tears welling in her eyes. "She was enchanting, full of energy. Bright of mind. She's not like that these days. I'd be careful, if I were you. She's undergone some sort of transformation." Some strong emotion made her eyebrows angle toward the center of her forehead.

Linda turned her head to scan titles on the closest shelf, though none of them registered. She wanted to give the professor time to compose herself. "It hurts you to be so angry with her, doesn't it?" she said.

The professor didn't seem to hear. "I can't trust myself," she said.

In the same moment, Linda spoke: "She admires Esther's work on the radio, but beyond that I think she has some sort of unhealthy interest in Esther's family and I—"

"Last winter," said Leticia Munizaga.

"—and I want to know why," said Linda.

"I developed a problem in my one good ear," the professor went on. "A benign tumor on a nerve. It got worse throughout the spring, and the operation to remove it stole all the hearing on that side. I can look out on a lecture hall of three hundred and see conversations everywhere, students leaning together, lips moving when they should be all ears."

The professor tipped her head back to lock Linda in a tight-eyed gaze. "This is my last semester. To tell the truth, I hardly care if they listen at this point. It's their choice. You, I see, are hanging on my every word." She stared at Linda's mouth. "Let's get specific about why you're here. You suspect her of committing a shocking offense. The *basis* of your suspicions is what?"

"I'm curious," replied Linda, "about Nina's connection to the Hebring family. Because of certain things Esther Hebring, the baby's grandmother, has said to me."

"Because of what?"

"Esther Hebring is something of a local celebrity, a radio personality. She told me Nina has harassed her by telephone, threatened her granddaughter, the one who was abducted. She thinks Nina is dangerous."

"This Esther has schizophrenia, from what I read in the *Register.*"

"That's true."

"I doubt she's reliable."

"Nevertheless, I have a hunch that it was Nina's interest in Esther that inspired her move to Linden Grove, not a job. Austin Benn hadn't yet relocated his business to town when he hired her back in June. Professor, are you sure she never mentioned Esther Hebring, or *Willing Suspensions,* her radio show?"

The professor removed her glasses. Without them, her eyes seemed watery and small. She rose to her feet. "I need to excuse myself for a minute. I have something to show you. Please don't leave."

*No chance of that,* thought Linda. "Professor Munizaga?"

*Mary Howard*

"Call me Leticia."

"All right," said Linda. "Leticia. I want to know why Nina lost her Ph.D."

"Yes," said the professor, a light of eagerness in her eyes. "That's what I want you to see. I'll be right back."

When Leticia returned a few minutes later, she brought a softbound manuscript. It was heavily fringed with yellow Post-It notes. She sat. "Let me show you what all the trouble was about." She opened to a full-page, color illustration of a primitive, puppet-like object with perfectly round eyes and a miniature-donut mouth, like a Cheerio. Below the chin was a handle-like torso with two straight-out arms.

The flat, ugly little face stamped itself on Linda's brain with a vengeance: this rustic object was part of Nina Sorba's passion, apparently. Linda's stomach contracted with a repulsion she didn't care to show.

"You see the convex shape of the face?" The professor spoke enthusiastically. "The way the mouth is built forward? The remnants of deep red color? The circles scribed around the dots of the eyes are very significant. This is a rare fetal mummy—"

*Fetal?* Linda looked away from the page.

"—painted with manganese first, then ocher paint. I found it myself, back in the sixties, long before you were born."

The thing gave Linda the creeps. She pressed the palm of her hand to her belly.

"It's called a statuette mummy. It contains a fetal skeleton, built out with bird or animal bones."

"Fetal," Linda repeated. "You mean unborn?"

"Or born before it was ready."

"A miscarriage, you mean."

"A modern word, Linda, but yes." Leticia's voice had a touch of scorn. "Nina had it X-rayed. It's painstakingly made, stitched together with human hair — an example of something whose purpose went beyond the funereal. It was meant to be admired." Leticia stopped to watch Linda raise her hand to her mouth. "I'm sorry," she said. "You want some water?"

"No thanks." Linda folded her arms over her stomach.

Leticia leaned back and closed the manuscript, but kept a thumb in it. "I forget, sometimes," she said. "In our culture people fear these sorts of graphic reminders of the dead. That's why movies about ghosts and vampires are so popular."

"I find stories like that childish."

"Well, they're not. They manifest a fear that if a departed spirit is not completely untethered from its body, it poses a danger to the living." Leticia seemed to be lecturing now. "It's fear of what happens to us after we die, an apprehension every person on the planet shares, regardless of belief. Religions have controlled people — or offered comfort — with answers to that question. I suspect the people who treasured this—" She tapped the picture of the ancient mummy-face. "—were afraid of hunger, weather, injury, but over death they must have felt they could achieve a modicum of control. They felt they could keep this lost child with them by means of careful preservation and embellishment. Keep in mind this was an *ancient* people, Linda. They didn't even have ceramics to decorate, or cave walls, but they decorated this. We can't know if they had a word for love, but they kept their dead in the family circle, preserved as objects like this one, marked with color and design. There's speculation that this is religious Art, the very earliest in human history. Nina is convinced of that. It's been her thesis." Leticia's eyebrows went up as she made eye contact.

"It's okay," said Linda. "I'm all right." *Just a little queasy,* was the truth of it.

This time when the professor opened the manuscript, she covered the small red face with her fingers, to Linda's relief. "These people lived eight thousand years ago — eight *thousand,* Linda. Think of it. Six thousand years B.C. They were hunters and gatherers who moved along the dry Pacific coast of Chile, hunting alpaca and llama and eating wild plants. They left no record of language or symbology, but they mummified their dead long before the Egyptians did. This is Nina's dissertation." She folded it shut into Linda's hands: *THE ICON MUMMIES OF CHINCHORRO: THE AMERICAS' FIRST RELIGIOUS ART.*

Linda wanted to change the subject, but the professor's enthusiasm was far from spent. "The faces of most of these tiny, so-called 'red' mummies," she said, "are actually painted black. This one is atypical, colored with the red ocher of Arica. I let Nina photograph it. She refused to give it back. That's where the trouble started."

"Just tell me this," said Linda, her impatience growing. "Do you think Nina is capable of stealing a baby and leaving it out in the elements?"

"I wouldn't think anyone would be capable of that," the professor said.

Linda refused to take that as a *no*. She paused before she said, "This subject isn't easy for me to think about." She pushed the manuscript back into the professor's hands. "Can we get to the reason Nina lost her degree?"

"This is it. Right here." Leticia ruffled the yellow papers fringing the edge of the manuscript. "Every one of these notes marks a place where Nina lifted entire paragraphs from my own articles, without any attribution whatsoever. It took a colleague from another university to report the plagiarism to the head of our department."

"But you were her major professor. Didn't you recognize your own words?"

"I would have, if I'd bothered to read this. I can't deny I was negligent. At the end of a career like mine, such a lapse is embarrassing. I trusted the quality of Nina's work, which has always been excellent. She didn't *need* to steal from me. Either I never knew her as well as I thought I did, or something happened to her to change her very character. I'm at a loss. Even more so with you here, making me doubt her even more."

The way Leticia Munizaga bowed her head to study the manuscript right then made her look especially heavyhearted. "I let her borrow this rare artifact to support her thesis. She could have *cited* my work, and that would have been fine. I can't imagine what came over her. Must be some sort of psychological collapse. But a kidnapping? An infant? Maybe."

The hesitation hung in the air: *maybe.*

"Some people believe," said Linda, "that an unimaginable darkness resides in some people. Latent, until something triggers it. Sometimes the devastating charm we love in a person is their way of holding back a capacity for doing harm."

"That describes Nina all right." The professor turned toward her desk and seized on one of the gold frames lined up at the back of it. "Here she is, the good Nina, when she was plump and happy." She offered the photograph to Linda. "Now she's like some half-starved, frightened rhinoceros."

Linda laughed. "Rhinoceros?" *Good Lord, now what?*

"The rhinoceros runs straight toward the object of its fear," the professor said, with dead seriousness. "It doesn't freeze, or run away, like you or I would do. Nina has that headlong brashness. That's what I mean. She is like a gun ready to go off."

Linda studied the three people standing close together in the color snapshot. They wore loose, sand-colored clothing and held brimmed hats in their hands — removed from their heads, no doubt, at the request of the photographer. A dark-haired Leticia Munizaga was in the middle, looking ten years younger. On her right was a tall, blonde man with a sunburned nose. To her left stood a woman with strands of near-white curly hair floating around her lovely freckled face. Her body rounded out the denim shirt she wore, unbuttoned at the throat. She had a tilt to her head and the start of a smile, as if caught in the act of flirting with the photographer. Linda pointed, to be sure. "This is Nina?"

"I know. She's changed. It's been a while since I saw her smile like that."

"I've been as close to her as I am to you right now," said Linda. "This person doesn't look familiar, except for the hair. I don't remember her being high-strung, though she did turn on her heels and leave — practically at a run —because of something I said." She stared at the face more closely. Maybe the eyes were the same.

"Like I say," said the professor, "she's like a gun—"

"Who's the guy?"

"Mitchell Compton. Mitch. Another grad student who worked with Sanchez."

"Who took the picture?"

Dr. Munizaga shrugged and shook her head. "It was taken eight or nine years ago, back when she had everybody charmed."

"I'd like to borrow it."

"Take it, then." The professor slipped the picture from its frame. "You don't need to give it back." The professor didn't bother a last look before she handed it over. "I should warn you: you may not be glad your search for her is over. I'd get the police involved before she shows up, if I were you. One minute she doesn't seem to have a temper, and then she loses it. Once she threatened me by saying she keeps a handgun in the glove compartment of her truck."

Linda had two hours to kill before she had to meet Will at the Linn Street Cafe. Restless, she wandered across the street from campus into the business district where she found the street-level door to Boisseau's Used and Rare Books. The stairs were narrow and steep, all right. She backed away and let the door go shut.

Strolling around the block, she looked in store windows and up at the sky, vaguely aware of the students she passed in low-slung shorts and t-shirts with words. By the time she returned to her starting place, she was almost ready to meet Jack Boisseau. She tried to think how to begin.

She made it halfway up his stairs before she paused to lean against the wall. Her excuse for stalling was to take one more look at the photograph the professor had given her — the stunning beauty of a plump and happy Nina Sorba.

The image stood at odds, in Linda's mind, with the pinched-faced drawing of Nina she had pinned to her studio wall, the look of malice incarnate, the woman she'd been looking for. *This* face, the face in the photograph, was exquisite in its symmetry. A "star," Annie had called her. Now Linda could see why. Nina had fixed the camera with a confident half-smile, mouth slightly open as if she were about to say something extremely clever. Her gaze transmitted a high level of intelligence — an utterly convincing characteristic Linda had never been able to analyze, but which she'd seen occasionally when learning portraiture years before, in school. Perhaps it was the person behind the camera who had inspired such thought behind the eyes, such openness in the countenance of Nina Sorba.

Perhaps that person had been Jack.

# Chapter 21

John didn't answer his office phone. After four rings, his secretary came on the line to say he was out for the afternoon. He forgot half the time to keep his cell phone with him, so Linda wasn't surprised when he didn't answer at that number, either. She left a message: "I'm turning my phone off in a minute while I meet Jack Boisseau, so if you call back, leave a message. I have an uneasy feeling you've been right all along. I may be out in left field, trying too hard to exonerate Esther."

Linda stood partway up Jack's steps, on the spot where Will had been smitten with Annie three years earlier. Now the specter of Annie Hebring appeared above and came clattering down in the tank top that had brought him the wide eye of her navel, the swell of her breasts, the tears welling up in her brown eyes. Linda turned her back on that secondhand memory and poked her home number with her thumb. John sometimes worked on articles at the house. It was worth a try.

He picked up on the second ring. The intimate timbre of his voice put her back into that morning's argument: "I am *not* overly emotional because I'm pregnant."

He laughed.

"It's not funny, Bender. It's something I resent."

"Sorry. I didn't really say that, did I?"

"Yes. You did."

"Well, if I did," he said, "I was out of line."

"And you went off to work mad. That's not good, John."

"I was trying to say your maternal feelings for Gracie are preventing you from getting past what happened to her."

"John, just—"

"You seem to feel that half the things I say are code for something else," he said, "as if you've forgotten all you know about me. Ever since you found Gracie I've been convinced there's something more—"

*Here we go,* she thought.

"—something going on you're not telling me," he said. "Whatever you're avoiding might be the key."

"To what?"

"The whole experience," he said, "has been harder on you than you realize."

"You really think I'm avoiding something?"

"By refusing to face the consequences of Esther's not taking her medicine, yes. All that time you used to spend with her in her kitchen, drinking coffee and talking, she was lucid, normal-acting, right? You used to tell me how delightful and smart she was, what good company. But she's not like that now, to state the obvious. Sickness in the brain can change a person's character. It *is* possible she could have done something awful, something at odds with herself, something beyond the pale— worse —than she's ever done before."

"She could have, but she didn't." Linda looked up the dusty stairway to the closed door at the top. "I called to ask your advice."

"I was thinking about you while I was painting, that's all," he said. "Then the phone rang and I started thinking out loud. Why are you whispering?"

"I'm in a stairwell. Sound reverberates."

"You're angry?" John asked.

"Apparently. Ask me if I've found Nina Sorba."

"Have you?"

"No, but I've talked to a couple people who know her, John. Apparently she's gone back to Linden Grove. Jack Boisseau is her husband."

"You're kidding."

"You see?" she said. "You're surprised."

"Yeah," said John. "Very. I'm going to have to think about that. I never knew he was married."

"I'm about to meet him," she said, "and I don't have a plan of what to say to him. I'd really like to know what's attracted him to Linden Grove."

"Besides a great piece of real estate that perfectly suits his needs? It may be as sim—

"—simple as that, I know," Linda said. "I was hoping to talk that through with you, but I'll just wing it. What are you doing home?"

"I decided this would be a good day to prime the basement walls. When you meet up with Will later, why don't you lay the day's new facts on the table? He'll help you think things through. I'll try to put the paper to bed early tonight so I can be here when you get home. I should be able to."

"I don't need Will to help me think," said Linda, still grouchy with self-doubt.

"You're wound too tight. Sweetheart—?"

She let the phone rest against her chin and closed her eyes.

"I'm sorry you're under so much pressure," he said gently. "I'm not trying to upset you."

"I'm taking a deep breath," Linda told him, and it really did calm her. She felt her love for him unwind her like a sigh. "What are you up to this afternoon?"

"After I'm done painting," he said gently, "I plan to wind up my last story and make a few calls." Before he came home, he explained, he had stopped at her studio and gotten the crib out of the loft. He figured they might as well start getting her workspace ready there at home. He'd worried the paint fumes might make her sick. "I've got the doors wide open down here," he said. "By the time you get back, the smell should be gone. I know you need to see this through, this theory of yours. I just want you to be okay." Linda could hear the slide of his feet walking up the basement stairs as he talked.

She heard a click. "What was that?"

"What?"

"That sound?"

"I opened a beer," he said. She imagined him wiping his mouth with the back of the hand that held the telephone. "Frank called a couple hours ago," he said, "on his way to Clarinda. The court has initiated commitment papers on Esther. He's upset about the idea that she could have held Annie's car key in her mouth. At first he didn't buy it."

"I still don't."

"He doesn't want people to be put off by her. On top of all the other problems, schizophrenia is so unflattering. You don't have to prove anything as far as he's concerned. He's so grateful to you for finding Grace."

"I don't deserve any credit for that." An arc of recollection leapt through Linda's mind, *four deer.* John was saying something about meeting Frank in town for a late supper, but Linda's mind was still on the deer that led her to Grace in the nick of time, or so it seemed.

"Did you hear what I said about not being here when you get home?"

"*Yes,*" she said. "You're having supper with Frank." The street-level door opened wide just then. With a quick good-bye, she disconnected him with her thumb. She pocketed her cell phone and moved her back against the wall so a United Parcel man could precede her to the top of the stairs, as if getting there first might make her feel like she knew what she was doing.

A stocky man with dark curly hair ignored Linda as she strode through the door as if she had all the confidence in the world. She headed off to her left toward a maze of bookshelves. Standing in front of a section marked Photography, she had her back to him. Out of breath from racing up the stairs, she listened to "How's it going, Jack?" and "We're headed for more Indian Summer, don't you think?" as Jack signed for his package and the UPS man left. She pulled a large volume off the shelf and sneezed. A hand over her mouth, she heard a deep grumble: "Bless you. That's scholarly dust you just inhaled."

The guy was a wit. She managed to say, "Thanks." Oddly, the place smelled sweetly fermented. Between where she stood and Jack's worktable was an open area with a dust-colored sofa and matching easy chair, both heaped with newspapers. He cleared his throat. In a grumble that implied *what a bother,* he spoke again without giving her so much as a glance. "I'm operating on a spine, but if you have a question, give a yell. I'll leave you alone otherwise."

That was just as well. Operating on a spine. He thought he was clever. She was left to stare at his profile before declaring herself. She watched him unhook a T-shaped instrument from a floor stand and bend over his work. His hair swirled at the crown and needed a cut. Bare toes gripped the rungs of a high work stool. At the knees his jeans were pale. Beyond him, on a counter beside a sink, lay a row of pages held flat by thick glass weights. Nearby stood some sort of torture device with wooden bolts at the corners, a book press. That was her guess.

Linda opened the large volume in her hands and pretended to look at it. She had expected Jack Boisseau to be dreamy-eyed and better groomed — not uncombed like that, with a wide, soft brow and toes that curled while he acknowledged customers he couldn't be bothered to so much as look at. A small cloud rose from his hand as he moved the steamer back and forth at the table edge. She shifted the heavy book onto her left forearm. "I'm Linda Garbo."

He swiveled to consider her over the wire rims of his glasses. His eyes were very blue. He rubbed a finger against a thumb, then extended that right hand anyway as he approached to shake her hand. He was a good four inches shorter than she and older than she had expected, closer to her age than to Annie's. His handshake was loose and hesitant. "You're the person I'm buying the building from," he said.

"Yes, that's right. I have to confess I'm a little jealous at the thought of your moving into my place. I thought I'd come by and break the ice. You're getting a good, solid building."

He pumped her hand again, a firmer grip this time. "I'll put it to good use. There's no problem—?"

"Ruby told me how well the place suits you."

His expression went slack.

"The realtor," she reminded him. "Ruby Best?"

"Oh, yes, of course. She's right." He held Linda in his steady, blue gaze. "Is Anne really okay, after that scare with her baby? Will called earlier." He shrugged. "Of course you know that. You were there in the car with him."

"Annie is doing well." Linda pulled her hand from his. "I'll tell her you asked." Linda let her shoulder touch the shelf behind — which made a row of books fall like dominos. She sneezed again.

He blessed her.

"Thanks. You were telling Will that you rang their doorbell the afternoon of the abduction."

Jack missed a beat, then nodded. "Don't think it didn't shake me up when I found out how close I'd come to maybe seeing the kidnapper. I did ring the doorbell. I wish now I'd kept it up longer than I did. I knew Anne was in there."

"How could you tell?"

"I could hear the baby crying," he said, "and Annie's car was in the drive. I knew it was hers by the vanity plates. I heard about the kidnapping on my car radio on my way back here that afternoon. Folks who might know something were supposed to call a number, so I did. I was relieved to hear on the news that night that the baby was okay. Anne was proud of her mother and used to talk about her a lot, but she never said anything about mental illness."

"That's something Annie doesn't like to talk about," said Linda. "The real reason I'm here is— I'm hoping you can tell me where Nina is. I had a conversation with her once, back in Linden Grove.

Since then I've been hoping to see her again. She's hard to find. I mean, I'd just like to get in touch with her."

Jack's face darkened. He resumed his work as if the conversation were over. Uncertain, Linda half-turned away from him and let a few seconds pass. "Maybe I'll just browse," she said. "I have some time to kill before I meet Will for dinner." She waited. "Sorry you can't make it."

"I have plans. I'll have to close up early, before five."

"Of course." By Linda's watch it was four thirty-nine.

Jack shoved his glasses higher onto the bridge of his nose. While Linda walked around the sofa to replace the photography book on the shelf, he continued shaving dark amber gunk from the spine of a book with an ivory-colored instrument. She approached him again, to watch.

Another hiss of steam released a feral, gluey smell. "Ruby told me I'd enjoy hearing you talk about your work," she said quietly.

Without raising his head, he glanced up at her over the top of his glasses, which were slightly askew.

"You take the book back to its original form," she said. "Is that the idea?"

"That's the modern ethic for this kind of work."

"To be as unobtrusive as possible."

"That's one way of putting it," he said.

"Another way might be to say that restoring its original state is to erase its history," said Linda.

His frown was momentary. "I prefer to see this as an art where the artist tries not to leave a mark." He explained he liked to use the kind of tools that were used in the book's own era, a purist's view. "This," he said, holding up the pale scraping-blade, is a bone folder made from the rib of a German cow. Lutheran, no doubt."

She chuckled along with him.

Jack's gestures were freer now, and more relaxed, as he put the tool to work again, pulling off the old hide glue in sticky strings. The crock-pot, he told her, was invented by a bookbinder to heat the glue. "Now-a-days we use P.V.A., polyvinyl acetate. It has the same horny look when it's dry, but stays rubbery for a lifetime. None of this brittle stuff."

He turned his head to lift the steamer from its stand again and proceeded to talk for a full five minutes about his work. Eventually, during a rare pause, Linda said, "I was talking to Leticia Munizaga this afternoon. She told me Nina has let everybody down."

Jack hung up the steamer with a downward jerk, like slamming a phone into its cradle. He pulled his glasses from his face, let them drop to the tabletop, and stared at Linda.

"She told me about the plagiarism," Linda added quickly, "how it's ruined Nina's career. That might explain why Nina wants time alone to lick her wounds, if that's what's going on. That, and if you and she are separated—" The cold look on his face stopped her. She'd gone too far, guessing like that. "Sorry," she said. "I'm getting too personal. I just need to know where Nina was while you were ringing Annie's doorbell."

"I don't like your tone," he said. "If I talk about Nina, it will be only enough to set you straight."

He resumed his work in silence.

It was two full minutes by Linda's watch before he spoke again. "First off," he said finally, "I don't know where you got the idea Nina and I were splitting up. In fact, we're getting back together. We're going to be fine this time." He paused for breath. "I suppose Munizaga told you all about her ugly little puppet-mummy."

"She showed me a picture of the thing."

"The good professor probably didn't tell you she stole it," he said. "In the sixties, from a dig in northern Chile." He continued working, the bone-blade scraping faster now. "The first time Nina saw the thing, she was a first-year grad student. It gave her the idea that was to develop into her major line of research."

Linda pictured the mummy's red, spoon-shaped mask, circles scribed around its eyeholes. A perfectly round, pouched-forward mouth-like-an-O. "I'm sure it's very interesting, but it gives me the creeps."

"Yeah, well," he said, "it's not my cup of tea, either." Jack's hands grew still. "She did a bunch of research over that summer. This was, oh, eight years ago, when we were first together. She developed her religious-art theory for one of Munizaga's seminars that fall. The professor translated two of Nina's papers into Portuguese and published them the following summer and fall under her own name, as single-author pieces, in a journal run by the Universidad de Chile." He looked tight-eyed, angry.

"You mean *Leticia* stole *Nina's* work and passed it off as her own?"

"You got it," said Jack. "Nina had dropped out of her program that Christmas to follow me to Denver, where I had an internship." He put down the bone tool made from a German cow. "We were gone almost three years before Nina decided to resume her studies here. She came across the articles last year when she was doing a routine literature search on her topic. They had never been translated back into English, but Nina—"

"—had learned to read Portuguese."

"Right," said Jack. "She tried to confront Leticia, but the professor wouldn't hear of it. So Nina stole them back, so to speak — her own articles — for her dissertation, making parts of them prominent in her chapter headings and using a huge chunk as an argument for something-or-other. In her citations she gave credit to the article, listing herself as author. Which she was."

"But a professor at another university recognized the research as lifted from an article published by Leticia Munizaga," said Linda, " and accused Nina—"

"—of plagiarizing Munizaga's article," he said. "Right. Someone from Central America who knew Leticia from years ago, when she did field work down there."

"And Nina lost her PhD," said Linda.

"She's turned her old professor in to the department here, to defend herself," Jack said, "but the problem is, Nina can't prove her case." He looked down at his hands. "Her original copies of the papers got lost along the way, so it's her word against the professor's.

Leticia refuses to absolve her by telling the truth. She's letting Nina hang. Nina worshiped that woman for the longest time. She feels betrayed. By everyone. She *was* betrayed. Now she's not taking care of herself, and she's not that well." His shoulders sagged.

"She left me for a guy named Mitch," he said. "Who dumped her when the plagiarism scandal made her lose her bid for an assistant professor job at Arizona State. She wants to make a fresh start, and I'm sure as hell going to try to meet her halfway. I'm going to see her through this thing. Not that any of this is your business."

Linda backed up to sit on the wide arm of the sofa. "You mean a lot to Annie," she said softly.

Jack met Linda's gaze.

"Maybe Nina found out you got in touch with her again recently," she said, "and saw her as a threat. She thinks Annie could come between you, like old times. That's it, isn't it? Nina is jealous of Annie."

Jack's stare intensified. "What in God's name are you talking about?"

Linda knew she'd gone way, way too far with her fishing strategy, but she figured she had nothing to lose: "I think Nina focused all her disappointments on Annie and decided to discredit her in the cruelest way possible— by casting doubts on her ability to care for Grace by putting the baby in harms' way. Maybe Nina's motive escalated from there and led to the idea of vilifying Annie's mother, or maybe that was an unintended outcome. Nina has harassed Esther Hebring in the past. I want to know where Nina was the afternoon of the kidnapping." She paused. She said, "I'm told she has a gun."

Jack's jaw hung loose, his face a portrait of agitation. He put his tools down with tightly controlled care. He stepped back from his worktable. He hunkered down to unplug the steamer, his movements methodical and slow — all of this without taking his eyes off Linda's face. "You're wrong," he said evenly.

He walked backward toward a messy desk against the wall, picked up a phone — the old, rotary kind — and dialed a number.

In a few seconds, he said, "Hi. No don't—" The disconnect was so loud Linda heard it five feet away.

Without a hitch, he dialed the phone again. "Linda Garbo's here," he said, turning to look at her as he listened. "Yes, I know I did," he said, "but this is different." He sounded tense. He turned to face the wall. "Yes," he said into the phone, "that's right. That you're the one who took Anne's baby."

He listened to the voice at the other end for long seconds, then seemed to lose his patience. "She's been asking for you all over campus, apparently. You can settle this now. — Why not? — I wish you would. I apologize for talking to this woman." Avoiding eye contact, he straight-armed the phone in Linda's direction. "Nina wants a word with you."

"Why are you bothering Jack?" said a nasal, southern Iowa drawl that for her next words slipped into a near-whisper, as if this were a confidence: "I guess you didn't get the e-mail I sent you." It was the same airy voice Linda had heard on the tapes in the police station four days earlier: *Imagine what could happen to a baby like that.* There was no mistaking it.

Linda held her breath while Nina's languid tones drew force from the very slowness of her speech: "This is just wonderful," she said with precise irony. "I seem to remember telling you that I admire Esther Hebring's work on the radio. How you got from there to accusing me of kidnapping the woman's granddaughter—" Nina's soft voice seemed to fail her. "I don't need this right now. I really don't." The next few breaths she took were audible, as if she were out of breath. "When will you get home? Tonight? Tomorrow? When?"

Before Linda could answer, Nina Sorba said, "All right, then, I'll surprise you. I know where you live."

Linda pictured the A-frame she could see through the trees from the north windows of her own house. "I thought you didn't live across the river any more."

"I moved back in. I'm surprised you don't know that. You're such a spy. I'll drop by later and settle all this," said Nina lightly. The line went dead.

At the far end of the shop, a light went out.

Linda hung up the phone as Jack emerged from the rows of shadowy bookshelves. *What's up with Nina,* she was thinking, *that she pretends to hold back something I must be dying to know, just to hook me? Passive aggression, the professor called it.*

"I need to close up now." Jack gestured Linda toward the door.

"Professor Munizaga told me Nina owns a gun," she said.

"That doesn't make her a kidnapper," he said.

*That's hardly the point,* thought Linda. The guy wasn't the brightest bulb.

"She's got her back up, but I doubt she has a gun. The only thing you're right about is that she's turned Annie into a scapegoat for all her misery. She's entitled to her anger," were his parting words.

# Chapter 22

Linda and Will arrived back on Isabella Circle, where Linda had left her car, well after dark. Driving toward home, Linda tried calling John again, as she had three times during the long ride back from Iowa City. Still no answer. She tuned the radio to a pop station, thinking how nice it would be to hear again, by chance, the song by a group called Counting Crows that Jessica Mann had played on Hebring's piano the night Gracie was found. 'A song for Gracie,' Jessica had renamed it. But the lyric Linda got as she sped along was *Do it up, it's on with Stella, What a way to finally smell her, Pick it up....* She clicked the radio off. In another twelve minutes she reached Limestone Lane. The dash clock said 10:42.

There was the tiniest sliver of moon that night. She was driving up their hundred-foot-long lane, a tunnel of darkness pierced only by a sprinkling of stars, when headlights swung around the bend up ahead and for a moment blinded her. A white pickup rushed by, rocking with speed on the rutted gravel. Linda watched it go in her rearview mirror. *Nina?* Linda suddenly felt cold.

The grove of ancient, knuckled apple trees was briefly underlit by Linda's own headlights as she rounded the curve. Contours of home came into view. Low to the earth, the house was built of river stones. A deep, pillared porch stretched across the front. The yard light mounted on a pole beside the house went on every day at twilight, automatically. Now it cast a golden glow upon the scene. Linda felt a chill of disappointment. The house was dark. John's car wasn't in the drive.

So he was working late after all, despite his hunch he'd get the newspaper to bed in record time after having dinner with Frank. Linda pulled through the open door of the old machine shed-garage and switched her headlights off. She listened to the silence before she unlocked the car.

On the dark porch, Linda smelled the savory fragrance of a chicken roasting, and her mouth began to water. Her dinner with Will at the Linn Street Diner in Iowa City had been a salad. She hadn't been that hungry then, but now she was famished. She fumbled to get her key into the front door lock, finally locating the keyhole with her fingertips.

Inside, the mouthwatering smell turned acrid, smoky, and her hunger turned to alarm. Something was burning. She flipped on the porch light, the dining room and kitchen lights, too. The chicken in the oven was burned to a crisp, the kitchen hazy with bitter smoke. The charred skin of the bird released delicious steam when she pierced it with a fork and pulled out a slab of white meat — which she left on a plate to cool. Although the oven was still hot, she realized with a start, someone had turned it off. *Nina?*

*Get a grip*, Linda told herself.

John wouldn't have roasted a chicken, when he was having dinner with Frank. She stared at the steaming carcass. The presence of that charred chicken robbed her of the relief of being home at last, after a long, confusing day.

She pictured Nina's white pickup racing away. She imagined Nina Sorba at the wheel, turning her truck around at Limestone Lane and rushing back again — mad as hell that Linda had figured out what she'd done to Gracie — a handgun lying on the seat beside her. Linda's fingers shook as she turned on the exhaust fan. Stock still, she listened for unfamiliar sounds inside the house. Her stomach growled.

The dark juices in the pan under the chicken were way past caramelized. Linda grabbed two potholders from the counter and carried the pan out the front door. She left it to smoke in the shadow of an oak. She propped the door open to air out the place and then thought better of it and locked herself in with the smoky smell. Holding her breath for the count of ten, she listened hard for whoever had turned the oven off. "My house," she said defiantly.

She stared at the steaming breast of chicken cooling on the fork, backing away from it. She poured herself a glass of milk and drank it while walking from room to room, raising blinds on the windows facing the river. *Here I am.* She wasn't going to freeze with alarm, or get back into her car and run away.

What *was* her greatest fear? It came to Linda then — far out in the country, alone in her house — the thing that terrified her and made her so determined. The insight straightened her spine. *Vulnerability.* Well, she'd have none of that.

Now she *wanted* to hear a truck in the drive. Again, she paused to listen. She opened the door to the basement.

Descending the stairs into the odor of fresh paint, she felt another chill. One of the sliding doors was open as far as it would go, letting in the cold night air. John had opened the door to air the room as he painted, in the warmth of the afternoon. Now Linda dragged it shut, locked it carefully, and pulled on it to be sure it was secure. Belatedly, she felt a chill of a different sort: she might not be alone.

The basement room, Linda's future studio, was brightly lit by two floor lamps John had carried down for extra light while he primed three of the walls a wintery white. The fourth bore the sketch of Esther. A line of primer, rolled up close to the crown of her head, showed how far he'd gotten when someone, or something, had interrupted him. *That would have been me,* Linda realized, *calling from halfway up Jack Boisseau's stairs.*

John had put the roller down into the paint tray, which now lay on newspapers at Linda's feet. The paint had a skin on it, and the roller was dry to the touch. Only a true emergency would have made him walk away from that; he was such a stickler for taking meticulous care of all his tools. She glanced toward the sliding glass doors facing the river, a mirror to her image in all that whiteness, a picture broken only by a tiny star from the house across the river — another farm light that went on automatically at dusk. Lights were on inside the A-frame, too, for the first time in three weeks.

Nina had moved back into that house, if she was to be believed. Linda raised a hand and waved.

She checked the half-bath and the storage space under the steps. She left both floor lamps on. As she went back upstairs she felt her anger rise again, furious that she should be so spooked. *In my own home.*

Right hand in her pocket, she grasped her phone. She crossed the living room, unlocked the sliding door, and stepped onto the deck. Off in the distance, on the interstate, a semi accelerated three notes up a scale, then faded. Shadows shifted in the trees and branches snapped — deer, or bobcat, or wind and gravity. Linda backed into the smoky-smelling house, wishing John had locked it tight before he left in such a hurry. *Why was he cooking a chicken, anyway? What had happened to his plans for supper with Frank?*

Some Tuesdays, when he had last-minute articles to write, John worked half the night. After he put finishing touches on all his stories, he had to import the copy for the Wednesday *Times* into Quark documents and do the page design. Sometimes as late as midnight or one o'clock, he would convert the pages to PDF files. He had to transfer them electronically to the *Des Moines Register's* printing plant in West Des Moines by eight a.m. But for once he had been so sure he'd be finished early.

Linda called his office. He wasn't there.

She called his cell.

Across the room, his phone played its happy tune, a sound that drew her to his jacket, on the back of a dining room chair. His phone had two messages, but she didn't know the retrieval code. Next, she went into their bedroom to check the answering machine. The first message was the one she'd left for him earlier in the afternoon. The second was in the now-familiar, breathy voice of Nina Sorba. *Hey, Linda, your husband answered the phone an hour or so ago when I called. Now it's six-fifteen. I guess when you get home, you'll be alone, for a good long while. I'll catch you then.*

Linda looked at her watch. It was eleven ten.

"Frank, it's Linda. Sorry to call so late."

"Is something wrong?"

"I just got home, and John's not here. He's not at his office. You had supper with him?"

"I had to call that off at the last minute. I just got back myself, from seeing Esther."

"So he didn't say where he might be?"

"No," said Frank. "I talked to him as I was about to head out the door, four-thirty or so."

"I called him, too, from Iowa City. Must have been right before you did." She walked over to the narrow window beside the front door and looked out into the yard. A streak of movement caught her eye — a ringed tail, two coin-like eyes. A raccoon was feeding on the chicken, she realized, as her heart slowed down. "John went off in such a hurry, he left a roller full of paint to dry in the tray and forgot to take his cell phone. Both of those things are out of character. I'd feel better if I knew how to reach him. Nina Sorba is back in Linden Grove. I talked to her this afternoon on the phone, and just now I found a rather cryptic message from her on our machine. She said she had called here earlier when John was home. I'm afraid she might have said something to him to make him rush away, to make sure I'd be alone. It's a long story, but she might show up here any minute."

"Surely not. At this hour?"

"She's angry and wants to meet me on her terms. That's how I see it. A pickup passed me on the lane just now, when I was coming in. We don't get a lot of drop-in company out here. If it was Nina, she'll be back. I'm wondering why she didn't just turn around and follow me in. If she's doing a passive-aggressive number to rattle me, it's working." Linda looked at her watch again.

"Do you want me to come over?" Frank asked. "I'm facing another sleepless night, anyway. I can be there in fifteen minutes."

"John burned the chicken."

"You want me to stop somewhere and get you something?"

"No, that's not what I meant. He left in a hurry, sometime before dark. He's such a stickler for locking the house, and the sliding door downstairs was wide open. He didn't think to leave lights on for me. It's like he thought he'd be right back. Or that he panicked, which wouldn't be like him either." She took a breath. "I would like your company. And Frank?"

"Yes?"

"I'm sorry about Esther. Truly, truly sorry her illness has gained the upper hand. I'm not sure I've ever actually said that to you, with all that's been going on."

"Yes you have, Linda, in a number of ways. You're the most constant friend she has."

"I've been trying to help her, that's all."

"I know you have," he said. "Let's say goodbye. I'll come stay with you until John gets home. I'll be glad, too, for the company."

Linda draped a washcloth over the faucet in the bathroom sink to run the bowl full of warm water without making noise. If there was a knock on the door, or a car outside, she wanted to hear it. As soon as she'd washed her face and brushed her teeth, she called the Linden Grove Police Department to see if something newsworthy had happened to make John run for the story. A fire, or a robbery.

"No, nothing much going on," the dispatcher told her. "Some kids partying loud, out in the new subdivision. Otherwise, it's pretty quiet."

Next, Linda called Detective Hansen at home, tapping her fingernails against the phone as it rang and rang. When at last he said hello, his voice was full of sighs. "Linda," he said hoarsely, "you know John's always got five irons in the fire. Before he married you I'll wager he was off somewhere almost every night."

*A slight exaggeration,* she thought.

"A public meeting, of some kind," the detective was muttering, still talking about John, "or listening to a story someone thought should be in print. He's probably chewing the fat somewhere. I bet he took his camera, right?"

"He keeps his camera in his car."

"Well, there. You see?"

*See what?* she thought.

"Don't rein him in so tight. I'm going back to sleep."

Feeling foolish, Linda ate a piece of toast with peanut butter and drank a glass of milk. She couldn't sit still. Her hands were cold. She paced.

She was mortified she'd awakened an off-duty police officer in the middle of the night because she'd lost track of her husband. When she heard the gravel crunch in the drive, she flew to the window, hands pressed together, hoping for John. After the headlights went off she watched Frank heft himself slowly into sight. As he stepped into the entryway, he opened his arms to her. He had a book in his hand. "Esther asked me to give this to you," he said. He had unbuttoned the top two buttons of his white shirt. His red-striped tie lay noose-like on the rise of his chest. The book was *Russian Tales.* "She marked a story for you. One she tried to tell you, apparently, about a man who sees the ghost of his dead son so he can say good-bye. That ring a bell?"

"She couldn't remember how it ended," Linda said. "Did you tell her I was in Iowa City, looking for Nina Sorba?"

"Yes, her radio fan. Esther's only reaction was 'I hope she doesn't tell Nina where I am.' You're right. That Nina person is the one she thinks has been stalking her. I can't see her new meds are helping her at all, as yet. If anything, she seems worse."

Linda left the book on the dining table and led him into the living room. "Ordinarily I love it out here in the country," she said, crossing the room to close the heavy drapes, "but tonight is different."

They settled themselves, Frank in John's extra-wide leather chair, she on the sofa. Her feet rested on a sand-and-earth-colored

Navaho rug. Almost immediately, she rose to open the fireplace damper and set a match to the kindling, all tented and ready. In less than a minute, flames sizzled and roared.

She told him about her visit to Iowa City. "I thought I'd gotten a handle on Nina until I met her husband Jack. His story is that the professor is the desperate, dishonest one. She was awfully eager to vilify Nina, now that I think of it; but Jack's the one I'd peg as unreliable. He's still in love with his wife. I take it they've had some serious marital trouble. He suggested they were about to get back together." She shook her head. "My theories are making me paranoid. That's what John thinks. I'm just anxious to see the puzzle pieces of Gracie's abduction fit together."

Frank's expression altered, as if he felt a fleeting pain.

"I'm afraid I'll blow it," she said, "if I get the chance to face Nina Sorba. You think Esther is worse?"

"She seems overly sedated," he said, "but the staff says she's not. She's in a kind of stupor." A log shifted in the fireplace, releasing sparks of blue and white. "This heavy silence of hers — maybe it's remorse for what she did to Gracie. Over and over, I've asked her if she took the baby. She shakes her head no in that frantic way that means, 'Don't ask.'"

"'She did not do this thing,'" said Linda gently. "Remember when you said that?"

Frank pulled at the loose skin under his chin. His girth made his arms seem short. "It's her schizophrenia that did it, not my lovely Esther."

"You want something to drink? Whiskey, coffee?"

"I'll wait until John gets here and have a drink then. Maybe a glass of water."

"Sure."

The lights flickered while she was in the kitchen. "One night we lost power for two hours," she called out to Frank, "after a car ran into a transformer up the road. At least we'll have light from the fire if the electricity goes out." She looked at her watch again.

"You may be wrong about this Nina person coming here tonight," he said when she returned to the living room. He rested the glass on his thigh. "She knows you believe she abducted Grace. Is that right?"

Linda nodded.

"And yet she invited herself here."

"Yes."

"That isn't the behavior of a guilty person," he said.

"Unless she wants to shut me up."

"Hurt you, you mean?"

"Maybe her troubles have gotten the best of her and made her reckless. What I'm most afraid of is that what she started with Gracie isn't finished. As a crime, I'm afraid, it's not only sick, but horribly incomplete."

"Or like something only a mentally ill person like Esther would do."

Linda fingered the fringe of the sofa pillow on her lap. What she had been going to say was that as a crime against a baby it seemed incomplete unless the abductor's motive had been to use blame to put Annie in prison for years, or put Esther away for good. But Linda kept that to herself. Frank looked as discouraged as she felt.

A sound from out front might have been a crunch of gravel, but it didn't repeat.

Linda shifted her posture, wishing she'd discouraged Frank from coming over. She hoped his silence didn't mean he was trying to come up with another way to insist her suspicions of Nina Sorba were airy fantasies. He was more at ease with silence than she. *He's a lonely man,* she thought. "I'm glad Elsa's your friend," she murmured sleepily. "I think she's in love with you."

"No, nothing like that," he said.

Roused wide-awake by her own audacity, she regretted speaking Elsa's name.

"As ideas go—" He gave Linda a solemn look. "Put that one to rest."

"She is very fond of you."

"And I of her. I don't know why that should need to be re-marked upon." Frank frowned at Linda for long seconds, as if holding back a thought. Then he smiled — suddenly and briefly — toward the fire. "I think I'd like that whiskey now."

"Of course." Linda called John's office on the kitchen phone while she made the drink. There was still no answer. Once she was settled on the sofa again, Frank seemed mesmerized by the blue-white flames, and she let the silence lengthen. She should have just locked the doors and gone to bed. Nina Sorba wasn't coming.

Ice shifted in Frank's glass as he tilted it. "—after she got her driver's license," he was saying. "Just turned sixteen."

Linda stared at his fleshy profile. "Annie, you mean? I'm sorry—"

"Not Annie. Esther. Six months after we started dating. She went missing for five months. That feeling of dread I'd never see her alive hit me all over again when Grace was missing." He stared into his drink. He took a mouthful of whiskey and swallowed. "She was gone nearly nineteen weeks," he said.

"Is that when she was diagnosed—?"

"Yes," he said simply. "'Something's wrong with my head,' she used to say to me. She called me her rock."

"I'm surprised that didn't scare you off."

"She was an extraordinary girl. She dreamed of a career beyond this little town. She should have had it. Instead, she was swallowed by a house." He stared into his glass. "My family warned me not to marry her, even after a drug got her stabilized. We married the day she turned eighteen." He smiled again.

"And was she—?" Linda began.

"—a theater major, no surprise," Frank said. "She made it through three years of college before she got sick again. Maybe in the beginning I'd mistaken a certain lack of inhibition as a sign she loved me."

*Sex, he means*, thought Linda.

"I think time has proved me right." He shifted his big shoulders in the leather chair, silent for a minute. Then he said, "Her father believed until his dying day that she ran away because she was ruined."

"Ruined?" *Sex, he means,* she thought again.

Frank sighed a quick, dismissive sigh. "He was ashamed of her. I never forgave him for letting her down that way. I'm feeling a little angry tonight."

He didn't sound angry. He sounded beaten down.

"He left her the family house," said Frank, "and enough money to cover putting her away somewhere. I promised her I never would. Now my hands are tied."

Linda sneaked a look at her watch. It was after one o'clock. "Why doesn't John call?"

"Obviously someone called to alert him to some sort of emergency," said Frank, "or sent an e-mail."

"He wouldn't have been checking messages," she said, "in the middle of painting a wall. But let's take a look."

Frank followed her into the master bedroom, where she touched the spacebar of the computer to wake it up. Her mailbox contained one message, sent the night before from the address Digart3@aol.com. Linda read the short message silently: *I've tried a couple times to call you, just as I promised I would, that day we met behind your studio. I thought we might become friends. Apparently you'd rather jump to conclusions and accuse me of stealing a baby, according to Munizaga. Believe me, you've struck a nerve. I won't have my good name tarnished anymore than it already has been. Don't bother going to Iowa City tomorrow to look for me because I'm right here. Nina S.*

Frank turned his face toward the crunch of gravel out front. So did Linda. They heard a car door slam.

"If it's Nina," she said to him as he followed her toward the front door, "I want you to go back to the bedroom, out of sight, so I can talk to her alone. It'll be less complicated that way." Through the narrow windows beside the front door, they watched Nina get out of her truck. "You'll hate yourself if you don't give me this chance to at least find out where Nina Sorba was that afternoon. I know it seems odd, but go back to the bedroom right now, *please.* I'll call out your name if I need you."

And so it was that Frank reluctantly agreed to stay silent and out of sight in the dimly lit bedroom behind a closed door. He looked too exhausted to resist. "Maybe this'll be the end of it," he said.

# Chapter 23

Through the glass by the door, Linda saw a familiar figure lean forward over the hood of a white pickup, as if she might be ill, bracing herself with both arms out straight. Nina Sorba's pale hair was loose around her shoulders. Beyond her truck, in the shadows of a massive oak where only its bumper caught the light, was Frank's black Lincoln. Linda stepped onto the porch. The screen door slapped shut behind her, and Nina stood up straight, lips parted expectantly toward the light. She was wearing the t-shirt with the winged horse that she'd worn the day Linda noticed her outside the church.

Nina waited by her car as Linda walked down the wide, stone steps and across the worn area in front of the house. The woman was smaller than Linda remembered. "Well, finally," Nina said, "you can accuse me to my face."

"You were here earlier, before I got home, weren't you?" Linda asked, the weight of annoyance in her voice. "I could tell you'd been in the house." Linda stepped to the side, so the light from the porch would fall on Nina's features.

Nina shrugged.

"Your boss Austin Benn has been trying to reach you," said Linda. "It seemed like you dropped out of sight when the Cantonwine baby was abducted."

"It only seemed like that to you," said Nina. Her weak smile gave way to a frown, and her pause was long. "You know," she said finally, "how sometimes people see Jesus in the shape of a potato?"

"What?"

"Or in a piece of burned toast?" Nina added.

Linda reacted with a nervous laugh and thought: *Nina's stoned. She's a stoner. Well that explains a lot.*

"—or the Virgin Mary," Nina said, "in a water-stained wall? Or where lightning scarred a tree? And think it's a visitation?"

"A visitation," repeated Linda.

"You've heard of that?"

"I've heard of such things, of course," said Linda. "It's not something I believe in, though. God doing magic tricks."

Nina shrugged again. "We all have our own explanations, don't we?" she said, "for what we don't understand. You certainly do."

"It's freezing," said Linda. "Let's go inside." She backed up a step or two toward the house.

Nina made no move to follow. "I looked across the river from my house," she said, "and saw your basement lights on. When I got here, the sliding door was wide open."

"So you just walked right in? That's trespassing, you know."

"I knocked," said Nina. "I called out. I made sure no one was home. When I got inside—" She took a labored breath. "I don't go for such things, either, holy apparitions. But for me, under the cir-cumstances—" Nina's face changed, a dreamy look around the eyes. "I was attracted, moved. A coincidence like that? It was meaning-ful, in a personal way."

"What sort of coincidence?" asked Linda, puzzled. Slowly, both women walked toward the house. "You're not being clear."

"The portrait on the wall down there," said Nina. "I've been thinking a lot about Esther Hebring, and there she was. No mistak-ing that face, magically seeping through the drywall." She chuckled. "For me, it was a sign that maybe Esther had been here, posing. She hardly ever leaves her house, and she's not much for visitors. I know that for a fact."

"That's been true all summer," said Linda. "Not so much before that."

"I had to get a better look at that face. It's not like I was breaking in. She looked the way I'd like to see her look, protective, peaceful, wise. And calm. I've only seen her once, up close, that day in church. The drawing is remarkable. You drew it?"

"Yes."

Under the porch light, the skin under Nina's eyes looked grainy. "I stared at it for quite a while," she said, "before I smelled smoke. A fire and brimstone sort of smell. Ha! The devil, in the form of a chicken, Esther might say." Nina aimed a wry half-smile at Linda. "I'm *kidding*," she said. "Lighten up." She stumbled up the top porch step.

Linda reached to steady Nina and felt the sinews of her too-thin arms.

"Thanks," said Nina. "I'm all used up. As I said, it's late—"

"—for a visit."

"Right," said Nina.

"Or a visitation."

Nina smiled again. "Nobody's god would bother to appear to me right now," she said lightly. "I'm not ready yet, for that. I'm far from finished. You should have smoke alarms, by the way. For two intelligent people— I don't know why you don't."

The smoke alarms were in a box in the spare room, along with supplies for a number of other unfinished projects for the house. A blur beyond the glass by the door had to be Frank, backing away. If Nina saw it, too, she didn't let on.

She was practically unrecognizable from the first time Linda had seen her outside the church with that silvery winged horse on her dark t-shirt. Her collarbones were prominent now. Her wrist bones, too, were sharp. So were the ridge of her nose and the point of her chin — a still-young face, but she didn't look good.

Neither did she look menacing, but as they entered the house, Linda gestured for Nina to go ahead so she could observe her from behind. The way the woman was dressed — jeans, loose and droopy in the seat — might very well conceal the gun Leticia had so explicitly warned her about.

A slight sound from down the hall made Linda wonder if Frank would keep his bargain and stay out of sight. The odor of burned chicken had faded quite a bit. Still, Nina lifted her nose, flaring her nostrils as if something had put her on alert. "Your husband still isn't home, I take it."

"He sometimes pulls all-nighters on Tuesdays," said Linda. "The paper comes out tomorrow. It's a weekly."

Nina nodded once, as if the information were old news.

For a moment, there wasn't so much as the sound of breathing in the house. Linda was more convinced than ever that Nina had told John something alarming on the phone when she'd called earlier, something calculated to send him flying out the door without his jacket, or his phone.

"I wanted to see you alone," said Nina, as if she could anticipate Linda's fears. She gazed upward with rapt attention, as if listening to the house.

After a long second or two, Nina lowered herself into a dining chair. "Could I have a little something for energy?" she asked. "Juice, or something? I didn't eat much dinner. I should know I can't get away with that. I've been unpacking, getting things ready for Jack. I don't seem to get hungry any more. I've been so indecisive. He says my ambivalence in love is chronic abandonment. I'm going to try and make amends, while there's still time." She took one of her wobbly deep breaths. "Don't you wonder why I'm talking to you this way?"

Linda backed into the kitchen. "All I want to hear you say is— Where were you on the afternoon of Friday, the twentieth?" She poured a glass of orange juice while she waited in vain for an answer. Linda spoke loudly so that Frank could hear her voice down the hall. "Jack told me he rang Annie's bell that afternoon, to deliver a book to her. So he was in town that afternoon. Where were you?"

Nina shook her head.

"Have you taken something?" Linda set the juice carton on the table. "Are you high?"

Nina's eye-blinks were slow. "I left something for you downstairs," she said. "A piece of paper. In case I didn't make it back tonight. It will answer your questions. First I have some other things to say."

"You came into my house without permission to leave me a note?"

"Yes, well— No," said Nina, "not a note. I've been wanting to visit the mental hospital in Clarinda, but Esther will never agree to see me. I'm hoping that after tonight we can go together."

"She's much too sick for that."

"But I'm much too sick to wait," said Nina. Her eyes closed in the slowest blink so far. She didn't open them. "The thing about an obsession is— I just can't help it." She winced, a weak attempt to laugh at her joke.

"I should call a doctor."

"No, don't worry. Nina stood, steadying herself with splayed fingers on the table edge. "I know my limits. The juice will perk me up. Give it two minutes. Three. It's all blood chemistry."

"Are you diabetic?"

"No. Don't try and guess. You are extremely bad at guessing."

Indignation straightened Linda's spine as Nina rose unsteadily and headed straight for the basement door. She was clearly familiar with the house.

Linda followed, observing Nina's fragile frame, her small rear end inside her baggy jeans. They descended into the bright white room where the two floor lamps cast ovals of light onto the gray carpet, covered by newspapers around the edge. The room was ten degrees cooler than upstairs. Reaching out for balance, Nina placed a hand on the railing of the crib John had moved from the studio and set up in the center of the room that afternoon. Linda stepped close, as if to steady the woman, but didn't touch her. "If you're seriously not well," said Linda, "I'll feel responsible, if something happens to you here."

"Yeah, well thanks for your concern for your own liability. Why the rectangles taped on the floor?"

"That's where my worktable will go," said Linda, "now that Jack is buying my studio in town."

"Jack," said Nina. She exhaled, a long sigh. "He likes this town. Odd, isn't it, if he ends up here alone, when I was the one who insisted on living here?"

Something shifted in Linda's mind, toward compassion. Nina's hands were shaking, and the blue veins showed through her pale, pale skin. "About that piece of paper," Linda said. "Why all the drama? Let's just settle something here. Tell me what's sapped your energy. Tell me what's wrong."

"That's better," Nina said. "That's the tone of voice I need." She swallowed. "I suffer from a bone marrow disorder. Myelodysplastic syndrome."

The eight, deadly-sounding syllables left Linda speechless.

"For over a year," said Nina, "I've been on the list for the National Bone Marrow Donor Program. Most patients wait a lot longer than that. The odds are one out of a thousand that a match will turn up for me. Wouldn't that make you desperate, if you were me?" She shook her head, as if she'd said enough, but then went on: "When the professor e-mailed me that you think I'm the kidnapper, I wondered what else could go wrong. You think I'd steal a baby and leave her out in the elements to die? You accuse me, with all the other blows I'm dealing with in my life? I think you owe me an apology for that." There was a snap of anger in Nina's narrow eyes. She lowered her right hand and tucked her thumb into the side pocket of her jeans.

"I'm sorry you're ill," said Linda, "but I know you've been stalking Esther and that you found a way to destroy her. Deny it all you want. I don't think it's admiration you have for poor Esther at all, but some twisted kind of hatred. I know what you've done. You might as well confess."

"I might as well?"

"I don't see the point of prolonging this." Linda moved around the crib toward the sofa, which John had pulled away from the wall in order to paint that afternoon. Running her hand down the sides of the sofa cushions, Linda came up with grit under her fingernails, a dime, and a quarter. She turned a cushion over and patted it. "Sit," she said.

Nina closed her eyes, ignoring the command. "Consider who planted that gun idea in your mind," she said.

"Professor Munizaga," Linda said flatly, "but you make it easy to believe. You're being so secretive, so evasive. So deliberately obtuse. You called the police to report Annie had left Gracie alone in her car. Nina?"

"I'm listening."

"I recognized your voice this afternoon, when we talked on the telephone. I've heard tapes of the calls. I have to say— I'm not surprised. I've thought for some time it was you. I had a hunch."

Nina's eye flew open. "A *hunch*? Is that what turned me into a villain, an ab*duc*tress? You had a hunch?"

"Not only that," said Linda. "Your presence in church the Sunday Gracie was christened caught my attention."

"I went to your church to see—"

"It's not my church."

"Well, you were there," said Nina, "with bells on. I'd asked around and learned that church was the only place she'd gone for months. I went there to catch a glimpse of her. I planned to approach her after the service, but she got so wild and upset the moment she saw me. She pointed her Goddamn finger at me. I hated her for that."

Linda turned away from Nina and faced the room's back wall, where night had turned the glass doors into a mirror. In the depths behind Nina's reflection stood the crib, and from the crib shone a tiny red light: the Fischer-Price Baby monitor Esther had hooked up the Sunday of Gracie's baptism. *All this time*, thought Linda, *this unit has been on.* As she turned around, eyes following the cord across the carpet, the phone rang upstairs and a thrill shot through Linda's chest. *John*, she thought. It rang again, then a third time, and a fourth. Six rings, and the machine would pick it up.

The ringing stopped on five. The caller had given up, or Frank had answered it. "Time to talk straight," Linda said to Nina, "about how much you hate Esther Hebring."

"You saw what she did," said Nina. "Singled me out in front of everyone. She went actressy and flamboyant as all-get-out in the middle of a prayer and *still*, I didn't get it. Why didn't I see she was a person suffering from mental illness and not just another religious enthusiast? For days after that I really did hate her for rejecting me in public, and with that devil-talk, of all things. And then I ran into you behind your studio and you told me she has schizophrenia. That changed everything."

"It's freezing down here," said Linda. "You're rambling. And you're cold."

"I'm— yes. I'm cold." Nina hugged herself. "But I'm not going anywhere."

Linda took a step backwards, toward the stairs. "I'll go up and get you a sweater. One for me, too."

"If I'd known she had schizophrenia—" Nina's features tightened. "Annie didn't recognize me that day in church because of all the weight I'd lost since she tried to steal my husband three years ago. To her, I was invisible. But not to you."

"No, not to me," said Linda.

"I might have stood up in church and begged people to sign up for the registry, to be donors. A bone-marrow match could save my life. Esther was going to be my last, best hope, with her voice on the radio, and all her fans across the county who might have answered a plea to help me out. I wanted to ask her to do that, but she pointed a finger at me and drove me out." Nina turned her head to stare at the portrait in the corner of the room. "It might have changed everything, if I hadn't let Esther run me off. It could have ended well."

Linda locked Nina Sorba in her gaze and said, "Why not get someone to help you organize a drive to find a donor. All this obscure drama won't get you what you want. I really don't see what Esther has to do with you at all."

Tears welled up in Nina's eyes. "I'm an anthropologist."

"I *know* that, Nina," said Linda. "Can we please not change the subject?"

"Anthropologists like artifacts. Evidence that might give away some old truth about people's lives, you know? I have some things that led me to Esther months ago, and I'm determined to get her to explain them to me. It's something she doesn't want to do."

Linda had one foot on the bottom step by then, not about to be moved by Nina's stories, when Gracie's safety was at stake. "I know you're the one who called the cops," she said, "to report Annie's baby was alone in the car. You made a *threat*, Nina. You warned something bad might happen to the baby, and something did."

In the master bedroom, directly above where Nina stood, Frank lay on the bed. The minute he saw Linda standing in the doorway, he struggled to a sitting position, lowering his feet carefully onto the floor. "Was that John who called?" she whispered.

"Yes. He's at his office." Frank yawned. "He said he'd be there for another hour, that he got a late start. He called earlier and got a busy signal, so he knew you were home."

"What sent him out of here in such a rush?"

"Some emergency with Ned Milhous and his son Bobby."

"Bobby Milhous is the boy John interviewed about his drug addiction."

"Right," said Frank, still whispering. "John didn't want to go into details right then. I told him you couldn't come to the phone. That I'd invited myself out here for the company, which is certainly true. I didn't figure you'd want him hurrying home in the middle of whatever's happening down there. Still, he won't be long." They both looked at their watches. It was one forty-five. Frank watched Linda drag open the bottom drawer of her dresser and pull out her favorite sweater — blue, a cable knit — and a green, wool cardigan, which she put on.

"I have this idea." Linda picked up the ivory, plastic baby monitor from the computer desk and turned the wheel on the side. The little red light went on, and white noise fizzed from the speaker. They heard Nina cough.

Frank stared at the sound.

"Esther hooked this up that Sunday you were here," said Linda. "The receiver's supposed to be downstairs for when our baby's up here sleeping, but she hooked it up backwards."

He still looked baffled.

"It's a one-way transmission," whispered Linda. "You'll be able to hear us talking downstairs. Nina loses concentration sometimes, or she's stalling on purpose. I feel like I can't push her too hard or she won't tell me what I need to know. She seems barely conscious at times, and doesn't seem reliable, but I think I'm finally getting somewhere. And there's something else." Linda took a green metal box down from the closet shelf. The presence of John's handgun in the house was something they had often disagreed about. Guns frightened Linda. Now she got the key out of his desk drawer. The gun was gray and blunt-looking, the metal quilted at the square-handle end. She'd never held it in her hand before. She liked the feel of it, not as heavy as it looked.

"Here," she said to Frank, giving it up quickly into his hands. "I've been told she keeps a gun in her truck. If she has it on her, I'm thinking she'd have pulled it out by now, but still— If I say, 'Frank,' that means she's finally told me what I want to hear, or that I need you to come downstairs and play hard-ball by waving this around to scare her into coming clean. I hope you aren't as scared of this thing as I am."

He took the magazine out of the box and pressed it into the gun with the heel of his hand. "I'm going down there with you right now," he said, "and get her to give you straight answers on the spot. I see no reason to wait."

"No," said Linda. "Let me keep trying first. She seems so fragile."

"But you think she's dangerous."

"Well, I'm not so sure. She's seriously ill with a blood disease. She says it's terminal. She's desperate— for what, I can't be sure." When Frank protested again that he should go down there at once, Linda's finger flew to her mouth to signify *Shhh*, without making a sound. "Please, stay out of sight. I know this is weird, but she has a fixation on Esther she's starting to talk about, and I want you to hear it. Remember, if I say your name—"

"That means you need help."

"Or that she's finally admitted taking Gracie, and you can come on down."

"I'll give you five minutes, is all," he said, "and then I head down, signal or no signal. And I won't be *waving* this, as you say. I know how to use it. Remember," he said. "Five minutes."

Linda pointed at the speaker on the desk and left Frank staring at it, John's gun in his hand.

# Chapter 24

At the top of the stairs, Linda leaned her head down to look over the railing to her right. Nina stood facing the far corner of the room, hands empty at her sides. As Linda proceeded down, Nina approached, reaching for the blue sweater Linda offered her. When she pulled it over her head and smoothed it down, the wristbands came to her fingertips.

"It's time," said Linda. "Come on. A straight answer. Where were you that Friday afternoon? The day Gracie Cantonwine was abducted?"

"My mother died last year," was Nina's response. "She left me a lot of land. In her safe deposit box, among stock certificates and other lists of assets, an envelope marked 'For Nina, after my death.' Inside were all my report cards from kindergarten on, my high school diploma, some snapshots of me as a baby, and adoption papers, listing my birth on June 12, 1965, at Mercy Hospital in Des Moines."

Linda's lips parted. "Where were you that Friday, Nina? Can we get to that?"

Nina turned her face toward a rattle of trees beyond the bluish glass doors.

Linda thought of Frank, listening upstairs.

Nina counted on her fingers: "Also in that envelope were a Max Factor lipstick, a shade called *Barely There*. A paper napkin with a list of numbers added up. An Iowa Driver's License issued in May of 1965 to Esther Spencer, with a Linden Grove address, the same house where Esther Hebring lives now. And an autographed picture of Esther my mom had gotten from the radio. A few months later I went to that address and asked Esther if her name used to be Esther Spencer. She was happy to say yes, but then she took one look at her old drivers license and threw me out."

Nina paused, eyes closed for a moment, and then she said, "When I went to her house a second time, no one answered the door. I walked around to the back, and there she was, inside a big kitchen window, wearing a hat and reading into a microphone. I stared at her and wondered if she could possibly be my mother. I had to know. That's how it started. Jack thinks I'm desperate for connections.

"I hadn't been dealing with it well," said Nina, "the way Esther had refused to talk to me, the way she hadn't even asked me where I got that drivers license the day I gave it to her, the way she had just put it in her pocket and pushed me toward the door. I was jealous of you that Sunday, standing up in church with the family. I wanted to be up there, holding Grace. I would have done anything to hold her the way you did."

Nina eye blinks slowed again. "I mailed a package off to Chile the other day, addressed to the professor who notified my department that I had plagiarized. Inside, wrapped in miles of bubble wrap, was an ancient artifact, a fetal mummy."

"You're trying to clear yourself?"

"You bet. The Chilean professor is a friend of Professor Munizaga's, from when they worked on digs together when they were young. 'The Leticia Munizaga you remember from the sixties was a thief,' I explained, in the letter I put inside the package. 'This tiny object that she took home with her belongs in a university lab, or in the museum in Arrica, not in Munizaga's attic." I explained how *she* plagiarized *my* work," said Nina, "and not the other way around. I finally got a reply from Chile on Saturday." Nina looked down at the folded paper in her hand. "I'll let you read it. I think it'll get me back my Ph.D."

"Esther says you harass her on the phone. She insists she saw you behind her house. Many times."

"I was back there once," said Nina, "not many times."

"Frank even took her to the police station," said Linda, "to see what could be done." *Uh-oh,* she realized. *Frank just heard me say his name.* She glanced up at the ceiling.

She heard a floorboard creak.

"The housekeeper told me the best time of day to try and see Esther was after eleven in the morning," said Nina, "and that I could come to the back door when Esther was still in the kitchen, after her broadcast. I tried that once. Esther wouldn't answer the door. I think she saw me coming. If I came to the front, in the afternoon, the housekeeper would let me in. She tried her best to help me out, to persuade Esther to come out of the kitchen while I was there."

"It's a lovely house," said Linda.

"Very," said Nina. "There's a Matisse over the fireplace. Have you seen that?"

"The woman gazing into the fishbowl, yes."

"It's an original."

"Surely not," said Linda.

"According to the housekeeper it is. Her name is Jessica."

"Yes, I know her," said Linda.

"And there's a primitive drawing of Moses in the Bulrushes," Nina said, "and a Gauguin watercolor in the library called something like Pepe Moe. I don't remember—"

"It's called *Pape Moe,*" said Linda, "Tahitian for *Mysterious Water.* I noticed it, in the library. It's a painting I studied in school." Linda heard another footstep overhead.

"I'm pretty sure it's original, too," said Nina.

Linda knew better, but didn't argue.

*Mary Howard*

"Every painting has something to do with water," said Nina. "In the hall there's a Japanese-looking print called *A Woman Bathing*, by Mary Something."

"Cassatt," said Linda. "Mary Cassatt. A print," she added. "Sounds like you've spent quite a lot of time in that house."

For the first time, Nina was calm, her posture more erect. She even smiled. "Jessie gave me a tour one day, while we waited to see if Esther might see me. The red pot by the piano in the living room is some rare Chinese terra cotta. I was treated to a cup of tea, but Esther never appeared. Here," said Nina. "This is what you've been waiting for. I'm all done talking." She looked down at a white piece of paper in her hand and offered it to Linda.

When Linda unfolded the paper, the printing was upside down. She was rotating it right side up when she heard Frank's heavy footfalls on the wooden stairs.

He stopped on the lowest riser. "I'm Esther's husband," he announced to Nina, raising his hand to show her he had a gun. "Just answer Linda's question, and don't say anything else. Where were you on the afternoon the baby was kidnapped?" He took aim at her.

Nina plunged her right hand into the pocket of her baggy jeans, and the gun went off.

Linda recoiled from the sound. Her nostrils flared to a burnt, oily smell. Well to the left of Nina's blond head, the glass patio door hissed for three full seconds — crazed like a spider web with a hole in the center.

Linda's ears were ringing.

Nina had covered her ears, too. A wild defiance flashed in her eyes as she took a step toward Frank, holding something out to him. To Linda, it looked like a paper napkin, the rectangular kind made to be pulled from a chrome dispenser. Frank took hold of it and looked shocked at what he saw.

He backed up, fixing a bewildered gaze on the ruined patio door, on the damage he'd done. "Esther lost our baby," he said to Linda, but her hands were still over her ears. He came close and spoke right to her. "She was sixteen. She ran away and was found days later sleeping in a barn on a farm near Macksburg, about twenty miles southwest of here, dirty and disoriented, enough to break your heart. She had a miscarriage," he said, "where they took her, in a Des Moines hospital. I was there. She hardly knew where she was, in a psych ward. We have to tell this Nina person she's not Esther's child. There's some kind of twisted motive in there somewhere for why she'd hate my Esther enough to take my granddaughter, do you think?"

"I can hear you," said Nina. "I'm standing right here. I grew up on a farm near Macksburg. I wanted to believe." She had tears on her cheeks.

Frank drew even closer to Linda so she could see a column of numbers on the napkin, in blue ink. "Holding this in my hand takes me back, my God," he said, "like yesterday. I don't know what to make of it. I was sitting across from Esther in a diner over on Third Street, where Mona's Pizza is now, one Saturday, in 1965. It's like yesterday. I added these numbers up, you see? This was my scholarship, here." He ticked off the blue numbers with a fleshy finger. "This is my loan, my part-time job. Then we subtracted this total, the rent and such. We were trying to figure out what we could afford for the two of us, and a baby, the week before I had to go back for fall semester classes, the week before she ran away." He stared across the room at Nina Sorba. Then he looked at the folded paper in Linda's hand. "What have you got there?"

Linda raised the paper, and the words "patient" and "red cell transfusion," jumped off the page. It was statement from University of Iowa Hospitals and Clinics, dated Friday, September 20, 2002, the day Gracie was kidnapped. Nina had undergone a blood transfusion that afternoon, over a hundred and fifty miles away from Isabella Circle. Linda studied every detail one more time, to comprehend it, to be absolutely sure. "Look at the date on this," she said to Frank, "and the time of day." She put her finger under the hour of admission, 2:22 p.m. The ER. An emergency.

*Mary Howard*

"I was wrong about her," Linda said, giving up the paper to Frank. She watched his face change as :t all sank in, Nina Sorba's innocence.

He crushed the hospital statement in both his hands. "God-damn it all," he said, "I'd halfway hoped you'd clear my Esther." He couldn't go on. He fixed Nina with another long, steady stare.

And then he moved ponderously up the stairs.

In a moment, up there, a door opened. Linda and Nina both looked upward.

The front door slammed shut, a powerful reverberation.

# Chapter 25

Linda shoved John's extra-wide easy chair closer to the fire and opened the green book, *Russian Tales*. The book fell right open to "The Insomniac," the old-fashioned story about a night-wanderer Esther had tried to tell Linda in the hospital. Esther hadn't been able to remember what had happened to Misha Michaelvich after he had walked around his village for an entire night, watching for a light in the barbershop, waiting for dawn. He had not wept for his son, lost in the war. It had seemed to be a story about unspoken grief. Linda remembered how she had touched Esther's hand to comfort her in her frustration, her forgetfulness — and how Esther had turned her hand over, clasped Linda's for a moment, and said, "I knew you wouldn't abandon me."

Way too tired and worried to read "The Insomniac" while she waited for John to get home, Linda turned to the last paragraph. *Why are you silent? asked the barber. Have you been walking again all night? Misha gave no answer. What do you need, Misha Michaelovich? The barber answered his own question: You need a shave and a haircut. He put both his hands on Misha's hair. It was a practical touch, but no one had stroked the head of Misha Michaelvich for such a long time, not since his mother, who was now old and very far away; and his distant, nearly -forgotten father; and his wife, who had*

*Mary Howard*

*packed up her own grief and hurried off. Misha Michaelvich knew she would never come back. He bowed his head under the unbearable tenderness of the comb. The barber said, I heard about your boy, and Misha wept.*

*So,* thought Linda. It was a story about human touch, and a kindness everybody needs. Esther had wanted her to see how the story ended. Linda thought then of her own story — one she had told Esther in exchange for this one — about the deer who had led her to Grace. Another story without an end. Linda closed the book and heard a car come up the drive.

As he walked toward her under the porch light, John's forehead gleamed, his breath white in the night air. His hands pressed gently on her hair as she tilted her head for a kiss. "It's so late. I was worried," she said.

As they walked into the kitchen together, John told her that even after spending time with Bobby Milhous and his folks, he had finished the layout for the paper before two-thirty. But when he had tried to post the file to the *Register's* transfer site, he couldn't get it to work. He wasted a few phone calls to Des Moines before deciding it would be best to put the pages on zip disks and have them hand-delivered. "The guy who usually does my running has the flu that's going around," he told her as he filled a glass with water at the sink, "so I made the trip myself. You know where the printing plant is."

"Almost to the Des Moines airport, right?"

"That's right. I'm surprised you're still awake." He drained the glass. "I stopped for some coffee for the drive home, and now I may be too wired to sleep. I don't know what else could have gone wrong tonight."

Twenty-five minutes later, at 4:10 a.m., Linda was sitting up in bed, wide-awake from telling John about her confrontation with Nina Sorba. She watched him pull on a pair of blue boxer shorts, his favorite ones to sleep in. "We'll have to get a new patio door."

"That doesn't seem like a huge problem right now," said John. His narrow chest looked dented down the center above his still-flat belly, his arms well muscled for a forty-one-year-old guy who didn't work out. His cheeks were dark with whisker-shadows.

"Frank left the house in a hurry, angry, ashamed—I don't know— without saying good-bye," she said.

"Maybe he was mad at you," said John. He yawned.

"At me?"

"For getting his hopes up. That Esther might be exonerated."

"I think he was embarrassed about losing his temper with a gun in his hand," said Linda, "scaring the life out of us."

"A lot more than embarrassed, I should think," John said. "It's out of character, to put it mildly, for Frank Hebring of all people to fire a gun at someone, even aiming wide. He knows better. He shoots with the gun club west of town. He's something of a marks-man, and he's a hunter. Such a solid guy. Now he's the one we should be most worried about."

"I have a design project to deliver to the bank tomorrow," said Linda. "I'll talk to him then. Now I want to hear about Bobby Milhous."

"It can wait. We're both exhausted."

"The short version, then," she said. "On the phone, you told Frank there was a problem with Bobby and his dad."

John sat on the edge of the bed and pulled the red rubber band out of his hair, releasing his ponytail and giving his head a two-hand-ed scratch. He told her the phone call he'd gotten at four-thirty in the afternoon had been from Ruthie Gustavson, from the parking lot of the outlet mall out by I-35. "Bobby was threatening to run off. Ruthie thought I could help. Bobby's dad was convinced the boy had been cooking meth in that empty building behind the grain co-op."

"The old bank."

"Right. Bobby insists he's never been inside that building."

"He trusts you, Bobby does," said Linda, "since that interview you did."

"That's what Ruthie kept telling me. I was a little out of my element talking down a furious kid like that, but Ruthie and I got

*Mary Howard*

Bobby back home. I convinced her to call Gus over there to help us all talk it through. It took a while."

John got under the covers on his side, his hand caressing Linda's pregnant belly. Even lying on her back, she had the beginnings of a bulge. "I think Ruthie knew," he said, "that if Bobby took off, he'd be getting high."

"Frank really opened up and talked tonight."

"Good," said John. "So did Bobby. Out of the blue, he blurted out that he wasn't part of it, but he knew who the guys were who used the building."

"You think he's bought from them?"

"Or he runs with kids who have. I didn't think meth was part of his pharmacopoeia. Tomorrow morning he's going over with his dad to have a talk with the Drug Task Force people. I promised to meet them there."

"Then we'd better get some sleep."

"It was quite a night." John moved his hand on Linda's belly again. "I even got tears in my eyes. But not until I was alone, driving through the dark streets. That's when I realized I'd left my cell phone here. I wanted to call you. I did, as soon as I got to the office, but the line was busy. At least I knew you were home safe."

"I made a few calls," she said, "right after I got back. I woke up Detective Hansen. I was looking for you."

"Why?"

"Let's just say it was my night for feeling foolish."

"Look at me," he said. His eyes were pink at the corners with fatigue. "It turned out Nina *was* up to something with the Hebring family. It wasn't for nothing you went after her."

"I was convinced I could save Esther from being blamed."

"I know. You want life to be fair. You feel the need to atone, somehow, for resenting your father's eccentricities when you were a kid, when he acted crazy and couldn't help it. Esther's a kind of *locum tenens*."

"Mm-hmm," she said, too sleepy to ask for a translation. "Let's turn off the light." He stretched to reach the lamp, and when he came back, she fitted her butt against him. "I've kept something from you," she said, under cover of dark. "A group of deer made me stop on the road where Elsa and I found Gracie."

"Deer made you stop?"

"There were four of them."

"You mean you almost hit them?"

"Yes," said Linda. "I had to slam on my brakes, and the car swerved on the gravel. I turned the ignition off to let my heart slow down. I was that overwhelmed by everything that was going on, and the deer were the last straw. When I started the car again, the headlights were right on Gracie."

Sleepy, in that comforting dark, with her back to John, Linda let him know that the only person she had told about the deer was Esther, in the mental hospital. "She said that God has many disguises. She'll probably repeat the story about the deer, and it'll come out that way, a family story to prove her faith. In a way I envy that. For a moment — well, more than a moment— more like a week— I've felt singled out, chosen, by some force, even though I don't really believe that. It's irrational," she said, "to think that the creator of the universe, with those deer in firm control, interfered with the randomness of my life and led me right to Gracie. I just don't believe it."

"It's the effect of a coincidence that matters," he said. "What we make of it, not what causes it."

"What I make of it is gratitude."

"It's four in the morning," he said sleepily, "and I'm fading."

"Mmmm." Linda felt her belly rise and fall under her husband's hand as weariness settled over her. She sighed.

He gave her belly a weary caress and murmured, "Deer."

"Four of them."

"Out of hundreds this year," he said. "It's a population explosion. It's little wonder—" Soon his breathing told her he was fast asleep, despite the coffee he'd drunk in Des Moines. Despite everything.

She drifted in the familiarity of his embrace and then knew nothing until he touched her shoulder and said her name and,

*Mary Howard*

"Sorry to wake you." He was standing over her. "Linda?" he said again. The windows behind him were framed with light around the shades. He knelt down so their faces were close and put something on the mattress. It was his metal gun-box, the small key in the key-hole. "I went to put this back up on the shelf where it belongs," he said. "It didn't weight enough." He opened the box and showed her it was empty. "I've looked all over the basement, and upstairs," he said. "Unless you know where Frank put it—"

She rose up on an elbow, barely awake. "What time is it?"

"It's after ten. I have to get going. Frank's not at home, and he's not at the bank. Did you say he was angry when he left here last night?"

# Chapter 26

Both Linda and John took Wednesdays off — John because he spent Tuesday nights putting the paper to bed, and Linda because she liked having the same day off as her husband. But on that Wednesday morning, October second, 2002, he left the house at ten-thirty to meet Bobby Milhous and his dad at the Madison County Drug Task Force office in Winterset. John was worried about Frank. "It was not at all like him to fire a gun right past a person's head like that," John muttered on his way out the door.

Sleep-deprived after her emotionally draining hours with Nina Sorba, Linda knew the best remedy for her mood was to drive into town and wrap up a couple of projects. By one o'clock that afternoon she had put the finishing touches on a corporate identity project for Singing Rooster Vineyard of Lawrence, Kansas, and had packaged it for mailing. Then she slipped three versions of her design for the Farmers and Merchants Bank into a portfolio for delivery to Frank Hebring. While she ate a tuna sandwich at her desk, her mind returned to thoughts of Nina, her deteriorating health and her sad obsession with Esther. Curious, Linda did a Google search for "bone marrow donation."

She had a two o'clock appointment with Frank so he could look at the ads with her. Right before she left for the bank, she called Annie to tell her about Nina's alibi. "She was in the hospital when

*Mary Howard*

Gracie was kidnapped. She showed up at my house last night with the bill to prove it. She did a number on me, stringing me along for hours to make me pay for misjudging her."

"Well," said Annie. "So now you know."

"You're not surprised it turned out like this, are you?"

"I guess I did have some hope for my mom."

"I should have trusted the police," said Linda, "and not played amateur detective. The reason Nina was in the hospital that day— She has a blood disease. She says it will be fatal unless she has a bone marrow transplant. She's been waiting for a tissue match for a year."

Annie didn't make a sound.

"I still want to see the prints you've been working on," said Linda, "so let me know when there's a good time, maybe right after five one day, when I'm done with work. How about tomorrow?"

So they agreed. Linda said, "See you then," and Annie said, "Yeah, bye," their voices quick and easy as if all the old tensions between them had been eased.

Suddenly very sleepy, Linda decided it might perk her up if she walked the six blocks to the bank, instead of taking the car. The day was sunny, in the seventies, and it felt good to stretch her legs, a portfolio under one arm, a padded envelope under the other. She was eager to see Frank, to ask him where he'd put John's gun, and to judge if he was at his wit's end, as John feared.

She arrived at the high-ceilinged F&M bank at two sharp, but Frank wasn't there. "He was in for a while this morning, Linda," said Amy, his secretary. "He got some things from his safe-deposit box and shut himself in his office until a half-hour ago."

"Did he say where he was going?"

"Back home, I think. He looked very tired. He asked not to be called unless it's important, but if you had an appointment—"

"No, don't bother him," said Linda. "I'll just leave this on his desk."

The secretary nodded. She gestured toward his office door.

The reddish-dark mahogany of Frank Hebring's enormous desk was polished to a gleam. On it lay an old fashioned box, the kind made to look like a book when it's on a shelf. It was splayed-open, empty except for a few age-yellowed papers. Linda withdrew her design work from the cardboard portfolio she'd carried it in and placed it dead-center on the desk, moving the box aside.

Leaning forward like that, she inhaled a musty, attic smell of dust and old paper. The green, marbled surface of the storage box was worn along the edges. She folded it shut to observe the spine and then studied the mottled topside. Scrawled there, in faded brown ink, was the signature of Nathaniel E. Spencer, Esther's father, who had once been president of the bank. What treasure had been stored inside? Linda wondered. Had Frank really gone home to sleep off his late night at her house?

Linda began to worry about the gun. Back out in the lobby, she paused to gaze up at Nathaniel Spencer's portrait. It hung behind the teller's cages, above the open door of the walk-in vault with its silver- and gold-colored gears behind panels of heavy glass. Esther had inherited her father's dark eyes, high cheekbones, and confident shoulders — *along with jewelry, paintings, Antique Chinese clay pots,* Linda was thinking as she headed toward the post office. *And a house big enough for a family of ten.* What was it Frank had said about Esther's dreams of a career in the theater? *"She was swallowed by a house."*

Linda walked down the street and around the corner to the post office, only two blocks from the bank, to mail her package. Inside, a line of four people waited at the service window. Taking her place at the end of the line, Linda glanced at the postal worker behind the counter. Linda looked away with some confusion, then returned her gaze to a familiar face. Though she'd met Hebring's housekeeper only once — at their house, the night Gracie was found — there was no mistaking Jessica Mann with her long dark braids and freckles, an immaculate gauze bandage the size of a playing card on her forehead.

Linda stepped forward, staring at the white bandage, trying to remember. How many stitches, had Jessica said? From her car accident the afternoon Gracie went missing? Five?

Now there were three people ahead of Linda in line. The man at the counter was there to pick up mail he'd had held, so Jessica Mann turned with a smile and disappeared into the back of the post office. By the time she reappeared, it had occurred to Linda to wonder if she could be looking at the person Jack Boisseau saw on Isabella Circle the afternoon Gracie was taken: "I didn't see anyone but the mailman."

Or had he said mail *carrier?* Linda couldn't be sure. The woman ahead of her bought a sheet of Breast Cancer stamps, and then it was Linda's turn. She put her padded envelope on the scale.

"Hello," said Jessica, with a warm smile.

"I didn't know you worked here," said Linda. "I come in a lot, and I've never seen you."

"I'm always in back. I'm one of the early-birds, sorting the mail, then I do a route in the country."

"And then you put in four or five hours at the Hebrings'?"

Jessica nodded. "It's a big house to maintain." Her smile faded. "It isn't the same without Esther. You want this to go Priority Mail?"

"That's fine."

"Frank called to say he didn't need me today," said Jessica, "and we've got someone off sick here. So I stayed."

Linda gazed at the white bandage on the woman's forehead as Jessica affixed the postage. "I'm sorry about your accident." Linda swiped her Master Card. "It's how many stitches?"

"Eight," said Jessica Mann.

Linda felt her hand rise slowly toward the woman's smile. "Hold still."

"What?"

"You have—" *A loose hair, some lint,* is what Linda had in mind that Jessica would think. "Hold still," Linda repeated. "There's something— I'll get it. Don't blink."

The woman combed back a stray hair.

Before she was sure she was going to do it, Linda seized the bandage and yanked down, cornerwise, revealing Jessica's skin underneath — as smooth and healthy as her freckled cheeks.

Jessica reared back with astonishment.

"No one goes to the trouble of telling a lie like this," said Linda, shaking the bandage in Jessica's face, "unless she has something awful to hide."

For two full seconds, neither of them moved.

Then Jessica Mann gave a fast glance over her left shoulder. She returned a horrified gaze to the bandage — insect-like, with adhesive-tape legs — as Linda dropped it onto the postal scale between them. Linda, whose impulse to rip the thing off Jessica's forehead had shocked even herself, finally found her tongue. "What were you doing," she said in a harsh, low voice, "serving tea to Nina Sorba in Esther's big living room as if you owned the place? Showing off Esther's art and antique ceramic pots as if you were entitled? Entertaining—"

Jessica glanced past Linda at the line behind her, then boldly looked her in the eye. "Who told you that?"

Linda continued her thought: "—entertaining Nina Sorba with tea and a tour of Hebring's house. Telling Frank the woman was part of Esther's illness and had *never been there*. It was Nina herself who told me how you gave her helpful hints about the best time to call, or come to the door around the back way, where Esther might see her from the kitchen table. You led Frank to believe it was Esther's sick brain that made her insist there was someone out there."

Jessica pressed her lips together.

"You probably even helped Esther tape those newspapers over the kitchen window," said Linda, "feeding her paranoia."

Jessica shook her head.

"Esther knows she can't always trust herself because of her schizophrenia. She has unusual insight in that way. What kind of woman would undermine her sanity for no apparent—?"

Jessica backed up a single step.

Linda pressed her weight onto her palms, hard against the edge of the counter between them. "You took Gracie, didn't you, to discredit Esther altogether? Using a fake accident for an alibi."

With that, Jessica turned and ran into the back of the post office, with its many partitions.

"It's easy enough to bang up a car on purpose," Linda yelled after her. "You should have sliced up your forehead while you were at it."

A man stepped into sight back there, two fists full of letters held waist-high.

"Where did she go?" Linda shouted.

"Out the back," he said.

By the time Linda got to the loading dock at the back of the Linden Grove P.O., there was no sign of Jessica. The man from inside stared from the doorway, curious. "Is her car in the shop, still?" Linda asked him.

"Far as I know. What's going on?"

"I just gave her some bad news. Where does she live?"

He pointed to the north and named a street near Isabella Circle.

Linda headed south on Second Street to the police station in long measured strides. The whole way, her mind played dreamlike versions of Jessica slipping into Annie's house in her postal-blue slacks with stripes down the sides, her braids tucked into an official hat with an eagle on the crown — only to emerge a few minutes later in Annie's yellow sweatshirt, hood up, carrying Grace. No wonder Burt Mack had thought it was Annie he saw that day in her driveway. She and Jessie were about the same size. The shirt had been right there in the back seat of Annie's unlocked car, a garment too warm for the weather, but just right for a disguise.

Linda walked faster. She could just *see* Jessica open the driver-side door to Annie's red car and hunker down to take the key from the floor mat, where Annie always left it. Jessie must know all kinds of Hebring family habits, from all the years she'd worked for them. Frank had grown fat on her cooking.

*Jessie planned all along to plant the key on Esther,* Linda was thinking, breathless, as she turned the corner and her destination came into view. On either side of the wide entrance, a pillar supported a glass globe bearing the word POLICE. Inside, Detective Hansen's secretary tried to head her off, but Linda pushed open the door to his corner office anyway.

There sat Frank, across the desk from Hansen. Both men looked up, startled, as Linda blurted out, even as she struggled to catch her breath, "Jessica Mann— Her car accident, the day of the kidnapping— It was fake. Five minutes ago I accused her of taking Gracie, and she ran like she was guilty. I'm afraid she'll get away."

The detective walked around the corner of his desk to pull a chair away from the wall. Linda sat. While her breathing returned to normal she managed to tell them about the bandage covering an injury that wasn't there. "What kind of monster is she, Frank? She seems so nice. Why would she want to destroy your family?"

She half-expected Frank to tell her she was mistaken again, that she had jumped to conclusions—*again*. Instead, he lifted a sheaf of yellowed papers in his right hand. "These," he told her, are certificates of authenticity and an inventory of original art and rare first-edition books." Also listed, he explained, were a couple of diamond necklaces and rings and other expensive do-dads that belonged to Esther's late mother. "And this—" He lifted a picture from the pile of papers on the desk and tilted it toward Linda so she could see. It was *Mysterious Water*, by Paul Gauguin. "I took it out of its frame at home this morning," he said. "It's supposed to be an original."

He turned the picture over so Linda could read what was stamped on the back, PicturePerfect.com. He dropped it angrily onto the cluttered desk. "Esther tried to tell me someone was breaking into our house and substituting one thing for another nearly like it. She said paintings and china knickknacks and such were growing, shrinking, changing color."

"She told me something like that, too, in the hospital," said Linda. "I didn't take it seriously."

"Because you thought it was her sickness talking," said Frank. "I did, too, and so did Jessie Mann. When Esther couldn't find her mother's rings one day, she actually accused Jessie of taking them.

Jessie was sure they would be right there in the safe where they belonged. Sure enough, they were, but they're not there now."

"Had Esther given her the combination?" Linda asked.

"Damned if I know. Probably. Jessie has keys to the house, and she knows the security code. She was part of the family."

Linda picked up the reproduction of *Pape Moe,* a picture of an androgynous person — a young woman, or a boy, it was impossible to tell — leaning to drink from a slender waterfall.

"I never looked at the thing." Frank leaned back in his chair. "It was just always there."

"She could have walked right onto Isabella Circle," Linda said to him, putting *Pape Moe* aside, "unnoticed in her post office clothes. The invisibility of the familiar. She had the whole thing carefully worked out. She could have learned from family conversation that Annie had begun working in her basement darkroom every afternoon, while Gracie napped." Linda turned to the detective. "And Jessie was at the Hebring house the night Gracie was found, remember? Making coffee and sandwiches, playing the piano. She could have slipped Annie's car key into the envelope of Esther's personal effects from when she was admitted to the hospital. Jessie was upstairs for a while, getting some personal items together for you to take to Esther. I remember that."

"Frank nodded. He clenched his jaws, deep in thought. "I wonder if Esther accused her again of stealing," he said, "and Jessie panicked, felt she had to discredit my Esther. That's all I can think. The value of the rare books in the library alone adds up to thousands of dollars. He ran a finger down the inventory list. "I checked them all this morning. If Esther was out of the house for good, I wouldn't have been hard to fool, when it comes to art, and books, and diamond necklaces. Those were never my treasures." He leaned forward again, absent-mindedly rolling the inventory list into a tube. "I measured the picture over the fireplace this morning. It's three inches too wide in one direction, and two in the other, according to this." He lifted the rolled-up papers like a baton. "That's Esther's favorite, the goldfish in the bowl. Her father bought it in the thirties. Every painting her family collected had something to do with water. Listening to Nina last night is what gave Jessie away, made me think that Jessie might not be the honest woman I took her for."

"We'll have to get into Mrs. Mann's house," said Detective Hansen. "For starters, I'll ask her to consent to a search."

"She won't," said Linda and Frank, in one voice.

The detective was halfway to the door. "She might if I tell her the alternative is a court order."

"First we have to find her," said Linda. "Fortunately her car is still in the shop."

"She has another," said Frank, "a vintage Mustang. She keeps it licensed so she can drive it sometimes. She won't be driving it today."

"I'll head over there myself, right now," said the detective, opening the door. "We'll can have a warrant before the afternoon is out."

"Just one second." Frank hefted the brief case from the floor beside him onto his lap, shoving papers into it. "I'm going with you."

"It's a police matter," said Hansen. "Linda, you too. I mean it."

"Of course you're right," said Frank. "We'll keep our distance." At that, he reached deep into his briefcase and drew out John's gun. Linda's heart thumped with alarm. Frank placed the gun on the desk. He stood. "I came this close to going after her myself."

Linda rode with Frank in his Lincoln Town Car. He parked two houses from Jessica Mann's yellow two-story Cape Cod on Barlow Avenue, a block and a half from Annie's house. The garage door was up. One black and white Linden Grove cop car was in her driveway. Another was parked at the curb. Every few minutes, Frank raised his left hand to the steering wheel, his right hand going for the key, still in the ignition, as if it were time to start the car and pull forward to become part of whatever was about to happen. But nothing was happening, his pantomime a nervous tic. He dropped both hands onto his thighs again and said, "You think it's a good sign they're in there so long?"

"Yes," said Linda, though she wasn't sure of anything. A breeze moving through the open car windows brought the balm of sun-toasted autumn leaves, banishing the Lincoln's new-car smell. A fragmentary thought flashed through Linda's brain: the answer to Gracie's abduction might be at hand, at last, and it was Nina's stories about Jessica that had given her away.

The police had been inside the house for fifteen minutes.

Frank rested his left elbow on the window. "My wife—" he said. "Think what it may have done to her that I brought Jessie into the house to take care of things and to keep her company. Jessie baked bread, she played duets on the piano with Esther, she kept things tidy, and all along she had a kind of nature we never saw? Do you believe a person could hide such a thing?"

Linda took her eyes off the yellow house and glanced at Frank's profile.

"A thief, and so much worse? An evil monster." Overcome, he had to pause. "Out of what," he said tightly, "greed and envy?"

"I suppose we'll find out she's got some sort of heartrending personal history," Linda said. "I won't want to hear it." Her voice rose, breathless with emotion. "I wouldn't let her off the hook by calling her evil. Evil makes it sound like she's the agent of some *force.*"

Frank raised both hands to grip the steering wheel. "Some force that opposes good."

"The opposite of good is bad," said Linda bitterly. "Evil is much, much worse. Jessie could have stopped herself. She got away with manipulating everyone for so long she began to feel entitled to play god, I guess. If we're right about her. If she did this thing." Linda reached for the door handle.

She had the door open and one foot on the grass when Frank said, "If you thought Elsa Silk and I were having an affair, you were wrong about that."

Linda pulled her right foot back inside.

"She's an old, dear friend," he said.

Linda pulled the door shut.

"It was Jessie who made me see what I'd been missing. At first I had no idea what I was encouraging. It went farther than it should have, and then I had to call a halt to it. I thought I'd stopped short of betrayal, but maybe not. Maybe I betrayed both of them." He looked at his hands, twisting his wedding ring. "A few hours ago, I was so angry I wanted to kill Jessie, but now—" He fell silent then. Linda waited, till he said, "I came here this morning with John's gun."

"Here?" Linda pointed at the yellow house.

He nodded. When he spoke again, he just sounded sad. "I had a terrible impulse to destroy her. For a few minutes I could have gone either way. I waited for her to come home from the post office, but she didn't show up."

"She filled in for someone, a sick person's shift. You wouldn't have hurt her, Frank. You're not like that."

"I felt enough entitlement to fire the gun four times." Frank turned toward Linda. "Into the tires of her car," he said.

Linda stared at him.

"I wanted to look for her on her delivery route," he said, "but I thought of Annie. I'm supposed to be the steady one." His smile was more like a grimace. "By reason of my own infirmity, I've come to know compassion," he said, as if the idea had just settled over him, a formal thought. Something remembered, perhaps. Some kind of truth. "Truth is," he said, "right now I don't know what to feel."

Linda watched Frank lean back and close his eyes. Then he caught himself. He resumed his surveillance. After a full minute of silence, he began to describe for Linda the absurdity of hiding out in her and John's bedroom the night before, listening to her talk to Nina Sorba in the basement below, over the baby monitor.

His reluctance, he said, to so much as jostle the bed frame, or place his feet on the floor, had filled him with a terrible restlessness; but he had known that any sound he made might abort the odd drama unfolding beneath him. He had strained to listen. And then all at once Nina was talking about how Jessica had entertained Nina in his library and living room — in his and Esther's home — as if she, Jessica, had been the woman of the house. And he had known at once that it was possible that Jessie had pushed Esther to doubt her waning sanity, to be sicker and sicker — sick enough to steal baby Grace.

It was nearly three-thirty. Linda looked at her watch.

Frank said, "Do you think Jessie could have driven Esther crazy enough to kidnap Grace? Esther may be guilty after all."

Unnerved by the question, Linda shifted her gaze from Jessie's house, glancing to the right in a gesture of avoidance and frustration — and caught, in the rearview mirror, a glimpse, in that silver frame, of Annie pushing Gracie in her stroller, at the corner of Barlow Avenue and Isabella Circle.

The stroller made a clicking sound as it rolled over sidewalk cracks. Linda got out of the car to explain, but Annie was staring past her, on her face a look — not of slack-jawed curiosity, but of mature fear. She stopped alongside the Lincoln. "What's happened to Jessie? Has something happened?" Linda turned her head to see what Annie must be seeing: two cop cars in front of Jessie's house, suggesting that something terrible had befallen her.

By then, Frank was out of the car. "Daddy? What are you and Linda doing here?" Annie watched her father slam the car door. "What is it?

Gracie began to fuss, probably because the stroller wasn't moving. Even the baby's revved-up mewing sounds didn't distract Linda from hearing a door close behind her. Detective Hansen emerged from the house and began walking toward Frank's Lincoln Town Car. Annie took three short steps toward the officer. Then, with an unexpected cry of surprise, she ran to meet him.

Annie's sprint toward the detective was so unexpected that Frank called out his daughter's name as if to stop her. She covered the distance quickly, but when she reached Hansen, she froze, head bowed, or so it seemed. She was, at any rate, looking down, her back to Linda and Frank. The posture of contrition.

Linda pushed Gracie forward in the stroller, following Frank, who with a breathless, rocking gait, was three sidewalk-squares ahead of them. When he spoke Annie's name again, she turned and stepped aside so they could see what the detective held in both his hands.

No one spoke the lamb's silly alliterative name; but even in its amniotic zip-lock evidence bag, it was definitely Lulu the lamb, the stuffed animal Annie had reported missing from Gracie's crib the day the baby was abducted. "It was stolen with her." Annie said to the officer. "Stolen with her," she repeated, a stunned look on her pretty face— and then: "What does this mean?"

Linda pointed. An officer was leading Jessica from the front door of her house to the cop car waiting at the curb. She had both hands behind her back.

# Epilogue

Now it's April, another Sunday afternoon. Three-week-old Alexander William Bender is bundled securely in Linda's arms. She carries him through a light rain. John, fist at his collar, rain on his back, holds an umbrella over his wife and son. The very moment they reach the shelter of Hebring's front porch, the skies open, delivering a thunderous ovation, a falling curtain of water. John and Linda laugh for escaping the deluge in the nick of time. Little Alex William sleeps through all the noise. They have named him after Linda's late father Alexander Garbo and John's best friend Will Cantonwine, who throws the door open wide to greet them now, in perfect sync with a thunderclap. From inside the house come Gracie's wail of fear and Annie's reassuring voice: "It's just the sky falling. You're safe as can be."

Linda has been a frequent visitor to Hebrings' big Victorian house since Esther returned home for good in February. Now the sounds of rolling thunder and lashing rain, and the bracing smell of ozone, diminished only slightly as the door is closed, make everybody talk at once. Will takes baby Alex from Linda while she removes her coat, streaming water onto the slate floor. Annie is right there, a wooden coat hanger in her hand. "Can you believe Dad's helping Mom in the kitchen?" she says. Beyond Annie, in the living room, ten-month-old Gracie sidesteps her way around the perimeter of the large ebony coffee table, reaching for objects that have been moved to the center, beyond her reach. Frank makes an appearance to kiss Linda, shake John's hand, and admire their sleeping baby. Frank is wearing a chef's apron printed with the bank logo Linda designed. He hurries back to the kitchen, looking worried.

"It's the gravy," Annie whispers to Linda. "It might have to be from a can. Mom'll be mortified if it comes to that."

Linda parts her lips to offer to help, but Annie seems to read her mind: "They're determined to do this dinner on their own, but don't be surprised if you end up in the kitchen. Mom thinks you're a miracle worker." Annie gives Linda a hug.

There's something different about Hebring's living room, even besides the promising fragrance of roasting meat and savory herbs. It's less cluttered than it used to be. The original oil painting found in Jessica Mann's small yellow house has been restored to its rightful place over the mantle, and the clocks are gone. A sudden show of sun dazzles the many-paned windows, casting rain shadows across the floor. John and Annie settle themselves on one of the sofas to keep an eye on Gracie. Back by the piano, in his cradle chair, baby Alex sleeps.

Linda and Will go to set the table in the dining room. Alone with Linda, placing forks and knives beside plates, Will lets his shoulders sag. "Annie's having a hard time again," he says, "like it just happened. The nightmares, the not wanting Gracie to be out of her sight, the way Jessie violated an almost sacred trust by concealing such depravity under her Earth Mother act. It's all come back. I'm not sure the counseling has helped."

"She'll be okay," says Linda. "It takes time, especially for someone who's unsure of herself like Annie."

Will nods.

"She has to re-experience her fear over and over," says Linda, "until she's faced it down, until she decides not to let what Jessica Mann did rule her life. And even then."

"It'll come back sometimes," he says.

It's Linda's turn to nod. "We have everything to be grateful for."

Will turns away, perhaps to hide his feelings, which puts him face-to-face with Esther as she comes through the swinging door from the kitchen, a jingling pitcher of ice water in her hands. He takes it from her to fill the water glasses. She looks beautiful, black hair swept back from her oval face, high cheekbones stroked with blush, brown eyes carefully outlined.

Esther's face has lost the puffiness from the neuroleptic drug she took sporadically last summer. Her new regimen seems to agree with her — and besides, she's come *through* something with the illness. Everybody says so. Her program *Willing Suspensions* is back on the air, more popular than ever. Linda listens to it every afternoon as she works in the studio downtown, which she decided to take off the market when Jack Boisseau withdrew his offer after Nina died in late October — Nina Sorba, whose anecdotes about Jessie Mann exonerated Esther and put Jessie behind bars. Annie has set up her photo workshop in Linda's loft. "Dear God, I'm glad you're here," Esther says to Linda. "I need your help. It's a disaster, and I wanted this meal to be just right."

It's no trouble at all for Linda to watch Esther whisk the lumpy gravy with a vengeance and pour it through a mesh sieve. It comes out meaty and rich from the roasting pan, with a hint of red wine, not a lump to be seen — and Esther's universe is in perfect balance. With a laugh of relief, she shoos Linda from the kitchen while Frank helps her finish up and *plate the meal,* language Esther has learned from her favorite cooking show. Linda meets Will at the foot of the stairs in the entry hall. Side-by-side they pause in the wide doorway to the living room.

When Gracie sees her dad and Linda standing there, she squeals, dark hair wild as ever around her face, a determined little ball of energy. "Gracie?" says Linda, stepping forward. The child stretches her arms to Linda, meaning *up,* and Linda feels her own spirit lift.

She carries the child to the fireplace to see the painting called *Woman Before an Aquarium.* "Look, Gracie, fish," she says. "Can you say fish?" The woman in the painting stares at the flashes of orange and gold in the bowl of water, vibrant in the convincing transparency of authentic pigment, as if the watery globe might show a future of great promise.

Gracie points to it and makes a marvelous sound.

# Acknowledgments

Writing *The Girl With Wings* stimulated my curiosity about book restoration, archaeology, child protection services, mimicry of foreign dialects, photography, portraiture, schizophrenia, and small-town journalism. For sharing their expertise with me along the way, I want to thank Terry Bird, Karen Bryan, Jo-Anne Boehmer, C.A. Croyle, Matt Donovan, Ivan Hanthorn, John Jugenheimer, Patrice Linke, Adam Meseke, Valery Shevchuk, and Bruce Smith. Thanks also to Barbara and Roger Bruene, and Priscilla and Charles Sage for letting me use their houses as writing retreats while they were away from Iowa for the winter. Brenda Fullick, Editor of the Madison County, Iowa, weekly newspaper *The Madisonian*, helped me bring the fictional Linden Grove and the Linden Times to life.

My perception of Esther Hebring's schizophrenia, particularly her level of insight into the illness, was expanded greatly by interviews with Nancy L. Hale, Psychiatric Nurse and Research Assistant III in the Department of Psychiatry, University of Iowa Hospitals and Clinics. For further insights I read *The Broken Brain*, by Nancy C. Andreasen, M.D., Ph.D.; *Surviving Schizophrenia*, by E. Fuller Torrey, M.D.; and *Schizophrenia Genesis: the Origins of Mad-*

*ness*, by Irving I. Gottesman. Parts of this book were written during a residency at The Ragdale Foundation in Lake Forest, Illinois.

*Pape Moe* (*Mysterious Water*), the Paul Gauguin painting featured in the novel, is a watercolor on ivory wove paper, c. 1893. The Matisse painting hanging over Hebrings' mantle strongly resembles *Woman Before an Aquarium*, painted in 1921. In the real world, both these paintings are owned by the Art Institute of Chicago.

Thanks to Brenda Fullick, Nancy Hale, Tiffani Howard, and Bob Bataille for reading this story in manuscript. And special thanks to my editor Mikesch Muecke for his generous editorial, design and marketing talents.

*Mary Howard*

www.ingramcontent.com/pod-product-compliance
Lightning Source LLC
Chambersburg PA
CBHW051245260626
47162CB00002B/625